M000288000

No
Witnesses
To
Nothing

Garry Rodgers

Copyright © Feburary 2013 by Garry Rodgers

ISBN 978-0-9917181-0-8

First Print Edition

Written and Published by Garry Rodgers, Dyingwords Digital and Print Media, Canada

All rights reserved.

This book is published for your personal enjoyment. Please respect the intellectual property of the writer. No part of this book may be infringed upon, pirated, reproduced, or transmitted by any means, in any form, or in alternate formats; electronic or mechanical, including downloading, uploading, recording, hard-copy printing, photocopying, or by any information storage and retrieval system without written permission from the copyright owner. The only exception is in the case of fair dealing by a reviewer who may quote brief passages in critical articles.Please contact the author regarding comments, discussion, or information about this story. Honest and impartial reviews are greatly appreciated.

Web/Blogsite: www.dyingwords.net
Email: garry@dyingwords.net

Also on:

Twitter: @GarryRodgers1
Facebook
Goodreads
LinkedIn
Amazon

Dedication

To Constable Michael Joseph Buday,
Royal Canadian Mounted Police Regimental Number 33631,
who gave his life in the line of duty
at Teslin Lake on March 19th, 1985.

Maintains Le Droit, Bude.

Author's Note

This is a book about karma.

It's the cause and effect of a true ghost story – The Teslin Lake Incident – the actual Royal Canadian Mounted Police operation straight out of The X-Files where many believe that paranormal intervention occurred. Everything took place exactly as told, except what didn't, and then it should have. The scene locations are precise. So are dates and times. The characters are based upon real people, still haunted by the events, though certain names are changed to respect privacy.

And there are no apologies for how any of them behaved. They had their reasons.

Murder most foul, as in the best it is:
But this most foul, strange and unnatural.

- The Ghost to Hamlet Act One, Scene V

Prelude

From Somewhere In-between The Darkness And The Light

Sergeant Sharlene Bate didn't believe in ghosts.

And the ghost didn't know that Sergeant Bate would investigate the informant murders.

Sharlene Bate knew a lot about murders. As a savvy, seasoned, and sensible homicide investigator, Sharlene knew the best thing about murders was that most have smoking guns. They're easy to solve, with nothing strange and unnatural.

Not like what went down here.

* * *

Most police officers don't believe in ghosts. Bate sure didn't. But that was before she exhumed some serious supernatural shit that happened to two young Mounties, which led to these murders.

You see, cops are natural cynics. They're skeptical creatures needing proof of strange things, such as witnesses. With a ghost – there's nothing to witness – so there's no witnesses to nothing.

No, Sharlene Bate didn't believe in ghosts.

Not till she investigated Constable Alfred Monagham and solved the mystery of why the informants had to be murdered.

Part One

The Informants

Chapter 1

Monday, April 30th, 2012
5:52 am
Southern West Coast
British Columbia, Canada

Sergeant Sharlene Bate of I-HIT, the Integrated Homicide Investigation Team, shifted foot to foot in a Vancouver Starbucks, elbow to elbow in the morning-rush lineup, awaiting her Grande, late for a briefing, and texting-off a scold to her daughter – oblivious to effects creeping out from the Gulf Islands death scene; effects causing grave repercussions for Bate's soul.

* * *

C-GSKE, Carmax Air's twin turbo-prop freighter, flew towards the crime scene at 278 knots, 3,140 feet over the Strait of Georgia, bearing 195 from Vancouver on its early FedEx run.

"YVR – SKE Cargo," the pilot radioed.

"SKE – Go ahead," the tower crackled back.

"Reporting a structure fire at a farm on Salt Spring Island. I'd give you the GPS read, but it's an easy locate. Right at Walker's Hook spit. East side."

"Roger that, SKE. 911 fire call?"

"Ah, 10-4, for sure."

* * *

Volunteer responders suppressed it by 6:40 am. Combined, two engines and two tankers killed the blaze without hooking to a hydrant. The captain would've greased his lieutenant for running slow, except both realized what was extinguished. They'd already called the cops.

It wasn't the first marijuana grow-op Salt Spring firefighters had seen, but this one was more sophisticated than others. The fire ignited in a diesel-powered generator building normally controlled by a caretaker. The greenhouse was a separate, large cinderblock complex with a double-insulated, hydronically-cooled, metal roof; not something that could burn, nor radiate a heat signature to be picked up by infrared. Inside were 1,100 BC Bud cannabis plants.

No one was around, which was telling. You'd think leaving an elaborate, expensive set-up unattended to the point of combusting seemed just plain careless, yet – here it was.

One of the volunteers was dousing a grass fire that spread to the perimeter of the secluded site. It was now bright sunshine, the fourth day of an early heat-wave. He was looking at a 21-foot Tango travel trailer set on blocks with a dirty old black GMC Suburban parked beside it at the west edge of the property, near the sandy entrance drive. A garbage pile under the trailer smouldered and he suspected the floor boards were hot.

"Hello?" he called out, closing in on the door. "Hello! Anyone here?"

It sounds absurd, calling out, given the commotion, but the volunteer was an insurance man in his day job and insurance men are cautious. He stepped up. Tapped the door. Turned the lever and pulled. The whoosh of rushing air hosed him like the stream straight out of a skunk's ass and he instantly heaved-up his guts.

"Hey! HEY!" he yelled, snotting and spitting. "There's a fuckin' dead guy in here!"

* * *

Constable Jill Prunty, of the Royal Canadian Mounted Police, was alone in her bathroom in her Salt Spring mobile-home park, fighting unruly red hair. Her pager beeped, reporting another found grow-show, something now epidemic in southern British Columbia. Prunty had six years with the RCMP in Ganges, the placid town center of Salt Spring – an island of ten thousand set in the Pacific Northwest between Vancouver and Victoria, just above Puget Sound and the greater Seattle area of Washington State.

It was far south of what had gone down in the Yukon.

Far north of what was going down in Colombia.

Far, far, east of what would go down in Australia.

It was a long way west of Cape Breton where Prunty grew up.

She'd policed Salt Spring since graduating from the academy; still single. Cop or not, she was a woman and quickly finished her make-up, then stretched on her uniform before heading out to the white Ford Expedition PC, Police Cruiser, which she took home when on call.

Prunty, like most B.C. police officers, blamed the erupting narcotics industry on the lax justice system that evolved in this notoriously liberal Canadian province. She knew it wasn't her place to comment. Not publicly. Prunty had to live here and enforce the law, but she'd watched it unravel. Even on sleepy old Salt Spring.

Least we're not Vancouver with the gangs and their drug war and all the friggin' shootin's, she thought, driving past a sheep-spotted pasture, then meandering her PC through an arbutus-canopied lane, making mental notes of what she'd need to dismantle this one.

When Prunty arrived on this piece of paradise, where hippies communed next to millionaires, marijuana was more of an annoyance than a problem. The hippies planted pot in small clearings, then, at harvest time, the police searched by helicopter to spot what the hippies allowed them to spot. The cops looked good on the six o'clock news, but, more importantly, their busts justified budgets and secured organizational positions. The hippies sold off what they'd not planted so publicly and the game would conclude peacefully – till next year, when they'd stage it all over again.

But times changed. So did the rules. If there were any left.

Drugs on Salt Spring were no longer controlled by hippies, who abhorred violence. The new grow-ops were hi-tech, highly funded, international business ventures run by organized crime.

Elimination by rivals was their fear and the threat from informants, their peril.

* * *

Prunty stood by the trailer and swung the door open with a long stick. She turned her head to one side, cupping her hand over her nose, inching closer.

It wasn't the look that repulsed her. It was the smell. It smelled like a rotting human being smells, and it was making her gag. The corpse was bloated, blistered, and purged brackish fluid which leaked to the threshold, then dripped to a congealed pool by a rock out of place on the landing. The volunteer had stepped in the ooze. Prunty pointed it out and he was back at the tanker, scrubbing scuz off his boots. Not sure of what she had, Prunty backed off, secured the scene, and paged the coroner.

* * *

Barbara McCormick took the ferry from Vancouver Island, a delay of two hours. She and Prunty had met on death scenes before, striking a great working relationship.

"Goood morning, Jill." Coroner McCormick smiled, getting out of her burgundy Subaru and setting her blue scene bag down on the damp sand. "What have you got for us on this wonderfully warm spring morning?" McCormick was a stout lady with a distinctive speech pattern that Prunty looked forward to hearing.

"Got a stinker for ya," Prunty said, pinching her nose and puffing her cheeks, walking up to help with equipment.

"Lovely! Have mask. Will travel," McCormick replied, referring to her HEPA filtered respirator, but saw it went right over Prunty's head.

Prunty was too young to remember the *Paladin* TV series and didn't get the cliché. McCormick realized she was showing her age, but wasn't concerned. She was comfortable with herself – intelligent, articulate, compassionate, and well known for a great sense of humour. McCormick was the senior field coroner in the region with no plans for retirement. She was still enjoying the job.

"I'd say a sudden cardiac event, the way he seemed to go down hard and never kicked again," Prunty told the coroner. She'd seen a lot of heart attacks on her island which was full of seniors. "Seems like he musta been runnin' this grow show, croaked in his trailer, then the generator caught fire. That's what brought us here. Pretty elaborate set-up for one guy, but it's all automated. The Green Team's comin' to take it apart, so all I gotta do is figger out who Buddy is."

"No name, I take it?" McCormick asked, pulling her clipboard and camera from the bag.

"Haven't looked through the trailer yet. Waited for you to get here. The plate on the Suburban comes back to some numbered company in Vancouver, which figgers."

"Well, let us go and have a little look," McCormick said, gloving-up and turning on her digital Pentax.

Knowing the odor would stick to her clothes, McCormick climbed into a pair of disposable, white Tyvek coveralls – the Bunny Suit, they called it – then slipped the respirator over her head, just above her face. She took shots, starting with the exterior of the scene, narrowing in on the door. Prunty, with only a surgical mask, propped it open with her long stick as they got a closer look at the corpse.

It'd been a large man. An older man. Not tall, but heavyset. The body was supine, lying on its back on the linoleum floor, just inside the trailer door. The face was barely recognizable; swollen and bearded in greyish-white. The exposed flesh had turned a green color. Not a light green, nor a dark green, but an intense green like the green of the Incredible Hulk. The lips were black bulges. The left eye squeezed shut, but the right was mostly open. Flies buzzed about; eggs laid, though their maggots had not yet hatched. Prunty shuddered with the heebie-jeebies. It was like the Hulk was winking at you.

The body was fully dressed. Worn, red sweat-pants with white stripes running down both legs. Greyish socks. Dirty unlaced hi-tops. A wife-beater undershirt that had been white once, and a soiled, partly-zipped, Adidas track jacket. Also, a filthy red and white ball cap with the number 81 on the front had been knocked off, now lying against the rear wall. The right arm was flung back with the hand palm-up, pushing at the ear. The left lay stretched out with fingers curled, and the right leg bent; knee pressing against a cabinet base.

Prunty saw no reaction from the coroner who'd attended over two thousand scenes in her career and was focused on determining the cause of death, not dwelling on the fact that it happened.

"Any idea how long he's been here?" Prunty asked as McCormick lowered her respirator, preparing for the head to toe examination that coroners do before a body is removed.

"Not conclusively, just by looking at this," McCormick said in Darth Vader breaths. She lifted the mask and stepped back towards Prunty, flicking her finger towards the remains. "We've got a rather heavy person here and the ambient temperature is high. Very warm. These factors contribute to a rapid rate of decomp, but see the greening of the exposed flesh areas?"

"Yeah. That's rude."

"Well, this occurs in a really fast breakdown which, ah, leads us to suspect that Buddy here is… correction… was… probably a cocaine user. We usually see this greening in deaths where cocaine is a factor."

"Hmm. An OD, you think? Too much coke?"

"Ahh, possible toxicity. But not necessarily too much. Cocaine deaths are not really dose-related, Jill. Two mechanisms can take place. Cardiac arrhythmia caused by direct action of cocaine on the myocardium, or cardiopulmonary arrest induced by cocaine on the central nervous system."

Prunty did a one-two with Kevlar-gloved fingers on her bullet-proof vest.

"But often we see the dangerous mix of cocaine and ethanol, or what is called cocaethylene. See all the empties?" McCormick swept the back of her hand to a mess of burnt bottles and cans scattered outside the trailer. "Boozing and blowing is much more toxic than doing either drug alone."

Prunty frowned. "Yeah, coke's nasty shit. It's everywhere these days."

"Oh, 'tis the evil spirit of the drug world, indeed."

"I don't get what makes it so friggin' appealin'."

"Outside of a good buzz, the principle mechanism is within the VTA, the ventral tegmental area of the brain. Nerve cells in the VTA signal the nucleus accumbens to increase activity. That's the key pleasure center. Going down on soft, Belgian chocolate or a hard, black Chippendale will do that to you, too."

"Gnarly." Prunty grinned.

"But bring on the cocaine molecule and it humps onto the dopamine transporter, blocking the normal recycling process and resulting in a build-up of dopamine in the synapse which starts a rather horny effect. You may call it the heavy breathing stage. This blockage brings on a large release of dopamine in the nucleus accumbens by neurons in the VTA. It's a cerebral double whammy and shoots everywhere like one long orgasm. The body says to the brain: That was fun! We must fornicate again real soon! And you're hooked."

McCormick paused. She looked at Prunty, who was chuckling.

"Oh, sorry for the lecture. You asked how long? Roughly, ah, three days. Four at the most. Notice there's no little, white, crawly-thingies on him yet. That's very indicative of time frame."

"Wow. I woulda guessed a week at least. Jesus! That's harsh."

McCormick grinned back at Prunty. "Cocaine is not a good thing. Apparently it makes one feel ree…ally good when one's alive, but it obviously makes one look reee…ally bad when one's dead."

With her respirator back on, now inside the trailer and standing overtop the victim, McCormick took close-ups of the extremities. Of the torso. Then of the face.

Something caught her eye through the viewfinder.

On the forehead, right in the center, she saw a unique signature – a small, star-shaped hole in the green.

McCormick stopped. She turned to Prunty.

"Ah, Jill… Please hold my camera."

She bent down. McCormick didn't need her magnifying glass to confirm what it was. She stood up, pulled off her mask, and looked straight at Prunty.

"He's been shot. We've got a homicide here."

Chapter 2

Most living people never visit the morgue.

Most never think of the morgue, except when watching *CSI*, *Bones*, or *Hawaii Five-O*. Television shows in hi-def and tells in surround-sound, but it can't broadcast smell. That's a good thing, or no one would tune-in and the actors would be out looking for real-life jobs such as cops, coroners, or forensic pathologists.

Vancouver General's morgue is like Costco for the dead. Stainless steel refrigeration crypts, stacked three high in two rows of nine, have shelving for fifty-four. The freezer unit stores eight and isolation for the stinkers takes six, sealed aluminum caskets. These tanks are also used for homicide cases, locked to preserve evidence. A grindy, overhead hoist shifts cadavers from wheeled gurneys that squeak about the fluorescent-lit room, touring them to and from metal drawers. Some are in-hospital deaths, brought down from the wards covered in warm blankets. Some are delivered by cold, black panel-vans handling coroner cases.

Not only were their physical lives extinguished before experiencing this place, their social status died in here, too. It didn't matter if they'd been the cabinet minister, now housed in 35, who had the big one screwing someone who was not his wife; the once-pretty teen in 22, who'd been texting while driving; nor the Salvadorian trafficker in 14, found plugged in his Escalade. He was just one of four hundred gunned down in Vancouver's drug war. Together, they rested at four degrees Celsius like meat in your kitchen fridge.

They'd waited their turn for a number and a name to be tagged to the toe, then got bundled in a white plastic shroud before being slid on their back to a shallow, perforated tray and rolled to the next vacant slot. The door was clicked shut and there they stayed latched, till the mortician arrived or the pathologist's knives were laid out.

There was no urgency now. Time was up for their bodies, but eternity carried on with their souls.

* * *

Jill Prunty accompanied her Salt Spring victim to the morgue, maintaining continuity – a test of law ensuring evidence on the body had not been altered, planted, nor contaminated along the way. The remains were removed from her island the night before, locked in a tank, and transported by van to VGH. It'd been late when she'd got to bed; much later when she'd fallen asleep. This was her first murder case.

Prunty had the only key, squeezing it tight as she walked towards the hospital from the Plaza Hotel, several blocks up on West 12th. The post mortem was set for 9:00 am, though Prunty was there at 8:15. She bided her time in a claustrophobic office off the autopsy suite, drafting notes, which she'd done twice over. The door opened and she heard a pleasant voice.

"Jill?"

Prunty looked up. "Oh, Hi."

"Sharlene Bate. Nice to meet you in person." Bate held out her hand.

Wow. She's a looker, was Prunty's first impression.

They'd spoken by phone twice the last evening. Sergeant Bate had been assigned as lead investigator shortly after the body was identified. No slight on Prunty's abilities, but murder investigations take more time and expertise than Prunty was currently able to give.

Bate, also an RCMP member, was attached to I-HIT, the joint-force homicide team based in the Vancouver suburb of Surrey. Salt Spring was slightly outside her jurisdiction, but she was taking over as this already appeared to be another gang hit.

"Nice to meet you, too." Prunty gave a light grasp and looked down. "Heard lots about you."

"None of it's true except for that fling with George Clooney," Bate replied with a laugh.

Prunty chuckled back. She'd heard of Bate's reputation, reading quotes in the paper and seeing TV clips with Bate as spokesperson for I-HIT. She was taken with Bate's semblance, though Bate was conscious that her maturity showed through. Bate was fifteen years senior to Prunty in service, but twenty-one ahead in age.

Sharlene Bate was twenty-six when the Mounties took her in and she could easily have been hired on appearance alone. It didn't hurt that she had the smarts and education to go with it. Bate was tall and proportionate in weight once again, but it was her flowing black hair, high cheek bones, and shining brown eyes that still turned heads. As the two women spoke, Prunty looked to Bate's eyes and could see the lines of time had advanced. Prunty figured stress of the job had taken its toll. Bate knew otherwise.

"Looks like we'll be here awhile." Bate smiled, removing her lusty-red trench coat.

Though the morgue was cool, Prunty perspired. She stepped aside, letting Bate drape her red coat over the back of the chair. Bate was in a black silk blouse and black slacks. Around her waist was a black leather belt holding her stainless Smith & Wesson, handcuffs, BlackBerry, pager, and her gold badge – all had been hidden by the calf-length coat. Prunty saw nothing on Bate's left ring finger, but couldn't miss the cross, sparkling with tiny diamonds, dangling by a silver chain from the neck. Bate set her laptop on the floor, snapped open her briefcase on the desk, removed a dossier upside down, and promptly dumped its contents on the floor.

"He's got a name," Bate said, scooping her documents and snagging a criminal record print-out.

The forensic identification officer at Salt Spring had scanned a thumb print through AFIS, the Automated Fingerprint Identification System, which came back with the ID.

"Gerard Joseph Dupris. FPS Number 149881 Alpha. Age seventy-two. Kind of old to be in the gang scene. Ever heard of him?"

Prunty thought a moment. "Nope. Can't say I have. I been on Salt Spring since oh-six and that name's never come up. Who's he?"

"He's a bad bastard. Or, should I say… was a bad bastard." Bate grinned, shuffling her papers. "Record has extensive entries since the fifties when he was a juvenile. Let's see. Manslaughter, armed robbery, rape, possession of weapons, possession of explosives, assault with weapon, assault police officer, drug trafficking, B and E, fencing stolen property, arson, buggery and indecent assault on male, counterfeiting, extortion, uttering threats…" Bate's eyes widened. "Fuck! Kidnapping, of all things."

Prunty listened.

Bate paused, then said "Funny. Everything stops around nine... ten years ago."

"Maybe he just got outta jail."

"Ah... I don't think so. Last entry was only a short incarceration and it shows him paroled after nine months. Here's his CPIC. There's an old outstanding warrant for parole violation. Also, he's on observation as a pointer person to Federal Drug Enforcement Branch. Hmm... Looks like an informant to me. Most of these assholes are. Look at how many charges were dropped over the years. I don't know. For some reason he'd gone underground..."

"Interestin'..."

"Another thing. The scene photos you emailed me? Something really stands out. You know that ball cap on the floor?"

"Yeah?"

"Red and white with the logo eighty-one? That's Hells Angels. Their corporate number and colors. Eight is for H, the eighth letter of the alphabet. One is for A. Also, he was wearing red track pants with white stripes. They do this shit to mark their turf, sorta like a dog pissing on a bush. You don't go around wearing this crap without Angel permission or they'll curb-stomp you."

"This guy was an HA?"

"No. Not a full-patch or we'd know about it. He's too old to be a prospect or a hang-around. He's definitely an associate, but there's something strange going on here. Fed Drugs must know something or they wouldn't have him flagged for so long. The date for entering him as a pointer is right when he's gone off the radar. This seems just a little too frickin' co-incidental to me. I'm thinking the witness protection program or agent status. They had some special interest in him. I'll bet he's a major fink or something like that."

"Big leagues," Prunty said, watching her.

"Oh, these fucking drug squad guys do this shit all the time. They got big-ass budgets to use up or they won't get them again the next year, so they go around changing people's identities, their looks, making their files disappear. You know... the spook type of stuff. Then, when we want information? They pull turtle. I'll have a better look later with an off-line search on his CPIC entries. We'll see who had interest in him. They can't hide that." Bate smiled, re-vamping her file. "Did you find anything more at the scene since we last talked?"

"Nope. Nothin' good. Searched everywhere. Couldn't find even a single receipt for anything. Lotsa cash, though. Over ten grand in piles on the table, like he'd been countin' it. His computer was fulla kiddie porn."

Bate quit smiling. Her face scrunched like she'd whiffed a hot and full Porta Potty.

Prunty continued. "Some coke. Personal use, looks like. We got a plate on the old Suburban."

"Yeah," Bate said. "Rick Portman, my Corporal, is following that up today. I'll bet my ass just where that goes. Anything else come up?"

"Well, there were no witnesses or nothin'. Only thing seen was a black truck that didn't belong there. That was Friday, the 27th, when the coroner thinks it went down."

"What's this about?" Bate opened her notebook, clicking her pen to jot it down.

"Well, our members did the usual neighbourhood inquiries and a lady from up the road remembers a shiny, like-new, black truck parked in front of the communal mailboxes which are right near the driveway to the scene. Only reason she noticed was it pissed her off 'cause it blocks the pull-off and she hasta stop on the road to get her mail. She knows all the local vehicles and says this one was definitely not from this parta the island. Guess they get this all the time with tourists parking there so they can walk down to the beach and it pisses-off the locals."

"Any better description?" Bate asked, picking her exploded PaperMate off the floor, screwing it back together, and starting in her notebook.

"Actually, yeah. Says it's a fancy truck. An SUV. A black, full-size, four-door like a Cadillac Escalade. Somethin' expensive like that. She even knows it's got a B.C. plate."

Bate looked up. Prunty grinned and kept on.

"You gotta understand these locals. They hates anyone from offa their island, never mind outta province or, God forbid, rich Americans. So she remembers it's an expensive vehicle, but cuts it slack when it's got a B.C. plate.

"Did she get the number?"

"Unfortunately, no."

"What time was that?"

"She's pretty precise. Just after 2:00 pm. She knows 'cause she takes the 1:30 ferry back to the island, stops in town, gets her mail, and is home to see Oprah."

"Hmm. Nice to have nosy neighbors. Okay. Black Escalade. Something like that. Typical of gangs. Good stuff. Strange vehicle. Near the scene. Around the time. I'll have Portman get vehicle makes for her to view."

"Uh, we're doin' that already." Prunty glanced down, then up again. "We got a member goin' over vehicles with her on the Internet today. Sorta like a high-tech lineup. Hopefully she'll narrow down the description. Also, we're lookin' at security video at the ferry terminals. We figger if this truck is from off island, then it hasta take the ferry and it oughta be on camera."

"Keep up that detective work and I'm going to be out of a goddamn job," Bate said with a toothy smile.

Prunty blushed. *Nice compliment. Especially from Sharlene Bate.*

* * *

The door opened and in squeezed Barb McCormick, followed by the pathologist, Dr. Elvira Esikainian, and Sergeant Ron Chamberlain, the forensic identification officer from the scene. McCormick introduced everyone.

There'd been extensive examination at the farm before the body was removed and transported to VGH, where the Coroners Service conducted forensic autopsies. Forensic is the fancy word for doing something scientific that's going to end up in court, and there were only a few pathologists, the doctors who study the process of death and disease, qualified to give forensic evidence in B.C.

Esikainian was one of them. She was Bosnian and spoke fluent English, but with a strong Slavic accent. She'd seen unspeakable atrocities during the genocide in her homeland when she'd served with the U.N., exhuming mass graves. The smells and the sights no longer bothered her. She was concerned about being contaminated.

"Thank you all for coming this morning," Esikainian said, shaking hands. "This process we will be doing today will not be pleasant, I understand. The putrification, it will have advanced even overnight and we will be taking some measures to control this. However, I will ask that you all change your dress as an appropriate precaution. I mean for communicable disease purposes."

Prunty looked at Bate and winced.

* * *

Forensic autopsies are attended by only those necessary. Today, Bate was handling evidentiary exhibits for processing at the lab. Exhibit-man was usually assigned to a junior investigator, but I-HIT was seriously short-staffed and Bate had done this job many times. Prunty stayed on, maintaining continuity of the body, which was great for experience as Prunty had dreams. It was Sharlene Bate's job she aspired to.

The group moved to a change room, robing-up in powder-blue gowns, black rubber boots, stretching on surgical masks and latex gloves, then pulling over poufy, cloth head-covers with clear plastic visors before stepping into the brightly-lamped, white-tiled, stainless-steel and antiseptic autopsy suite.

McCormick presided over the post mortem as she was the coroner having jurisdiction, and it was her responsibility to rule on the cause of death. McCormick didn't care who did it or why. She'd leave that to the cops and the courts. Besides McCormick, Prunty, Bate, Esikainian, and Chamberlain, who'd photograph and video the process, was a radiologist to X-ray the body, and also Lito, the little Filipino *Diener*, or morgue attendant, who did the majority of dissection.

Prunty fished out her key, released the lock, and stepped back, shivering in the coolness of the suite. Lito unclasped the tank, wrestled the lid, scissored off the shroud, then misted the corpse with isopropyl alcohol, knocking the waft back to a manageable level. He and Esikainian tipped the tank, sliding the body face-up onto the metal examining tray where the radiologist expediently X-rayed it, then hastened off to develop images.

Although this pathological examination was termed forensic, the procedure was routine. Autopsies start from the outside with a visual inspection, recording everything from your identifying marks like clothing, moles, birthmarks, tattoos and scars, to your trauma indicators such as needle pricks, ante or post mortem injuries, and multiple gunshot wounds. Your internal exam jointly opens your thorax and abdomen, ending in exposing your cranium. It's scientific – definitely not a family event.

* * *

Aside from the obvious defect on the center of the forehead, Esikainian indicated two small perforations in the garments at the middle of the chest. Lito slit away the track jacket following the seams on the sleeves, preserving the mid-section for GSR, gunshot residue. The undershirt was retained similarly. With the corpse stripped, Esikainian dictated a gross external examination recording abrasions, contusions, and lacerations in conjunction with identifiers. The radiologist returned, curtly discussed the exposures, then scrammed.

The pathologist turned to the group.

"As I can see on the X-rays, we will be looking for a total of three bullets. Two of them, I can see, are intact and will be found behind the heart, against the spine. Then, we will look for the third, which I see is in the front and center of the brain. This bullet, it has broken, and is in three pieces. Probably this is so because of the greater resistance offered by the skull as compared to the softer sternum."

Esikainian first focused on the double torso punctures, cognizant that they were entrance wounds. She described their correct anatomical location into her voice-activated recorder and placed a plastic medical rule adjacent to the holes, noting both diameters as 9 millimetres, 2.6 centimeters apart, axis to axis. Taking two thin steel rods, she probed the missile cavities, protracting the angles of passage relative to the horizontal surface of the tray, then dissected a wide circumference of the lesions and tacked the dermis to a corrugated poster-board to dry.

She nodded to Lito. Lito smiled and nodded back. Taking his scalpel, he sliced a Y-incision, opening from the tip of each shoulder, above the nipples and across to the sternum, then in one long sweep down the center, terminating at the pubis. Because this had been a fat man, Lito's next cuts were multiple strokes, exposing a thick layer of corn-yellow celluloid holding over the radish-red breast plate. Using a hooked linoleum knife, Lito loosened the plate, then snipped the ribs clear with orange pruning shears. The sternum was dislodged and he set it aside; the bullet paths being imprinted through the cartilage.

Lito removed the organs, lifting out the lungs, then the liver, the heart, and so forth. Each was weighed on his suspended, metal, dial-scale like the one you use in your supermarket produce department, and he scribbled the gram results in green dry-erase on a large whiteboard, screwed to the wall above his stainless dissection bench.

Esikainian found both chest bullets embedded within the spine right after Lito detached the heart. The aorta had burst and the cord was severed by the two projectiles, which she knew caused immediate immobility and instantaneous death.

Why was it necessary to put a third bullet to the brain? Esikainian briefly wondered, already knowing it was fired last. She motioned to Sergeant Bate.

"Mark this one to be first," Esikainian said, releasing her forceps and letting the lead chunk clink into a sterile glass container which Bate held out. "And this second."

Bate saved the other in a separate clear jar.

When the cranial exam started, Prunty shied away.

Lito propped the head with his black, plastic V-block, then swiped his scalpel from the base of one ear, traversing to the other and peeling the scalp back in two directions – dragging one section over the face and the other down the neck. He switched on his Stryker saw, severed the skull in a small cloud of fetid bone dust and pried off the cap using a miniature chrome bar, relieving the pressure with a suck like opening a quart pickle sealer, exposing the brain.

Lito glanced at Prunty. She watched, half in pall, as he clipped the brainstem, extracting the glob of grey matter from its smooth, bony bowl, letting it squish like a silicone implant onto his Teflon chopping board on top of the bench. Esikainian dislodged the three lead fragments, which Bate secured in glass vials, then spent the next hour securing specimens of blood, urine, vitreous humor, stomach contents and bile, cross-sectioning organs, and exscinding tissue to fix in formalin. Finally, she nodded to Lito who took the visceral material from his white ice-cream bucket, pouring the offal into a green, plastic Glad bag, twist-tying it, and returning the entrails to the abdominal cavity.

Esikainian motioned for the group to move out to the gowning area, disrobe, and meet in her office. She thanked Lito for his help and left to wash up. Lito stayed behind, whistling the theme from Andy Griffith and skilfully stitching his Y-incision with brown, butcher twine looped through a sail-maker's needle.

* * *

"You can record in your reports that I am completely satisfied this man died as a result of trauma caused by multiple gunshot wounds, and there is no evidence of a natural disease process which may have contributed to his immediate death."

Bate penned in her notebook as Esikainian continued.

"As we now know, there were three bullets shot to him and all three would be immediately fatal on their own. I cannot be certain which of the two that we recovered from behind the heart were fired first, but I am certain that the broken one, the one that we recovered from the frontal lobe of the brain, was the last. I say so from the angles.... the trajectories or the paths that the bullets took. Let me see the photos again that show this man in the position in which he was found."

McCormick patched her Pentax to her laptop, scrolling up images.

"You see there."

Bate looked as Esikainian pointed at a likeness taken from outside the trailer, viewing through the doorway, and showing the body supine.

"The angles of passage through his chest are from lower to higher, and they are exactly the same for both cavities. It is not far from the skin of the chest to the spine but, anatomically, we see about seventy-five degrees of incline using the assumption, of course, that this man was upright and he was struck as he opened the door. We again have to make the assumption that the door was, in fact, open as there were no bullet holes through it. Correct?"

McCormick smiled. She liked Esikainian's dry humour and ability to drop medical terminology so a layperson could understand.

"She must be great with a jury," Bate whispered to Prunty.

The pathologist continued. "I can also say that the anterior torso wounds, the front ones in the chest I should say, were caused from some distance. More than two meters, because I cannot see gunshot residue on the clothing like I can clearly see on the forehead wound. I can say the forehead wound was from an almost ninety degree of angle, anatomically, and at very close range. Less than half meter. This is conclusive."

Bate sketched in her book. Esikainian motioned to her.

"You can base your investigation on my conclusion that this man was shot with two bullets. Twice. Very rapid in succession, through the center of the chest, which basically caused the heart to explode and the central nervous system to collapse. Then, for some reason, once this man was dead on his back, on the floor of this mobile type of home, he was shot once again with a bullet, directly from overtop into his brain."

Esikainian pointed at Bate's glass jars.

"There is something else that is of a puzzle to me, and this is probably better for your people in the laboratory to explain. The bullets we have recovered, they are all of the same in this man, but they are not like the usual bullets we see. Like the gangs people, they use. These bullets have no copper wrappings. Jackets, I think is the correct term. They are just soft lead, and I would think they would stop very quickly."

Again the pathologist showed her humour.

"I don't know if this, your killer, could not afford to buy very good bullets, but you can say for sure that your killer stood outside this doorway and, when it was opened, he shot this man in the chest. Twice. Very fast. Bang-Bang. Then he walked up and killed this man a third time, directly in the forehead. For what reason, I don't know. But I know that is exactly what was done."

"Jesus," Prunty said. "Somebody sure wanted this guy dead."

"No shit," said Bate.

Chapter 3

Ghosts were the furthest thing from Sergeant Bate's mind as she flashed her badge and signed in at the Forensic Lab, stating her destination as the Firearms Section.

It took Bate twenty minutes to load up and drive over after the autopsy. She hung an unescorted visitor ID around her neck, grabbed her laptop and exhibits, riding the elevator to the basement where she buzzed a big, steel door. She stared up at the camera, smiled a mouthful of winter-white teeth, waved, and the electric lock snapped open, allowing her into the largest gun-show in Canada.

"G'day, Sweetums," Bate greeted Brian MacAllister, a civilian member of the RCMP. He'd been a firearms examiner thirty-one years, all in Vancouver. She'd nicknamed him after the big, hairy, loveable character on the Muppet Show.

"Hey there, Shar," MacAllister called from his workbench in a side office that smelled like a redneck's bedroom. "Stuff from Salt Spring?"

"Yep. I'll type a request. You get your book."

She slid her laptop onto his government-surplus desk, knocking over a dented, stainless mug and dumping his blacker-than-black coffee into a warped, wooden drawer housing a blue, three-ringed binder. MacAllister leaped and rescued his exhibit ledger, sponging it off and shaking his head. It wasn't the first time she'd drenched it. They'd done this process many times, taking it serious, as it was vital to record evidentiary chains of possession. The lab tried a computer system, abandoning it after a series of crashes, and going back to a handwritten log. Some things can't be improved upon, despite Starbucks stains.

Bate began turning over sealed, plastic packages to MacAllister, who initialed the labels.

"Gonna have to air dry these fabrics," MacAllister said, setting them aside. "They're pretty rank and contaminated. I won't be getting at 'em for a week or so anyway."

"I've got five vials here with bullets," Bate told him.

"Five?"

"Actually just three bullets. Two are whole. One's in three pieces."

"Thought you might be going for a record." MacAllister smirked, thinking back three months when a Red Scorpion gangster was shot four times at a busy Chevron. That one wasn't going to trial. The assassin was smoked a week later in a pre-school parking lot.

"You know Brian, this bloody drug war is getting worse all the time. They should drop the British and just call this province Colombia."

"You read that article in the Economist too, eh?"

Bate looked up from her notes with a big, brilliant smile. "Ah, shit. I thought I could take credit for that line."

"This one gang related?"

"Oh Christ, yeah. Hells Angels this time."

Bate went back to her notebook. MacAllister sat still.

"Really?" he asked.

Bate kept writing. MacAllister was thinking.

"Different," he said. "Rarely see the Angels shooting each other out here. They usually leave that to their fuckin' idiot brothers in Quebec."

"Oh, this guy wasn't patched. He was just caretaking one of their grow shows. Somebody whacked him, but I'm not sure why."

"Don't seem like they need much of a reason these days. A rip?"

"Nope. Grow show was intact. Actually, a ready crop. Big one, too. Around eleven hundred plants, worth maybe a half-million bucks. Not a robbery, either. Still wads of cash in the open. No, this was targeted." Bate stayed writing. "He must have pissed someone off."

"They always do," MacAllister said, finishing his markings. "Like I said, it's gonna be a week or so before I get around to 'em."

"Works for me."

"I'd ask if a weapon was recovered, but I guess you'd be handing that over, eh?"

"I'd hand over the fucking bad guy if I could." Bate glanced up with a wink.

"That'd be a first." MacAllister locked the exhibits in a ventilated metal cabinet, placed the key in a separate safe, shut the door, spun the dial, and turned with a grin. "So how's IHOP treating ya, Shar?"

* * *

You had to know the acronym for International House of Pancakes would show up after the politicians named I-HIT, set up to handle the pandemic of gang murders that took off in the quagmire of overlapping police jurisdictions in British Columbia's Lower Mainland, two years before.

No one prepared for the Colombian cartels combusting, lighting up Mexico and throwing flames north at Canada. Most of the authorities had ostriched their heads, letting Vancouver get butt-ended. Enforcement, prosecution, bail conditions, and especially sentencing for drug traffickers were exceptionally lax in B.C. That lured some major world players. Low risk was a huge business incentive, and it was just a pleasant bonus that Vancouver, with its surrounding Gulf Islands, had sun-tanning weather and some of the most eye-pleasing scenery on the planet.

Vancouver's underground smoldered with the unfiltered, free-trade drug industry. Intoxicating profits were inhaled from an exchange of hydroponic marijuana, grown in commercial venues like Dupris on Salt Spring was caretaking, being traded straight-across for Colombian cocaine smuggled in from the States via Mexico. Cash was used less and less at the wholesale level. Now, all too often, a bag of hot guns was dropped into the deal.

Politicians were willfully blind to the build-up. The Premier had spent two terms prepping his priority, the Winter Olympics, leaving his Attorney General, a former appeal court judge, to make sure the drug troubles didn't embarrass this world-class event. The AG handled it the only way he knew how – by defending the status quo and making excuses for leniency of his learned friends on the bench who wouldn't hammer home a hard line. The federal RCMP management had become a carrion of incompetence and the municipal chiefs vultured over who'd turn that carcass into a regionalized force. Only the new boss of Vancouver City PD had the balls to build order from chaos when it blew up in his streets like a Taliban bomb.

The Canadian Government was far from innocent in Vancouver's mess. In February, they took-down Operation Xcellerator, a multinational investigation targeting the Sinaloa drug cartel, which controlled central Mexico at the American border. It was a huge bust by anyone's standards – hundreds of suspects arrested – seizures of $59 million in cash, 12,000 kilos of coke, tons of weed, a meth lab cranking out 12,000 pills per hour, plus Hummers and Cessnas and SeaRays and Sigs. This followed Project Reckoning, set against the Gulf cartel, terminating the previous September. It hit them much harder – scooping a fast-talking, top-member of the Cardenas-Orejuela crime family.

Worse for the Gulf... back in March, they were punched a one-two within forty-eight hours, costing a half-billion dollars in cash and product. Nineteen tons of cocaine, enroute to Mexico from Colombia, was intercepted by the U.S. Coast Guard from a Panamanian-flagged motor vessel, the Gatun. The same weekend, $207 million was seized in Matamoros, in the eastern state of Tamaulipas, destined for the Gulf's chemical broker who supplied huge quantities of the precursors required to manufacture methamphetamine. Mexico – specifically the Gulf cartel, financed by the Canadian-based Art Williams Organization – was the source of eighty percent of the world's meth and a vital ingredient needed in production had been removed.

Cash.

No system of supply and demand could withstand the hit that the Mexicans took. They fought back. Brutally. Their fight was not just against authorities – it imploded within their ranks over market access. The Gulf aligned with Tijuana's cartel, while the Sinaloa propped-up their once arch-rival in Ciudad Juarez. The drug war turned so ugly that Mexico's President unleashed the army in support of the municipal, state, and federal police agencies which, themselves, reeked of corruption and collusion. The traditional white-powder trail – Colombia – Mexico – the States – to Canada – quickly grew over.

The first swirl in flushing British Columbia's narcotic toilet started with its cocaine tap being turned off; not just by seizure of product and money, but because so many Mexican distributors had been shot dead or locked up. Few in B.C. had pockets deep enough to warehouse product. Then again, who'd anticipated the drought?

Supply virtually stopped. Demand continued. Prices shot up.

Old timers, like the Angels who sat on top of the hierarchy triangle, had no contingency. They had tons of Bud available, but the purchasers, now used to trading in blow, were cash strapped. Credit was a touchy issue and government bailouts weren't available for criminals without white collars.

The door opened wide for new players – gangs like the Red Scorpions, the Independent Soldiers, and the United Nations – all who lived for only the day and the thrills, the clothes and the chicks, the clubs, the guns, and the rides. The universe unfolded as it does, and the war to secure profits took off in Vancouver.

Right where the chief financial officer of the Art Williams Organization quietly lived out her life.

* * *

Bate took time to reply to MacAllister's question.

"I'm getting tired, Brian. Sure I get lots of overtime. The money's good. Prestige is great. But... I've been doing this shit way too long. The hours are a bitch, and I'm ready for a change."

"How's it affecting Emma?" He referred to Bate's daughter.

"She's okay." Bate didn't make eye contact. "She's the big reason I'd like a weekday job now. Em's a good kid, but thirteen is the age where they can go one way or the other. I need to be there at night and on weekends for her. God, I'd give anything for a normal, balanced routine for once in my life." She paused to swallow. "Just to be happy at work and at home."

Emma was becoming a real handful. It sank in last Sunday when she screamed "*You love your fucking job more than me!*" Bate knew it wasn't true. She also knew it sure looked that way.

"Jim?" MacAllister asked.

"Makes his payments on time and calls her when he gets around to it."

Though MacAllister had been Bate's colleague for years, he'd known her ex even longer. Jim Bate was Emma's biological father and, for five years, Sharlene's husband.

"Seems like it's working with Graham." MacAllister grinned at her.

In most work-place relationships, MacAllister would have been way out of bounds with that comment, but he'd introduced Bate to the new man in her life. Graham Sheehan was a prominent lawyer in Vancouver – one of the good guys that wore a white hat – a prosecutor well-connected with an eye on high office. At fifty-six and just appointed head of the Organized Crime Prosecution Unit, he treated Bate like royalty, and she loved the perks that came with her tall, handsome Graham.

"Gotta thank you for that one." She was all smiles.

Bate had been suspicious when MacAllister insisted she come for dinner one night in Kerrisdale where he and Carolyn MacAllister had their home. The Bates and the MacAllisters had been close prior to the divorce, but Carolyn naturally took Sharlene's side in the melee. She'd been Sharlene's close friend since high school. By no coincidence, Sheehan was a guest that night and the two quickly became an item, despite her tipsying a glass of Cab-Sav on his crotch.

"We're getting away for a few days, starting this weekend. Going boating."

"Oh yeah. Where to?" MacAllister asked.

"Vancouver Island. Cool little fishing village called Bamfield on the west coast."

"I know where that is. Kinda out of the way. What's the attraction there? Whales?"

"Nope. Just to get away someplace different. I love the Island, but places like Tofino are getting way too god damned touristy. We're taking that working freighter out of Port Alberni, down the canal to the Broken Group at Pacific Rim National Park over in Barkley Sound and getting off in Bamfield. It's about a four hour sail 'cause the ship stops a lot for people and packages. We're spending two nights at some place a little rustic, which suits me fine. Then we'll come back on the same boat."

"I've heard about that trip. Suppose to be one of them hidden gems. Guess the road in sucks so not many people go there."

"Exactly what we want," Bate said, making more notes.

"Nice there's still little places like that around, ya know. Off the beaten track, where no one's in a rush and nothing big ever happens."

"Yeah, it's becoming more popular with divers and kayakers. Whale-gawkers and the spa-wienies, they stick to Tofino and Ucluelet. Graham's been fishing at Bamfield a couple times and says there's a place called Brady's Beach on the outside that rivals Hawaii and there's just nobody there."

"Just the two of ya?"

"No, we're taking Emma and one of her school chums along. I'm so looking forward to this. The girls can beachcomb. Graham and I... you know... cold bottle, hopefully two, of Pinot Gris... woven Red-Ridinghood picnic basket... checkered blanket on the sand..."

"Sounds romantic."

"And you know the best thing?" She shut her notebook and looked up. "No goddamn CrackBerry."

"I hear ya. You really been going hard since I-HIT started. Anymore on getting promoted to a white-shirt?"

Bate rolled her eyes. "Still hurry up and wait."

* * *

There's a lot more you must know about what made Sergeant Bate tick.

Sharlene started out a Constable like every young Mountie does, going through basic at Depot, the RCMP Academy. She'd been Sharlene Fletcher back then; older than most recruits. Born and raised in Burnaby, next door to Vancouver, she graduated high school with principal's honors. Her mom, Donna, was an operator with Telus and her dad, a line-man with Hydro. Ed Fletcher was a full-blooded Oweekeno First Nations member from Rivers Inlet on the central coast, well north of Vancouver.

They'd earned good income as labor people, providing well for Sharlene and her younger brother, Terry. The family took two trips per year; one local with nature and the other exposing the kids to culture – Europe, Egypt, Japan, India, and four times to Disneyland. The Fletchers were strong in the United Church, which Sharlene remained loyal to.

Following senior secondary, Sharlene spent a year on her dad's home reserve up in Oweekeno, being schooled in the ancient ways by her grandfather, whose traditional name was *Heiclaamaax*. She exchanged with other aboriginal settlements in Australia and South America through her church, returning to Canada and enrolling at UBC, earning her degree, a BSc. Honors. Her goal for years had been the crime lab. Forensics captivated Sharlene, but the recruiter suggested she get street-cop experience and then branch-off to the lab. Staffing looked at her profile. Nearly perfect they assessed, and she was hired immediately.

Sharlene graduated in December; red-serge tunic, spit-shined high-brown boots with gleaming chrome spurs, yellow-striped breeches, and a white glove saluting off the brim of a tan Stetson. Her parents, grandparents, brother, and close friends came to icy Regina to watch her 'Pass Out'. That's Mountie-speak for getting her badge. She was below average in physical training – two left feet, her drill instructor wrote – but scored top in academics.

Posted to the harness, or uniformed duties, back in the Lower Mainland, Sharlene started in Richmond under a field trainer, attending traffic incidents, domestic disputes, shoplifters, and the usual petty crime. Her abilities were recognized. Soon she rotated on Street Crew, the plainclothes unit focusing on the problem of the day – a rash of

B&E's, crack-houses, weenie-waggers, or car-boosters. She was seconded to stints with VIP security at YVR, Vancouver International Airport, which flowed with high profiles – politicians, movie stars, royalty, the mega-rich, and the list-topping crime bosses that NCIS, the National Criminal Intelligence Service, loved to psych out.

Sharlene never returned to the harness. It wasn't that she looked down on her colleagues in uniform. Her aspirations never lay there at all. She'd abandoned forensics, setting her sights on the Serious Crimes Unit which investigated the hierarchy of crimes. Murders. Her career plan changed. Work homicide. Get commissioned. Climb the hangman's rope of management. Then, run off and join the circus of politics.

At thirty, Sharlene transferred to the General Investigation Section, where she met Inspector Jim Bate, eleven years older. Their working relationship became personal and, in less than five months, Sharlene Fletcher became Mrs. James Bate. He was twice divorced with a couple of boys as baggage who'd spend three weeks with mom and one week with dad. Sharlene sold her condo, moving in with new hubby and a pair of mouthy, young twerps.

Two years later, Emma was born – not planned at all. Sharlene nested as her stork-shock subsided. She put her career on hold; decorating the nursery, taking pre-natal, and shopping for baby. Carolyn MacAllister coached at the birth. Jim Bate was away on some management course; mandatory for those with commissions. The first six months were sleepless for Sharlene, but time whipped right by.

She returned to a dayshift at Sex Crimes in Surrey – the Bronx of the Lower Mainland. Lowlifes and hardcores hovelled in the City of Surrey, set against the American border. She bit her lip, accepting the job; hardly a choice if she were to play out her career. They needed a woman on Sex Crimes, not just politically. This place was out of control and teemed with traumatized kids. Sharlene got her promised promotion, supervising a stressed squad of four.

The work was disgusting. At day's end, she'd stop and gorge ice cream, go home exhausted, heat frozen dinners, and read *Harry Potter* while tucking her girl into bed. Then, after one-too-many glasses of red-evening-alone, she'd weep off to sleep; fifty-five unwanted pounds with no room for a third in her marriage.

Corporal Sharlene Bate moved to Serious Crimes the next spring. She'd proven herself, not just a good investigator, but as a leader, which is what management should be looking for. She knew this, trying to balance a career plan while raising Emma alone. Sharlene and Jim Bate had long parted.

This section was a flat-out run. A meat grinder. The drug war had yet to start, but this cesspool gave them three cases a week. Most were just idiots. A bread knife through the heart following an argument over the toaster. The shit-kick from black Dayton boots. Then they'd get kinky stuff, like the guy who was autoerotic-asphyxiating and died with his head stuck in a mix of wet drywall plaster.

Sharlene was promoted to Sergeant just before I-HIT was formed. She'd earned it. Her colleagues respected her. And by now the RCMP white-shirts were chronically dysfunctional, affecting public image and private morale.

The white-shirts are the commissioned officers in the police business, named for the difference in uniform between labor and management. Mountie management was an old boy's club. It hadn't changed in a century, and it wasn't serving anyone well anymore.

Sharlene thought about MacAllister's white-shirt question. *It's my career dream, and I can offer a lot of change.* She knew the constables, and most of the NCOs, held the white-shirts in contempt. The us-against-them division was eons-deep from a leadership lake stagnated in autocracy.

She thought something else. *My weakness has never been exposed.*

Bursts of energy and highs of emotion seemed normal to her, and so did the lengthy periods of darkness; a bitch for a balancing Libra. Like her mother, Sharlene self-diagnosed – compensating by maintaining control, over-achieving, and obsessing with things so well planned out.

* * *

"Getting promoted to Inspector will take time yet, I guess," Bate told MacAllister. "I really, really want it, but it'll probably mean a move back east and I gotta think how that'll affect Emma. She's my priority, no matter what. And there's a couple of things working against me. I got no Admin time, and I don't parlez-vous da Francais."

RCMP command was administered in Ottawa, the bilingual nation's capital.

"Where do you see regionalization going, Shar?"

"Between you and me? I'm keeping my options open. Just look at what's falling out from the Z Inquisition."

She referred to an immigrant who died after being Tasered by four RCMP members at YVR. That perfect storm had been coming.

Vancouver suffered a series of questionable deaths in RCMP custody, and public confidence in the federal force was crumbling like a fistful of dry feta cheese. A local replacement seemed inevitable.

"That's just a total fuckin' mess," MacAllister said. "You know, I get crap from civilians and I'm not even a real cop. There's some major hostility against us out there, and I don't think it's gonna blow over."

She thought a bit, then folded her laptop. "Graham tells me they're already drafting legislation for Vancouver Regional."

"Where do you sit in it?"

"A player, hopefully. But I'm not willing to sell my soul for it."

* * *

Selling her soul would not be Sergeant Bate's peril.

Having it stolen would.

Chapter 4

Thursday, May 3rd, 2012
4:15 pm
I-HIT Office
Surrey, British Columbia

"PRIME is the stupidest goddam thing they ever come up with, and I've seen some boneheaded shit in my time." Sergeant Bate shoved her laptop away; the Police Records Information Management Environment operating system was frozen solid.

"Try bootin' it." Corporal Rick Portman gave her a slight grin. He'd just walked into their hot, cluttered office after spending two days hounding-down leads on Salt Spring.

"I'd like to boot the bozo who made this thing," Bate said with a scowl. She picked up her cup, leaning back in her chair. "So? Whadda ya got?"

"Buncha stuff," he said, making space for his computer bag on the desk, unplugging a radio, and calling it quits for her afternoon talk-show. "For starters, the grow-op property is, like you called it, registered to a numbered company... whose sole director is?"

She watched him do an air drum-roll and hit the cymbal.

"Robin Ghomes."

Bate turned to the side, stuck a finger down her throat, and fake-puked.

"You remember Mister Ghomes, don't cha?" Portman said with a huge grin.

"President. Nanaimo Chapter. Hells Angels. Biggest fucking asshole I ever met."

"The old Suburban at the scene is also registered to one of Ghomes's companies."

"So why's he keeping his name so close to the action?" Bate's brow raised.

"I have no freakin' clue." Portman shrugged. "But it's typical of Angels to use holding companies. Tell you what. I'll go knock on the clubhouse door and get him to call you."

"Yeah. Sell the dickhead some tickets to the ball at the same time."

"You think Ghomes mighta had this done?" he asked.

"Ghomes would never shit in his own nest. Never. But talking to Ghomes is going nowhere. Trust me. So, what do you make of this Dupris guy?"

"He's a piece a work. They pretty much wrote the Criminal Code for him." Portman pulled out his Panasonic. "Interesting he vanished for so long and just shows up now, snuffed."

"I've been giving that some thought." Bate fiddled with her tea bag string. "Doesn't seem to fit the witness protection profile. Strikes me he's been out of the country. U.S. jail, maybe? The old possum's been layin' low for some goddamn reason. Scumballs like this don't just shelve their career for years, then pop up dead. Right? Something's going on, for sure. What else?"

"Okay. There's something in this black truck thing," Portman said, whining-up the computer. "The mailbox woman seems positive on the make after looking at a pile of vehicles on the Internet. It's a good idea these guys on Salt Spring had. Never heard of an on-line line-up, but I don't see why an ID like this wouldn't be clean evidence."

"Ahh, fuck!" Bate yelled.

"What?" Portman looked, then just shook his head. She'd dumped the cup on her lap. He was used to it and carried on. "She picked out a new Ford Expedition, four door, four-by-four, completely black, including the side windows. She's also positive of B.C. plates. Get this. She was so pissed about being blocked, she looked to check out the plate."

"Prunty told me about that." Bate was mopping with a McDonald's bag she'd fished from her garbage.

"Yeah. The old gal was going to write a shit note. There was no front plate, so she went around rear, saw it was a B.C. tag, then backed off."

"And didn't write it down." She pulled at her slacks.

"No, or it'd be Christmas. Now, where this gets good is security video at the ferries. Long Harbour. The local guys came through again by reviewing video streams stored on hard drives at the three terminals. Information from the past weekend here could be a gold mine."

Bate tugged at a liquid wedgie.

"Here. Look at this." Portman brought up an image of a parking lot partly-filled with vehicles. He placed the cursor at the end of the line-up and clicked, editing the image. "See this. A blacked-out Excursion. Bigger than an Expedition like she indicated, though. But watch." He pulled up an image showing the front. "No plate. Keep watching." Another appeared, again showing the black truck from the back. "Note the rear plate numbers seem to be wiped over with something." He zoomed in on the bumper.

"Looks like it's B.C. resident." She squinted at the grainy screen.

"For sure. I'm gonna send this to the video enhancement geek and see if he can tweak it. Also, we got a similar vehicle boarding at the Tsawwassen terminal and got it coming off at Long Harbour. Same thing. No front plate, but the camera there didn't pick up the ass end. That's a no-brainer, though. If it got on, it got off."

"Times?" She dabbed with printer paper.

Portman flipped back in his notes. "Going over to Salt Spring we got it boarding Friday, the 27th at 10:10 am. It's gotta be the same vehicle. This model's rare. I'll get to that."

Her interest was up. "Anything else that fits?"

"There's a blacked-out Suburban, like our Emergency Response Team guys use, on one boat, but that's not what she saw."

"You're sure?"

Portman kept on. "But coming back, it's boarding the 6:30 am on Saturday, the 28th. So it musta over-nighted, cause the last direct sailing to the mainland was 4:30 pm on Friday and it sure-as-a-dick-goes-soft wasn't on that one. There were other sailings to Victoria and some of the smaller islands, but no vehicles even close were on those. Nope. This gotta be our guy."

"Why you so sure?" She hunted for something better to use as a towel.

"Look at the close-ups of the driver." Portman clicked, zooming at the windshield of the black Excursion leaving Salt Spring. "Watch this fuckin' guy."

She squinted again.

"This guy's dirty," Portman said. "The visors are down. He's got a ball cap on. Sunglasses at daylight. Look at his right arm. The hand. It stays up covering the right of his face the whole time, blocking the camera. He clearly knows it's there. He's last in the line-up. Never gets out. No front plate. The back one looks like it's been smeared by sheep-shit, yet the rest of the truck is shiny clean. I mean, Special O could take lessons off him."

Special O, for Observation, was the RCMP's secret surveillance squad. They did nothing else these days except follow gangsters, waiting to intercept the next hit.

Bate put the picture together. "Okay. So we got some hole-in-the-ground, old dirtbag whacked at an Angel-run grow-op. No witnesses or nothing. Coroner thinks he was done three days before. That puts it about Friday, the 27th. Mailbox lady sees a black, gangster truck there at the time, ya-da-ya, and... we got some spook caught on camera driving one on and off the island in the right time frame. Good stuff."

"Hopefully we can develop the plate, but I don't expect magic."

"You said this model was rare?" she asked.

"Yeah. There's not many Excursions made. Actually, they've been discontinued. This one was the last year. I checked with Brown Brothers Ford and showed 'em the clips. They found a few more things that narrow it down. This one's fully loaded with unique identifiers." Portman read from his notes. "Six point eight diesel Powerstroke, chrome running boards, a Blocker Beam undercarriage protector, twenty-inch, seven-spoke wheels, monochrome appearance package, towing mirrors, powered moon roof..."

She looked at the ceiling. "Spare me the used-car pitch. Have the Motor Vehicle Branch do an offline search."

"My hand has been moving faster than yours as always, Master Bate."

"It's Madam Bate to you, Mister Jerk-off. How many are there?"

"Survey says... thirty-two in British Columbia. Seven of them in the greater Vancouver area. But I'll betcha there's only one with this." Portman clicked up the image showing the rear end of the ferry terminal black truck. "See the hitch."

"Yeah?"

"Not factory. It's a CURT industrial-duty receiver hitch that's been installed on the aftermarket. Expensive piece of equipment used for towing something real heavy. It'll jump right out when we track down these trucks."

"Starting tomorrow," Bate ordered. "But make sure mailbox lady sees this video so we know for sure we're talking about the same black truck."

"Monday. Got court tomorrow, and I'm finally taking a week-end off and going dirt biking with my kid."

"Ahh, good for you, spending time with your family. You need a break." She chucked a soaked paper-ball at the garbage can. It missed, bouncing back to attack her.

"Not as much as you," Portman said, watching her crumple it tighter for a punt across the room.

"Well, actually, I am getting away for a bit. I absolutely need it, too. But I'll be back Wednesday. So get right on your black truck thing."

"Yeah. I'll check the rest of the Salt Spring motel records, too."

"Yes, but stay on the black truck lead. I agree. There's something in this."

* * *

Sergeant Bate was right.

There certainly was something in a black truck prowling Salt Spring.

Part Two

The Kushtaka

Chapter 5

Thursday, April 22nd, 1982
1:50 pm
Dwyer Hill Training Facility
Carlton Place, Ontario

*B*a-*Bang*

Baang

"Staaand easy, lads!" Warrant Officer Malcolm Atkinson barked a frosty breath-cloud down to RCMP Constable Mike Buday and his partner, Al Monagham, who were paired on the mock hostage-rescue inside the *Killing House.*

Atkinson, or Akker as he was known to the guys, stood on the dimly-lit, gun-smoked catwalk inside the Close Quarters Battle Building where he watched over live-fire scenarios. He was one of three instructors seconded from the British Army's 22nd Special Air Service Regiment based in Herefordshire, England, to train the RCMP's Emergency Response Team near Ottawa, Canada's capital.

"Too slow. Too slow. We'll go another round."

Monagham holstered his Sig Sauer P226 pistol and glanced over at Buday whose left hand was up, thumb vertical, and forefinger pointed at Akker. Buday squeezed two air shots. Akker batted them off like a Jedi Knight.

"The Force is strong in this one," Buday squawked in a Yoda voice, then muttered something about it being the eleventh time they'd practiced the hard-entry that day.

Who Dares Wins is the official motto of *The Regiment*, but those inside the British SAS know it's really Who Trains Wins. This week's training was on honing instinctive shooting skills. Buday and Monagham went outside to reload for their next try at getting the double-tap right.

Buday – Bude, as everyone called him – took a swig from his Thermos, tore open a new box of Federal 9 millimeter ammunition, and snapped brass cartridges into his fifteen-round magazine. Monagham grabbed a green, logo'd army bag he'd swapped off Akker and dug around inside.

Dressed in Black-kit – Nomex combat suits with carbonate helmets, Bolle goggles, and black balaclavas – they were faceless figures intended to instill shock and awe on their targets. Though this was practice, both wore complete tactical gear including the twenty-two pound Spectra-Shield body armor.

The Beast, they called the vest, had a black, ballistic nylon cover with pockets on the upper right back, holding portable radios hardwired to flesh-colored earpieces and key-activated throat mikes. In the front were their tools – a Fairburn-Sykes fighting knife, Flash-Bang stun grenades, packets of C4 plastic explosive with SPD detonators, OC and CS gas canisters, extra mags, a Laser pointer, flex-cuffs for prisoner restraint, compression bandages, duct tape, hay wire and cutters, a Mini-Mag flashlight, spare batteries and, in Bude's case, a small tin of dirt.

The 1982 trainees tutored on firearms of the time. The prototype Sigs. The Heckler & Koch MP5 sub-machine gun. The Colt M16, which was Monagham's favourite. The Remington 12 gauge Brushmaster. Also, on several sanitized weapons which were stashed in storage.

Bude laughed, seeing Monagham pull a sanitized piece from his duffle bag. "Where the fuck did you get that?"

"Stole it from the fuckin' armory," Monagham said. "They won't miss it." He loaded the 9-mm magazine, tapped it on his kneepad packing the rounds, stuck it in the Cobray MAC-10 machine pistol, then slapped the bottom of the mag with his palm to seat it.

The sanitized guns weren't inventoried or traceable. They were just for experience. Part of the curriculum was so candidates would experience the limits of weaponry and this weapon was definitely off limits. There was no serial number on this little murder weapon as it'd been home-made of parts seized at the border and kept at Dwyer Hill for pure fun.

The Ingram, as a Cobray is also known, looked like a blackish-grey metal box with a short pistol grip holding a thirty-two round magazine, a retractable steel stock, and a short sound suppressor. Its four-inch barrel had no rifling twists so there'd be no identifiable ballistic markings on precisely hand-cast, sub-sonic, all-lead, and non-jacketed bullets. A black nylon bag on its ejection port caught the spent casings, and it had a selector switch to the left of the trigger with three pole positions; safe, semi, and fully automatic. The light weight, eight pounds with a full load, let the Ingram work with one hand, and its silencer squashed the report to a *Pe-teuwt* sound, no louder than you'd hush your baby nite-nite.

An Ingram is the perfect execution tool.

Monagham held the Ingram in his right hand, barrel pointed up. He grinned and nodded at the Killing House. "Bude. Maybe we should go fuck Akker up. No?"

The twelfth entry worked. Bude, much more powerful than Monagham, booted the door. Monagham came in low with his Ingram, picking off the first bad guy, instinctively planting two 9-mm bullets to the chest. Bude nailed the second with his Sig right from the door, flying forward from the kick's inertia. Two more shots. Also one inch apart. Middle of mass. Four rounds in total. Two terrorists dead and Monagham's fiberglass target keeled over.

Then, with the signature unique to the British SAS, Alfred Monagham put one more round to the forehead. Right in the center. He looked up, flipped Akker off with his left middle finger, clicked to fully-auto with his right, and ripped twenty-nine more to the mannequin's guts.

The Ingram went back into Monagham's green army bag and stayed there.

* * *

Like Sergeant Bate, there's things you must know about these two swagmen.

Bude was what the movies wanted in commandos. A body builder. 5-10. 220. All muscle. Zero fat. His cardiovascular system was extraordinary. Flexibility amazing. His eyesight was perfect. Hearing exceptional. Reflexes instantaneous. And that immeasurable ability, situational awareness – SA, it's called – outstanding.

But far north of Hollywood sets where Schwarzenegger fought the predator, Stallone drew first blood, and the Blackhawks went down, Bude grew up a Catholic farm boy near Tilley, Alberta, made Grade 12, and then asked the Mounties for his ride out of Dodge. He joined the Force a few months before Monagham and, destined as friends with their future foretold, they met on this course and turned teammates.

Akker saw Bude's abilities. He also saw something in Monagham.

It was his eyes. Akker saw intensity in Monagham's eyes. Monagham wasn't a ladies' man; not like Bude. He didn't have Bude's bedroom eyes, nor Bude's other manly attribute.

Actually, Monagham was not a good-looking guy – certainly not as Gentleman's Quarterly has them. At 5-11 and 165, Monagham looked thin, almost gaunt. His azure eyes shone like spotlights, his busted nose remarkable, as was his craggy complexion. He'd suffered acne as a teen which left its mark, but what also left its mark was his parent's compassion; not something you'd expect of a cold-blooded killer.

To Akker, Monagham never tried to be anything other than what he really was – someone born to be a warrior. This was beyond a learned ability. It was something you get passed down in your genes. Everything Akker looked for in an SAS soldier he saw in Monagham, except for one small flaw. Monagham was intense. Somewhat solitary. It was noticeable, but far from disqualifying him from the team. Akker worried the lad would burn out.

* * *

The RCMP ERT is a paramilitary unit within the world-renowned police force. Bude and Monagham were two of sixteen members selected for the year's initiation, screened from the 17,000 member organization. There was a minimal physical standard which all finalists exceeded but, more so, an exceptionally high mental standard was mandatory. It included the key ingredient that keeps a functioning unit together.

Loyalty.

The principle of loyalty applies to every successful unit, be it armies, political parties, police departments, families, religions, ethnic communities, intelligence agencies and, of course, professionally-run criminal organizations. There is no monopoly on loyalty, but the lack of it is a death-knell to all groups. Bude and Monagham needed no instruction on loyalty.

The RCMP began their ERT program in the seventies, responding to a growing need to effectively deal with armed and barricaded persons in their Walmart model of policing service, which they provided to federal, provincial, and municipal jurisdictions across Canada. They also took on the national security mandate; protecting airports, embassies, dignitary entourages, and economic summits from subversive groups bent on terrorist actions. ERT instruction included counter-terrorist tactics – extreme actions – and the Force contracted with the world's most extreme of instructors. The 22nd Regiment of the British Army.

The SAS.

The sixteen candidates had been immersed fourteen weeks, soon to be deployed on operational units around the nation. Though their role was containment and diffusion of volatile civilian incidents, the military tactics taught by the SAS were vital. Weaponry, concealment, diversions, explosives, and communications were integrated through teamwork. Teamwork required loyalty, and these two would never have graduated if not loyal.

Grad ceremonies from Dwyer Hill didn't include pomp, pageant, or family. Families didn't even know where Dwyer Hill was. Bude, single like Monagham, was ready to go home to see family but, for Monagham, there was no home or no family to see. He was an only child. The last in his legitimate lineage.

* * *

"Alfred. How about coming to the farm for a week?" Bude asked, toweling-off the brute after showering at the end of the day.

Monagham thought before replying. "That might sound good. Like to meet the family. You talk about 'em so much. That farm must be a good place, too, or you wouldn't pack around that can of dirt like you do."

Monagham's voice sounded like a weed-stoned Bob Dylan. Bude loved to imitate it.

"It's me Lucky Charm." Bude winked.

One would think the world's best trained would be above superstition, but it's a quirk of the breed. Akker, of all people, kept his three daughters' first teeth in a baggie tucked in his tac-vest. Monagham regretted not bringing a vial of saltwater.

"Least it's not cow shit." Monagham grinned.

"Or fish piss," Bude shot back.

Alfred Monagham knew nothing about farms. Water was his thing. When it came to the choice between cows and fish, he decided to spend the down-time alone on his boat docked at Ganges on Salt Spring Island. He'd just spent three and a half months with fifteen other burping, farting, stinking men, and he needed his space.

They'd been posted to the Northern B.C. team based in Terrace where they'd face more bush work than those heading to urban teams in Vancouver, Edmonton, Winnipeg, Ottawa, and Halifax. That suited them just fine.

"You know. I'm gonna pass," Monagham said, thinking out the offer. "But whadda ya say, maybe we split a place when we get up north? Neither one of us got no baggage or nothin'.."

"Not a bad idea, Alfred," Bude replied, referring to his call-sign; a ritual like fighter pilots had. It was easier, and a lot safer, to use call-signs in action. Call-names were clear. Individual. Unforgettable. They were earned by a mannerism, ethnic background, a twist on name, screw-ups, or sometimes just plain bad luck. Bude was a natural handle. Others became Digby, Razor, Crow, Wiener, Burnout, Mazzie, Finn, Rocky, and so on. Bude call-signed Monagham the morning they met and it went like this:

"Mike Buday from Alberta." He introduced himself.

"Al Monagham. B.C. Looks like we're bunkin' up."

"Sounds like the plan. Al… What's that short for?"

"Alfred."

"You're fucking kidding?"

"Ah, no." Monagham looked at him.

"A sweet, innocent, pink baby and your parents called it Alfred?"

"You don't like it, no?"

"Where the fuck did they come up with that?"

"It was my dad's and my grand-dad's. I'm named after them."

"They did that three fucking times?"

"You know? I'm kinda proud of them." Monagham gritted his teeth.

"Okay. So your name's Alfred."

And it stuck.

Within a week, they bonded; pairing on scenarios, on the firing line, and at the mess table. Monagham saw the big farm boy was way more intelligent than he let on and was seriously close to the family – his Pa, Frank; his Ma, Margaret; brothers Frankie and Bob; and his little sister Janet. As they talked, late into nights, behind a closed door, cleaning weapons and mending kit, Monagham felt Bude was like having a brother.

* * *

For the first time they could relax.

They'd passed SAS tactical training, but were still not allowed to go out. Public access, or even discussion of Dwyer Hill, was forbidden. Akker and a big Brit instructor, call-signed Tubbs, snuck in two kegs of beer, six jugs of rye, and a pair of vodka 40's for the grad party, which was supposed to be dry. The knob who ran Dwyer Hill conveniently disappeared for the night, leaving the troops home alone. This pleased

Bude to no end, and he was the first with his face in the pail. Monagham lagged behind, making sure his gear was together so he didn't have it to do the next morning.

Bude was the most popular guy on site and the mess crowd was around him when Monagham showed up. That was no surprise. Monagham hadn't known what to make of his big roommate at the start because, with Bude, you saw the first take.

Bude was fitter than most instructors and would often lead the morning workout. He lived the no-man-left-behind and would be back-of-the-pack on the 5:00 am run, encouraging stragglers on. The instructors were impressed. That excused a momentary lack of respect for government property when he nearly destroyed a black ERT Suburban after chucking in a live CS tear-gas grenade while the instructors were hunkered inside eating lunch.

But Bude earned penance the week later by rescuing a feral cat which wandered down-range and was smacked by lead fragments off a metal target frame. He shut down the line, capturing the stray and commandeering the same black truck he'd bombarded, taking the cat into town where he footed the vet's bill from his own pocket.

Tonight, Bude's table captured the kitchen and cleaning ladies. They lived on the base; the only civilians cleared to be in there. It was getting loud and Bude was already feeling his liquor. He and Monagham were at the makeshift bar now. Bude for his third. Monagham for his first.

"Get mine packed too, Alfred?"

"Gottanuff shita my own," he replied, snooping the bar.

Monagham was careful around alcohol. He didn't handle it well and had a history of going overboard when drinking. But tonight was the night, he reasoned, and poured himself a long, tall Sally. He'd earned this, even though he knew he'd pay for it later, and he was quite right.

"Alfred," Bude said, putting his big bicep around his partner's bony shoulder. "Gotta say I'm fuckin' sorry I made fun of your name when we met. I didn't know."

"It's awright." Monagham looked away.

"Naw, fuck, it's not. I'd no idea about your dad and your grandpa."

The stories came out late one night as they were building their *ghillie* camouflage suits for a stalking exercise. Neither recalled how it started, but Monagham opened up about how his fraternal line had been war vets. Alfred Monagham, Senior, had been a ground-pounder during the First Great War, immigrating to Canada in 1919, minus a few body parts, but with some medals and a pair of bad lungs to prove it. Monagham's dad, Alfred Junior, was a veteran of Bomber Command during the Second. He'd had enough of airplanes by war's end, and returned home to British Columbia to raise Alfred Monagham III on the sea.

Bude listened as Monagham related stories of Passchendale and Ypres the old man had told of The Great War, and of air-combat white-knucklers his father brought back from the next.

But what Monagham didn't reveal – how as a little boy sleeping over at his grandpa's, he'd waken to screams for a medic and, as a teenager, he'd watch his dad sit in long stares till the butt of a cigarette burned him back into reality.

* * *

Monagham settled at Malcolm Atkinson's table.

As the evening progressed, it brought over Bude and the ladies. Akker was getting pissed and his favor for Monagham showed through. He knew Monagham was a fellow Brit, though long removed from the homeland. He also knew of Monagham's father's and grandfather's service to King and Country, respecting that enormously.

Akker told the tale of Operation Nimrod, the Iranian Embassy siege occurring in London almost two years to the day. Monagham sat, quietly zoned out, reading The Regiment's motto scrolled across the blade of a winged sword tattooed on Akker's right bicep, which only those trained by the SAS can wear. What impressed was the confidence. There was zero conceit. No air of superiority. Just a man who totally had his shit together.

"We had three days to mock-up," Akker told his audience. "We made a model of the embassy based on blueprints and practiced the assault all night long. We had excellent Intel where the sods were. Hah! Even today no one knows how we got it. We could actually see and hear the fuckers inside."

Monagham listened.

"Diversions can be wonderful things, lads."

Akker stopped, raised his mug in a toast, quaffed, and continued.

"Air traffic from Heathrow was sent low over the area. We had British Gas move drilling equipment ever closer. The noise got louder. The pricks didn't clue in."

Akker took another pull.

"Right when we stormed, we sent in two Harrier jump-jets from each direction right over the fucking roof. Got the bastards to look up. Then we blew eighty liters of diesel lit by C4 out the back lot. You should have seen the light up, lads. It made old people fuck."

Monagham was diverted by something else at the table – Kathy Wedge's big tits.

She was a cook at Dwyer Hill, and they'd been making eyes since the start of the program. Wedge was single, too, but older than Monagham. She was heavy; disproportionate to her height and self conscious, but her pretty face made up. Wedge and Monagham threw flirts as Akker held his table captive, recalling Prime Minister Margaret Thatcher and her husband visiting The Regiment for a thank-you after the mission.

"Denis had this big grin on his face and said 'you let one of the bastards live'," Akker recalled. "We failed in that respect. We just stunned the cocksucker with the double-tap. Fucker had a ballistic vest under his jacket, and we didn't finish him off with a head shot."

Akker paused, locked onto Monagham, and pointed.

"Don't you ever make that fucking mistake."

They moved on to discuss the trouble between Great Britain and Argentina over the Falkland Islands in the southern hemisphere.

In an effort to boost popularity, the Argentinean military junta invaded those barren islands off their east coast which happened to be under British sovereignty. General Leopoldo Galtieri doubted Britain would put up a fight, but seriously misjudged the size of the cojones on the Iron Lady, Maggie Thatcher. A full-scale retaliation was now underway. Akker and the other two Regiment instructors were on notice that their G Squadron was deployed, salivating to see action again.

That's what they trained for.

* * *

Around midnight, Monagham pulled out a disposable camera. Photos weren't allowed at Dwyer Hill, but doing things not allowed didn't exactly bother Monagham.

Kathy Wedge, now crammed beside him, giggled at a rye-hammered Bude who was hitting on an equally-cut cleaning lady. Monagham took aim, swaying. Wedge grabbed his hands, steadying the camera, just as Monagham turned to chomp a fake chew on her shoulder. The shot fired off, though the print turned out somewhat blurry.

The photo seemed no big deal at the time.

Akker was passed out with his face in a plate of fried rice. Finn was behind, bent down between Bude and his score, giving a big, shit-eating grin. Rocky was at right, squeezing Mazzie's cheeks, forcing his lips to a pucker. Bude's eyes were half shut, a string of spit drooling down. It appeared innocent enough. Just a bunch of drunks with no sense of their doom. The night went on. The music got louder. Inhibitions dropped. By morning, Bude was out cold on the cleaning lady, and Kathy Wedge woke up with Alfred Monagham in her bed.

* * *

At dusk on May 19th, 1982, Warrant Officer Malcolm Atkinson died along with twenty-one other SAS and support soldiers.

They were cross-decking from HMS Hermes to HMS Intrepid, sixty-five nautical miles north-east of the Falklands when their overloaded Sea King HC4 helicopter from 846 Naval Air Service sucked an eight-foot, black-browed albatross up the intake. The aircraft was under full power when both engines quit, dropping three hundred feet to the freezing water in four seconds.

Monagham was at the house he now shared with Bude in Terrace, northern British Columbia, when he got the news that a bird-strike took Akker out. He excused himself, going off to the garage before throwing up and then breaking down.

Tragically, there was a lot more bad news coming for Alfred Monagham.

Chapter 6

The Legend From September, 1836
An island on *Kusso-a* (a lake called the long narrow water)
Ancestral territory of the Inland Tlingit People
Sixty-one miles south of today's community at Teslin
Yukon Territory, Canada

The ghost story began long before Sharlene Bate's, Alfred Monagham's, and Mike Buday's time.

It was long before the conspiracy to murder the informants. Before the drug war broke out. And before cocaine, which caused the war, was even known in North America. It started with scrapes of wooden, funeral canoes being dragged off the island's cold, gravel beach leaving *Kaash Klao*, the Shaman, to begin his eternal watch.

The Shaman's body had been dried, bound, and placed in a sitting position, inside a bent-box under a young evergreen, within a pavilion of piled rock, facing north-west – a strategic spot overlooking the lake and the only direction from which invaders could approach. Behind him were the *katakede*, the grave houses.

The mourners paddled back through the chop of the waves into dusk, towards the smoke of their village, a mile and a half southeast where the river met the lake. The *ann* was an old village. How old? No one knew. The Teslin Tlingit, called *Deisleen Kwaan* in their own language, measured time by the day, the season, and the generation. For generations the village had been there, and for generations the elders passed down the oral history of the Tlingit people. The stories told of how the Shaman would protect their souls in life and in death.

Kaash Klao, left to guard the mortuary island, was the last Inland

Tlingit Shaman, or *icht'a*, to exist before Christian contact. The invading missionaries saw the Shaman as the manifestation of paganism, which they would not tolerate. By the latter nineteenth century, their crusade and smallpox, intentionally spread by the authorities, decimated the Tlingit.

The new Shaman, Kaash Klao's apprentice, could not defeat the white man's disease. Most who survived lost faith and converted, believing in a new deity – one called Jesus Christ. They listened to the missionaries. Shamanism was dangerous. Heathen, the whites said, and must be forgotten. The people accepted the new stories; those of a miraculous man, born of immaculate conception, resurrected after death by crucifixion, and ascending bodily to the heavens where he sat to the right of God, watching over them. Their souls would join him in everlasting life, the missionaries promised, as long as they believed.

Christianity went back less than two thousand years. The Tlingit had been there, their tale told, since *Yehl*, the creator, turned two blades of grass into the parent race. They prospered, became a great people, spreading far and wide. But they fought over who was good and who was evil, so *Yehl* sent a great flood bringing death to all except two, whom, after the waters receded, gave life to all those now in existence.

Before the white man interfered, the Tlingit observed a positive and negative system of dichotomies. Good and evil. Life and death. Order and chaos. Those sorts of things. They knew that reality was composed of the world of the living and the world of the dead. They practiced animism, knowing both worlds were controlled by spirits. Everything, they knew, possessed a soul. A life force. *Khaa yahaayi*, they called it. The essence to existence. The conduit of consciousness. The intangible field of intelligence that connects with all else including humans, animals, plants, celestial bodies, and the forces of nature.

They also knew the other world held mystifying beings.

The Kushtaka (The kush-Taw-ka) was a mystic being – a shapeshifter that took human or animal form. It was evil. Deceitful and deadly. The Kushtaka was Wildman-of-the-Woods, who ate only raw meat. It tricked you. Killed you. Stole your soul. Or invaded you alive – riding parasitically inside – sometimes for decades – till the energy of your essence expired.

A Shaman was a protector of souls – an intermediary in the world of the living and the world of the dead, and also the ghostly world in-between where souls got trapped.

In-betweens were dysfunctional souls, not enjoying life among the living, nor finding rest with the dead. They were minds without bodies, who anguished horribly and strove to be set free.

Freeing *khaa yakghwaheiyagu*, trapped souls, was a skilled task – an ancient task – which only a Shaman could perform.

* * *

In life, Kaash Klao fought The Kushtaka in battles over souls. He knew the power of The Kushtaka. He knew the power of a Shaman. He knew the forces of good and evil. Order and chaos. Life and death.

His final performance – in mortality, that is – came after a new moon following the first sharp hoar-frost of autumn. Late in summer, the food-gatherers became terrified to paddle down-lake to the rich fishing grounds at the narrows. The first party had been found slaughtered on a point of land sheltering the fish-trapping bay, and the Tlingit people knew it was no massacre by humans from a warring tribe.

It was The Kushtaka.

It appeared in the form of a haggish old woman. Tricked them. Circled. Attacked from the back. It cut their throats and opened them up like the Ripper just autopsied them – then carved out their souls and packed them off to its cache squirreled away deep in the world in-between.

* * *

Winter was approaching and the ice-over would soon come. The traps weren't yet set as the people knew The Kushtaka lurked about. Without a supply of *uchut hin-takat*, dried fish, the tribe faced starvation.

The elders summoned Kaash Klao, now old and frail, to battle the entity and defeat its existence for all time. The Shaman doubted his strength, but knew of his duty. He called on two warriors to assist him from the seclusion of his cramped *gau-hit* hut and cross the village to a massive log-and-plank structure called the *da ku*. As always, his Shamanic performance would be public, in the warmth of the *da ku*; not like The Kushtaka that was cowardly and disguised itself in deceitful shapes, callously concealed amidst the thick chill at the edge of the forest.

At sunset, hundreds of spectators flowed into the *da ku* through a large communal entrance facing due south. Elders and the *angaschi*, the ones of nobility, were seated on spruce-slab benches in rows semi-circular to an enormous fire which blazed in a boulder hearth in the middle of the big-house. Thirty feet above, a retractable flue in the *ti*, red-cedar shingled roof let smoke vent to the open sky. Those lesser of status stood back, at the east and west walls, while youngsters sat cross-legged on woven *ti*-mats scattered about the earthen floor.

Ceremonial attendants filed in from a small ingress, a private one at the north – sixteen prime-of-life men, nearly naked, and sixteen pre-pubescent boys dressed in festive clothes sewn of dyed *ketl* dog hides decorated with shell buttons and garlanded with fresh, aromatic conifer twigs. Since dawn of the fourth day before, the adult attendants fasted of food but imbibed on *tutsch-tleku*, a juice laced with *rat-ak'e* emetics, causing them to vomit and defecate profusely into long, slippery bags of intestine, purging and purifying their own innards.

Over the portal loomed a scaffold built of peeled *chlatl*, pine logs, lashed tight with braided cords of *wo-tsig*, caribou gut. On it stood the village-master, the *ann s'aati*, his face and chest painted rich green, red, and black. He wore a tan breechcloth and a gray timber wolf pelt – its stuffed head atop his – front paws draping his chest from the shoulders with hind feet dangling down his back, tail stroking the split-log slats. A *tsak-sset* noosed his neck, gleaming yellow with grizzly bear fore-claws separated by a piano key contrast of polished argillite stones and slivered abalone shells, matching those of his armlets.

Four fire-tenders sealed the main entrance, darkening the house to only light from the flames which snapped and popped like water dropped in a hot, greasy pot. Crowd noise dipped to a rippling murmur as four, fat-fuelled, *kan rajek* torches flashed orangey-blue, high up each corner of the platform, dimly foreshadowing the scene staged below.

* * *

"*H*oiittchka! Hoiittchka! Hoiittchka! Hoiittchka!" the master shouted, welcoming the crowd, arms high and open. He paid immediate respect to the elders – the *ach-chlilchku*, who were the Grandmothers, and the *ach-elch*, who were the Grandfathers – tossing a buckskin pouch holding *kantsch*, a tobacco offering, to the cherry-red coals, and beginning a low, slow beat on a taut skin drum.

Boom – Boom – Boom – Boom

Two men dressed as *yeks*, the Shaman's spiritual helpers, appeared from behind a woven, *ti*-bark curtain cloaking the base of the stage. They carried a regalia box made of *ti*-wood, brightly adorned with painted images of lesser *yeks* and spirit animals, placing it before the elders. Inside were Kaash Klao's tools – *tsche-schuch* rattles of bone and hard shell, carved masks, *icht'a gau* drums, rawhide ropes, wands, crystals, stones, pendants, an antler dagger, charms and wooden whistles, feathers, claws, grasses, herbs, seeds, and ivory soul catchers.

Natural light was gone. Temperature soared for crammed, salty spectators as tenders forced fuel on the fire. The master drummed faster – *Boom Boom Boom Boom* – commencing a chant calling elders to song. In monotonous monosyllables of "*Hi-Ha*", wrinkly old women wailed high, mournful tones while woolly old men grunted "*Ha-Hi*" with deep, guttural bellows. Eight adult attendants joined in, drumming harder – *BoomBoomBoomBoom* – as others formed an arm-locked axis arrear, shaking clenched fists and stamping cinched ankle-rattles, partially packed with pebbles and pods of *pchachta* seed. The youths stood still at attention; boy-soldiers submissive to the shadows of the men.

Slowly. Purposely. Four figures appeared, shrouded in red, white, and black robes – faces hidden in masks carved of *chlach*, yellow-cedar, bearing long, stringy, *ti*-bark hair with hollow cheeks painted late-dusk's cobalt blue; mouths barring sharp, white, wolverine teeth glistening in open jaws, and elliptical jade eyes bulging from full moon sockets. They moved to the beat of drums and smoky hot chants, singing and coaxing at the blackness from which they'd emerged.

Blocked by the curtain, Kaash Klao summoned physical strength. He slackened a draw-stringed bag, sprinkling a powder of crystallized leaves from the *achta* plant to a cockle-shell bowl. Bent, he snorted the dopamine enhancer through a hollow reed.

Up one nostril. Then up the next.

His rush was instant; energy smacked like the tip of a whip cracked at the base of his spine.

Drums stopped. Mantras subsided.

"*YAIiiiiiiiiiiiiiiiiii!*" A stone-splitting shriek shattered silence.

Kaash Klao burst from the dark, wailing and hissing and spitting into the light. He spun four times to the direction of the sun. Four times away. Four again to the direction of the sun.

He braked and fell silent.

Crouched on his haunches, he leaped, pirouetting a single axel, recovering with both feet, square-on to the crowd, haggard hands holding high, calloused palms thrusting forward.

Spectators gasped – *BOOM BOOM* – as drums pounded.

His hair – never washed, cut, or combed – flung loose from its topknot pinned with a bone; the ashy-grey mane cloaking his back, hanging down through his legs like a thick, thorny mat. His weathered face was tattooed, smudged by charcoal. Ears and nose looped with sinew. He wore a royal-blue tunic soaked in rancid fish-oil, displaying brilliant designs of greater *yeks*, and a bronze seal-apron adorned with sun-bleached puffin beaks and orange, deer dew-claw appendages. His headdress – a black crown of mountain goat horns. His leggings and moccasins – fringed moose hide.

Today, he'd be an astonishing sight.

* * *

"*W*oetsch! *Ach-i-re-tan!* (Spirit! Appear before me!)" Kaash Klao screamed.

Drums stopped.

Then started – *Boom Boom Boom Boom* – their beat lower, yet faster, as attendants launched a throaty incantation. "*tsige-kao dek-kona, TSIGE-KAO DEK-KONA, tsige-kao dek-kona.* (Ghost of the near-dead)."

The Shaman donned a mask which a greater *yek*-helper hauled from the regalia box – the Wildman-of-the-Woods with its hideous face and fiery eyes – wrapping a ragged, brown bear-shawl about his shoulders.

He circuited the fire in a direction away from the sun, dropping to all fours, scampering around the blaze. Backwards four times. Forwards four times. But always away from the sun.

"*Woetsch! Di-kr'-i-ta-ge!* (Spirit! You will not sleep!)" Kaash-Klao hollered, goading The Kushtaka to materialize.

A posse of four dressed as *kushtas*, land-otters, rushed in, chasing the dog-running Shaman, pelting him mercilessly with a flogging from sticks of green willow.

He stood. Turned on them. Snarling challenges to the *kushtas*, till four shaggy shapes with great grizzly bear heads pounced from all sides, punting him to the ground, casting a braided net over the groaning Shaman, dragging him off to be swallowed by the blackness of the north.

The chorus stopped.

Drums went silent.

Time excruciatingly passed.

Kaash Klao reappeared in a burst of phosphorescence from the south, wearing a black, feathered cape with a helmeted beak-mask resembling *jelch*, the raven trickster. He ran bird-like – upright around the fire – now four times in the direction of the sun, taunting the phantasm to be seen.

BOOM-BOOM-BOOM-BOOM. Hard drumming and fast rattling resounded.

A bucket of urine, used to eradicate The Kushtaka's defilement, was sloshed on the hellish-hot hearth boulders by a lesser *yek*-helper, driving an acrid stink up the nostrils of the crowd.

The beat broke again.

Human blood, arterially drained from a *kuchu*-slave to prevent the shapeshifter from amassing human form, griddled on the rocks as the small, crippled *yek*-helper ladled the putrid, coagulated slop from a baked-clay urn, drizzling it about the circumference of the pyre.

"*Tasse-ju klelch! Ach-i-re-tan!* (Your form! Appear before me!)" Kaash Klao shrieked.

BOOM-BOOM BOOM-BOOM. Drums began pounding.

He snatched a glowing-red *ssit*-pine log, three forearms in length, throwing it high toward the smoke-space, shooting stars of sparks across the ceiling's black backdrop.

Quiet fell.

Squatting, the Shaman balanced on his heels and sputtered a series of staccato challenges for The Kushtaka to appear. He pleaded to *kiyek*, the upper spirits, to *takiyek*, the middle spirits, and to *tekiyek*, the lower spirits of which The Kushtaka belonged, then engaged the local-consciousness of spectators, pleading them to pull as if paddlers in a spiritual canoe.

"*Tu kinayek!* (To all spirits!)" Kaash Klao howled.

"*Ti kinayek!* (From all spirits!)" the crowd bellowed.

"*Kush-ta-ka! Kush-ta-ka! Kush-ta-ka! Kush-ta-ka!*" Kaash Klao cried, vexing the fiend.

The crowd reciprocated, four-fold in intensity. Clamor soared – the Shaman leading the *da ku* with the intensity of a tent-full of hellfire and brimstone revivalists.

* * *

An inversion formed in the smoke-hole.

Invisible at first, it began to haze and swirl in a direction away from the sun.

A chill rained over the sweltering house, hushing the crowd to a concurrence of pounding hearts, heaving lungs, and sobs of small children overwhelmed.

The cloud accrued color.

First indigo. Then aquamarine. Then blends of goldenrod mist, fluttering with creamy-green gas, mimicking the dancing hues of northern lights. It emitted a crackle, modulating like static electricity. Beginning to cyclone, it formed a tumultuous tempest turning lineal – a tangerine trapeze of electromagnetic tentacles radiating high voltage, high overhead.

The shape shifted.

Now a gelatin funnel, it spun a half optic spectrum, flashing chartreuse to saffron. Instantly, the apparition flashed itself as a vortex to the bull's-eye of the fire, exploding in a kaleidoscope, showering the spectator's scalps under a torrent of crimson sparklers.

* * *

Shaking as an old man with Parkinson's, Kaash Klao reached to his regalia box, grabbing an oyster-catcher rattle, a rawhide rope, and a dagger carved from deer antler. He hoisted these artifacts of the ancients to his crowd, displaying them as high as he could. They roared approval, but he turned – succumbing to a fit of wheeze.

A greater *yek*-helper pulled off the *jelch*-trickster mask and feathered cape, handing him the *alkatsk* bowl with remnants of *achta* powder which he snorted once more.

Energy blasted back.

He stood. Bare-breasted. Square-on again to his tribe.

The master beat a rapid tempo – *BOOOM-BOOM-BOOOM-BOOM* – as attendants barked back. The Shaman signaled spectators to follow, driving decibels above thunder rolling on a hot August night.

Kaash Klao half-wheeled, pounding his rattle at the conflagration, incanting "*Kushtaka*" at the apex of his lungs – an embodiment of Yehl berating a fiend from hell's angels.

* * *

The phantasm metamorphosed.

Infuriated, it leaped off the tongues of the flames, seizing the Shaman, demonically spinning him twice in a direction away from the sun, violently accelerating and cinching a ghastly ligature around the neck of the stricken old *icht'a* – fanatical foes flailing and flogging, slashing and shiving, breaking, binding – collapsing – convulsing – ceasing – flat-lining to ethereally exist, now one form en masse.

Time seemed to freeze.

Like an ice-age passing, the spectators glacially thawed from the shock of their awe.

Slowly, they craned towards their Shaman – contorted in a fetal ball – puffs of mauve and teal emitting from his orifices. The wisps increased, permeating to an iris-blue hue, encircling his body, becoming a halo of olive drab smog.

The *da ku* erupted.

The murk diffused, levitating above the fire, transfiguring to an oily-slick scum – the banana-ripe glow of the skunk-cabbage flower – polarizing, magnetically suspending, taunting the embers as if to pick an unprovoked quarrel.

The master struck hard – *BOOOOM* – frantically ordering the attendants to follow. Dozens of drums. Hundreds of voices. Bashes of beats and core-chilling chants of "*Kush-Ta-Ka*" smashed off the *da ku* walls.

The film of sleaze bubbled.

Condensing to a greasy-gold smutch, the apparition churned atop of the flames, forming a slippery column of serpentine slime, showing its primary spectrals – part cyan, part magenta, part yellow.

The crowd went primeval.

The sludge manifested as oxblood plasma.

"*Woetsch! Di-k'ri-ta!* (Spirit! Death to you!)" the master shrieked.

It elevated, orbiting the ceiling – twice in its whirlpool away from the sun – spontaneously ejaculating hot spurts of demonic seed, spastically spraying the gaping crowd in a despicable violation of their spiritual dignity – its satanic spawn sickly swallowed by the gagging mouths of all those within, no matter the status. Adolescent or elder. Boy. Girl. *Kuchu* slave or *ann s'aati* master.

The entity decelerated.

Collected at the smoke-hole.

Then vanished somewhere in-between the darkness and the light.

* * *

The legend concludes that Kaash Klao died that night – in physical form, that is – on the ground in that *da ku*, an old man exhausted from a metaphysical match which sent the shapeshifter spiraling back to a corner of the paranormal. But he remained loyal, keeping watch a hundred and forty-nine years until The Kushtaka returned to the narrows. This time in the form of a man.

Immense spiritual forces battled again, that day in 1985, on the edge of that frozen lake, trapping two young police officers, Mike Buday and Al Monagham, transcending their souls to that world in-between – the world of ghosts – ghosts that would come to haunt Sharlene Bate and deliver the informants to exactly where they belonged.

Into the flames of eternal damnation.

Chapter 7

Tuesday, March 19th, 1985
10:55 am
Sixty-four miles southeast of Teslin
Yukon Territory

Seventeen years before the first informant was shot and a thousand miles north of Sharlene Bate, who sat yawning in her university class, Monagham and Buday hovered at nine hundred feet in a Bell 206, watching their target mush a packed, sun-lit sled towed by two dogs southbound across that white, frozen lake. They stayed back a mile and a half as it was armed with a high-powered rifle, already trying to shoot down the first police aircraft spotting it.

"This is fuckin' nuts," said Monagham.

They were discussing that point of land where the lake narrowed and was choked by a stretch of open water, planning to cut off a madman wanted for murdering a trapper and suspected in the disappearance of others. Bude was serious. More than Monagham had ever seen him.

"Got a bad feeling on this one, Alfred," Bude said over the helicopter headset. "If he makes it past that point, he's home-free for a straight run to the bush. That'll be a fuck of a lot worse than trying to take him on the ice."

No one ever thought this up as a training scenario.

The mad-man was Michael Eugene Oros, a Kansas draft dodger who escaped the Vietnam War and hid in Alaska, before wearing out his welcome and fleeing to the Yukon. Oros roamed this vast wilderness for thirteen years, living off the land and raiding trapper's cabins and trail caches. He'd become a legend in the north, known for his bush savvy and ability to survive in the harshest conditions, often exceeding thirty below.

The whites called him Crazy Mike, who'd appear from the dark at a campfire, point his rifle at pants-pissing people, and ramble on about the CIA poisoning his water and spraying him by air with mind-altering chemicals. Clinically, he'd be diagnosed as a paranoid schizophrenic – more so a perilous psychopath with homicidal neurosis.

But the Tlingit people knew more about Oros.

A lot more.

* * *

The hunt started three days before when Oros burgled a cabin and was spotted down-lake near the narrows by a terrified local who reported it to Constable Jack Watson of the Teslin RCMP detachment. Watson had spent two years, on and off, pursuing Oros after Gunter Lishy, a trapper, was found shot in the back and the vanishing of others began.

Watson set out to locate Oros in a fixed-wing, Pilatus Porter PC6 ski-plane piloted by Ed Haines, who owned Wolverine Air in Teslin. Both knew the area. They'd a suspicion where to find Oros, though they'd no intention of confronting him on their own. Watson already alerted the Commanding Officer in Whitehorse, requesting ERT to standby.

Normal for this time of year, the weather was cold and the skies were clear and sunny – perfect for flying. The Porter circled the ransacked cabin where they picked up a sled trail heading south. Watson knew of another cabin eight miles down Teslin Lake, which was actually a large widening of river, nearly a hundred miles long and two wide.

Sure enough, that's where the trail led. Haines yoked the plane in a starboard bank, giving Watson a broad view out his window. As they flew low, 300 feet over trees, Watson spotted Oros standing atop a ridge near the cabin.

"Look out!" Watson shouted.

Oros pulled the trigger on his .303 rifle. Haines heard the shot above his engine drone. Watson saw Oros work the bolt.

"Hang on!" Haines yelled. He evaded, full-throttling the Porter, turning tail, minimizing its silhouette, and waggling the wings.

Two shots were enough for Jack Watson. He called the CO, who reluctantly activated ERT.

* * *

It was a Monday, pushing five o'clock. Monagham and Buday were heading to the Skeena Hotel in Terrace for a drink after the day's training when their pagers went off.

"So much for getting pissed tonight," Bude said.

Getting pissed was routine now. Fire and Gasoline, their senior NCO called the pair. Work hard and play hard was the lifestyle up north, and these two were as good as it got. Monagham bought a house, which Bude paid him rent for, and it was party central at times. Actually, most of the time. No one got hurt, but the stories of what went on became epic, including the time Bude chain-sawed the front door down – buck-naked.

They kept their own space, each having a bedroom at opposite ends which worked-out well, and they shared a kitchen, one bath, and a living room. For two single guys, they survived quite all right and were smart enough to hire a cleaning lady. This one was hands-off though. She was a big Polish woman, tough enough to ass-whoop a water buffalo, and she put up with zero bullshit, including the time the old hose-monster found Monagham passed out on the couch with a grilled-cheese stuck to his head.

For two years, Monagham and Bude lived, worked, and played together until one day Monagham went and got married. You'd never think it would happen. A tall, dark, and strikingly pretty Italian girl, who worked as a police dispatcher, took Monagham away, but only as far as a new house down the street with a suite in the basement. For Bude, it was win-win. He kept his brother and adopted a new sister, Maria Monagham, who would put up with their bullshit.

* * *

There was no bullshit today.

Monagham and Buday were backed up by two other helicopter squads of three; the second holding north of the target, also out of firing range; the third about to lift off at Teslin. Their nine-man team left Terrace late at night by the Force's Twin Otter, setting down in Whitehorse right at midnight. Due to a weight limit, they shipped with minimal equipment. Someone had the bright idea to leave the portable radio repeater behind, as a second was in stores way up north.

Watson had a game plan in place before ERT was deployed. It was simple. Keep Oros on the lake and stop him from getting in the bush.

He and Haines held surveillance from the Porter all afternoon, except for a trip to refuel. Towards dark, they watched Oros make his way across the ice towards Big Island, the traditional Tlingit cemetery at the lake's center, three miles north of the narrows. The Jennings River estuary was southeast by the old village and the high mountain, Klunuctiway, was due west; neither a viable escape route. Straight south lay a camp at Hutsigola Lake where they suspected he'd flee, except for one obstacle – the narrows with its wide-open water. The Porter circled high out of rifle-range till dusk forced them down at their strip. It was a new moon and would be black soon, unlikely Oros would break before day.

* * *

Their target saw them leave. Standing at the tip of the island, it unhitched the dogs, letting them pace, waiting for food. It took an axe, shifted shape, gliding trackless overtop of chest-deep snow to a crest where a large, old evergreen kept watch. Back in man-form, it chopped boughs, making its bed at the base of the tree against a pavilion of piled rock, facing northwest – a strategic spot overlooking the lake and the only direction from which invaders could approach. It wouldn't build a fire. That'd make heat, smoke, and light. It fed the dogs frozen moose, keeping a fresh squirrel for itself, eating it raw. Then, it shifted in with the shapes of the night, rifle at ready, knowing they'd be back come the light.

* * *

The Porter was refueled, the repeater delivered by road, and all were in the air at dawn's crack. As ERT mustered in Whitehorse's wee hours, one hundred sixty-four miles to the east their target broke camp and went south.

Now the clusterfuck began.

The CO was new in from Ottawa; an administration guy with no operational time. The Yukon was a post he'd held his nose at, though it was deemed prudent for his white-shirt's progression. He didn't need to exorcise the poltergeist that Oros presented. He'd no idea of options to exercise, and he'd an ego far too anal to ask. He waffled on Watson's plan, checking policy and procedure, unsure of how ERT used their force.

As he mangled his manuals and massaged his waxed moustache, the Otter sat still on the tarmac. Someone had to authorize overtime to refuel it. Someone's truck wouldn't start, so they hitched a ride back to gas-up. Someone bumped the plane's plug-in and its batteries went cold. Someone forgot to call the co-pilot. Someone lost the case with the maps. Someone locked-up the guns, and the ammo, and then sauntered on home with the key. And they all awaited a decision from someone in-charge; someone sound, sound, asleep on his books.

Clusterfucks get people killed.

* * *

It was nearly ten by the time the team mobilized from Whitehorse to gear-up in the Teslin police garage before transferring to helicopters for an assault down the lake. Moose, the team leader, was dictating blood types for a standby ambulance crew, when Jack Watson called to Corporal John Greer, the Detachment Commander, who was scrawling them down.

"John. Someone out front needs to see you."

"Not now. Have them come back tomorrow."

Watson came up, whispering, "It's Eunice Johnston. You better go talk to her."

If it were anyone else, Greer would have ignored them. He handed Moose the pad, went to the front door to let the Tlingit elder in, and helped her to his office.

"Policeman," she said. "I have seen in a vision of what is to happen. Oros. He is The Kushtaka. He is tricking your warriors to kill them and steal their souls."

Greer's swallow stuck half its way down his throat.

"The Kushtaka has invaded our sacred burial grounds and violated the grave of our ancient Shaman, Kaash Klao," she said. "The Shaman, he must stop The Kushtaka, and a battle will take place before noon. Your warriors must know this, for they are in great danger and must take caution."

Greer had been a policeman in the north for twenty-eight years and had immense respect for the Tlingit people. Knowing this elder, her ways, and the location of which she spoke, Greer took her message seriously. Very seriously. He gave her an offering of tobacco, clutched her hands, thanked the Grandmother with his eyes, and she slowly went on her way. Greer forced his breakfast to stay put as he went back to the men in his garage.

They'd only laugh if I tell them.

* * *

Moose divided them into three groups of three, each assigned to a Jet Ranger chartered from Whitehorse. Squad One – Tubbs, Sonny, and Shambo were to stay north. Squad Two – Bude, Alfred, and Ozzie were to go south. Squad Three – Moose, Mother, and Deet would stay east, in a holding pattern.

The Ops Plan, finally endorsed by the CO, was no different from what Watson wanted. Keep the target on ice. Contain it from shore. Use bullhorns to order surrender. And shoot it for failing to comply. The first two teams would land at the shoreline, ahead and behind, prepared to fire, and the third would box it in from the lake. The plan also gave the green light to hostility, authorizing discretionary use of deadly force.

It sounded good in the briefing room, especially with the group's insurance – the Porter keeping watch – relaying through the repeater on board.

* * *

"He's headed between that open water and the west shore," Bude said over his ERT headset, transmitting on local, not repeater. "Fuck. I wouldn't do that. What's he doing?"

"Tryin' to suck us in," Monagham came back, barely audible above the high-pitched, whiny chop of the aircraft's main rotor.

"*Fuuck.*"

"It wants us on the ground."

"It, Alfred?"

"Sumpin real weird goin' on here, Bude."

"What're you saying?"

"Dunno what it is, but the only safe way to do this… take the door off the chopper, and I'll take the cocksucker out from up here. Goin' a round on the ground with that fuckin' guy is suicide."

"*Fuuuck.*"

Moose was just lifting at Teslin, so Bude was in command down the lake. Practically – he knew Monagham was right. Legally – he couldn't justify it.

"Okay. We gotta cut him off at that point." Bude clicked to repeater. "Tubbs from Squad Two."

Tubbs, or Big Jim Claymore, who'd just converted to the police from the military, was in-charge of Squad One.

"Go, Bude."

"See that point jutting out where it narrows and the open water is? We're going down there."

"Copy. Where do you want my lads?" the huge man called back.

"Best place for you guys is… make your landing behind him. That north bay back of him. Make lots of action. Do the diversion. We'll touch 'n bail just south of the narrows."

"Copy"

"Keep on repeater. Don't switch back to local," Bude ordered, knowing the squads were nearly a mile apart and dependent on the Porter; not just for eyes, but for ears. Bude looked at Monagham in the rear seat beside him, then to Ozzie upfront. Still on repeater, Bude directed "Okay. We'll buzz-saw."

This was a standard containment tactic where, like teeth in a saw blade, all points covered one another.

Bude's voice came back on the earpieces. "He's what? Eight hundred yards out from that point? Heading right at it, going slow with the dogs. At that speed, I'd say we got least an hour."

The helicopter held hover as Bude laid it out.

"We'll do a wide sweep, come up from the south at lake level, exit at the shoreline just behind the point, then the chopper will head out as if no unload. You guys keep pushing him right at us, Tubbs. We'll cut him off."

"Right, lad."

"We all good?" Bude roll-called.

"Tubbs. I am good to go."

"Sonny. Good."

"Shambo. Good."

"Ozzie. Good."

A pause.

"Alfred?"

Another pause, then, "I'm good, Bude."

Everything seemed good.

But, thanks to the clusterfuck, the Porter drank itself dry on fuel, forcing it back to Teslin. The only repeater, its electronic air hostage, went skyjacked along, and its only battery was dying.

"Go south-east for two miles," Bude told the pilot by intercom. "Make a wide circle back north, then descend just above lake level. Fly tight to the shoreline so we're outta his sight. Hold just before the point, then go right to surface, hover, and we're out. You leave the same way."

"Watch the surface in the bay," the pilot cautioned. "Doesn't crust like open lake."

"Just get us down. We'll go from there." Bude switched to repeater. "Tubbs, we're going in."

A garbled signal came back. "Copy, lad."

Monagham was watching their target. "Bude. The fucker done sumpin funny. Fuckin' guy left his sled, went in the bush, and come back out. I don't like it."

"Copy that, Tubbs? Target off sled, to shore, back to sled," Bude radioed.

"Probably testing snow conditions," the pilot cut in.

Bude glanced up. Monagham's eyes stayed on their target, now back at the sled and slowly southbound.

"Tubbs?"

Claymore had seen it, but couldn't respond.

Bude called again. "Tubbs?"

Nothing.

"Tubbs? Copy?"

Silence.

"What the fuck? The repeater's down."

They raised the Porter over aircraft frequency, confirming it was done for two hours.

"Lovely," Bude cursed. "Just fucking lovely."

Monagham was still on their target. "Don't see we got no choice, Bude. Squad One's already grounded."

"*Fuuck.*"

Five minutes later, Alfred Monagham was the first to leap out, expecting to be off on the run. He felt like he'd been dumped in the ocean. The snow was powder, chest deep; its fluff forcing a fast, frontal crawl. It was fifty yards to shore, but the surface firmed-up with each stroke. Ten minutes were lost before Squad Two hit the crust.

"Oz. Take the east. The tip of the point," Bude directed. "Alfred. Take center tooth. See the big tree? Highpoint? Midway in-between tip and timber?"

"Yup."

"I'll take west flank against thick stuff and stop any circle. Alfred, you take the horn and challenge when he gets close. Ozzie, you fuckin' smoke him when he don't comply."

They looked like ghosts in the forest – camouflaged in white, military oversuits, moonboots, shooting mitts, and white balaclavas. Monagham and Bude held M16's; between them, over 200 rounds. Ozzie had the team's sniper rifle, confident in a head shot, anytime, out at 300 yards. His job was simple. Give the team protection at a distance and that's what they wanted. The target at a distance.

Bude signaled Ozzie to go. Oz struggled, half belly-crawling, keeping low till reaching a brush clump at the point's icy end, sixty yards to the east. Monagham and Bude crouched, rifle checking – mags full, breeches locked, barrels clear.

And they stood. Silent. Staring right into each other.

"I know what you're thinking, Alfred."

Monagham cast his gaze at the snow. Bude grasped his partner's bony bicep.

"If I don't make it out, you can have my chainsaw." Bude's smile was weak and his wink only half.

Then they split-up. Monagham had forty yards. Bude, a bit further.

Jim Claymore couldn't raise Squad Two. Through binoculars, the powerful man was observing their target. It was observing him back.

250 yards north of the point, it changed snowshoes, grabbed its rifle, left its dogs on the ice, feinting once again to the bush.

Claymore knew what was happening. It was the oldest of tactics, and he'd done it himself. He swore, immediately ordering Squad One to advance fast on foot.

Monagham saw it fade into thick green, just as he got to his big tree.

"Watch your flank, Bude. The fucker's comin' for us."

"Got 'er under control."

Eight minutes passed.

Monagham believed if anyone had 'er under control, it was Bude.

The only thing he felt secure of was Bude. On the flank.

Six more minutes.

Air still. Sun brilliant. Temperature neutral. Silence total.

Monagham was never this alert.

Adrenalin shot as he saw a shape shift through trees.

"Bude. One-fifty out. West timberline. Sumpin's there," whispering in the mike.

"Copy."

Four minutes.

"Bude. Watch your flank."

"Got 'er."

One minute.

Monagham caught a flick over his left shoulder.

Back to the scrub brush. South towards the noon-day sun.

Nausea burst from his guts as a ghostly glow formed in the gray wash of the brush, forty-four yards behind.

Monagham blinked.

The glow stayed, becoming a hideous face with fiery eyes set on ragged shoulders.

"BUDE! IT'S RIGHT BEHIND YOU!"

BANG!

* * *

For Monagham –

Time stopped.

He viewed the world from outside his body.

As if perched on a limb of the big tree, he saw everything with absolute clarity.

Like a slow motion picture –

Frame –

By frame –

He watched Bude go down –

The Kushtaka work its bolt –

Turn at him –

Pull its trigger again.

Monagham's M16 snapped up and fired one round to the center of the shapeshifter's head.

* * *

Mike Buday lay in silent death, on his back with his eyes wide open, while the snow all around them turned red.

Alfred Monagham screamed and buckled over.

Gyrating from quantum imbalance as his core's conduit cut clean, Monagham was spiritually eviscerated as The Kushtaka spun out his soul and packed it off with Bude's to its cache hidden deep in the dark world of ghosts.

* * *

Big Jim Claymore laid Bude in the Porter.

Al Monagham sat on the floor through the flight back to Whitehorse; anatomically intact, but no longer with essence of existence.

He gripped Bude's stiff bicep, speaking just under his breath. "Bude. I promise to go home to the farm and tell the family what happened. I promise that can of dirt'll be in a pocket of your Red Serge we'll bury you in. And I promise. No matter what. No matter how long. Somehow… I'll find our way out."

* * *

Jim Claymore stayed back and strapped their target to a sled, dragging it up-lake by snowmobile, leaving the body on the concrete floor of the police garage.

Oros was dead, but The Kushtaka sure wasn't, and it needed a new ride.

Claymore shut off the light and went towards the warmth of the station, not aware of something creeping right up from behind.

Chapter 8

Friday, December 20th, 2002
6:15 pm
Ganges Marina
Salt Spring Island, British Columbia

Jingle Bell, Jingle Bell, Jingle Bell Rock
Jingle Bell Chime in Jingle Bell Time
Dancing and Prancing in Jingle Bell Square
In the Frosty...

"Fuck off!"

Click. Alfred Monagham shut off his boat's radio.

He was miserable. Christmas was a bad time for him, but it wasn't carols he was sick of. It was life. He was sick of his life and he'd made the choice to check out.

He stared at the half-empty forty, then reached for one final drink. After Bude was gone, whiskey became his best friend. They stayed friends seventeen years, but now it was time to say bye. It wouldn't be hard. Monagham finally had enough.

He'd had lots of drinking buddies over time. Most were superficial, like the two informants he'd got pissed with up in a cabin near Atlin nearly two decades before.

Before things with the informants went so horribly wrong.

Or those at Moby's, the bar above his wharf, where he lushed his last days away.

But some had been deep, like those in the photos he'd taken from a waterproof container and laid out on the galley table.

His boat – his only home – rocked and creaked against the wooden float, sloshing the rye in his cracked, plastic tumbler. The wind came up, making the dark air much colder. It felt like the rain may turn to snow, but he didn't care. He no longer cared about the weather. He no longer cared about shaving and showering. And he cared less that he'd missed the medical board.

You need to know that he cared about the investigation, though.

And he cared about two other things, though he'd no idea how they'd ever come back.

He made sure his affairs were in order and it would appear accidental. A done-himself-in ruling would void the insurance set aside for a pair from his past. His will was updated, and he trusted the executor. His credit card balance was zero. His fuel bill and moorage were paid, as were his cell phone and satellite TV accounts. Same with his postal box.

Alfred Monagham planned to go out clean.

* * *

He'd learned lots of psychiatric terms by now.

He knew NEC was short for neuroendocrinology, an all encompassing term for a multi-disciplined study which included PTSD, post traumatic stress disorder, and that was old hat. Combat stress reaction was real, he knew. He'd learned they used to call it *Shellshock*, which was why the old man screamed for a medic in the middle of the night, and why his dad had *The Thousand Yard Stare*. He'd researched the shit out of PTSD and knew that wasn't his issue – just the look in his eyes showed his life force had long been spun out.

At the direction of two doctors, he couldn't recall which ones, he'd undergone a DEX, a dexamethasone suppression test that determined his CRF, corticotropin releasing factor, concentrations were high. This suggested an abnormality in his HPA, hypothalamic-pituitary-adrena, axis and an increased sensitivity of glucocorticoid receptors. They advised long term exposure to high levels of norepinephrine and lower levels of cortisol.

Monagham listened, shook their hands, and thanked the pair.

He'd had lots of psychotherapy that promoted stuff like CBT, cognitive behavior therapy; GET, group exposure therapy; PET, prolonged exposure therapy, and some others that were part of CISM or critical incident stress management. One treatment created a special program, prepared just for him, that had a method of factors identifying six symptom clusters they thought may have been the source of his torment.

He found EMDR particularly puzzling. It involved eye movement desensitization and reprocessing, but was told it would be discontinued as it had an iatrogenic effect. Someone did a meta-analytic comparison and found both EMDR and CBT protocols were indistinguishable in terms of effectiveness.

Monagham politely listened to those doctors, too. Only his conclusion was much simpler. *Bullshit.*

Standard prescriptions were the first drug approaches they tried. It started with SSRIs, selective serotonin reuptake inhibitors; citalopram, sertraline and paroxetine, as well as triglyceride antidepressants, TCAs, and other autonomic medicines such as propranolol, a non-selective beta blocker, and clonidine, an alpha-adrenergic agonist. Some of these prescriptions relieved the depression but induced anxiety, so they tried him on benzodiazepines; diazepam, ativan and oxazepam. He threw most of the pills overboard because they didn't mix well with alcohol, which worked.

Monagham's disorder was real, but it wasn't dysautonomia like they thought. It was not mental. It was not physical. It was something far, far, more serious.

He'd become an expert on neurasthenia: headaches, diarrhea and nausea, night sweats, spasms, palpitations, hypotension, extreme fatigue, and exhaustion, followed by periods of hyper vigilance. He could write a book on non-psychotic hallucinations: flashbacks, visions, and night-haunting visits by demons and spectres and ghosts of all kinds. He went to extreme lengths at disassociation, avoiding occupational and social settings that would trigger the episodes.

Oh, his disorder was real all right. But it was only understood by a small fraternity, schooled in the ancient ways, who'd been treating it their way for thousands of years.

* * *

Alfred Monagham stood in dim light, in the warmth of the wheelhouse, worshipping his photos. One had been snapped at a drunken party, twenty years before. It was blurry, well worn, and he held it by the edges as he'd so often done.

Finn stood behind the group. He'd been killed in Chang-Mai, Thailand, on a classified operation. Rocky fell to his death when a carabiner snapped during a rappel entry. Mazzie should never have got it. He took a .22 round to the side, in that gap between the panels of his

Beast, fired by a distraught farmer who'd never hurt anything else in his life. Bude sat with his arm around the cleaning lady; the string of drool hanging down from his lip. Akker was passed out on his plate.

Monagham took a sip.

He anguished over not being loyal, failing his partner and promise. He anguished why Bude died. Why he'd lived. He anguished about the misfire. He knew the shot returned couldn't be done again in ten thousand tries. He knew of his near-death experience, and he knew that his time had stood still. He knew of his debt to the Shaman. He knew of his score with The Kushtaka. And he knew that was far, far, from settled. He'd researched the shit out of that, too.

Monagham took another sip and flashed back.

He saw the brains of a cornered escapee explode like a cantaloupe in his cross-hairs, before harm could be done to a child. He felt the sear of a petroleum blast set by a nut-case, which he immediately took out. He smelled magnesium smoke from Flash-Bangs and tasted the recipe for diversions – sour diesel and the sweet paste of C4. He heard the smash of hard entry when a meth freak shot one hostage and went for another. He cringed from the media frenzy over his instinctively double-tapping the freak's chest and then signing one onto his forehead. He felt scorn for the white-shirts – the carpet cops, he called them. They'd abandoned him, even though they'd trained him that way.

He fell back into the soul-stealing terror at Teslin, then stared at his winged sword, sadly mouthing the motto scrolled across its broad blade. He thought of the first life he created, but chose to neglect, and he shook at the icy-cold death Akker bought.

Deep in alcoholic ecstasy, Monagham thought of a lot of things. Order and chaos. Good and evil. Life and death.

He remembered his good things that died unnecessarily. Shorty, his spaniel, squashed by the moving truck when he was ten. His dad dropping beside him at nineteen. Granddad in the crosswalk, and his mom wasting of cancer. Bude. Akker. The other guys in the photo. They didn't deserve to die. Not one of them. But the ones he shot all deserved it, and there still was one more yet to go.

He'd spent his last days thinking. Sober sometimes. But mostly drunk. And mostly he thought of his wife, Maria, and their daughter, Gabriella. They never left his mind no matter how much he drank. He stared at their photos and wondered just how different his life would be if they were still here.

* * *

He knew it was time.

He dressed, took his last drink, and put the photos away. He slipped into rubber rain pants, fastened the suspenders, pulled over his slicker, and went out on the float. The engines were running and warmed up. He cast off the lines, stepped back on board and pushed hard away, then dropped his boat into gear and idled out of the harbor, beyond the lights of the breakwater, into the wind-driven chop and the sleet.

Like a barrel in his mouth and a finger on the trigger, Alfred Monagham powered up and headed at the reef.

Part Three

The Illusions

Chapter 9

Brian MacAllister punched-in her number.

"I-HIT, Sergeant Bate speaking."

"Shar, Brian here. Hey, how's the trip to Bamfield?"

"It was the worst fucking weekend of my life."

"What? Why? What the hell happened?"

"Pretty much anything that could go wrong did."

"What?"

"First of all, the goddamn ferry's late getting in and Graham gets a chinsy speeding ticket going over. So we still make it on time, but Emma's friend leaves her stinkin' backpack on the boat, so she's all torqued outta shape. Then she gets seasick on the freighter ride and upchucks all day. Graham, he burns his hand trying to light a romantic fire at the lodge, and we have to go find a first aid station in the dark with a dead flashlight. Next day, I get stung on the foot by a jellyfish, and it swells up the size of a bull's bag. Emma, she steps in steaming-fresh dog shit with bare feet on the beach and sets up a screaming session that woulda got-off a slasher."

MacAllister just kept quiet and grinned.

"Let's see, what else? Oh yeah, the bloody freighter boat breaks down, so we have to hire some retard off the reserve to drive us ninety miles back to our car, down that windy, bumpy, shit-for-a-road in some beat-up Jeep Cherokee that reeks of stale beer. Emma's friend now gets carsick, so we have to stop every ten miles to let her puke. And, Emma, she was a total snot the whole time. She hated the place 'cause there's no mall and no texting. Oh! Did I tell you it poured the whole goddamn trip?"

"Aw, that sucks." MacAllister was snickering. He knew Bate so well that the scenes played out in the theater of his mind like the Griswolds from *National Lampoon*.

"And now I get back and find out that Portman, my partner, broke his leg, arm, and collarbone in a motorbike accident, and he's gonna be off for Christ knows how long. So good fuckin' mornin'."

"Aww, no! Is he gonna be okay?"

"Yeah. I talked to his wife last night. He's still in hospital, but I'll go over and see him in a bit. He'll be okay. He's tough and has a good attitude. So I'm on my own for a while. There's sure as hell no one else available to help out."

"Give him my cheers. Hey, the reason I called so soon this morning. I had some time yesterday and looked at the bullets from Salt Spring." MacAllister's tone changed. "Tell me, Shar. How was this guy shot?"

"Duh? With a gun? Like, is this a trick question or something?"

"No, shithead. I'm serious. Where were the bullet wounds?"

"One in the forehead and two in the chest. Why?"

"Reee...aaaly..."

"Really what?"

"I've seen this exact same thing before. I can't yet say if they were conclusively fired from the same weapon, but I'll tell ya, this has gotta be more than a coincidence."

"What are you talking about?"

"Ah, wait... Hold on. Better come over and see me in person. This is real sensitive."

"Kay. Be right there, hon."

* * *

Bate hit 'end' on her BlackBerry. She grabbed her briefcase, laptop, and red trench coat, heading for the door and taking the coat-tree down behind her. It took her an hour to get to the lab, driving-thru for a coffee part-way. It was still pouring.

Honestly, the traffic is getting worse in this bloody city. How do you blind a friggin' immigrant? Yeah, put a windshield in front of him, Bate muttered, getting out and dashing for the Lab. She went through the sign-in routine, again granted privilege to the government's giant gun store.

"Let's go in my office." MacAllister led her through a short hall to the solvent and sulfur smelling, windowless room plastered with posters of pistols in place of centerfolds. He closed the door. She set her Starbucks on his bullet-scarred desk. He strategically slid it to a neutral zone at the rear.

"Okay. You got my curiosity up," she said.

"Sit down. I got something to tell ya."

Bate rolled out a chair, pulling at an electrical cord caught up in the wheels, then sat and opened her notebook.

MacAllister pointed at it. "Ya might wanna hold off on that."

Bate closed up. "Okay. What the hell's going on?"

"This goes back about ten years. You know where Atlin is?"

"Vaguely."

"Well, Atlin's about two hundred miles outta Whitehorse, just at the Yukon border. It's like a stone's throw over from Teslin in northern terms. Little town that started in the Gold Rush."

"So?"

"Anyway, this skinny old guy's found shot dead in a cabin out on a remote gold claim. I did the ballistics. Never did find the weapon, but there was something very, very, specific about the bullets themselves. They were solid lead. Not factory loads. In fact, they were clearly hand-loads that had no jackets, or ah, no copper or metallic encasements, eh? They were all nine millimeter, weighed a hundred and fifty-seven grains each, and were definitely composed from the same lot of lead, with a small ratio of antimony and tin. Nothing a factory would ever use, you understand, but something someone extremely knowledgeable would do for a specific purpose."

Bate frowned, folding her arms.

"The real unique thing. There were no rifling marks on the bullets, but I could see the mold impressions from the castings. Two were intact and one had fragmented, but there was nothing at all on any bullet to identify it to the firearm that discharged it. You know what I mean by rifling, eh?"

"Ahh, grooves you guys see under a microscope?"

"Right. Well, there was no fuckin' rifling on the weapon that shot these, I can tell ya. The bore of that barrel was as smooth as J-Lo's ass. That just doesn't happen in factory firearms. Like, I mean, look at what was going on there. Someone hand-cast heavy, nine-mil, all lead bullets using a metallurgical compound that allows a very soft, very quick stopping, and shallow penetrating missile. This is the exact same thing I see in your Salt Spring case. The two intact bullets come from the chest. Right? And the fragmented one's from the head?

"Yeah."

"Yeah. Well, they were made to do that."

"Help me out here."

"It's gotta be the same thing as Atlin, Shar."

Bate had never seen MacAllister this intense.

"Look, your guy on Salt Spring? I'm goddamn sure his bullets are identical to Atlin. Hey, don't quote me yet. I'm gonna to try a new technique to be positive. Bullet lead compositional profiling through Gaussian distribution and neutron activation analysis are old science now. They were never a hundred percent conclusive."

"Never much cared for them myself."

"We'll do 'em anyway, but there's a new kid in town and I'm gonna run these through it. A company called Forensic Technology has a serious breakthrough out... part of IBIS, our Integrated Ballistic Identification System, called the Bullettrax 3-D Sensor. It makes the tiniest of irregularities in the barrel show up like peaks and valleys in a satellite image. We don't need rifling to get a match with this puppy. It's way superior to the old comparison microscope I'm still using but, so far, the Force hasn't bought me a Bullettrax."

"Uh, you're speaking gun-speak to me, Brian."

"Sorry. Ah... this thing is way bigger than you realize."

"Okay..."

"Look at how your guy on Salt Spring was shot. Two to the chest and one to the head. Same with Atlin. Two in the chest. One in the head. Same MO. Bullets used in both look identical, and they're extraordinarily unique. Ah, gimme time and I hope to prove that, ah, not only are the bullets cast from the same batch of lead and the same mold, but they're from the same weapon. It fired 'em all. I fuckin' well know it."

"Okay. I'm with you."

"Tell me. There's no casings found at Salt Spring, was there?"

"Not that I know of. They would've been turned over to me."

"Well, there weren't at Atlin neither. Nine-mils are all automatics, Shar. They eject casings. Not like a revolver that contains 'em. Look at all your gangland killings. You had casings all over the place. Right?"

"Right."

"So either your scene search missed three casings, which I seriously doubt, or your bad guy stopped and picked up all three. More likely he'd a catch mechanism on the weapon. So what we got in both Atlin and Salt Spring is two shots to the chest. One to the head. Both nine-mils. No casings. No rifling. Same bullet composition. You followin' me?"

"With you."

"Okay, take it a step further. The MO. Each guy's shot at their door at a secluded location. Right? There's no witness. Neither victim's armed. So these were carefully planned, technical executions. Way, way, above your standard hit. But it's the method of execution that reee…ally stands out."

Bate stayed silent. MacAllister pointed at her.

"How far apart were your chest wounds?"

"About an inch."

"And I suppose the forehead one was dead center?"

"Bulls-eye."

"Yeah. Well, there's no fuckin' way this is a coincidence. We got the exact same MO and, don't quote me yet, the same firearm and same ammunition, but a decade apart and a thousand miles away? Don't you see something really out of the ordinary, Shar? Like extraordinary?"

"What's this two bullets to the chest and one in the head thing?"

"Exactly."

Bate squeezed her chin with her left hand, her elbow with her right.

MacAllister gazed straight through her. "No street criminal. No gangster. No Hells Angel. Not even the vast majority of cops would know about this, but it's as obvious to me as rifling. Look at the bullet composition. They load their own. Personally."

"Wha…?"

"It's all personal for these fuckin' guys. For close quarters they cast a soft, heavy, lead bullet that packs a helluva punch. These bullets stop and kill immediately with no exit and no collateral damage. They shoot them to the center of mass. Twice. Then put one to the head."

"Who…?"

MacAllister stared as he spoke. "It's instinctive for them."

"Who are 'They'?"

"There's only one outfit in the world that does this. The SAS. The British Special Air Service."

Bate's hands flung palm up. "Wha…at?"

MacAllister just looked at her.

"Okay, you got me." One palm slapped her forehead. "We're late for, what, April Fools? You're telling me the SAS sent a hit squad to

Salt Spring to cap an old biker?"

"Shar, I am totally fuckin' serious. Look. Let me explain what's going on here. Like I said, this thing's real sensitive."

She squinted.

"Back in the early eighties the SAS trained our ERT teams in Ottawa. They were working up for the national counter-terrorist team, SERT, the Special Emergency Response Team, which followed the old HARP, the Hostage Assault Rescue Program of the seventies, but it got into a political mess and was handed over to the Canadian Forces. Now it's JTF 2. Okay?"

She nodded slightly.

"Our early ERT guys were just finding themselves back then. All their techniques were SAS based, but the Force stopped working with the Brits because they were just too, too, hard-core. The SAS are a total military strike unit. They have only one objective. Kill the enemy. Take no prisoners. And make sure there's no witnesses to nothing."

Her mouth opened.

"That's their code, Shar. Nothing to identify them and no witnesses left to testify. They're like a buncha ghosts."

She rolled her chair forward.

"Our Force is different, eh? We're paramilitary. We contain and diffuse civilian confrontations, not military ones, and we neutralize the bad guy, not fuckin' execute him. The SAS learned real early, back in World War Two, that all threats had to be eliminated. They developed a technique called the double-tap which is two shots to the center of mass. That's the large and vulnerable part that takes the target down. Like right now."

His fingers snapped. Hers locked.

"They followed up with an immediate, direct shot to the head to make sure their target was done. Permanently. Fuckin' for good. This shit happens in seconds. The ERT guys still train this way with the double-tap, but that final head shot thing is taboo. Only the early guys from the SAS program practiced it, but they got in a bucket of shit once when they killed some druggie that way."

Her jaw clamped. His throat cleared.

"The inquest ripped us over excessive force. The member testified the head shot wasn't intentional. He claimed he just reacted to his training. The jury called it overkill, and the press cried murder. I felt sorry for the guy. And he got screwed over by headquarters. Big time."

"Brian. What the fuck is going on here?"

"This stays right in this room, but you got yourself in the middle of some major shit storm. I don't know what the fuck happened on Salt Spring, but it hasta be connected to Atlin."

"So commandos killed that guy up north, years ago? Now they're back and did my guy on Salt Spring? That's what you're saying?"

"I'd stake my job on it."

"What the fuck? Who's behind this?"

There was a very long pause.

"You and I work for 'em, Shar."

Bate rolled back, smacking the desk, sending his phone and her coffee flying. "Fu...uck off!"

"I am one hundred percent serious."

Bate gasped like she'd been double-tapped herself.

"Told you this was sensitive. I'm just blown away that it's happened again."

She started taking oxygen. "Aw, come-on. Are you telling me the RCMP ordered a hit on someone? And don't fucking bullshit me."

"No doubt someone in this outfit did. The Atlin investigation became super secret when they thought our ERT guys did the shooting. You know, I commented about the MO at the time when I looked at the bullets. I saw it right away. I guess that's when they started looking into the connection."

"Who..."

"I don't know who the suspected members were. They kept that real quiet, but I heard from a very good source they thought it was some kinda black ERT operation."

"Huh?"

"We're not supposta do those things, you know. Also, it was sanctioned by those in high places, or at very least, covered up by them. I got no idea what the reason was, but I know it's never been officially solved."

MacAllister paused, looked away, then back at Bate.

"And now it happens again."

"Holy fuck." She swallowed twice. "I'm... having a very hard time getting my head around this. Just who was the victim at Atlin?"

"I really don't know. I heard he was some kinda big informant, but, like fuck... we don't go around killing off our finks, right?"

"Who handled the file?"

"It was transferred to headquarters. Serious Crimes. Everyone involved in the investigation, me included, was ordered not to discuss this case with anyone other than a delegated investigator. Even then, only under written instruction and everything down on tape. I actually had to sign a direction under the Security of Information Act given by the CO personally, acknowledging dismissal and prosecution if I disobeyed it."

"Whooa…"

"I could get fuckin' fired, even jailed, for telling you this. Never seen that done before. I'll tell you, though, senior management had their assholes majorly puckered."

"God! I never heard about this, and I've been around Serious Crimes a long time. Nobody's ever let a peep out about this."

"For good reason. It'd cost them their job. And some time. That's why you never heard this from me."

She reached and touched his knee. "I'm just floored and, no… I didn't hear it from you."

The two sat silent, trying to comprehend what went down. Bate was the first to speak.

"Who else knows about this connection between Salt Spring and Atlin?"

"No one. Just you 'n me," he said. "I really don't know where you go from here. I don't even know who's handling the Atlin file no more."

Bate thought a bit. "You said you heard something from… what'd you say? A very good source?

"The lead investigator back then. And he's bulletproof now. Retired a few years ago. You know him."

"Who's that?"

For the first time, MacAllister smiled. "Fred Mahle."

"Oh for fuck's sakes!"

Chapter 10

Sharlene Bate was only eight when the infamous Art Williams met the little man in the rumpled, green suit with the mile-wide smile who showed him the plan.

Art was skeptical at first, sitting there at his kitchen table. You would be, too, as most prospects of Amway are. But Art was on the look-out for something – not sure of what – as things weren't going all that well for him at the moment. Art sipped his tea and studied the plan as the pimply, wee man drew circles, connecting them with lines, all the while scribbling on a yellow pad with a leaky, red pen.

The terms *upline* and *downline, consumable products* and *residual income* were foreign to Art, but he followed the concept. The harelipped, blonde man suggested the potential of phenomenal wealth, which those in his own upline kept promising. Art nodded in agreement. He didn't sign up as an Amway distributor, but he bought some soap, thanked the toilet-breathed man and helped him jump-start a mufflerless, pumpkin-orange Datsun.

Arthur James Williams would become a crime legend – known to the locals as The Wizard of Ladysmith or, to those in law enforcement, by the less flattering name – The MDA King. This seaside village on the east coast of Vancouver Island, once voted the prettiest little town in Canada by *Conde Naste* travel magazine, hardly seemed like the place where one of the world's most profitable, international, drug-trafficking organizations would begin.

But, then, empires have to begin somewhere.

It took that one page from a small, sweat-stained sage for Art's light to flash on like an arc welder. He got the brilliance of Rich DeVos and Jay Van Andel when they conceived the Amway network-marketing giant in their Michigan garage years before. Only Art didn't see soap in his downline. He saw one fundamental flaw in the Amway plan. They focused on creating loyal, repeat customers by efficiently supplying them with condensed, consumable cleaning products. Art planned to create loyal, repeat customers by addicting them to drugs.

Then control their supply.

* * *

Like the other characters you've met so far, there are things to know about the key players in the Art Williams Organization and how they fit into this ghost story.

Art was a Brit. He'd been an Army soldier who'd seen active combat in France during WW2, operating a flame thrower; once bragging that he could hit any window from over a hundred yards, every time. He immigrated to Canada by way of Mexico after the war, in his youth, with no particular vision yet. His IQ topped the chart and he liked to show it, which tended to piss people off.

Art bought property south of Ladysmith in 1955 and renovated the house for himself and his new wife, Margarita Cardenas-Orejuela, who was half Mexican and half Colombian. She was a Hispanic beauty, about to give birth to their first child – a girl. Initially, Art earned a decent living from patenting and selling inventions, one of which was a line of laminated archery bows that he manufactured in his garage and sold around the world.

At first, things went well in Canada for the Williams family. Their daughter, Tracillina Cardenas-Orejuela-Williams, was Art's joy, and she went to the local Catholic school. Art had learned Spanish during his two years in Matamoros, Mexico, on the Gulf coast where he and Margarita met. Although Margarita gradually spoke English over the years, she preferred her native tongue and wanted Tracy fluent in both languages. Tracy would get plenty of English at school and with her Canadian friends, her parents reasoned, so they spoke only Spanish to Tracy at home.

While Art was busy making some money, he neglected a blood-sucker that crawled up and latched onto his sack. The Tax Man had been prospecting Art as well, slithering in one day to freeze his accounts and lien all his property. That absolutely enraged Art. His battle with the Feds caused his archery strings to snap, forcing Art to take his other ventures underground. Literally. That was a wise move on Art's part, as one of them wasn't exactly legal.

Art had been manufacturing 3,4, methylenedioxyamphetamine – MDA for short – which was banned under the Food and Drug Act as a highly addictive chemical, in vogue with the hippies. He'd learned about entheogens during his time in Mexico, and he started his clandestine Canadian drug operation small, also in his garage, like Jay and Rich – actually as a sideline – not to his bankrupted, bow-building business, but to his interest in mushrooms, of all things. These weren't the red-reishi mushrooms with medicinal properties that he bullshitted the bureaucrats into believing. No, they were magic mushrooms. Psilocybin ones, that grew wild in the fields and sent the hippies floating up to higher planes of awareness. The strange thing was, the magic mushrooms were still legal, and Art was attempting to mass-cultivate them for a legitimate market. Not like the MDA business, which kept him looking over his shoulder.

His 'red-reishi' venture showed so much promise that Art was able to get a government research grant for his new company, the B.C. Institute of Mycology. Art didn't mind getting money from the government. He just hated giving it back. All this was going on when he met the mini-messenger from Amway.

Now that Art had some quality, consumable products to sell, he needed a proven distributor method and the flatuant, thin man with the rusty car's plan of upline and downline and residual income was a god-send.

For distributors, Art recruited some local boys that he rode Harleys with. Art wasn't a biker in the sense that the 101 Knights were, but he loved the thrill of a ride on a hard-tail. He loved the vibe that passed through his nuts, just like he loved hauling-ass in the air. Art's other passion was flying, and he kept a small Cessna 172 along with his Hog at the nearby Cassidy airport in a hanger the Revenuer knew nothing about.

There were three young bikers that Art trusted – Dale Everett, Robin Ghomes, and a big American by the name of Raymond Ridge. Art saw their loyalty to the club and to each other. Loyalty, Art knew, was the key ingredient necessary to ensure success of the international organization he was building.

* * *

Ghomes never tried to be anything other than what he really was – someone born to be a criminal. This was beyond a learned ability. It was something you got passed down in your genes.

Everything you'd want in an antisocial personality disorder, you got in Robin Ghomes. He was a half-blood from the Huu-ay-aht First Nations at Pachena Bay, south of Bamfield, and was raised by his maternal grandparents, taking their surname like a lot of reserve kids did. His mother was not one bit stable, spending most of her time in Port Alberni, the closest town with a bar that juked-out old Hank. Ghomes' biological father was a violent Quebecois who'd been out on the west coast, robbing cash-buyer fish boats, but fled back east, hounded by a horde of warrants, long before getting shot by a cop.

Ghomes was educated till grade six in a residential school run by priests who gave him lessons on things of which he'd never speak. He was bullied as a kid; partly from his girly-sounding name; partly because he wasn't a 'real Indian'. The pecking order on the reserve was worse than in a white community, and it turned Ghomes out tough. Real tough. He was intelligent – good looking for a 'Chug' as the 'Honkeys' called him, using it to full advantage with giddy 'tween girls who spread wide for his cool, rebel image.

Ghomes' first go-round with the law came before his year-clock struck twelve. Three long-haired Dachshund puppies at Huu-ay-aht were found gut-shot and hung from trees by fish line, mortifying the elders who got two small boys to squeal on Ghomes. They took him before council, who called-in the cops. Other incidents of dog and cat torture cropped up once Ghomes returned to the reserve, but the police deferred his case to Social Services, who placed him in the care of an alcoholic aunt and a pedophilic uncle. Within a week, both tattletales were beaten so badly that one lost nine of his teeth and his only good eye; the other's skull fractured with one ear sliced-off and jammed-up a raw, bleeding rectum. Neither could recall who'd assailed them.

Ghomes hit reform school at thirteen, entering custody's revolving door, convicted of assaults, break and enters, car thefts, a contract arson, and chronic drug trafficking. Most in the legal system viewed YDC, Youth Detention Center, as a finishing school for young hoods and it was here that Robin Ghomes met Dale Everett, doing time for similar crimes. Everett was seventeen and a seasoned little con-man. A lot like the Artful Dodger from Dickens' *Oliver Twist*, Everett had been out on probation till police-dog teeth nabbed him with money from a Salvation Army Christmas kettle.

Movie night at YDC was mandatory for young inmates, but they looked forward to turning these into sessions on pulling-off scams and not getting caught. One Friday evening the boys sat back to watch *Easy Rider*, the classic biker flick starring Peter Fonda as Wyatt and Dennis Hopper as Billy. That night, Everett and Ghomes made a pact – they'd pursue that outlaw life of freedom and adventure, planning the club they'd dub the 101 Knights.

By '72, the Knights were a presence on Vancouver Island. Everett was President, Ghomes appointed Sergeant-at-Arms, responsible for discipline, and Raymond Ridge trusted as treasurer. In the beginning, they made mistakes. Misfits like Gizmo Walls, Billy Finch, Wilf Dreschell, and Zeke Mitchell were recruited by the club, but became liabilities. The true Knights instinctively followed the old biker creed – loyalty being so important that acts of betrayal were punishable anywhere from a quick thumping for insolence, all the way up to excruciating death for informing.

Some of the bikers weren't gearboxes, though. Big Wally would've aced a PhD if he'd wanted it. Randy Scott dropped out of Med School to join the Knights – to his parents' horror. Pussy was his thing. Lee Sheppard loved his Harley, the camaraderie, and the business networking. Lloyd Sturgis was their old man. They called him Grumpy after Snow White's dwarf, but Sturgis was no dwarf, nor was he snow white. There were others with proven loyalty, staying with the Knights as they evolved into the Satans Angels, then patched-over as the Nanaimo charter in the royalty of outlaw motorcycle gangs. The Hells Angels.

Always the alpha, Robin Ghomes moved up to become president.

* * *

Raymond Ridge was a different kind of biker. Growing up in Queens, he played with the cut-throat Hispanics and spoke their language. A large, quiet, and bright boy, Ridge read a lot, which was unusual in his neighborhood. His oldest sister raised him in the projects – that failed social experiment which concentrated crime and poverty in New York – doing her best to instill beliefs of a decent, dependency-free life.

It was February 7th, 1964. Free love was starting and the Fab Four were live on Ed Sullivan. Raymond Ridge stood in the chill, outside the Manhattan theater, hoping to catch a glimpse, while an Army recruiter worked his way through the crowd. Ridge felt something when the black Sergeant grasped his arm, suggesting a way out of the hood – education, pay, travel, and adventure – a better deal by enlisting than by awaiting the draft. He forgot about the Beatles, laying awake all night in his icy-box room, knowing he'd been called to serve the big picture.

Ridge deployed to Vietnam the first time in June '67. He earned a green beret with the 5th Special Forces Group, secretly sent to monitor Cambodia as part of Project GAMMA, reporting on Viet Cong subversives. His second tour, in '69 as Sergeant First Class, was even more clandestine.

Ridge went through a bad spell, arrested as part of a group accused of executing the VC double-agent, Thai Khac Chuyen, who was feeding American intel to the Commies. Understanding he'd take the fall as a patsy, Ridge went to the CIA, who were running the show, and told them something. The Secretary of the Army, facing a national media flogging over the incident, soon announced all charges were dropped in the interest of national security and the Green Beret affair was over.

Ridge was quietly discharged from the United States Army on March 31st, 1970. To ease his transition back to civilian life, the Central Intelligence Agency gave him a sizeable amount of cash, a motorcycle, and entry into Canada with the understanding that they'd keep in touch.

The warm, west coast was a haven for displaced Americans in the 70's. Most were draft dodgers with no loyalty to the homeland, which justified their being watched in the interest of national security.

Ridge enjoyed his freedom, growing his hair and his beard very long. All of the people out there were from somewhere else and he fit right in. He paid for a lot of drugs, but nobody noticed he didn't do the stuff himself. People flocked around and he got connected.

It wasn't long before Robin Ghomes invited Raymond Ridge to ride with the Knights and introduced him to the man named Art Williams.

Chapter 11

Wednesday, May 9th, 2012
1:25 pm
430 West Crooked Stick Drive
Casa Grande, Arizona

Retired Staff Sergeant Fred Mahle was clipping the end off a fat, black Cuban by his backyard pool after a good morning ruined from an eighteen-hole hack with some other old codgers, as he'd put it, when the phone tweedled.

Mahle was enjoying being out to pasture after thirty-six years with the Mounties, all of it as a detective. His retirement party would've been huge, except Mahle and his wife slipped away to their winter home, which didn't surprise the few he kept close.

He'd investigated some of the highest profile cases including convincing that maggot-spunk, Clifford Olson, to confess and turn over the hammer-killed bodies. Taking credit wasn't Mahle's thing. He left that to the rookies and the white-shirts. He was old-school – a gumshoe right out of a dime novel – knowing you get more bees with honey than you do with vinegar. A long time partner said the only difference between Mahle and a polygraph was that Fred liked to shake hands and drink scotch.

Violet Mahle answered it. He'd heard the thing ring, but paid no attention. Ten minutes passed as he sat in the shade, quietly savoring a most-excellent smoke and choking-down *USA Today*, till Violet popped out on the patio.

"Fred, I've got a surprise for you!"

He frowned as she handed him the handset.

"Hi Uncle Freddy!" said a laughing voice that he'd recognize if it came from the moon.

"Chiclets! How the hell are ya?"

Sharlene Bate and Fred Mahle weren't relatives, but she adored the older man. Mahle had been in charge of investigations at Richmond when Bate started on plainclothes and looked after her again while at Surrey. In all, ten years as Bate's mentor. He'd nicknamed her from her perfect set of teeth. Anytime she needed a favor, she'd ask 'Uncle Freddy'.

They'd been out for dinner last fall, just before the Mahles flew south before snow-fly. It was Bate's chance to introduce the new man in her life, nervously seeking Mahle's approval. She knew dammed well how he felt about Jim.

"Great!" she answered. "So, how's your game?"

"Hfff. Know why they called it golf?"

"No."

"Cause the word 'fuck' was already taken. So, how's my little princess?"

"Good… actually, nehh, Fred. I'm having my trying times with her. Teen and Mom stuff, but that's for another day."

"Well, I don't suppose ya ever give yer folks grey hair. I know I didn't," Mahle said with a chuckle that sounded like he ate gravel with his corn flakes. "How's yer Graham doin'?"

"That's going great. Really great. We still got separate places, but we click."

"So when's he gonna be Attorney General and kick some of them pansy judges right up the ass?"

"He's working on it, believe me. I'm getting my eyes opened as to what politics are about."

"How's the officer program goin'?"

"Slow process. Who knows with those guys. I passed my final exam. Yeah, I told you. I'm strongly sponsored, and I really want it, but what's hurting me is… I've got all operational experience. All criminal. I've never done the Fed side or any Admin shit, so I'm kinda, how do I say it? Limited?"

"Ya got what fer service now? Twenty-one? Just the right time. They need people like ya up in management." Mahle cleared his throat with a deserty cough. "God's sakes they got enough fuckin' idiots up there. Think about branchin' out soon. Go to a Fed Squad or one of them new Security Sections."

"I've applied for a few, but right now we're so strapped on I-HIT they won't even give me time to fart, never mind let me go anywhere."

"I been watchin' yer gang mess from down here. That's gonna get a lot goddamn worse before it gets better."

"Oh fuck, Fred. It's nasty. Are you getting any spill over from all the Mexican shit?"

"Naw, not right here. We got more danger from some geezer croakin' behind the wheel of his motorized chair and runnin' ya down at the mailbox. That actually just happened to our neighbor."

Bate broke out laughing.

"Violet and I went over the Mexican side at Nogales last week. Ya'd never know nothin' from there. Them locals are just hooked on siestas, not drugs."

Bate kept laughing.

"It's not like Ciudad Juarez at El Paso where they're all fuckin' crazy. This drug war was bound to happen when they put the army up against the cartels, ya know. The stupid fuckers took a baseball bat to a hornets nest, but had no goddamn plan to deal with the hornets."

"Thank Christ Vancouver's not that out of control. But, yeah, it's the same thing. It's all that goddamn coke. The balance of power's upset."

"Well, I'm glad I'm outta it. So what's on yer mind, Chiclets?"

"What makes you think I'm up to something, Uncle Freddy?" she asked, still giggling.

"Cause yer callin' in the middle of a weekday on yer government phone. I got a clock and call display," the gruff ex-detective replied, taking a puff.

"Okay, I'm going to try out your memory, old timer." Bate changed tone. "Atlin. An old guy shot in a cabin out on a gold claim."

There was a long, long pause before Mahle answered. "Now why would ya ask me 'bout somethin' like that?"

"A little bird told me to call you."

"What kinda bird?"

"One that likes guns."

"Yer little bird is gonna get his fuckin' beak chopped off. What's goin' on there, Sharlene?"

"I got handed a murder file last Monday, the thirtieth. Victim was running a sophisticated grow-op that was Hells Angels backed. Ah, he's not a known club member, but definitely associated. Coroner thinks he got whacked on Friday, the twenty-seventh, then lay there stinking in the heat all weekend till he was found by firefighters when a generator went up in flames. There's no witnesses or nothing much to go on, except a lead on a black truck which looks promising. We got ferry line-up video on it, but can't ID the driver. He looked dirty, though. Clearly aware of the cameras..."

Mahle cut her off. "What's the connection to Atlin?"

"The MO. My guy was shot twice in the chest about an inch apart, then a third time right smack in the center of the forehead. Brian's sure it's the same gun. Same bullets. Nine m-m, hand-cast leads. No jackets. No rifling. No casings left. He's convinced it's the same as Atlin."

"Serious?"

"Yeah."

There was another long pause before Mahle growled again. "What more do ya know 'bout Atlin?"

"Nothing really. Just that Brian is absolutely convinced the two are related. He's saying Atlin had something to do with an ERT operation gone bad? Also, he thinks there was something going on at the top. Some kind of cover-up? Apparently a gag order was issued?"

"Who else knows 'bout this connection?"

"No one. Just the three of us. Brian insisted I talk to you before going any further."

"Who's yer victim?"

"A guy named Dupris. Gerard Joseph Dupris. Age seventy-two. A fat, old guy. Long-time FPS'r. Mean anything to you?"

Mahle thought a bit. "Naw. I don't recall that name comin' up. The age is interestin'. What's on the system?"

"Ah, besides a long record and a pile of aliases, he's a pointer to Fed Drugs. Also lots of charges dropped over the years."

"Hmm."

"Other thing kinky is this guy went right off the map just when Atlin went down. He was on parole and never heard of again. Till now. What do you make of that?"

"Ah... could be a buncha things, but sounds like another informant."

"I thought about that. Also agent status or witness protection. The pointer person to Drug Squad is suspicious, but I haven't checked into it yet."

"Well, if he is, they'll know already. First query on his name will set alarm bells ringin'. Anyone contact ya yet?"

"No. Nothing. What do you mean by 'another' informant? What's going on here, Fred?"

"Well, ya can say ya heard this from me, Chiclets, 'cause I don't have a career to give a shit for no more." He took off his glasses. "We were all ordered to shut the fuck up 'bout this. Keep Brian outta it. He's still got a few years to pension. Wow! Same fuckin' MO, eh? Fuck!"

Bate was silent. She opened her notebook as Mahle took a deep suck on his Oscuro, exhaled, and started right in.

"April 22nd, going on ten years now, a coded informant, E - Eighteen-Oh-Four, a guy by the name of Eugene Jacques, a skinny old guy, was found shot to death in a cabin at Surprise Lake 'bout twenty-five miles east from Atlin. Out in them gold fields, ya know."

He paused, taking a pull off a cold Sam Adams that Violet had just brought him.

"They're a rough buncha bastards up there. Any number of these people coulda had reason to want old 1804 dead, but this one was different. Like MacAllister identified, and good fer him, the MO was one of a kind. Just like yers. Hmmph. Bullet types. Sequence of shots. Placement. We got involved right after Brian asked the first investigator if he was lookin' at stuff from an ERT shoot-out. Ya know, it was so fuckin' obvious when ya looked at it objectively."

Bate was all ears as Mahle kept on.

"There is no one, and I mean no one, else who'd use this MO. It ran away real fast... up to the CO at the time and he panicked, thinkin' this was some kinda black ERT op against some rogue informant. We were tryin' to get a grip on this thing, but them gag orders come out and, ya know... lookin' back... so they shoulda. By the time we got somewhere close to the bottom of this mess... Hmmph... I don't think he was far off."

"Ho...oly fuck!"

"Now it looks like ya got the same thing. Ho...oly fuck is right."

"Anyone ever charged in the Atlin thing?"

"Naw. We developed a strong suspect, but never identified anythin' even close to a fuckin' motive. I'm still baffled by this. I know your next question, so I'll go ahead n' answer it."

Mahle took another pull, set the bottle back on his pool-side table, and leaned ahead in his chair.

"Oh, the suspect was one of our guys, all right. You mighta heard of him. A bit of a legend in the Force. The guy who pulled off what they called the amazing shot in the Yukon, back in eighty-five where ERT went after the second Mad Trapper."

"Ah, sorta. That was before my time. Who is he?"

"Al Monagham. Constable Alfred Monagham. Regimental number 34604."

"Name's not familiar. Wow. A 3-4 number. He'd have what for service? Thirty-two, thirty-three years?"

"Woulda."

"What do you mean?"

"He's long dead now."

Bate paused, wondering *How could a dead man shoot my victim?* She'd also opened a Coke, which fizzed out over her notebook, and was searching for something to sponge it.

"What happened to him?"

"I'll get ta that. The investigation basically stopped after he died, but the suspicion it was a Force-sanctioned hit and certain people in high places were involved, didn't end. That never went anywhere with us, though. Them commissioned bastards closed ranks when they thought some of their own were dirty."

"God, Fred. I can't believe what I'm hearing."

"I couldn't either. At first. But the facts support it. I don't mean direct evidence. There's none. But the circumstances were there. It was him and they fuckin' well knew it."

"What did you have on this? What'd you say his name was?"

"Monagham. Al Monagham. We got onto him when it became obvious someone with SAS type trainin' did this. Brian musta explained that to ya, right?"

"Oh, yeah. But I never heard of that before." She jotted down the name.

"Don't feel bad. Neither have 99.999 percent of all the people on this planet," Mahle said with a grunt. "Anyway, we identified the guys who'd been trained this way. The head shot was tellin'. That was a short lived tactic taught to only about thirty instructed right by the SAS. We profiled and alibied them all, and come up with only one viable guy. Monagham." He hooked the ash off his stogie. "Alfred... Fuckin'... Monagham."

"Well, what about it being some other guy out there with the same training? Like even an SAS himself?"

"Naw. Ya gotta remember this took place way up north, still in winter. Not the sorta place ya'd be passin' through. Anyway, there's more."

"Okay." Bate was making notes.

"We could place Monagham in Atlin at the time. We found him registered under a phony name at a motel in Whitehorse, and we identified a call made from a pay-phone in Atlin, same day as the murder, back to that motel. He'd rented a four-by-four from a local garage, not a legitimate rental company. Actually, the clever bastard went to a lotta work to cover his tracks, but a similar truck was seen on the road to Surprise Lake. Only one way in. One way out. Funny how these locals notice the smallest shit that's outta place and remember it."

Bate smiled, listening to Mahle say that.

"Fortunately, the truck plate was recorded by a watchman at the motel, and we found it. Ah, the mileage matched the distance to Atlin and back. Tires were same as marks found in the snow by the road above the scene. Also, we identified footwear impressions consistent with the moon-boots like the ERT guys were issued. But, of course, we never found his."

"Okay. So what happened to him?"

"Oh, we found Monagham all right."

"Where?"

"Well, he'd turned into a sad case and was put on medical disability by this time. PTSD was the diagnosis... and alcoholism. I read his personnel file. Uh, he'd had a lot of serious stress in his service. A partner killed before his eyes under some real weird... some say supernatural circumstances."

"Huh?"

Mahle chuckled, reaching for his ale. "Yeah, some bizarre shit happened there, for sure."

"Wha..."

"Also, he had three other ERT friends killed in operations. He, himself, was responsible for four duty-related shootin's. All justified, but they musta took their toll. Poor bastard's wife and kid were killed in an accident."

"Ouch!" Bate winced. "What happened?"

"That was bad. Real ugly. She and the little girl were headin' from Richmond to pick him up from a bar in Vancouver. He'd gone drinkin' with the boys after work. It was dark. Right before Christmas. Rainin' heavy. They got clipped in an intersection and spun across the oncomin' lane, then flipped over." Mahle took a pull and set it back. "One of them tippy, short wheel-based SUVs."

"Yeow."

"They got outta their belts, but them kid-proof locks wouldn't release. Then it burst in flames and, ya know, I guess the screams were just fuckin' horrific."

"Oh God, Fred! Oh the poor things. The poor guy…"

"Can't imagine how hard that was on him…"

"Oh God! That is just awful!" Bate shuddered, envisioning Emma.

"Never went back to work after it. Took medical leave, then started drinkin' heavy, or I should say, heavier. He was no stranger to the bottle before losin' his family, but it got a lot worse. Pretty much cut himself off from everyone after that."

"Yeew." A huge pang of sympathy shot through her.

"No relatives. Lived alone on a boat. I interviewed him twice. Once formally at headquarters, then another time I went over and just dropped by his boat to see how he was doin'. That was right before he died. Ya know… he was a likeable enough guy. Quiet. Co-operative. At one point, on that second time, he come close to makin' an admission. I think he wanted to tell someone why he done it. It was one of them cases where we both knew, and he just played dumb."

Bate nodded in agreement.

"He made a real weird comment, though. He'd been drinkin', but seemed to be thinkin' clear enough."

"What'd he say?"

"Get this. He said I shouldn't be lookin' at him. I should be lookin' for a ghost."

"What? That's strange!"

"No kiddin', eh? I asked if he had a little help from beyond, and he just give me the spookiest look. He started to say somethin', then just shut up and never said fuck all after that."

"What was his motive?"

"Like I told ya. I got absolutely no fuckin' idea why he done it."

"You think he was officially ordered?"

"Fuckin' seemed like it but, naw, I just can't never see that happenin'."

"Money? Like a contract?"

"Oh, hell no. The bastard was rollin' in it. He inherited a large family estate and was quite the knowledgeable investor. Plus insurance from losin' his family. A bit of a tightwad, I understand. Quite a complex guy, actually. We did an extensive psych profile on him. Pictured him as a loner and intelligent, but with some serious, serious shit goin' on inside him."

"So what happened to him?"

"Boating accident. Drowned. Some think it mighta been a suicide, planned to look accidental, but I don't believe that. But, ya know, no body was ever found, so no autopsy was done."

"So how do you know he's dead?"

"Oh Christ, there's lotsa evidence. It was a witnessed event. He was pissed and ran his boat into some rocks, then fell in the water. Some tugboat guys saw him disappear under the waves. It was dark, cold, rainy. Just before Christmas."

"So how do you know it was him?"

"DNA. There was blood on the boat."

Bate frowned.

Mahle picked up his beer, taking another drink. "I know what yer thinkin', but I looked into this real close. I don't see it being some kinda setup. That water was way too fuckin' cold. It was a ways to shore and, ya know as well as I do, someone goin' down in the salt chuck stands little chance of bein' found. Crabs get 'em in a day or two."

Bate shivered.

Maile put down his bottle, keeping on. "Naw. He never surfaced again. His bank account was never touched and there was a pile of money in it. Ya know how it goes. Eventually there was an inquest, and it was conclusively ruled an accidental drowning brought on by, let's face it, a drunk drivin' a boat. Case closed on Constable Monagham. Take my word for it."

"Okay." Bate stayed speed writing.

Mahle burped. "He's dead. Ya can rule him out for yers. Unless his fuckin' ghost has returned."

"Okay. Yeah. Looks tight. So what about this commissioned officer thing?"

"This was never resolved. Suspicion centered round 1804's handler, a young Inspector by the name of Dirk Haugland. Ever heard of him?"

"No. Should I have?"

"He was one of them golden boys around headquarters. A drug squad high-flyer. One of them undercover guys who made a name for himself on international cases and got his commission early. He's long since been transferred out, and I don't think the fuckin' guy's even in the Force no more. He took a lotta heat over this."

"For?"

"Well, our suspicion was old 1804 blackmailed Haugland and threatened his family, so Haugland had him rubbed out before he could get at the kids. We never got to interview Haugland, though. Like I told ya. Them white-shirts looked after that and reported back to us."

"So how was Monagham connected to Haugland?"

"Well, this is where it gets interesting. Haugland was handlin' 1804, but the informant had been cultivated by another officer who was Haugland's boss at the time."

"Who's that?"

"The OIC of Federal Drug Enforcement Branch. Superintendent John Moloci. Know of him?"

"Just the name. Seen him around HQ. Why?"

"Well, 1804 was originally Moloci's fink and got turned over to Haugland to run. They used this guy for a number a years. With good results I understand."

"Okay?"

"Ya said yer scene was an HA show?"

"For sure. The property belongs to Robin Ghomes."

"Now that don't surprise me."

"And you know who that fucking low-life is," Bate said.

"Everyone knows who that fuckin' Ghomes is," Mahle replied.

"No shit, eh?"

"The Atlin scene was also HA connected. Not to Ghomes, though. Did the name Archibald Wiggers, Archie Wiggers, come up in yers?"

"Wiggers? Nope. Who's he?"

"A Newfie who owned the Atlin property."

"An HA?"

"Not color flyin', but thick as thieves with them. He's a sea captain with an interest in gold mining."

"That's different," Bate said.

"Oh, Wiggers is fuckin' different all right. He done a lotta marine importin' for the Angels. He's also connected to Moloci, but we were never sure just how. Probably another fink."

"Sounds like Moloci was at the center of this. So how does this tie into Monagham?"

Bate almost heard Mahle grinning over the phone.

"Monagham was Moloci's brother-in-law. He was married to Moloci's sister, Maria. The one killed in the car crash."

"Oh... My... God! Oh God. This is so dirty! Oh, no wonder they closed ranks."

"Ya got it, Chiclets."

"So who the Christ killed my guy?"

"I got no fuckin' idea, but I can tell ya, it sure wasn't Monagham.

Unless ya believe in ghosts. Naw. There's somethin' deeper, a lot deeper, goin' on here. The MO is just way too unusual. It's gotta be some guy trained in SAS tactics."

Bate kept on scribbling.

Mahle stopped and re-lit the Cuban. "I find it interestin'... ya said yer guy... what's the name again?"

"Dupris. Gerard Joseph Dupris," Bate told him.

"Dupris? Frenchman too, eh? Hmm. Ya said he was a pointer person ta Fed Drugs?"

"Yeah, no contact listed, though."

"Interestin' he's gone in a hole since Atlin. Nothin' on him at all?"

"Just the warrant for violating parole."

"Well, he wouldn't be in jail then. Least not in Canada. If I were ya, first thing I'd check out is the Source Unit. Find out for sure if this Dupris was coded and who was handlin' him. Sure sounds like he was some kinda rat. You'll know soon as ya start pokin' around. My guess is old 1804 and yer guy were some kinda snitch-partners run under the same handler."

Bate stopped writing to process it all.

Mahle stifled a burp with a throaty rumble. "Probably Moloci. Probably both killed for the same reason."

"Hmm. What do you make of this shit, Fred?"

"Well... I got no doubt Monagham done in 1804. Why? I don't know. He had his reason, and I guess he took that to the bottom of the sea. I'm not satisfied Moloci done anything direct, but he had to know Monagham was dirty."

"Sure sounds like it."

"But I'll tell ya, though, there was nothin', absolutely nothin', goin' on in this investigation that Moloci didn't have his fuckin' mitts on. He's a control freak. My speculation is that Haugland was behind it. There's no proof, but for sure them white-shirts knew way more than they was tellin' us poor flat-foots. I'd love to find out."

"You know... I'm just gobsmacked over this."

Mahle took another swallow. "Well, go out and smack 'em, Chiclets. But just be careful around that Moloci. He'll make or break yer career real quick."

"Now what makes you think I'll be talking to Moloci, Uncle Freddy?"

"Cause I trained ya, dipshit. Just do yer homework and be real cautious, or you'll end up walkin' the plank. Remember, them gag orders are still in place."

"Har Cap'n," Bate said with a snarl. She started to sign-off, then something struck her. "Ah, Fred, you said Monagham's death was confirmed by DNA. How'd that happen?"

"Well, there was blood at the scene. He got cut up when the boat hit the reef. They took a sample and matched it."

"Where did they get the control standard from? Didn't you say there were no living relatives?"

"Oh. Sorry. We didn't look after that. There was no charges in his death, so it become a coroner's case. They looked after ID."

"So?"

"Oh, fuck, sorry. Monagham had a bastard son. He knocked-up some broad years ago. They got DNA to cross-match. He never had nothin' to do with the kid other than makin' support payments. Also, he left his estate to that woman and the kid. Quite a large insurance policy I understand, but we never looked into that. It weren't relevant."

"Where's this son now?"

"Don't know. They tracked him down back east. He was in the Army then, but where he is now, I don't know."

"Name?"

"Don't know that either. It'll be on the coroner's file. What're you thinkin'?"

"I'm not sure what I'm thinking, Fred. But I'm with you that there's something much deeper going on here."

They were about to hang up when the old detective realized that he'd missed something. "By the way. Where's yer scene?"

"Ganges. Salt Spring Island."

Mahle let out a long whistle. "Hoooly fuck! That's right where Monagham died."

"No fucking way."

"Quite the ghost story ya got yerself into, Chiclets."

Chapter 12

Monday, August 8th, 1977
4:45 am
10884 Westdowne Road
Ladysmith, British Columbia

The pre-dawn raid caught Art Williams in his nightcap.

He and Margarita were nestled all snug in their bed, visions of sugarplums dancing in their heads, when their back door came down. It kicked easy, as Art had nothing to hide but a limp dick in the main part of the house. The cops crashed in, screaming and yelling with Model 10's pointing, Brushmasters racking, and German Shepherds ki-yii-ing. It scared the shit out of Margarita, and also Tracillina Williams, who cowered down the hall in her room.

Art was absolutely enraged. He stood there half-naked, swearing and demeaning the officers for a quarter hour straight – instinctively knowing the best defense was a good offense – and Art came on like Chuck Norris.

There was a junior constable by the name of Giavano or John Moloci with the raiding party who'd been assigned to contain the Williams family in their living room while they sat out the search. Art was smart enough to tone down once he was made to understand that the police were serious about this operation. He kept to the couch with Margarita and their now adult daughter, Tracy. He also kept eye contact with Moloci, attempting to intimidate the youthful cop. It wasn't working.

For a young lad he's composed, yet this must be the biggest thing he's seen so far, Art surmised. *Probably way too loyal to be corrupted the usual way.*

But Art knew that we all have our price and, not being able to do much else at the moment, he started a conversation that seemed innocent enough to Moloci at the time.

"You look nervous." Art nodded at him. "Must be your first big one."

He waited for a response. Moloci didn't bite.

"Don't worry about your safety, young feller. The only guns here are yours. Same with vicious dogs."

Art smiled at Moloci like a boa about to constrict. Getting no reaction, Art applied a different twist.

"This is a farce, young officer. A farce. There's nothing here to find."

The raid would've been a farce, except the police were so sure the Williams Organization had their meth-lab somewhere on the property, that they just kept on looking.

* * *

Art, and his then-small group, had been under investigation for drug trafficking since 1972 when the U.S. Bureau of Drugs and Narcotics identified a shipment of Isosafrole, a precursor or key chemical ingredient in the manufacture of MDA, addressed to the B.C. Institute of Mycology on the west coast of Canada. Knowing this molecule didn't grow mushrooms, they put Art's institute under the microscope.

The first investigation identified Art as the mastermind and named three co-conspirators, Raymond Ridge, Robin Ghomes, and Dale Everett as distributors; alleging a market network through North American outlaw motorcycle gangs. The authorities staked out a farm rented to Everett, which was a nightmare to surveil. Besides being remote and alarmed with trip wires that activated spotlights, Everett kept it guarded 24/7 by relatives in a lookout tower and two grizzled, old crossbreed hounds. But it wasn't the traps, or the dogs, or even the human eyeballs that made approach impossible. About the property roamed a flock of domestic geese that honked like New York cabbies at the first sign of intruders.

The Mounties realized how sophisticated the Williams Organization was, so they stepped back and slipped inside the Knights, looking for the weak link in their drive-chain which they jammed and sprocketed into an informant. The police busted Everett's place, finding drugs. All four were arrested, but their lawyer slipped them out on bail within the week. And that was when the purge of the Knights began.

Suspecting they had a rat infesting the clubhouse, the bikers began a process of fumigation that would set a new standard for loyalty. Ghomes never trusted Billy Finch right from the get-go and figured he'd be a good place to start. He suckered Finch to a meeting down at the river and nearly drowned the man, till satisfied Finch was only guilty of failure to pay for two beers from the clubhouse fridge.

Wilf Dreschell, it turned out, had a little more to conceal – like the issue of skimming from a club-sponsored heroin deal. He pleaded personal use, but the club didn't need a hype in the house, and they decided to set an example. Two bikers tied Dreschell to a workbench in the clubhouse garage while Ghomes heated a machete with a blow-torch, burning off all tattoo links to the Knights, as well as the tip of his dink.

Ghomes' suspicion finally fell between Gizmo and Zeke. Who the informant actually was, only the police would know. But one thing for sure – neither Gizmo nor Zeke ever talked again. Ghomes made bloody sure of that.

It took two years for the charges to get dropped against Art, Ridge, and Ghomes. Everett took the fall, pleading guilty, as the goods had been found on his farm. Their lawyer made a slippery deal and got the others off, but Everett got slapped hard. Ten years. He served just under two; their lawyer getting the sentence slipped back on appeal. Everett slid out on early parole and the Williams Organization set about improving efficiency.

The cops continued to work their informant, which led to the search of Art's home. They'd been warned the place had booby-traps, secret passages, spring loaded staircases, disguised doors, and locks that would puzzle Houdini, but they were floored when one of the searchers activated a bookcase which revolved like in a Hollywood haunted house, leading down a long ladder to the lab.

The operation was beyond anything the authorities anticipated. It wasn't the amount of MDA stockpiled, or the capacity of the factory to put out. It was the brilliance of the controls – the lighting, the heating, the ventilation and air conditioning, the cooking, the mixing and encapsulating equipment, and the security. Art linked a motion sensor to a video monitor and audible alarm at the lab's entrance. It let two doors seize tight, giving anyone inside time to pig-trot through a yardstick-wide culvert, running to a dry creek where a gassed-up Jeep lay in wait in the bushes.

The police took it all in. Not just in the brilliance of the operation, but in a methodical recording of exhibits. Art, Ghomes, Everett, and Ridge would be charged again. The evidence seemed overwhelming, but once their lawyer got his fee, he'd slip the four out on bail in under a week.

* * *

Art eyeballed Moloci while waiting for someone to decide when his family was going to jail. He thought he'd have fun with the young cop and try the recruiting formula that the little green man from Amway had showed him. It made sense to Art. The network marketing gnome called it FORM for Family, Occupation, Recreation, and Message; claiming it worked like a hot-damn for setting up prospects.

"Where are you from?" Art asked.

Moloci paused. *Can't see harm in making small talk. If anything incriminating is said, I'll record it as evidence.* "Montreal," he answered.

"Nice city. Sophisticated and cultured. Born there?"

"Yes."

"French Canadian?"

"No, actually Italian."

Art was looking up, estimating Moloci's height to be at least 6-5. He'd assumed the post-card Mountie was French from the dark skin and heavy growth but, of course, now he could see the Mediterranean.

"Family still there?'

"Yes."

"Parents born in the old country?"

"Just my mother."

"Speak the language?"

"Raised in it."

"French, as well?"

"I'm from Montreal."

"Married man, are you?"

"No." Moloci smiled for the first time. "Too smart for that."

"Lots of pretty girls in Montreal." Art had seen Moloci sneak glances at Tracy, who was not enjoying this at all. He nodded towards his daughter. "There's a few out here, too."

"I can see," Moloci replied.

Tracy was twenty now and had turned into an absolute knock-out. She'd been blessed with her mother's looks and her father's brains.

"How long have you been on the Force?"

"Three, just about four years."

"Rank?"

"Constable."

"Corporal's stripes soon?"

"Not likely in this outfit," Moloci said, shifting feet and thinly frowning.

Art detected dissatisfaction. "You're somewhat junior to be a plainclothesman, are you not?"

"A bit," Moloci replied, hands moving to his hips.

Art probed for that weakness in John Moloci, who was still assigned to uniform, but had been temporarily moved to Drug Squad for the raid.

"You must be competent to achieve this so early in your career."

"I like to think I earned it."

"Certainly. Speaking three languages is an asset. You sound well educated."

"I've got two degrees."

"Tell me." Art smiled. "What in?"

"One in political science and the other in karate. Black." Moloci grinned.

Bingo. Art found the vanity streak.

"I suspected as much," Art said with a hearty laugh and a fast wag of his finger. "See, Tracy. This is the catch you should have. Handsome and athletic. Intelligent and worldly. A good job with a steady check and a pension forthcoming." Art lowered his head. "Not a poor and simple working bloke like me."

Tracy stared away; arms and legs crossed, nearly crushing herself. Margarita stayed stone-faced, knowing exactly what Art was up to. She'd already decided they were heading south.

Art looked up at Moloci. "Are you allowed much relief from your case load, Constable? What does a young copper do when he's not chasing gangsters?"

Moloci smiled. *Okay. He's going somewhere with this.* He'd read the intelligence file on the Williams Organization and knew Art was up to something. *Two can play this game.* "I like the city life. Spend some time in Vancouver, but I like to get away elsewhere."

"Where is your favorite get-away, my new friend?" Art asked.

"Believe it or not, Mexico." *Bounce that ball back.*

"Really?" Art looked like he'd just scratched and won. He gestured towards his wife. "Margarita, here, is Mexican."

Margarita sat like the Sphinx.

"Wonderful." Moloci seemed pleased. He turned to Margarita. "Which part?"

"Matamoros," Art replied for her. "On the Gulf side, at the Texas border. You should taste her chili!"

Margarita gave Art the stink eye.

"Under different circumstances, I'd love to." Moloci winked.

Art moved to the message. "Tell me, a bright young man like you. Are you to make a full career in government? There are other opportunities, both in pay and in benefits, never mind networking, enjoying an adventure, and perhaps serving a much bigger picture."

"I enjoy what I do. And I like to think I'm doing some good."

Moloci and Art locked eyes, two chess-masters making their moves.

"Well, I look at it this way," Art continued. "Some of us are much better compensated than others. Life can be long, or it can be short. You should make the most of it."

Moloci got the message. There was a long, long, silence as he waited for Art to finish his bribe. The stalemate was shattered by a Sergeant with news that they'd just found the lab. The Williams family were stood and readied for jail.

Art continued to study Moloci. He was impressed with the young cop's credentials and calculated his next recruitment move. Art needed police contacts within the Organization. It was going to be huge one day, and he could see a place in it for Moloci. Call it insurance. Call it intelligence. Or you can call it just good business strategy. Art knew his empire would be limited without including the enforcement and intelligence worlds.

He'd found a flaw in this quarry, but Art knew that Moloci could not simply be bought. There'd have to be proper compensation, of course, but there'd have to be motivation to start.

That would be a woman. Men like Moloci always had that weakness. The second would not be money. Money would never motivate someone like Moloci. It would have to be something greater. Like a purpose. The belief in a much bigger picture. That Art understood.

The Sergeant directed that the Williams family be marched to a prisoner van. Moloci ratcheted cold, steel cuffs on Tracy's silk wrists as Art was escorted by.

"I don't believe I've caught your name, Constable." Art extended his shackled hand.

"Moloci," he replied, instinctively reaching back, being met with a two handed grip from old Art.

"Muhloshi?"

"Pronounced Maw Law See. John Moloci."

"It's been a pleasure chatting with you, John. I'd like to continue our conversation sometime."

"It may be some time before you're free to do so." Moloci grinned.

* * *

It's going to take some work to get him onboard, Art thought as he, Margarita, and Tracy were placed in the paddy wagon. *I'll let Ghomes look after the details.*

Chapter 13

Most police officers at Headquarters have never investigated a murder.

Many have never seen a dead body, let alone smelled one – especially not one in Dupris' condition. That's a good thing or a lot of these carpet cops would be out looking for work they could stomach, such as politics, law, or other acts.

HQ was a big and busy place on a week day. A lot of important things were going on. You'd need a guide, or at least a map to get around, then have to navigate colors for security clearance. Green for this. Blue for that. And red for where things really got interesting. Like the Source Unit.

Sergeant Bate didn't need a map or a guide. She knew the route. She'd been to HQ many times and was security cleared to everywhere except the Source Unit. Few were. That required an Enhanced Reliability Status to the highest of secrecy. This was the place where informants were coded, agents were handled, witnesses were protected, and identities were changed; some cases being so intricate that their immediate families would never find them, nor recognize them again – if they could.

* * *

Balwinder Dhaliwal was temporarily in charge of the Source Unit, and he loved it. The reedy-built Corporal received Bate at the lobby desk where she'd stood fidgeting, forty minutes past their appointed time. She huffed as Dhaliwal puffed, signing her in. He snailed her up a curry-fumed elevator, checking through two more stations, first blue, next red, before showing her to his supervisor's office where he snubbed her to a stiff metal chair with one leg a bit shorter than the others. He shut the door, sliding into his boss's squeaky seat, across the pressboard desk, with his back square on to Bate.

"So what would you be needing from me, please?" the bespectacled man asked in his Punjabi accent, folding his arms before turning to face her.

Bate handed him Dupris' criminal record printout, which she'd scotch-taped back together. Dhaliwal snatched it and scanned with a snide smile. She saw the whitest of teeth shine through a dark, bearded face.

Arrogant little prick, she thought.

"I was expecting someone much earlier than this." Dhaliwal tossed the papers back, re-folding his arms.

"Yeah, well, I like to do my homework first." Bate gritted the chiclets.

"I understand this man met with foul play. How unfortunate. What can you be telling me about this crime?"

"I think it's the other way around. What can you be telling me?"

"I am very, very sorry, but our information is very, very sensitive, and I cannot be at the liberty to be disclosing anything without proper approval. I will record your interest and get back to you."

Bate was now pissed right off. "Listen, you frickin' dweeb. I'm investigating this guy's murder, and you have information I need."

"I am very, very sorry, but I cannot release anything to you without proper approval. You will have to wait for this to be cleared through my superior."

She pushed on her chair and stood up. "You know what? I sense you're obstructing justice."

Bate pulled back her red trench coat, unsnapping her handcuff case. Dhaliwal's palms shot straight up.

"Oh, please, please, you won't be needing to get that upset."

"Look, asshole. Who was handling him?"

The administrative Corporal's eyes were like a pair of Titleists sand-trapped in a cloth bunker. He kept smiling.

"Yes, thank you. I can be telling you that he did in fact have a number, but that is all that I am allowed to disclose. Please do not be upset with me. I am only doing my job. I am certain you would be able to understand that."

"What's his code number?"

"He will be known to you as E - Seventeen Forty-five. But that is all I can say without proper approval."

"1745? Same handler as 1804. Right?"

Dhaliwal looked like he'd been caught with his cock in his hand. "Yes, yes, of course. But that would be a different case which I cannot discuss."

Bate had enough of this guy. She took a gamble, chucking her card at Dhaliwal.

"Here. Tell Moloci to call me."

His turban nearly untwirled. Dhaliwal raced Bate down to reception, then scurried back up for the phone.

* * *

Bate also used the phone, then crossed the street to the Administration and Personnel building where she landed on friendlier turf.

"Is Peri-Ann around?" Bate asked at the front counter of A&P.

"Who should I say?" The old Commissionaire croaked out his question.

Bate told him.

"Just a minute, dolly." He forced himself up and creaked off. A minute passed. Bate heard a commotion coming from the back.

"Sharlene!" Peri-Ann Litzenberger rolled through the door, throwing her saggy arms around Bate and giving a huge, squishy hug. "Oh, it's been too long. How ARE you?" She stepped back, holding Bate by both arms. "Oh, you look sooo good! Ohhhhh!"

After small talk that lasted twenty minutes, Litzenberger asked Bate what she needed.

"A service file. I'd like to take a look at it." Bate gave her the name.

Litzenberger left. She returned much quieter. "It's Protected C," she said.

That was another term for Top Secret which some drone thought up.

"I've never seen this before on a personnel file. What's going on, Sharlene?"

Bate took her aside, partly confiding.

"Okay. But you never saw this." Litzenberger left Bate standing in a poll-booth sized file-stall with the door shut tight.

Bate put on her Pharmasave glasses; used when no one was

watching. She opened the dossier jacket, beginning with basics stamped on the inner face.

```
Alfred John Monagham. Regimental #34604.
Born 19October1956. Ladner,British Columbia.
Deceased 20December2002 Ganges Harbour.
```

Bate was sure about Mahle's conclusion that Monagham shot 1804 and was, himself, long since dead. But she was also sure 1745's homicide was connected. Same strange MO. Same special weapon. And Dhaliwal's goof confirmed that both were informants run by the same handler.

It's definitely a different shooter, but it has to be the same motive. She was looking for the link.

"So what the hell's going on here?" Bate asked herself, starting into a pile of documents as thick as its folder was long. It began with his application.

Looked like a good candidate, she observed. *Young, fit, Grade 12, Anglophone, Naval Reserve experience. Good score for placement. Seems to have done well in training.*

Bate read the academy record.

Academic scores seem okay. Law, History, Human Relations... B's all the way through. Hmm... Public Speaking, C minus.

She found a note indicating a slight speech impediment and his flow not being smooth. She scanned his physicals and the instructors' comments.

```
Drill - B Not impressive in uniform but attentive in
class.
P.T. - A Excellent for never having a formal program.
Swimming - A Strongest aquatic subject in this troop.
Firearms - A+ Outstanding.
```

Bate learned that he'd been awarded Crown pistol and rifle badges, meaning perfect scores. A jot from the firearms instructor recommended Monagham be monitored as an ERT candidate. She turned up something from his troop counselor.

```
   Cst. Monagham is far from a typical recruit, I mean
the typical idealistic one. He presents as more mature
than he visually appears. He shows little interest in
general policing duties and states his primary career
objective is being attached to a marine section. He
```

```
seems above average in IQ and has excellent physical
abilities but is reported to be solitary and at times
quite withdrawn. I view him as an excellent candidate
for undercover duties.
```

So what was this guy all about? Bate wondered, knowing something led this rising star to implode. She held an assessment from his field trainer.

```
Well suited to duties.
Picks up on detail quickly.
Good attitude. Good potential.
```

Bate saw the trainer's name and nearly shit.

"Constable John Moloci? Holy fuck!" she said out loud. "Okay. Okay. These two go way back. There's more to this."

She dug further.

Little, almost no uniform time, so probably didn't think like a typical cop, at least not one jaded by the system. Went pretty much straight to the boat, then to Ottawa.

She got Monagham's ERT training assessment, signed by Warrant Officer Atkinson.

We don't have Warrant Officers in the Force. Is this maybe an SAS instructor like Brian said?

She finished the summary, swallowed, and whispered, "Jesus. This guy was talented in that stuff."

* * *

Sergeant Bate had no idea how Emergency Response Teams or Special Forces units operated. She assumed they attracted macho, trigger-happy jocks – the guys who liked to dress up and play army. She had no idea of the level of commitment required, no idea of the danger these professionals were trained to face, and she had no idea that meeting up with some of the world's best would not be fun at all.

* * *

She went on to absorb the Teslin Lake tactical operations debriefing report:

```
…Oros was observed proceeding south towards Squad
#2 and, as he got to within 250 yards of their location,
he stopped his dogs and sled, removed a rifle and
proceeded in a near southerly direction from the sled
to the bush area north of Squad #2's location. Oros
```

111

could be observed as he proceeded through the light underbrush and then was lost from sight. Within a few minutes Cst. Monagham, not seeing Oros again, felt that Oros could have went past their location in the deeper bush and perhaps had continued on south of them or by now may have doubled back behind them. As Cst. Monagham observed the area behind him he noted what he described as 'a face strangely glowing' approximately 40-45 yards behind him to his left. Cst. Monagham advised Cst. Buday either orally or by use of the portable ERT radio that Oros was behind him. At this time a shot rang out. Cst. Monagham observed Oros to be what he felt working the action of a rifle and, seeing only the face and head area of Oros, shot through the brush separating them at which time Oros disappeared from sight. Cst. Monagham did not know at this point if Oros was hit and he tried to make communication with Cst. Buday by his portable radio and also orally with no response coming from Cst. Buday. Squad #1, led by Cst. Claymore, proceeded into the bush down along the trail Oros had left from the ice. This led Squad #1 to a point approximately 150 yards northwest of Cst. Buday's position at which point Oros' trail in the snow inexplicitly stopped. A sweep-search of the area by Cst. Claymore found Oros' body lying on its back 30 yards directly behind Cst. Buday with absolutely no connecting tracks in the fresh snow, rifle in his hands. Upon examination of the .303 British Army rifle, it was found to contain a live round, the bolt closed, and the primer of the round having had been struck by the firing pin. Cst. Monagham had fired his round with the M16 at a distance of 132 feet through the thick underbrush seeing only the head and face of Oros, striking him directly in the center of the face. Cst. Buday was found deceased having been fatally shot through the neck from behind.

It should be noted that subsequent forensic testing of Oros' rifle and the round from its chamber found both in proper working order. The reason for this misfire cannot be explained, nor can the break in Oros' trail in the snow. The instinctive shot returned by Cst. Monagham was fully justified however a duplicate feat is considered virtually impossible. From a re-enactment of Oros' movements, it is now clear Oros was ready for a confrontation with the police on their arrival. He had set up a camp on the island on Teslin Lake in such a location as to afford him maximum advantage should the police come after him. His subsequent actions clearly indicate that he had tricked Squad #2 into a trap, circled around, and ambushed them from behind.

```
Had Cst. Monagham not reacted in the manner he did, the
situation would have turned out far worse.
     Oros was not a sane human being.
```

"Whoooa!" Bate gripped the table, her fingertips turning white. "Ho... Lee... Fuck!" Then she found the Vancouver Sun article covering the inquest.

Strange things are done in the midnight sun but nothing much stranger than what has emerged during testimony at the inquest into the deaths of RCMP Constable Mike Buday and his killer, Michael Oros, the 'missing link' of Teslin Lake; the mad trapper who police said lived like a wild animal in the bush.

The setting was the exquisite and uncomplicated beauty of the Yukon. On that March 19th morning, along the shores of Teslin Lake, the air was crisp and cold. A deranged individual was moving with amazing speed through the bushes, yet he was barely making a sound and leaving no tracks.

The objective of the special RCMP Emergency Response Team camouflaged in position on the ground was to capture and arrest Oros – an American draft-dodger-turned-bushman who earned a reputation for alarming and bizarre behavior. For 13 years, the suspicions surrounding him were plentiful and included murder.

The RCMP members did not expect Oros to be arrested quietly. And no one was kidding themselves by expecting it to be easy! Oros's survival skills were astonishing and legendary. Skilled with a gun, he was known never to miss a shot. And he had openly expressed an intent to kill policemen!

Oros had spent the night on Big Island. This was disquieting to the Tlingit people in the area because by doing so, Oros had trespassed on sacred ground. The island was in fact the gravesite of a Tlingit shaman. They knew this was sure to disturb the spirit of the shaman buried on the island and there would be consequences for Oros. Serious consequences.

Sadly, Oros was able to completely circle around the Mounties and attack from the rear – a feat believed to be physically impossible for any human, given the bush and snow conditions. Oros instantly killed Cst. Buday with his first shot. In the same motion, he turned, reloaded, aimed at Cst. Alfred Monagham and pulled the trigger. Simultaneously, Cst. Monagham caught movement in the bushes and saw what he described as 'a face strangely glowing'. He raised his rifle and fired at the almost imperceptible glimpse of Oros's face through the tangled tree branches. The bullet struck its mark precisely. Oros was dead.

Cst. Monagham should have been, too.

Oros had fired first! What happened to prevent the second officer's death? Subsequent investigation proved the gun was fired and worked perfectly. Miraculously, the bullet didn't. The percussion cap had an indentation where it had been struck, yet something prevented it from firing.

And how was the bullet that Cst. Monagham fired able to find its mark? The odds are astronomically against it! The 5.56 caliber bullet that Cst. Monagham fired could easily have been deflected by a twig or even a raindrop. Expert marksmen shook their heads in amazement when they viewed the path the bullet travelled.

'It is impossible,' they said.

'No. It is not!' said Tlingit elder Mathias Tom, testifying before the six person coroner's jury.

'Oros was the manifestation of The Kushtaka,' Tom said. 'The Kushtaka is the Wild Man of the Woods who tricks you, kills you, and steals your soul. The Kushtaka had violated the grave of our ancient Shaman, Kaash Klao, who stopped the bullet meant for the second Mountie. Then Kaash Klao guided that policeman's bullet to destroy The Kushtaka in its human form.'

Perhaps the Tlingit people were right all along. They believe that Devine Spiritual Intervention was at work, that day on that frozen lake.

"OH... MY... GOD!"
Bate cupped her palm over her open mouth.
"Oh My God!"
She stared at the paper.
"Could Grandpa Heiclaamaax have been right?"
Sharlene Bate knew exactly what Shamanism was, and she'd been warned of The Kushtaka. Her grandfather had schooled her in both.

* * *

The file recorded that Monagham was awarded the Commissioner's Commendation for Outstanding Service for his presence of mind and quick action in ending the Teslin Lake incident, saving the lives of other ERT members by taking the madman out. Bate read of the other fatal shootings Monagham was involved in. Their debriefing reports included one where he was severely criticized in the media for killing a deranged methamphetamine addict.

There's that shot to the center of the head thing again, Bate noted.

Her throat constricted and eyes moistened at the collision analyst's report on the incident claiming Maria Monagham and their eleven year old daughter, Gabriella.

"Oh God! That is just awful!" Bate said out loud, trying to shake off the image of Emma.

She leafed till she got to his medical chart, stopping at the first psychiatric report where he'd applied for a counseling session to discuss PTSD. That ignited a fireworks of referrals. Documents described a chronic, progressive decline in his mental state. One memo turned down Monagham's request for treatment at an American Indian center with a proven track record. Another was from a forensic anthropologist he'd contacted. She'd recommended treatment at a Carrier First Nations spiritual retreat. A squiggle across the letter's face denied Force reimbursed mileage to attend their sweat lodge ceremony, citing no recognized therapeutic value. The next note did authorize something – something a bearded and bonobo-like shrink had prescribed – ninety days, all-paid, at a drug rehab camp. That Monagham flat-out refused.

One report was just plain weird. Monagham was briefly committed to a psychiatric institute after being arrested for drunk and disorderly inside the University of British Columbia's Museum of Anthropology, exhibiting bizarre behavior by drinking from a metal cookie tin, then drumming on it, chanting, dancing, and cursing at an ancient, carved Bakwas mask.

Now that's interesting. Bate wrote it down. *That's very interesting*.

The last entry was his failure to show for a police medical discharge board, and the file ended with the coroner's report, ruling the cause of his death being drowning, antecedent to blunt force trauma resulting from a boat crash; impairment by alcohol being the contributing factor.

Bate let out a whistle, closing the folder. *No motive why he did in 1804. No clue who took out 1745. But absolutely no doubt they're related.*

* * *

It was lunch time, but Sergeant Bate avoided the HQ cafeteria. She knew too many people there, wanting time alone to think. She drove a few blocks, stopping at Subway, sliding into one of those smooth, yellow, plastic booths with her cold-cut trio sub and a watery Coke. She doodled on a napkin, drawing circles, lines, and squares – the link-analysis she'd learned on a conspiracy course.

The key was identifying the lowest common denominator and work outward. She knew it was the wounds – the double-tap and the head shot. That linked the events. The bullet type and lack of casings linked the weapon. The MO linked the scenes. The Source Unit linked the victims and the tactics linked the 22nd Regiment of the British Army.

The Special Air Service.

Monagham was trained by the SAS, and he's long dead, but he wasn't the only one trained that way.

By now Bate knew the shootings were connected and that her Salt Spring killer came from that school. She also knew the victims were old coded informants who, she suspected, had once been jointly controlled by now-Superintendent John Moloci. Bate wiped mustard and mayo off her blouse, waiting for the phone call to confirm it.

So who's the frickin' ghost in the black truck? Her gut feeling said something in Monagham lived on – something so compelling that his purpose was exhumed and carried out.

* * *

A police officer's hunch is not evidence in court, but more cases have been solved from this tool than from all of the new and cool forensic breakthroughs combined. Bate's gut took her over to Burnaby and the headquarters of the Coroners Service. She'd phoned ahead for her contact, Tej Sangha, who she'd met on a pathology course. Monagham's death file was pulled when she got there.

"What's with this guy?" Sangha asked.

"Cold Case thing. Won't be long."

"No worries. Just leave it on the desk when you're done. I have a tele-conference starting."

"Thanks, Tej."

Bate closed the door, settled-in at the desk, opened the docket, and unhooked her reading glasses from her red coat pocket, bent after sitting on them in the car.

She flipped through the few documents. A judgment of inquiry by the local coroner. Photos of Monagham's up-right boat on the rocks. Some hand-written notes. A faxed police report citing two men on a tug witnessed the crash, but no names and no statements. A lab report on his DNA.

Not much here. Must be more on the Serious Crimes file that Fred looked into, but I can't get my hands on that.

What Bate did find, though, was a lead on Monagham's only next-of-kin. The coroner's investigation located the bastard son, as Mahle called him, at an Army base in Ontario. Sure enough, the son had been the DNA donor, confirming blood on the boat was genetically linked. Bate didn't know how this mattered to Salt Spring, but the hunch kept her looking. She found it on the hand-written notes.

C40-334 son Ryan Wedge, mother Kathy Wedge
Dwyer Hill, msg passed 5 B to JTF 2

Another note.

Cpl. Ryan Wedge, JTF 2, temp/at CFB Petawawa
Contact Garrison Duty Centre, Warrant Milcott, 1-613-687-5511, Ext 5611

There's that term. That acronym again. JTF 2. I've heard that before.

* * *

Bate finished with the coroner records, positive Monagham was dead, but now his haunting began.

She left the docket on Sangha's desk, went to leave, but she'd been locked in. She banged on the door for help, waited, finally phoning reception from her cell for release, then grabbed the elevator out to the parking lot where she sat in her car. Thinking.

It was a term Brian used. A commando thing.

Bate pushed speed dial.

"Firearms. MacAllister."

"Hey, Sweetums. I'm curious. Remember when you were telling me about how the SAS operate. You mentioned something… JTF 2… What is that?"

"JTF 2?"

"Yeah."

"Joint Task Force 2. It's our Canadian Forces equivalent to the SAS. The military's Counter Terrorist and Special Ops regiment. Why you asking?"

"Do they train the same as the SAS?"

"Far as I know they're pretty much a carbon-copy. But they're all so secretive no one ever knows for sure."

"That double-tap thing?"

"Yeah, they all do that."

"How about the head shot?"

"That's a Brit tactic."

"Would JTF 2 do this?"

"Well, I don't know, but they'd sure be aware. They cross train with the SAS all the time. Why you asking?"

"Like you told me, Sweetums. This is sensitive. Thanks."

Bate hit 'end' and followed her hunch. She punched in 1-613-687-5511. A computer voice answered. 5611 got a live human being.

"Garrison. Warrant Officer Milcott."

"Uh, Sir?"

"Yes, Ma'am."

"My name's Sergeant Bate. Calling from the RCMP. Sorry to call you under these circumstances, but there's been a death in the family."

"Oh NO!" Milcott's anus snapped shut.

"Oh, sorry, Sir. Not in your family," Bate lied. "No. Sorry. It's someone in your command."

Milcott pinched off his bladder. "Who?"

"A Corporal by the name of Wedge. Ryan Wedge."

"Aw, fuck! No!"

"Is he in your command?"

"Well, sort of. Oh, No! What... What's happened to him?"

"Oh, sorry, Sir. No. Corporal Wedge is fine. At least I think he is. No, it's someone in his family."

Warrant Milcott had taken an emotional kick in the junk and was staggering. "What do you need? Sorry, I didn't catch your name."

"Bate. Sergeant Bate. Where can I reach Corporal Wedge?"

"You can't," Milcott said, still on the ropes.

"This is JTF 2, right?"

"Well, yeah, but... but he's not here."

"Where is he?"

"On the west coast."

Holy Fuck! Bate recoiled.

Milcott rebounded. *I hope to Christ no one hears I leaked this out.*

"Where abouts on the west coast?"

"Sorry. That is classified. Who... who are you again?"

"I understand, Sir. Please have Corporal Wedge call me. It's an urgent family matter." She gave her name and number.

Bate was waiting for two calls now. The first came in nine minutes from a blocked number.

"Sergeant Bate."

A strained voice said "Ah, yeah, Master Corporal Ryan Wedge. What's going on? Is my Mom okay?" Wedge just tried his mother's cell, but got voice mail.

"Oh, Corporal Wedge. Thanks so much for calling back promptly. Don't worry. Your mother's fine. So is everyone else. No worries."

"What... What the fuck? I got a message about a death in the family."

"Sorry about that, but it's very important we talk right away, and this was the only way I could get through to you in JTF 2. With you being on the west coast right now, I'd like to see you today, and I'm in Vancouver so you're probably out in Chilliwack, but I can head out right now and meet you in two hours."

"Hold it. Who the fuck are you?"

"Okay, Ryan, let's cut the bullshit. My name is Sergeant Bate. RCMP. I'm with I-HIT. You know what that is. Don't you."

A long silence.

"Ah, sorry... No... what... what did you say you were?"

Bate's spidey sense was on high. She came on hard. "Integrated Homicide Investigation Team. I only call about murders."

"This is some kinda sick fuckin' joke. Right, bitch?"

Bate held her phone back. *Pretty aggressive for someone who's dirty*, she thought, but her police gut said there was no way Ryan Wedge was a coincidence. "No joke, Corporal Wedge. You know exactly why I'm calling."

"Look here, lady. I don't know who the fuck you are, or what the fuck you're up to, but this conversation is done."

"Hold it, Corporal Wedge. Or should I say... Monagham."

There was another long silence before Wedge replied, "Now why did you say a name like that?"

"So we've found some common ground here, Ryan."

A long pause with no reply.

"You have information I want, Ryan. It would be very much in your interest to meet me immediately."

Another long pause, but this time he answered, "Go on..."

"We need to talk. You and I. Alone. Tell me where you are, and I'll be right there."

Wedge's pulse pushed 180. "You're... you're from Vancouver, right?"

"Yep. But it's best that you come to my office in Surrey. I'll meet you there."

"Not going to happen," Wedge said. He'd already decided any meeting would take place on his time and his turf.

"Okay, where are you?"

"I'll give you this. On the Island." Wedge took control.

Bate suspected the base at Esquimalt near Victoria. "Okay, my headquarters there is on Blanshard, downtown Victoria. See you there at ten tomorrow morning."

"You just come over here. I'll call you and tell you when and where."

So he is in Victoria. Bate squeezed her phone. *Yeah... Right next to Salt Spring. Convenient, buddy. Bet you drive a black truck, too.* "Very well, Corporal Wedge. I'll be there. You've got my number. I need yours just in case."

"Not a fuckin' chance."

"That's okay. I got it on call display."

* * *

Wedge knew this woman was bullshitting again. He ended their conversation and immediately instigated another.

Chapter 14

Wednesday, October 19th, 1977
7:05 pm
Parking lot behind the Patricia Hotel
Nanaimo, British Columbia

Constable John Moloci sat in the passenger seat of Robin Ghomes's musty black Suburban, staring at grainy snaps in the chilling dimness of the interior light. His guts twisted and turned like snakes in a mating pit, and he tasted his own bile.

The photos were real, Moloci knew. He'd enjoyed every second screwing the girl in them. A Ghomes girl, it turned out. Now, not only had the Honey Trap bombed in his face, it could nuke his career.

You'd think Moloci would've realized it was too easy a bust when he'd arrested the bubble-headed bleached-blonde for possession of cocaine. Back then, possessing coke was a big deal. But, she offered her honor, and he honored her offer, and as the joke goes, all night long he was on her and off her. Moloci was young, and human, and that night his little head did the thinking. The existence of the photos was bad enough, but who the girl was, would be worse. This was John Moloci's debut on the world stage where the Art Williams Organization would perform.

Moloci was suspicious when Ghomes called him earlier in the day, saying he'd information that'd be worth Moloci's while. For Moloci, good policing involved good informants. Information was a commodity, like money, in his crime fighting world.

For Ghomes, though, crime was all about control. Money was a commodity to Ghomes as well, but in his world, money was just another tool to gain power.

And to keep it.

* * *

"So what do you want?" Moloci asked, appearing calm and staring down the brown-skinned biker who wore his Hells Angels colors, adding to intimidation.

"This is a fuckin' message from a friend of mine," Ghomes said in his Lucifer voice. "Someone I play bows n' arrows with."

Moloci knew who. He just glared at the dark Angel.

"He wants you ta help us out."

The wheels spun in Moloci's head. His pulse buried the needle, but he simply kept eye-balling Ghomes and asked, "Why?"

That was not the response Ghomes expected. He replied the only way he knew how.

"Why is 'cause yer fucked, asshole."

Ghomes sat up and bulked in. Moloci could smell both liquor and BO.

"How is what you n' I gonna talk about."

"Fly at it," was all Moloci said.

Ghomes knew Moloci was playing head games, despite how hooped he really was.

"Work with us and yer little fuckin' problem'll go away."

"Go for it…"

"Simple. Just let us know what we needs to know. Not only will yer problem dry up, you'll be looked after."

"Meaning?"

Ghomes cut to the chase. "You know fuckin' well what I mean. Look. Yer fucked. Awright? You n' I both know it, so quit pissin' around. All of us'll be better off if we work this together. Look. You got yer expertise and you got yer network. So does we. You just do yer job and make fuckin' sure it stays away from our job. We'll feed you shit to take down. Don't worry. You'll look good. You'll get yer fuckin' stripes. As long as you make fuckin' sure no shit falls on us. Unnerstand?"

Moloci never expected this to happen. As his mind raced, subconsciously his hand slipped towards his hip where his .38 was holstered. Ghomes sensed it, striking across, seizing Moloci's arm.

"Don't… Even… Fuckin'… Think about it."

The clean-shaven Angel nodded out the windshield, to the darkness where the cold wind blew wet leaves on the glass.

Moloci snapped back to reality. *For sure Ghomes has someone covering. This thing'll get real nasty if I do something stupid.* "Take it easy, dickhead," Moloci told the black-haired biker. "I'm getting a card from my wallet."

"Slowly, man. Slowly," Ghomes growled.

Moloci took out his wallet, holding it up in the low light. The windows had fogged, and he didn't want some jackass to think weapons were out.

"Look, I need a bit of time..."

"There IS no fuckin' time!" Ghomes roared. "It's Now or this fuckin' porn show goes straight to yer fuckin' boss."

"Cool it, for fuckssake. Geezus, guy. Take a fuckin' valium." Moloci took out a business card, clicked a pen, scrawled a number, and shoved it over.

Ghomes leaned back on his door. Moloci saw the glint of gold teeth as the burly outlaw fingered the card.

"So what's this?"

"Private number. Not traceable. You get me there."

"You know. You got some fuckin' balls." Ghomes grinned, changing his tone. "I like that. Okay. Let's fuckin' mellow. So we agree to do business? Right?"

"Think I got much choice?"

Ghomes kept grinning. "Look at it this way. You scratch my balls. I scratch yers. We both feel good."

Moloci stared at him.

Ghomes dropped the grin. "Fuckin' don't take it personal, man. I'm just takin' care of business. Right?"

Moloci continued the stare.

"That's how it works," Gomes said.

They kept eyes locked, till Ghomes broke away. He glanced out to his cover, then came right back at Moloci.

"You know. What fuckin' pisses me off about you fuckin' cops is you always look down yer noses on us bikers like we're fuckin' stupid or sumpin. You don't give us no respect. You don't unnerstand we got a way stronger code. Way more fuckin' loyalty than youse guys do."

Ghomes thrust a thick finger at Moloci.

"I seen a lotta cops come, n' a lotta cops go. You might got more fuckin' members in yer club but, what we do in our club... we do it for life."

Moloci stayed silent. Ghomes smiled through his gold teeth.

"Like Art says. Life can be long, or life can be short. So make the most of it."

* * *

Moloci knew there was a vice grip on his nuts. For now. He'd square up with Ghomes one day.

But, over the years, as John Moloci got to know Art Williams and worked with the other key members of the Organization, he'd come to respect that there was a much bigger picture to the world of drugs.

Chapter 15

Friday, May 11th, 2012
10:44 am
Parking lot behind the Tudor House Pub
Esquimalt, British Columbia

Sergeant Bate had no sense of being watched – never mind by what, or just how sophisticated the eyeball was. It was at 32,800 feet in altitude, but its discreet imaging SAR, Synthetic Aperture Radar, could see she was wearing what appeared to be a silver cross embedded with tiny diamonds.

Bate had other things on her mind this morning than trying to scan the sky for some ghostly thing of technology. She yawned and rubbed her eyes as she'd lain awake most of the night, mesmerized by the Teslin story and how it fit with Grandfather Heiclaamaax's teachings, which she'd long since dismissed as folklore. Running late, she suffered another fight with Emma before dashing off, fearing she'd miss the ferry.

Forty minutes earlier, Bate had been zoned out, thinking of Emma and of Monagham, when her BlackBerry toned. Ryan Wedge's voice directed her to a bar parking lot in Victoria's suburb of Esquimalt and to stand outside the car. That didn't surprise her. She figured Wedge was at the Navy base, three blocks away. Fifteen minutes passed while she watched traffic; third Grande in hand and getting uncomfortably warm, as it was already high seventies, Farenheit. But she kept her red trench coat on – open at the top and tight at the waist, concealing her sidearm and a body-pack digital recorder.

A blacked-out Expedition circled, braking hard in front of her Grand Am. Civilian plate from B.C., she noted, not a government marker which the Armed Forces normally displayed. Her knees locked. A second black Expedition roared in from the back, boxing her bumper. Bate knew what was happening. She'd been set up.

"Oh Oh! Oh, how goddamn stupid trying this alone."

Her chest pounded and fingers punched 911. Nothing. She tried a second time. Nothing. Her signal had been jammed.

"*Fuuuck!*"

A third black truck barrelled right up, squealing to a stop. The front passenger door flung open and a very fit figure in black combat pants, boots, and a turtleneck stepped out, driving a 9-mm sub-machinegun at her breast and, in one motion, opened the rear door with his free hand.

"Get in."

Bate felt like her bowels would let go. She'd lost control and a panic attack came on. Her mind turned tricks. Like in a dream – a Jason Bourne movie – her kidnapper became Matt Damon. She screened the scene as if on the roof of the pub; her world becoming a slow-motion picture. Frame by frame, she watched the figure grip her arm, floating her onto the back seat.

The slam of the door snapped Bate back to consciousness.

The driver was a black man, disguised with a black ski mask. Beside her was another faceless, black figure holding an FN P90 weapon. Matt Damon got back in front. In seconds they moved out, turning west towards the base; the first Expedition leading the convoy, the third black truck guarding the rear.

They bypassed the main gate at MARPAC, Maritime Forces Pacific, speeding downhill to a secluded area and sliding through a thick mouth of leafy alders before getting gulped by a concrete and metal, windowless building. A powered, steel, overhead door rolled down behind, echoing with the soul-crushing smash of an Alcatraz cell.

Ryan Wedge moved from up-front, opening the black truck's back door.

"Get out," he ordered.

She complied. P90 man slid his big frame through, still covering.

"Face the wall and spread eagle."

She stumbled from wobbling knees and a fibrillating heart.

"Do it now!"

She did.

Wedge frisked Bate, removing her Smith, cuffs, badge, BlackBerry, and body-pack. He looked at the recorder, turned her about, burning a long, searing stare in her eyes.

She swallowed hard, but held contact.

He broke first, nodding to P90, who hauled Bate by the arm through a cinder-block corridor, shoving her into a beige, Javex-smelling room, lit by four, bare incandescent bulbs and furnished with a grey, banged-up metal desk and two purple, hard plastic chairs. She sat in one. Trembling. Badly having to pee.

P90 left. The door locked. The lights quit. In death-like blackness, an electronic voice squelched from a small, silver speaker mounted high-up by a lens on the cold, concrete wall.

"You are under arrest. You are in the custody of the Canadian Federal Government. You are charged with attempting to infiltrate the Special Operations Command. An offense under the Anti-Terrorism Act. Spying under the National Defense Act. Treason under the Criminal Code. Your charter rights do not apply in a national security case. Communication with the outside is prohibited."

The lights flashed on. Bate forgot having to pee, now wanting to puke.

Oh God! How am I ever going to explain this? I broke every rule laid out to prevent what I just tried to pull off.

She fingered watery eyes, praying this was only a nightmare – not the reality where cloth-hooded spectres loomed like Grim Reapers.

* * *

The Commanding Officer of JTF 2 shut off the mike, but he continued to monitor Bate by audio and video. Colonel Dave May was impressed by reaction to this infiltration scenario. It proved just how fast his Dwyer Hill JTF 2 units – bricks, they were internally called – could respond. They were in Esquimalt running insertions and extractions on RHIBs, Rigid Hull Inflatable Boats, preparing a new marine commando regiment to go operational.

This is different, May thought, but he was used to being tested with scenario shit spontaneously chucked at them. *Some clever bastard has thought of using a fake cop to infiltrate my command, attempting to get one of my soldiers alone and take him hostage.*

May was immensely proud of his command, once quoted in the press describing them as 'very highly trained people who are trained in anti-social skills – they're trained to kill people in various ways.' The Colonel took a puff on an Old Port and a taste from a Timmies, sitting back to watch it play out on his screen.

* * *

Sergeant Bate might have been an expert on Vancouver homicides, but she was out of her league in the world where nations were overturned by armed coups or held helpless by the barbaric actions of a fanatical few. JTF 2 were the experts here, and they took their role seriously. Very seriously.

The RCMP did the nation's counter-terrorist work until they were relieved by the military after the police high command was unable to resolve their paradox – the necessity to kill versus the desire to serve and protect. Originally, the RCMP hired the SAS to train thirty-two select Mounties, who'd earned their winged swords, but the white-shirts put an end to that program once one in Vancouver used a military tactic to end a civilian incident. It was two shots to the chest and a third to the forehead – one Alfred Monagham trained for scads of times.

But the white-shirts ran scared, lobbying hard to the Federal Government of the time. The Feds heard the Force and, in the interest of national security, directed the military to take over counter-terrorist control. So it was that in fifteen years, the tarnished and bruised old Airborne Regiment of the Canadian Army evolved into, arguably, the finest Special Forces unit in the world. Joint Task Force 2. The unit was richly funded, highly motivated, and quietly recruited the best that Canada had to offer. Ryan Wedge was one of those.

Wedge grew up near the small town of Carleton Place, Ontario, where his mother grew up. Kathy Wedge had cooked at Dwyer Hill her entire career, raising Ryan on her own. Many times the young Wedge interacted with RCMP members, then with JTF 2 soldiers after their takeover. At sixteen, he joined the Army Reserves; at nineteen, converted to the Regular Force – now a combat veteran of two tours in Afghanistan.

His peers saw Wedge never tried to be anything other than what he really was – someone born to be a warrior. This was beyond a learned ability. It was something you got passed down in your genes.

* * *

Captain Armand Lange stood across the grey desk, holding the P90, still wearing his balaclava and blocking Bate's run for the door. Wedge also stood – examining her badge, identification, and business cards. He looked through Bate's purse. It contained what you'd expect from a woman. He looked at her cuffs and at her stainless service pistol, seeing *RCMP* engraved on the breech. He looked at the recorder, then at Bate, then back at the recorder, and he swallowed hard.

This shit's real, he thought.

He'd traced Bate's phone the previous evening. It took time, but

Wedge found it registered to a government account. That meant nothing.

Obviously they'd never use a civilian for a training scenario. And she's targeted me personally. That never happens in scenarios. Worse, she'd said my father's name along with that term. Murder.

Wedge had picked up a secure phone to call an old police contact, but he stopped and thought it out. Long and slow.

That's a last resort. No way I'm opening that crypt which holds my old man.

So he took a gamble – mustering his brick, which moved out hard and fast. And now, Ryan Wedge gambled again.

"You said we need to talk, you and I. Okay, talk."

Bate swallowed deep.

Wedge came on big. "Who put you up to this?"

Bate knew she was pleading for her career. "There's been a terrible misunderstanding here. You are Master Corporal Ryan Wedge, aren't you?" She looked at the dead-ringer for Matt Damon.

Armand Lange motioned to Wedge, slicing his finger across his throat.

"Doesn't matter who I am," Wedge replied. "Who the fuck are you? Really?"

Bate's wits were returning. She'd lost control and knew that her only way out was to level with these guys, but she had to go in the worst way. She cut a deal. The truth for the toilet. In six minutes, Sergeant Bate was back in that hard plastic chair.

* * *

She'd had time to think. It was something Wedge said. 'Who put you up to this?' *They think it's a training thing. A scenario.*

Her cop sense had returned to her now. She told them about an investigation, convincing them she was a real cop, investigating a real murder, but she left out key-fact evidence like the double-tap, the head shot, the bullet composition and, of course, the ghostly black truck skulking Salt Spring.

"I'm just following a Crimestoppers tip that some military guys may be involved," Bate lied. "I had no other avenue but to cold call and see who showed up. I thought it might even be a hoax."

She glanced at Wedge, who glanced back. She saw him blink. Bate knew the military had no idea of how police investigated murders. She also sensed P90 was in charge here, probably an officer. She looked in his eyes, the only thing visible through the black mask.

"This thing has gotten out of hand, Sir. For all of us," she said to

P90. "None of us needs this shit."

Captain Lange tightened, and she caught it.

"I mean, like you can't go around pointing firearms at police officers either. And kidnap them." She watched P90 jolt. "Right?"

Lange looked at Bate. Then at Wedge. Then at the camera. Colonel May winced hard, too.

"Your shit seems legit," Wedge said, appearing collected.

But his mind roller-coastered. He knew this woman was a bullshitter, although there was no way he would call her on it – unleashing the monster which was his father's past. Bate wasn't going there either. She just wished she was back at Bamfield, suffering something less painful like her jelly-fish sting.

"Ah... Sir?" Bate addressed P90. "We all work for the same outfit, right? We gotta get along here."

Captain Lange was confused. So was Colonel May, watching his monitor. They knew this didn't add up to a training scenario. It sunk in that this good-looking lady was a real cop they'd grabbed off the street. The officers were now thinking about their careers, having abducted a police officer at gunpoint. Lange motioned to Wedge, and they left Bate on ice in her cold, purple chair.

* * *

"What the fuck?" May asked.

"Fuckin' weird," Lange said. He jabbed a finger at Wedge. "Why d'fuck she go after you?"

"Haven't got a fuckin' clue," Wedge replied. "She just fuckin' called me outta the blue and come on hard. I thought it was a fuckin' training thing."

"Fuckin' weird," the big Frenchman repeated.

May interrupted. "Look. Some kinda shit's happened here. It's obvious she's gone outta her bounds, too. But she's not going to say a fuckin' thing cause she's shit-scared for her fuckin' job, and I think we oughta be, too. Like she said, none of us needs this shit. Whatever the fuck's going on... It's over."

The last thing the Colonel wanted was to lose control and have this thing blow up in Ottawa. As far as May was concerned, the scenario was done and, in the interest of national security, would not be spoken of again. He ordered Lange and Wedge to put Bate back where they found her.

* * *

"Fuckin' weird," Lange said as they watched Bate fumble her keys, pick them up, and set off her car alarm.

Ryan Wedge had the feeling that he'd not seen the last of Sergeant Bate.

Chapter 16

Wednesday, November 30th, 1977
7:35 pm
One mile south of the Canadian Boundary
Semiahmoo Bay, State of Washington

If Art Williams was nothing else, he was a figuring old scoundrel.

And Art figured twenty years, if he stayed the course. That's what Sydney Sleeman, Esquire, also figured Art would get. They discussed it again, that fall afternoon, at their Vancouver meeting which Art flew over for in his Cessna.

Slippery Syd, as the cops called him, was a big-shot, downtown lawyer. Syd knew that Art stood no chance of getting off again this time, though he'd managed to slip Art out on bail. That's why Syd fried up some spam.

Syd cut a deal with the prosecutor where Art would plead guilty to being the kingpin in his drug-trafficking conspiracy, and all that was left now was to negotiate time. The deal included an irrevocable agreement letting Everett, Ridge, and Ghomes walk – irrespective of what went down with Art.

* * *

"Mayday! Mayday! Mayday! Cessna one-seven-two. Mike Lima Tango!" Art's panicky voice cried over the 132.300 aircraft frequency.

Vancouver International's tower heard his distress.

"MLT. YVR. State your emergency."

"Engine failure. Setting down in the water. Mayday!"

"MLT. State location and altitude."

Nine hundred feet. Semiahmoo Bay. Non-filed flight. Boundary

Bay enroute Cassidy. Wheel-plane in the water. Mayday!"

"Got one dropping at seven-fifty," the controller told her supervisor. "Bearing one-six-six."

"MLT, YVR. Confirm location and altitude," the supervisor radioed.

No response.

"MLT, YVR."

No response.

"Aircraft at seven-five-zero over Semiahmoo bearing one-six-six. Identify."

No response.

The aircraft at 750 was not Art's. It was a biker-piloted bogey; a small Piper Cub nosing-over in the dark, vanishing into ground clutter at YVR's radar threshold. One hundred feet above Semiahmoo Bay, the decoy flared to level flight, heading towards a thumpy, grass strip at Birch Point in Washington State.

Repeat calls to MLT were futile. The tower notified RCC, the Rescue Co-ordination Center, who dispatched the responders. A fixed-wing Buffalo lifted off at CFB Comox, a hovercraft blew south from Richmond, and a U.S. Coast Guard cutter raced north out of Bellingham.

The weather was perfect for a late-autumn night search. Bright waning moon. Temperature cool. Seas calm. They quickly found the crash site, strewn with MLT's wreckage; marked things you'd expect to be floating, like seat cushions, lifejackets, and a watertight briefcase with Art's papers and passport. Impact was pin-pointed from the wreckage position, calculating in currents and tides. There were no witnesses – nothing independent to verify the incident – but the location was precise. No doubt it went down in the States.

The Canadians had no jurisdiction in American waters, and the Yanks held a different standard of thoroughness in this case. They'd had enough of narcotics smugglers using the old Boundary Bay airstrip, just north of their border, and the Federal Aviation Agency wasn't prepared to look into the demise of an intruding aircraft flown by a foreign drug trafficker. The FAA washed their hands of the investigation, turning it over to the Whatcom County Medical Examiner, who relied on Canada for information. Bureaucracy being what it was, none of the northern authorities – police, coroner, nor Transportation Safety Board – were prepared to do anything except assist the Americans, who'd asked the Canadians to do it all for them.

Bureaucracy is a crook's best friend and in slid Slippery Syd, who promptly provided the ME with everything that she needed. He slipped across the line with an affidavit, swearing he'd been the last to see Art alive, alone, airing the doomed plane at Boundary Bay, which he swore backfired south into darkness. Robin Ghomes shotgunned along with Syd, swearing Art never arrived in Cassidy, where he swore he'd been waiting. Both swore the voice on the Mayday tape – a tape they'd not listened to – was, in fact, that of Art Williams.

Ghomes and Syd slunk back to Canada by night with Art's death certificate – the cause being drowning, antecedent to blunt force trauma resulting from an airplane crash; engine failure being the contributing factor. All charges were stayed, and Art's police file was closed.

* * *

Aside from the small club of Canadian conspirators, there was a large American club who knew exactly how the plane crash went down. The United States Navy.

The Art Williams Organization, still in its infancy, had cleverly picked a strategic spot to stage the show in Semihamoo Bay, which was on the flight path out of the old runway, clearly in U.S. waters and deep enough to make recovery of the heavy parts of the wreckage difficult for divers. It was also a strategic spot for SSN689, the USS Baton Rouge, a Los Angeles class nuclear attack submarine, to sit – silently waiting its foe, a Soviet Victor II class ballistic sub, to make the next move.

1977 was well into détente of the Cold War, but the U.S. Navy took the red threat, approaching from Canadian waters towards their new Trident base at Bangor, Washington, seriously. Very seriously.

The STS, the sonar technician on the Baton Rouge, was well aware of a small landing craft drifting above him; monitoring it, among a number of other things, from a sonobuoy skulking up on the top. He could hear voices, but didn't care who Art and his loyal lieutenants – Ghomes, Ridge, and Everett – were or what they were up to. His concern was the acoustic listening device he'd set for the Victor might be damaged or, worse, stolen by these clowns.

The Baton Rouge's Radioman of the Watch intercepted Art's Mayday, instantly knowing it was from an aircraft bandwidth that'd been broadcast right on the surface of the ocean, not at nine hundred feet like the bogus caller claimed. The COB, the Chief of the Boat, took control when they realized something strange was going on. They isolated the Mayday as coming from the landing craft but, in less than a minute, four jettisons came from the craft, sending immediate alarm through the sub. The CO ordered General Quarters.

The signatures of the descending objects showed as large and metallic, profiling like obsolete depth charges. There was no time for evasion. Two torpedoes locked onto the threat. The skipper was ordering fire just as the objects passed within a half-boat length of the Baton Rouge, harmlessly settling into the ocean's mud floor.

Once the sub crew pulled their shorts from their sphincters, they checked passive sonar, seeing the charges were actually an engine, fuselage, and two detached wings from a four-seater airplane. *What the hell?* the CO and the COB wondered, then laughed how angels watched over the jackasses bobbing above. Seconds more, they'd have vaporized the landing craft, and Art Williams really would've been dead.

Outside the soundproof, double-hulled Baton Rouge, no one else ever knew of the incident. In the interest of national security, the crew ignored the Williams Organization, silently awaiting the Victor's next move.

Art's next move was back to Mexico.

Chapter 17

Tuesday, May 15th, 2012
7:10 am
RCMP Headquarters
Vancouver, British Columbia

Superintendent Moloci knew about the hit on 1745 well before Sergeant Bate did.

* * *

He was back in his office now, checking e-mail and phone messages after two weeks away, picking up the one from Dhaliwal as well as a few others regarding his informant being terminated.

So Sergeant Bate from I-HIT wants a call, does she?

He knew who Bate was. He also knew the Officer-in-Charge of I-HIT, Bate's boss, who could decide if she stayed on the case.

Well, let's see what's been going on... Officially.

He switched computers, entering his Protected C code, checking the I-HIT file and reading the investigation reports; noting references to key-fact evidence, including who was privy to it. Moloci saw MacAllister was on the list.

Hmmm. That's the same lab guy.

Suspicious, Moloci pulled up the Atlin file, which was SUI, still under investigation; its access severely restricted. Sure enough, there were recent attempts to hack-in. He did an off-line search, implicating Sergeant Bate.

Okay. So she's onto 1804, too. Hmm... Tried to get in on May 9th starting at 2:43 pm. He smiled, penning down the figures, clicking some more. *Persistent. I like that quality... Just not snooping after me.*

Moloci keyed back to the Salt Spring file, checking dates and times. *Found on April 30th,* he noted. *Identified that evening. Fits. Looks like the usual background checks.* He left the investigation screen, entering 'Gerard Joseph Dupris' on CPIC, the Canadian Police Information Centre database. *Okay, the pointer is still just to my unit, not to me personally.*

The CPIC pointer person feature automatically notified Moloci immediately after 1745 was first queried. It didn't matter where he'd been. The message would've reached him instantly, anywhere in the world that had cell coverage, and it was a message he'd been patiently waiting years to receive.

There were a few recent references to Dupris on the PRIME system. All seemed routine for what you'd expect on a homicide victim, but Moloci looked for that link that led Bate to the Atlin case, then to the Source Unit, and how she knew that he'd once handled the expired informants. He suspected MacAllister had something to do with it, as he knew there was history between MacAllister and Bate. There wasn't much around Headquarters that John Moloci didn't know.

So how'd she connect me to 1745 and 1804? Moloci knew someone gave Bate a tip. He made a short call – call it damage control – on his secure line to a sensitive acquaintance, then attended to unrelated business. At 8:30 am, Moloci walked down the hall to the Source Unit where Dhaliwal stood shitting his pants.

"Please believe me, Sir. I was very, very surprised when she knew you were the handler. I would not be telling her that. She is a very, very aggressive woman, and she just threw her card at me and told me to be having you call her."

"So how'd she know, Corporal?"

"I do not know that, Sir. Please believe me. I called you as soon as it happened."

Moloci was satisfied that Dhaliwal was truthful. He'd known the obsequious little member long enough to read him like a Neon sign in Times Square, so he left Dhaliwal quaking in his oxfords and returned to his office.

All right. So MacAllister's made some connection to Atlin and shot his mouth off to Bate. He wouldn't know the handler though. No. Someone else in this bunch talked to her.

Moloci opened the drapes and stood at his window, stroking his Clark Gable moustache and running his fingers through slicked-back, silver hair – planning on busting Bate off at the knee-caps. It took a bit, but then he decided that his best course was to first take a swing at her head. Moloci picked up the phone.

"I-HIT. How may I direct your call?"

"Your OIC, Superintendent Vedder. Superintendent Moloci calling."

Moloci was on hold for three minutes.

"Mornin' John. Sorry. I was in the can. How's things?"

"Great, Ted."

"Get everything ready for the move?"

"Pretty much. As much as you can get Mexicans to move anything."

They laughed. John Moloci and Ted Vedder went way back in the Mounted Police, both now just short of retirement. Moloci spent his career in Drugs. Vedder in Serious Crimes. It was no secret that Moloci had a place in Mexico, soon moving south. He'd been going there for years and, rumor was, he'd a lady-friend down in Matamoros.

"Ted, what do you know about a murder on Salt Spring? One of our sources got it over there while I was gone."

"Yeah. Running an Angel grow-op. An old guy like us."

"Yeah, real old. We'd lost track of him for years, but the guy used to be productive. What happened there?"

"From what I know it was just another hit. They got some hold-back, but I can say he was shot. Fucking near everybody is these days."

"Any idea who's behind it?"

"Nope. We had a briefing last Thursday morning. There's no suspect or witnesses. Nothing yet. What do you guys know?"

"If I tell ya, I gotta kill ya." Moloci replied, chuckling with that corny, old police line.

"Well, keep it to yourself then. I've got less than six months, too, and I wanna live to see pasture."

Moloci changed tone. "Bate, one of your Sergeants left me a direct message while I was gone. Pretty blunt. Wants me to call her personally about the victim. That's a little outside the chain of command I'd say, Ted. What's she all about?"

Vedder thought a bit. *Strange that a Sergeant would call a senior officer directly.* "Don't know, John. She's a top-notch investigator. Very aggressive. A no-bullshit type, but she knows the system. She's on the list for a commission, you know. I'll call her and find out why she did that."

"Na, that's fine Ted. I'll call her back myself. Just wanted to clear it with you first."

"Cleared. I'm heading out the door for two weeks leave, myself. Late already."

Good timing. Moloci smiled about the gag orders.

* * *

Bate was changing lanes on the merge ramp to a bridge when her BlackBerry toned.

"Sergeant Bate."

"Superintendent Moloci."

It was the other call she'd been expecting, but she was late – heading to a new scene and she'd had a bad weekend. Bate got home from being kidnapped by commandos to find out that Emma ran away.

"Sir."

"You dropped your card."

"Ah, yes, ah, sorry Sir, I'm in traffic."

"You said I should call you."

Bate groped for a line. "Sir, you're aware one of your sources was shot?"

There was no pause. "This is not appropriate to discuss on a cell phone, Sergeant. And there's a helluva lot more you've been doing that's not appropriate. You are to attend my office and speak to me directly about this. Do you understand?"

Moloci came on hard, taking the upper hand and throwing a bluff. Like many things he'd learned from old Art, Moloci knew the best defense was a good offense. He also wanted time to check out his foe.

"Yes, Sir... When?"

"Four pm. Sergeant. Precisely." Moloci hung up.

"Aw... FUCK!" Bate slammed her hands on the wheel. "I don't need this shit today." She had an appointment with Emma and a counselor at four.

* * *

Moloci leaned back in his oxblood, leather swivel chair, reflecting on the meticulous office he'd soon be leaving. The rich taupe and cherry-wood paneled walls were decorated with diplomas, photos of him with high-profile people, trophies from takedowns, and citations from international agencies. A lot of successful cases happened for John Moloci since the night he sat in Robin Ghomes's musty black Suburban, but there was still one last case to conclude. It was huge – tricky and complex.

Moloci picked lint off his woolen trousers. *The last thing I need right now is someone like Bate nipping at my heels.* He got up from behind his massive mahogany desk and went out, speaking to his secretary. "I'll be over at A&P for awhile."

* * *

Moloci walked across the street to the Personnel office, asking for Litzenberger who he'd known since he was a constable. She knew almost as much about what was going on around HQ as he did.

"Ohhh, good morning, Johnny, I mean Sir John, soon to be a Mister John." Litzenberger giggled.

"I'm gonna miss ya, Perriwinkle."

Moloci spent fifteen minutes in small-talk, getting the latest gossip. A curious lady with a search-engine memory, she'd once been a clerk in his unit.

"Could I see the file on Sergeant Sharlene Bate, I-HIT?"

Litzenberger's lips lapsed. *Sharlene recently looked at the file on John's deceased brother-in-law. That's strange.* She stayed silent, knowing she'd breached a security classification.

Moloci read her reaction. "You know her well, don't you?"

"Yes. Yes. She's a sweetheart."

"Well, I'm going to let you in on a little secret." He put his arm around her shoulder. "She's shortlisted for the next commission, and I'm sitting on her promotion board. I'd like a little head start, if you'll help me out." Moloci squeezed tight, smiling. "You'll keep it quiet, won't you?"

"Ohh, Ohhh! Of course."

A relieved Litzenberger fetched the records, gave Moloci her office, and steeped him a cup of tea; so happy for her friend.

* * *

The folder on Bate was thick and Moloci took his time. *Hmm... Intelligent, educated, travelled. An experienced investigator who's loyal, discreet, and ambitious.* He skimmed twenty years of performance appraisals, zeroing-in on her fault. *A perfectionist. Exactly what I'm looking for.*

Moloci had something in mind for Plan B on his final project. Plan A, the simple one, went off the rails last September when a long-time informant, a challenging informant – the Goofie Newfie, Moloci called him – got caught and was squeezed by the DEA in San Diego.

Moloci browsed the papers, looking for who'd informed Bate on 1804. He picked up on her long-time supervisor.

Ahh... I'll bet that's who it is. Fred Mahle. She'll know about

Monagham then.

Wanting to be sure, Moloci returned to his office, booting his desktop, getting the Supply & Services database, querying Bate's BlackBerry records, and going straight to the afternoon of May 9th.

Okay. 1:25 to 2:36, one hour and eleven minutes. 520-421-0993.

He wrote it down, checking a previous note. Bate's first attempt at accessing the Atlin file was 2:43.

Seven minutes. Just enough time to get off the phone and the throne.

Moloci changed screens back to A&P, dragging up the retired member directory. Mahle's number matched.

Okay. Let's see who else she's been talking to.

The remainder of May 9th was quiet. Calls home, to a video store, to a hair salon.

May 10th was revealing. Moloci confirmed Dhaliwals's story of Bate calling first. There was almost an hour gap, then a call to Headquarters. Moloci checked the number and extension. Litzenberger at A&P.

Okay, so she's read Al's file. No big deal. He's dead. Moloci smiled. *There's nothing in there.*

The call at 1:34 was to the Coroners Service and then, an hour and three quarters later, one to Firearms at the lab.

Yeah, MacAllister.

What transpired next tweaked Moloci's interest. 613-687-5511-511. He queried it.

Canadian Forces, Petawawa. Oh-oh. What's this?

The next call to Bate was incoming, blocked, and try as he might, Moloci could not identify this one. Four more outgoing calls remained for the day, three to her home, one to the ferries reservations. The digital trail told Moloci she'd booked a sailing for Victoria early the next morning.

The May 11th records were strange. First call was at 6:38 am to the ferries. Then a bunch in succession to her brother, Terry Fletcher in Burnaby – all incomplete. At 10:04 there was another incoming from the blocked source and, between 10:41 and 12:06, her signal had been electronically disabled. He knew there was only one outfit capable of jamming. The military.

What the hell has she gotten into?

Moloci saw Bate was back on her phone at 12:32, calling the ferries for a ride, then twenty-plus calls to her home and to Terry Fletcher – none connected.

Something's upset her. This'll upset her even more.

He called the Commanding Officer, then spent the remainder of the afternoon on regular business.

* * *

Bate paced outside Moloci's office like a tumor patient waiting biopsy results. She'd no idea what she was in for, hadn't slept decently in five nights, and now it was 4:25.

"You may go in."

She rattled the bronze levers, opened the right side of the solid oak doors, peeked through, and stepped onto the shiraz carpet. Moloci stood; back to her, arms folded, left hand under his chin, facing the window. She advanced to the desk, stopped, and stood to attention. Perspiring.

"Sir."

"Sergeant."

Moloci turned. He seemed seven feet tall. Like the Teflon Don, he was dressed in a blue-black power suit with a bright-white, cuff-linked shirt and deep-red silk tie. She couldn't see the suspenders or his 9-mil slung in a black, nylon-webbed shoulder holster.

"You've been out of bounds."

"Yes, Sir. I apologize."

"You, Mahle, and MacAllister have all committed a serious breach of the Security of Information Act."

Aw Fuck! He knows everything. Bate started wobbling. "Sir, I, ah, need to explain…"

"Like explaining what you were doing with the Canadian Forces?"

She felt disoriented as a one-eared bat. "Sir… I need to sit down."

Moloci was curious about the military contact, really curious, but steered clear and pulled out the rug. "Oh, fffuc… Go ahead."

Bate grabbed for support on his pedestal globe. It spun, spilling her into an upholstered wing chair before he'd finished his words.

"Sergeant, you don't look well, and I'm not going to keep you. This matter is far from over. I've discussed it with the CO because your supervisor is gone for two weeks." Moloci eyed Bate, smelling her blood in his water. "We'll get to the bottom of this before Superintendent Vedder gets back."

"I am so sorry," was all that came out.

"I have some papers for you." Moloci opened a dossier on his desk, pulling out the Security of Information Act order for the Atlin file. He laid it on his blotter, handing her his pen.

Welcome to the club, Moloci thought, seeing Bate's hand vibrate as she signed.

"Stand up, Sergeant Bate."

She was not expecting this.

"Under the authority of the Royal Canadian Mounted Police Act and at the direction of the Commanding Officer, I hereby suspend you of duties pending the outcome of an internal investigation."

She was speechless and turned to go.

"Ah… Sergeant."

Bate looked back. Moloci flicked his finger at her waist.

"Yes, Sir."

She removed her sidearm, handcuffs, and badge, setting them on his desk.

"Cell and car keys too. They're government property."

"Yes, Sir."

* * *

Sharlene Bate left John Moloci's office. Through waterfall eyes, she found a pay-phone and called for a cab-ride home.

Chapter 18

Thursday, September 8th, 2011
2:15 pm
Washington Square near Greenwich Village
Lower Manhattan, New York City

The street performers by the fountain paid no attention to her, but many in the crowd did.

Tracillina Williams weaved through the people, to the Hanging Tree at the north-west corner of the park where she'd sat many times; many times thinking it ironic how this peaceful bench under the old English Elm had once been the site where criminals were executed.

She waited in the shade, sipping her ice-cap, aware of a young couple on the lawn playing Scrabble and some tourists buying overpriced gelato from a cart vendor. She read the review of an Off-Broadway play she'd see that night. Her iPhone toned. She checked a text from her assistant and went back to the review.

Tracy loved New York City. Like Glenn Frey wrote in '*You Belong To The City*' – Nobody knows where you're going and nobody cares where you've been – You're just a face in the crowd. They call it the city that never sleeps, but Tracy's interest wasn't nightlife. It was arts and finance; the real heart of the Big Apple. She would've made Manhattan home, except for her business and someone special back in Vancouver. Tracy smiled slightly at the review, knowing one of the actors well and looking forward to dining with her after the show.

Her contact was late. *Probably the traffic*, Tracy thought, but she wasn't worried he hadn't called. She'd worry if he did. They kept meetings like these away from any possibility of electronic eavesdropping.

Raymond Ridge sat down on the bench and Tracy embraced him with a long hug. The big American appeared a lot different now, compared to when she'd first seen him back in his biker days. Today, he was clean-shaven with close-cropped grey hair and dressed in a black Armani suit with a white embossed shirt, gold silk tie, and Versace watch. Tracy held him, her eyes welling. He wasn't her father, but she adored this older man, and Art had recently passed on. She raised her head from his shoulder, stood, and removed her Wayfarers. Ridge took in her figure as she dabbed her eyes, always thinking Tracy appeared somewhat of a caricature – 5-5, busty, with a teeny waist flaring to wide hips, tapering back to shapely legs.

Tracy was fifty-four now. Any Fortune 500 company would have hired her on appearance alone, but it didn't hurt that she had the smarts and the education to go with it. She was heavier than in her youth, though her Hispanic gifts – jet-black hair cut over pearl-studded ears and shaved at the neck, high cheek bones, chestnut skin, and deep, deep cocoa eyes still turned heads. As they spoke, Ridge looked to Tracy's eyes and could see the lines of time had advanced. Ridge figured stress from the Organization had taken its toll, and he was quite right.

* * *

"He was not the same after the death of my mother," Tracy said, staring at the grass.

"He aged so fast," Ridge replied. "Sad to see such a brilliant mind break down…"

"He would not speak of business at the end. He would only speak of freedom," she said, barely audible. "He spoke of freedom of a soul being a wealth far greater than money and authority…"

"This drug war broke his spirit, for sure. To see so much of what he accomplished taken away. Destroyed by violence and deceit…"

"Freedom of a soul." Tracy kept gazing down. "I believe that, Raymond. I so believe that is the truth."

Ridge turned away. "These people today… They are monsters. What the Sinaloa did in Ciudad Juarez is despicable. They cut their heads off, Tracy. I mean, they cut off their fucking heads and rolled them out on the nightclub floor. We never operated like that."

"I read of that horror." She sat beside him again. "Also of the massacre in the day-care."

Ridge looked back at Tracy, pausing to appreciate her carriage. She removed a tissue package from her long-strapped bag, its matt-gold sheen accentuating an ecru linen, sleeveless blouse tucked into sashed slacks, hemmed just above low-heeled, sling-back pumps.

"You can no longer trust the downline," Ridge continued. "There's little loyalty left in those people. And look at your younger cousin, Ezekiel Cardenas. I'm sure he made a deal once he was taken into custody. You can't tell me that he had nothing to do with all the arrests and seizures. Who knows what he's said to save his slimy skin. And the sonofabitch still thinks he's running the Gulf from inside prison walls."

"I fear for the worst." Tracy's voice faded off.

"We have decisions to make," Ridge said.

"Yes. Yes of course." Tracy composed herself. She was here on business and this meeting was vitally important for the future of the Williams Organization. She looked at the Scrabble couple nearby, who seemed to pay no attention. Out of caution, Tracy switched to Spanish. She knew Ridge was fluent, despite being of African descent. Besides, it was the language of their business.

"The Xcellerator loss, and now this one they call Reckoning, have hit us hard," Tracy said.

"The loss of product and equipment can be absorbed," he said. "People are the problem. Our cash situation?"

"We have serious shortfalls. Our reserves are tight. We have been relying on product trade far too long. And the BMPE, the Black Market Peso Exchange, has ripped us royally. I should never have bought into that. Thankfully, most of our wealth is electronic, and there is almost no way to steal that."

* * *

Raymond Ridge had returned to New York in 1979 to look after the Art Williams Organization's international interests, as well as some things of his own. Ghomes stayed back to control the west coast, and Dale Everett was sent to work with Tracy's Colombian relatives, the Orejeula family, who were the Cali cartel.

After her father's disappearance, Tracy began studies at New York University in lower Manhattan, across from Washington Square where she and Ridge sat. Margarita quietly relocated to Mexico within six months of Art's 'death' and funds were set aside, ensuring Tracy's education. She took an apartment in neighboring SoHo and, by twenty-five, obtained her chartered accounting degree, continuing at NYU's Leonard N. Stern School of Business to earn her PhD in accounting, taxation, and business law. Aside from academics, Tracy pursued her love of watercolors, finding hours of solace in paint. At twenty-nine,

Doctor Tracy Williams returned to Vancouver, taking over the finances of her father's rapidly expanding syndicate.

Tracy had spent the past twenty-three years laundering money for her father's conglomerate and its close affiliate, the Gulf cartel. She hated cash. It was risky, never mind dirty, and she felt it downright sleazy.

The principle of money laundering was simple, though the practice was complex. Bulk cash required *Placement* into legitimate industry or financial institutions. This was the risky phase. Established countries like the United States, Canada, and Great Britain, had enacted strict reporting laws for high value transactions. Even Mexico and Colombia had their forms of control, but the controllers could easily be bought. The problem, from a criminal's point of view, was that few could be trusted. The same applied to law enforcement agencies – except in Tracy's case. She had a priceless contact high inside the RCMP, long ago cultivated by her father.

Another problem was the sheer size of cash transactions. $1 million U.S. worth of near-pure cocaine, at current New York market price, weighed thirty-four kilograms. $1 million U.S. in cash, paper bills, weighed one hundred sixteen kilograms. Cash transactions were heavy, slow, and extremely vulnerable to theft and seizure. Electronic ones were weightless, instantaneous, and mostly secure.

Layering is the second step of the process. It's safer, but time consuming, and requires creativity. Tracy was brilliant here. Once funds had been placed in one institute, they were divided among others, changing form to foreign currencies or commodities. Tracy created nested accounts with global institutes that had friendly bank-secrecy regulations; Hong Kong, Panama, Bahamas, Bahrain, Cayman Islands, Antilles, and Singapore. She avoided the high return on shady systems such as Hawala in Pakistan or China's Fie Chen. She also dodged a bullet with Luxemburg's Clearstream International when an investigative reporter identified her and the name 'Tracy Williams' recently appeared in *Time* magazine. It scared the living shit out of her.

Integration is the last step, where money is repatriated into the mainstream economy – investing in overvalued jewels, art, yachts, or in one of Tracy's recent projects, $8.6 million for the purchase of an old fish cannery at Bamfield and the $1.4 million purchase of patent rights to a revolutionary scuba diving tank. These funds she'd safely stored in an offshore account established in her assistant's name, labeled 'Retirement Fund'.

Technology evolved over the years as Tracy practiced her profession. She started small, laundering with the tried and true 'Smurfing' technique where she placed cash, daily, into numerous accounts at numerous banks around Vancouver. The cash came shipped by various means – from a human mule arriving at YVR with a stuffed duffle bag to an enormous couriered piñata, smashed open with a sledge hammer she'd gone out and bought at Home Depot. She was careful to keep below the reportable limit but, as the Organization grew, Tracy became exhausted of time and energy to keep up.

Two huge breakthroughs changed Tracy's life. One was the Internet. The other was a trusted assistant. She had Moloci to thank for the second.

The Internet brought unprecedented opportunities to the crime world. Not only did it let the world interact instantaneously, it let business transactions go unnoticed. Millions of international transfers now occurred each working day. The lack of account holder relationships allowed anonymous transfers of unlimited funds across global payment networks. Money Services Businesses, MSB's, flourished. Digital currencies, mobile payments, wire remittances, prepaid cards, global debit and credit networks, internet gambling, online dating, porno sites, and virtual worlds were the new cleaners in the cyber laundry business.

Internet-based technologies brought more than just inimitable financial services and products to the world; they brought novel forms of communication. Social networks like Facebook and Twitter were free, anonymous, and relatively secure. The Internet was a criminal's dream.

The Internet brought unprecedented nightmares to the intelligence, law enforcement, and regulatory communities. The cutting-edge technologies evolved so rapidly that the laws and regulations governing them were non-existent or, at best, undefined. The IMF, International Monetary Fund, and the World Bank were shackled, leaving individual countries to restore order to the chaos. The United States took a lead role with the Bank Secrecy Act, the Money Laundering Control Act, the Money Laundering Suppression Act, the U.S. Patriot Act, and now the vicious and all encompassing Foreign Narcotics Kingpin Designation Act.

All of the Cardenas family, Tracy's Mexican cousins who headed the Gulf cartel, were designated Kingpins. When captured, they faced extradition to the U.S. where they'd be imprisoned for life.

* * *

"Our investments must be liquidated, dispersed, and we must flee," Tracy said.

Ridge winced.

"I know. It will take time." She absorbed his reaction. "But we must stop. Quit while we can. The Kingpin threat is far too great. I am so terrified that I am going to be next."

"You know what the others will think..."

"You know what I think, Raymond? It does not matter to the others what I think."

Tracy bent forward, wrapping her gold-bangled forearms about her shoulders.

"My life... It has been ruined by this business. I could not marry. Bring children to my world? Let them grow up in this? My parents died prisoners of their success. They were not able to go outside the compound for fear of being shot or blown up. They had no freedom. And I have no freedom. I have never done anything good in my life. I feel I have sold my soul, Raymond. I anguish so horribly inside. Every time I see a stranger... look in the rear-view... hear footsteps on the dock... I expect to be arrested again."

Ridge put his arm around Tracy. She turned, pushing her face to his chest.

"I am so trapped... I do not want this anymore. I never wanted to do this. I just want out."

Tracy wept in silence. A minute passed before she spoke.

"All I ever wanted of life was to bear children... and make them happy. I have a piggish amount of money, but I could not buy happiness."

"I understand you, Tracy. Completely."

She sat back, letting his eyes contact hers.

"But there are others who are not as well off for retirement," he continued. "They need the chance to rebound. We can't abandon them. They were the loyal ones to your dad and they devoted many years to him. They deserve our loyalty now."

Tracy knew who Ridge meant.

"I know how faithfully my father served them," she said. "And, of course, I know the allegiance which he demanded in return. But the others' commitment has collapsed with the drug war, and it has put the Organization in peril. Yes, winding down slowly is prudent, though I am painfully aware of the consequences. And I struggle with the loyalty that my father would still expect of me."

She tissued her nose, staring at the Scrabble couple, wondering, *Can my life ever be as peaceful as that?*

"It is also the violence, Raymond. It makes me just sick to see what has become of Vancouver. They are shooting each other in the streets. And they are just children, for God's sakes. You expect that in Colombia. Even Mexico. But not in Canada."

She turned back to Ridge.

"It is our product they are killing for."

He took her arms.

"No, Tracy. It's the lack of our product. That's why they're killing each other."

* * *

Tracy knew Ridge was right. She'd been born in the business and groomed from her teens to become comptroller of the fortune that her father generated. She'd resigned herself to this destiny, much as a child of royalty or a Kennedy would accept the curse of their lineage. As much as she despised the business, Tracy would do nothing to dishonor her family.

It'd been her maternal grandfather, Juan Nepomuleno Cardenas, who founded the cartel in the city of Matamoros across the border from Brownsville, Texas, on the Gulf of Mexico. Juan was a harmless, old scallywag who peddled bootleg whiskey across the American border. He'd made lots of money. He never hurt anyone. And he never got caught.

Juan took the odd trip to Colombia to get a new product called cocaine. It was in Cali that he hooked up with the Ouejeula family and married one of the daughters, bringing her back to Matamoros where they raised six children including the second oldest, Margarita, who was Tracy's mother.

Art Williams joined the Cardenas family quite by accident. He'd been a young traveller, motoring through Matamoros after the war and ran into Juan Cardenas. Literally. Art got a job driving Juan's banged-up truck, soon trusted to smuggle daily booze deliveries into Texas.

Juan saw intelligence in the young Englishman – something beyond a learned ability. It was something you got passed down in your genes. He introduced Art to the peyote cactus, an entheogen that lifted Art to a height he'd never known – an altered state of consciousness. Juan acquainted Art with others who'd mastered the sacred succulent, and Art realized he could become stupendously wealthy by selling psychoactive substances to the world.

Juan trusted Art. At night, Art would stay at the Cardenas compound where he met Margarita. An unwed pregnancy was frowned upon by the Roman Catholic Mexican society, so it was thought best if Art would take Margarita away for a while. Art always dreamed of living on Vancouver Island, trading the hot, sticky Gulf coast for the cool rainforest, much like his home on the British Isles.

* * *

"I agree it's time to retire," Ridge said. "But we need an exit plan. We need to abandon the manufacture of MDA and finish off solely on coca product."

Tracy knew this was the proper business direction, though it would never have happened as long as Art was alive. He'd built the Organization with MDA as its core product and had only taken on cocaine as a value-added sideline. To Art, MDA and its cohort, MDMA or Ecstasy, allowed the user to expand their consciousness and learn from their experience, unlike coke, which gave them stupidity in spades. Until the drug war, caused by the cocaine industry, the Williams Organization was immensely profitable, and Art kept it sequestered from the enforcement eyes which the high-profile, coke-head scene seduced. Art was a firm believer in the business philosophy that you don't fight your enemies – you buy them – and Art had a lot of well-paid enemies.

"What will Everett say?" Tracy asked.

"He thinks we should have got out of chemicals long ago. There's far, far more demand and way more return now in blow. He just had too much respect for your dad to say so. He'll be okay going alone, but he still needs our help with the Canadian route."

"You are very confident in this," she stated.

"We all know importation through Mexico has to be abandoned. The place is nearly out of control, close to becoming a narco-state. It's only the leadership of the current Mexican President holding it together." Ridge glanced around, lowering his voice. "We also know shipping large volumes directly to the United States is far too risky with the U.S. government entertaining federal legislation to execute Kingpins. Polls confirm voters support it."

"How confident are you in the plants?" Tracy asked.

"Completely," Ridge replied. "The extraction is consistent now. The technique took longer to stabilize than anticipated, so we have a mountainous stockpile of impure product at Santa Barbara. Shame it'll go to waste, but the purity is so bloody erratic, there'd be ten times the war if we put this shit out on the street."

"How reliable are the boats?" she asked.

"Sea trials had issues, but most of the kinks are worked out."

* * *

For nine years, Dale Everett had built the Organization's Colombian venture independent of the Gulf and Cali cartels. He'd refined a genetically-modified strain of coca plant and a process of condensing the potency.

Everett's team also developed a sophisticated, stealth transportation system, delivering huge quantities of product by water from their factory, cloaked in the mapless jungle of western Colombia – bypassing the chaos of Mexico, the lethal potential of arrest by America's War on Drugs, and landing the contraband safely on Canadian shores. Here, the concentrate was bulked in their warehouse, then diluted and distributed in controlled amounts to downlines spanning continental North America.

It made for a strong business case, supporting a much bigger picture, and was approved by an agency layered deep in a labyrinth of secrecy, operating entirely in the interests of national security.

* * *

"When will the next shipment leave?" Tracy asked.

"Wiggers is already back in Colombia for a second load."

"Wiggers." Tracy smirked and shook her head.

"Yeah, Wiggers." Ridge grinned, shaking his too. "The operation at Bamfield?"

"Bobby is on it."

"You put a lot of trust in him."

"I trust him with my life."

"You better be right. I always found it suspicious how he just showed up, and Wolfgang found nothing on his background."

"John also trusts him," Tracy said, knowing far more about her assistant than she'd ever tell Ridge.

"How is Moloci?"

"On top of things and controlling everything, as usual. He is retiring next summer."

"He's made his decision?" Ridge asked, already knowing. He and Moloci kept in contact on things they'd never tell Tracy.

"That is another good reason to quit." She clasped her hands, focusing on some small, random stone below the bench. "It is only because of John that we are not all in jail."

"It's worked well for him, too."

"Ghomes?" She looked up.

Ridge paused. Tracy knew what Ridge thought of Ghomes.

"How is he going to react to us shutting down?" she asked.

"He needs to be dealt with."

"I am scared of him, Raymond."

* * *

It wasn't that Ghomes had 3,600 Harley-riding brothers that scared Tracy. The Hells Angels had over one hundred chapters in twenty-nine countries, including nine in Australia where she'd planned to retire. Tracy had a greater reason to be scared of Ghomes. So did everyone in the Art Williams Organization.

For years, Ghomes practiced mutually-assured destruction. He'd recorded and documented all of the Organization's transactions, swearing notarized depositions which incriminated each and every member, keeping the evidence in a vault controlled by the executor of his will; his lawyer – Slippery Syd. In the event of Ghomes' death, the depositions were bequeathed to the Solicitor General of Canada and to the Attorney General of the United States. Ghomes made sure they were all well aware.

* * *

Ridge checked his watch. He had an appointment shortly at JFK with an old German flying in on another matter.

He looked up, saying to Tracy, "We need an exit plan for Ghomes."

Chapter 19

Tuesday, May 22nd, 2012
8:55 am
RCMP Headquarters
Vancouver, British Columbia

Superintendent Moloci stood in his office and stared out the window. He'd given Sergeant Bate the week to think about her job. Her old one. Not her new one. He also took the week to calculate.

Moloci was a believer in the philosophy of Sun Tsu, the 400 BC Chinese military strategist who said 'Keep your friends close and your enemies closer'. He was no longer going after Bate's head.

No. Quite the opposite.

Moloci had a major operation unfolding, and he now needed an adjutant – a trusted assistant – someone to take over coordinating his most sensitive agent until the takedown was done. He also needed the Salt Spring and Atlin investigations to back off until he was retired and long gone. Taking Sergeant Bate under his command would accomplish both.

* * *

Sharlene Bate sat in her Richmond townhouse, slumped in front of her Mac with a mountain of crumpled Kleenexes overflowing the desk. She'd spent the week in anguish, and it didn't help that she'd picked up a wicked cold and sore throat right at the time when her monthly friend paid its visit. Her phone rang. She looked. Saw a private number. Hesitated. Then let the machine take it.

You've reached 604-274-0329. Please leave a message.

"Ah, Shar, Brian here. Just got in and see you been trying to get a hold of me..."

Bate leaped at the handset, banging over the prized Japanese bonsai that her mother left her, punching the talk button to override the recorder.

"Thank God you called! Where've you been? You wouldn't answer your cell. You don't even have voice mail!"

"I drove to Portland to bring Carolyn home," MacAllister said. "I already cleared the border before I realized I forgot it. You know her sister's in palliative now, eh?"

Bate paused to cough. "Oh God! How selfish of me. I'm so sorry. Yes. Carolyn called and left the message, but I didn't want to burden her with my shit, too. She's got so much on her mind. I'm so sorry. I didn't know you went to get her."

"What's with you?"

"Oh, God! Where do I start? I've done something I never should've. And Graham, he's gone on a conference, and Emma, she's at my brother Terry's, and she won't even talk to me anymore. I've never felt so alone," she said, sniffling.

"What the hell happened? You sound awful."

"The Salt Spring and Atlin things. Oh God! Have I screwed up royally this time." Bate was barely able to frog out the words.

"What the hell'd you do?"

"Moloci. Has he contacted you yet?"

"No. You mean Moloci? The boss at Drug Enforcement Branch? Why would he?"

"He knows everything," she blurted out. "He knows you told me, and he knows Fred told me, and he found out about me going after JTF 2, and he got the CO to suspend me, and now he's started an internal on us over the Security of Information breech..."

"Whoa! Whoa! Whoa! Hang on here. How'd he find out? Wait. What the fuck's he got to do with this, anyway?"

"I did something really stupid. I went to the Source Unit, and I tried a bluff 'cause I found out the guy on Salt Spring was an informant just like the guy at Altin, and I put two n' two together, and I figured Moloci was handling both finks so he had to know who was behind the murders, and it just blew up on me like some kinda giant shit-bomb..."

"You... You said... *Whaat*? You went after JTF 2? Where the fuck did that come from?"

"That was the dumbest thing I've ever done. I nearly ended up in prison!"

"This is way too much for me. Did… Did you just say you were suspended?"

"Even took my gun and badge away," Bate said, choking up.

"Okay, okay. Ca… calm down. Start from the beginning."

"The suspect in the Atlin murder is Moloci's brother-in-law, and he's one of those SAS trained guys you were telling me about, but he's been long dead so how the hell could he have done in my guy on Salt Spring? So it must have been the bastard JTF 2 son, but I got no idea why or what the hell is happening any more…"

"Are you fucking losing it?"

"No," she said, quietly snuffling. "This thing is way bigger than I thought. There's something really, really, weird going on here."

"How did Moloci find out we were talking?"

"I don't know," she whimpered. "He's got informants all over the place. Maybe he even tapped our phones."

There was a long pause.

"Hang on, Shar. I'll be right over."

* * *

What Bate never told MacAllister, as they privately tried to sort out their predicament, was what she was beginning to believe – what she thought was really going on.

She'd cried herself out the first day of suspension, then turned to the power of prayer. First at home. Then in her church. Then somewhere sacred to her First Nations roots.

She thought a lot over the week, and she'd had a lot of time to think. She thought about her career, and she thought about Emma, and she thought about happiness. She thought of Carolyn, and her terminally-ill sister. She thought about Graham and about her brother, Terry. She thought of her Christian God, and why she was placed in this world. She thought about her parents, Donna and Ed, who'd been grounded in both worlds; white and aboriginal. She thought of stories from the Bible and of stories from Oweekeno legend. She thought about potlatches and about searing-hot sweat-lodges where her spirit soared free.

She thought of Grandfather Heiclaamaax, ridiculed for practicing the ancient ways and how he stayed true to his beliefs. She thought about Kaash Klao and his battle with The Kushtaka. She went to the library and she went to the bookstore and she went on the Internet. She read *Descent into Madness* by Vernon Frolick, the story of Oros and what led to the tragedy at Teslin Lake. She telephoned an elder of the Desileen Kwaan, riveted on the line for two hours, then she called her aunt Evelyn up in Oweekeno, and stayed glued to the phone for three more. She bought a print of the memorial painting to Mike Buday, titled *Sheep-Standing-By-Himself* by Ed Hill and Roy Henry Vickers. She learned how the spirit of Kaash Klao inspired the artists, and she was captivated watching Brian Coxford's Global Television documentary showing this vision. She studied Tlingit and Carrier and Navaho beliefs as Monagham had done.

She went to the Museum of Anthropology, and she stood where Monagham had stood, she'd seen what he'd seen, she read what he'd read, and she learned what he'd learned. She confirmed some things were not of this world, as Grandfather Heiclaamaax and Auntie Evelyn had said, and she realized that she'd neglected their teachings. She tried to comprehend what went down, that day, on the edge of that frozen lake, and the more she thought, the more Sharlene Bate became haunted by the ghost of Alfred Monagham and the secret of why the informants had to be murdered.

* * *

An hour after MacAllister left, Bate was still in her yoga pants, back researching Shamanism on the Internet, when her phone rang. She checked call display. Grimaced. Then picked up.

"Hello?"

"Sergeant Bate?"

She knew the voice.

"Yes, Sir," she said, still sniffling.

"I'd like you at my office. Four pm today. We need to discuss your situation."

Bate knew Moloci couldn't fire her. But she accepted that it would be the end of her officer program, and she was prepared for a transfer to some place that didn't even have a name yet. She showered, wiped on a bit of foundation to lessen the redness, dressed, and chugged down three Cold FX tabs with hot, blueberry tea before shuffling on out into public.

It was pounding rain and Vancouver traffic turned uglier than an ape with acne on days like this. Her one-hour drive pushed onwards of two. Bate ditched her CRV in the HQ lot, bailed out, and cracked her umbrella. She nearly pulled a Mary Poppins before it sprung inside out. She bunched its bent carcass back through her door, slamming the seatbelt in with the hasp and solidly jamming the lock. Hitting the wrong remote button, the panic alarm freaked out. She prodded away till its hissy-fit halted, then made a bolt for the building, braking to re-capture a shoe. She hit Moloci's office dead on four, soaked as a swamp rat, hair flat as an old road kill.

"You can go right in."

Bate started through the oak doors. She stopped as if encountering an alien.

Moloci was dressed in D&G jeans and a white, open-neck polo shirt, treading in tan Cole Haan slip-ons from behind his desk, greeting her warmly as she sloshed on his carpet.

"Today will be a little less formal than last Tuesday," he said, tanned face seemingly pleasant.

Bate stood, mouth catching flies. Moloci gently guided her by the arm to the upholstered wing chair where he held his fireside chats, settling into another – purposely placed at a right angle. Perplexed, Bate forgot that Moloci had years of undercover experience; U/C operators being masterful actors.

"Sergeant Bate... Ah, Sharlene, I've had time to look into what you've done and... You know what, Sharlene? I would've done the exact same thing if I was doing your job. Sometimes investigations just can't be done by the book. Right?"

Bate had no idea what to say but "Yes, Sir."

Moloci's leg crossed the other, hands clasping his knee, expression most inviting.

"I appreciate you were not under written order on the Atlin file. However..." he said, grin instantly gone and pointing his right index finger, "You were duty bound to at least go to your supervisor when you became aware that others were. Fred Mahle is retired and somewhat removed from the Force, but Brian MacAllister is still employed. I'm sure you'd like that to continue."

Bate swallowed. No further explanation was necessary.

"Contacting me direct is not exactly policy, but it's not an offense either. Actually," he said, suddenly chuckling. "It's pretty bloody efficient. You got my attention."

Moloci stayed away from the Canadian Forces episode, but he was curious. Very curious. *That has to involve Monagham, but no way I'm opening that crypt and raising the dead.*

His tone tightened. "You realize of course, Sharlene, the Atlin matter is Protected C and for good reason. This is no longer your concern. Whether it relates or not to the Salt Spring investigation you were assigned to, that will now be up to someone else to decide."

* * *

Here it comes. Her nails clawed into the chair. She was sure she saw horns on his head.

Moloci's brow clamped over iron-grey eyes. "I've had the chance to review your performance evaluations, Sharlene, and I've talked to people. I see you've long been rated as high potential, and you've been shortlisted three times for your commission."

Moloci wasn't bullshitting her.

"I spoke to the CO again about your, ah, situation."

She was about to get sick.

"We both feel it's the right time in your career, actually, for some added responsibility. Let's say some grooming towards your move into management. Call it payback for twenty years of loyal service."

Bate was completely bamboozled. "Sir?"

Sternness stopped. "We're offering you reinstatement, Sharlene... and a change of venue. Management has trust in you and there's a major drug project underway, coming into the west coast of Vancouver Island. It's close to fruition, now needing someone with your skills and background."

Bewilderment stayed. "Sir?"

A wide smile broke. "It's a, let's say, coordinating role, based right out of my office here in Headquarters. Highly classified. In fact, the highest profile, most sensitive investigation of my career. Good one to go out on."

Dumbfoundment set in. "I, ah..."

Delighted, he got up. "I'm retiring at the end of it, you know."

"No, Sir, I didn't."

The wide smile vanished. He stepped toward the doors. "Hours will be normal, though towards the end, will require travel to Bamfield and a few erratic shifts. It's international in scope and will expose you to other agencies. Excellent opportunity to make contacts." Moloci half-turned, icicles impaling her from the sides of his eyes. "It's what you know that makes your career."

"Yes, Sir. I understand that one."

Moloci grinned as he ushered her out to the hall. "Expect the duration to be no longer than four months and, pending your performance and a successful conclusion, Sharlene... the Commanding Officer is prepared to promote you to the commissioned rank of Inspector. She has something in mind, but that's for another day."

* * *

Bate was blown away, like winning the lotto, going from zero to hero in no time flat.

But Sergeant Bate had no idea that this would take her straight for a go-around with The Kushtaka.

Part Four

The Diversions

Chapter 20

Monday, October 10th, 2011
9:35 am
San Diego County Jail
San Diego, California

Why did the informants have to be murdered?

* * *

Archibald Wiggers knew, but he didn't give a fat rat's ass about that as he squirmed in the interrogation chair. His left leg vibrated like a barnacled old prop, and he tapped away on what served for his right. He was in a bind. A snarl, the relic Newfoundlander would've called it back home on 'The Rock' but, then, Archibald Wiggers had been in snarls before.

Wiggers had been minding his business on September 30th, 325 nautical miles off the Guatemalan coast when intercepted by a United States Navy guided missile frigate. He tried scuttling his narco-sub, but the remote fused out. Wiggers, the sub, seven tons of cocaine, and his mother ship, *The Big Easy*, were hauled by the scruff into San Diego for detention. Permanently, if the U.S. Drug Enforcement Agency had its way.

It was actually shithouse luck, good or bad – depending whose side you were on – that the U.S. Navy EA-6B Prowler locked onto him. The reconnaissance plane was part of a routine, national security patrol deployed under Operation Panama Express, a long-running project of the American OCDETF, the Organized Crime Drug Enforcement Task Force comprising the DEA, the FBI, the USCG, and the ICE, or Immigration and Customs Enforcement, targeting cocaine shipments sneaking out of the watery South American jungles.

Wiggers had left a western Colombia river mouth, bearing north, when the Prowler soared over. At 37,600 feet apart, neither he nor the jet's crew could see much of each other with the naked eye, but the crew didn't depend on naked eyes. They had a system onboard worth more than a CEO's severance package to see for them.

The Prowler paid no attention to *The Big Easy*, Wigger's 107 foot, 225 ton, re-fitted tugboat, built forty years earlier in Helsinki by Oy Wartsila. There were all kinds of tugs coming and going from Colombia, and they were of all nationalities, including Liberia where *The Big Easy*'s flag of convenience claimed she was from. Any tug could've been chock-full of coke and the authorities would never have known without surface checking each one. That was the main method of interdiction before they started blitzing with Operation PanEx.

Now, they assumed a trafficker would no longer be brazen enough to load up his tug, so they set their system to spot *The Big Easy*'s sidekick – a Self Propelled Semi-Submersible – SPSS for short. These were the leading edge of contraband movers, and the Americans were passing laws targeting them specifically.

These smuggling boats were powered, but not truly submarines; not designed to travel completely underwater. Except for the surface of the deck and control module, the structure was submerged for the sole purpose of evading detection by keeping the profile off radar.

Wiggers' narco-sub was one of a number, hand built in the seclusion of the Colombian jungle with pieces imported from around the world. The vessels ranged from forty feet to nearly eighty and carried two to twelve tons of cargo. At first, they were manned by two, three, or sometimes four, conscripts. They cost upwards of a million dollars, per, and took the better part of a year to construct. The early ones had limited range. They were unreliable in navigation but, like everything else, the new and improved models increased efficiency.

Every SPSS had one thing in common, though. They were a one-time-only operation, destroyed by the delivery team once the cargo was offloaded at its destination. Unless, of course, one was intercepted enroute. Then it was bombed – scuttled within minutes, taking the ship and its contents to the bottom – provided the remote controlled explosives went off.

Wiggers didn't invent the SPSS. He just capitalized on it, like Wiggers did with everything else. Credit for inventing the SPSS went to the infamous Colombian shrimp-boater, Enrique 'Captain Nemo'

Portocarrero, nicknamed after the Jules Verne *20,000 Leagues* character. He saw the go-fast, surface boats of the 80's as being stupid, *Miami Vice* TV-stunts, like waving a red flag in front of a bull with full balls. Nemo understood naval technology, historical and emerging, and stayed ahead of the authorities. He also had a frothing budget to work with – part of it courtesy of the Art Williams Organization.

The first SPSS to be seized was ninety miles southwest of Costa Rica, carrying five tons of near-pure cocaine and slinking northwards to Mexico. The U.S. Coast Guard called it 'Bigfoot'. There were lots of rumours of the subs but, till then, none had been photo'd, let alone captured. This was an early model. It was crude and still manually operated. What gave this boat away was its heat signature, as obvious to the Prowler as a zit on a prom girl's nose.

Wiggers got caught skippering a next-generation vessel. His SPSS was fifty-nine feet long, bow to stern, and exposed less than two feet of freeboard. The lower structure was steel, but the topside made much use of fiberglass, shielding it from radar. Nemo dealt with the infrared issue by lead-lining the engine compartment and water cooling the exhaust ducting. He camouflaged the topside with a chameleon paint scheme, and he ordered the boat to be run slow during the day so its wake was small, but to max out at nine knots in the dark.

What Nemo overlooked, though, was the ventilation apparatus that exhausted via a PVC snorkel to the surface. It was the CO_2 signature that the Prowler picked up this time.

Wiggers' sub was unflagged. It was also unmanned and remotely operated by a joystick from a laptop through GPS guidance. Both tools had been high up in the wheelhouse of *The Big Easy*, but were now down low on the floor of the Pacific Ocean. The sub should have been there too, along with its cargo. But, as Wiggers found out, sometimes shit happens.

* * *

DEA Special Agent Garfield Woods unlocked the door, letting his partner, Eileen Ziegler, back in the interrogation room. She'd left to check a legal issue and came up, whispering in his ear. Woods glanced at Wiggers, seeing an about-to-be-struck-with-a-blunt-instrument pair of eyes, resembling black-eyed peas, stare back at him through a bristly grey face – looking much like an unwilling racoon being mounted by an old porcupine.

Ziegler whispered again.

Woods's expression changed.

Wiggers's did, too, as Woods whispered back.

"Told ye I's right, old cock," the caged-critter said.

They'd been arguing the validity of the Drug Trafficking Vessel Interdiction Act, the DTVIA, which he'd been arrested under. Wiggers was better versed in law than most agents were, and he'd been relying on Article 5 of the 1958 Convention of the High Seas to protect him on the nationality issue. It worked well for him in the past.

"Not entirely," Woods said. He was one of a few black agents who spoke fluent Spanish.

Woods had been with PanEx since its concept, and he'd known Wiggers back from the Joaquin Valencia-Trujillo trial where Wiggers gave State's Evidence under the name Jose Castrillon-Henao, which convicted Valencia, permanently removing him as the last head of the Cali cartel. Art had ordered it. Raymond Ridge made the plan. Dale Everett set it up. Wiggers sucked him in. Woods presented the evidence and no one on the Florida jury questioned why the star witness spoke Spanish with a Newfie accent.

Wiggers had been in a snarl back then, too. He figured he'd paid his dues and was squared up with Woods. But he knew it was not so with Moloci. Or with Ghomes. Certainly not with Ridge, and especially not with the old German, who knew everything that was going on.

"Let me read you something right from the preamble to the Act," Woods said.

'Congress finds and declares that operating or embarking in a semi-submersible vessel without nationality and on an international voyage is a serious international problem, facilitates transnational crime, including drug trafficking, and terrorism, and presents a specific threat to the safety of maritime navigation and the security of the United Sates.'

Wiggers' head cocked to one side. "I's hardly a tret to the States."

"Here's where you done," Woods continued.

'2285 (b), Evidence of Intent to Evade Detection; the presence of any of the indicia may be considered, in the totality of the circumstances, to be prima facie evidence of intent to evade detection.'

"You passed the coasts of Colombia, Panama, Costa Rica, Nicaragua, Honduras, El Salvador, and Guatemala, heading toward Mexico. That pretty much covers the international requirement."

Wiggers knew exactly what prima facie meant. Unless he could prove otherwise, he was fucked.

"See, b'y. I's only a lookie-loo here. Darn near run into the liddle boat. Never seen such a ting in me life. I says to the b'ys. Would ye look at that! She's harf sunk n' harf afloat. Let's watch how far she'll go. Wouldn't know ye were thinking the same thing. How's a b'y to know she's carrying cocaine."

"Your operating signals were recorded by our aircraft. We filmed you ditching the remotes. It's on CD. Doesn't matter. We got the sub. We got the coke. And we got you."

Wiggers was no stranger to law, nor to law-enforcers. The hoary old swagman had popped up here, there, and everywhere for five decades, usually around the water, but sometimes in the gold fields when work on the sea ran slow. He was a small man by stature, but immense by ego, and a survivor to the core. It was instinct for Wiggers to test legal position. He didn't need a lawyer to tell him if their case would hold. If it looked solid, he'd call in a marker. Then, cut a deal.

Wiggers had cut lots of deals and he'd had lots of markers, including one in charge of the RCMP Federal Drug Enforcement Branch in Vancouver, but he tried an obtuse angle before appealing there.

Woods stood Marine still. He read Wiggers' fidget, but couldn't help being amused by the veteran reprobate; something you'd see as cartoonish – an emaciated dungeon-man hanging from wrists by chains on a medieval Keep's stone wall.

"It's a mute point," Woods said. "You're still in a conspiracy."

"No, b'y. Only if ye can prove I knew about it," Wiggers said, wriggling. "Asides. Ye's got an issue with yer Act. As I sees it, it ain't quite a law till the President signs it, and it weren't signed when ye nabbed me."

Ziegler could bluff too. She was the senior DEA agent in San Diego. She had the authority to cut a deal, within reason, and she had a reason to cut a deal. She'd left the room to check on whether the Act was actually legal yet. PanEx had been ordered to immediately and aggressively target the SPSS threat under the DTVIA, which passed the U.S. House of Representatives on September 29th. Wiggers was right. It was still on the President's desk.

"He's also got your Kingpin order to sign," Zeigler replied. "And the death sentence bill."

Wiggers' hoop cinched. He wasn't going to call that one.

"Now ye wouldn't be needing to do that now, old dear."

"Archie, let's cut the bullshit," Woods said. "Whadda you got for collateral this time?"

Wiggers sat there. Calculating. He'd contracted his informant services out for a half-century now. He'd not a lick of loyalty, but he recognized an opportunity, and this one could keep his arse off the lethal injection gurney.

Woods and Ziegler watched Archibald Wiggers stop his squirm and start a toothed-deprived smile.

"How would ye likes to hear about a big deal heading towards Bamfield on the west coast of Canada?"

Chapter 21

Tuesday, May 22nd, 2012
12:40 pm
37 miles north of the village of Solano
By the Rio San Pedro, near the Equator
Caqueta Department (State), Southern Colombia

Nectario Gomez was taking a shit when he heard the ATV's approach from down by the river. He wiped up and limped out, letting the outhouse door spring shut. He passed the tin-roofed shanty that sheltered his family, crossed the field, making his way along the dirt path towards the steaming, thick green foliage blocking the water's edge.

They were earlier than expected, but he was ready, having the bales of dried and compressed coca leaves stored on pallets under a green, camo'd tarp. It was hot and humid again today, but not too hot and humid – just the right combination that made his farm perfect for growing coca plants. Especially these coca plants.

Gomez hobbled to the fringe just as three, blue Yamaha Quads punched through, two towing squeaky metal trailers. The visitors shut off the rattling machines and dismounted, removing their gloves, then their goggles. It wasn't the sear of the sun and the whip of the willows they needed protection from. It was the flies.

Colonel Noe Suarez Rojas, aka Grannobles, greeted Gomez in Spanish, thanking him and wishing Gomez and his family well. Gomez saw Grannobles had the usual one-eyed gofer with him but, for some reason, he'd brought the scientist along; the gringo they called Everett.

Gomez didn't like the guy. Everett was overly friendly and spoke pigeon Spanish, but Gomez put up with him because he paid immediately and he paid well. Especially well since Gomez began growing the new plants.

"Senor Everett is pleased with the progress," Grannobles said, his melonous cat-face grinning; rodent-like incisors bucking from a mess of tobacco-stained whiskers. "He's come to look at the plantation again for himself."

Gomez offered a gnarled hand. Everett shook it with North American zeal, saying how appreciated Gomez was. After compliments, they got on with business, strolling through the coca rows, inspecting the next crop.

"The proper amount of water is critical," Gomez told his visitors. "These are young plants. They have not built up drought or disease resistance. It takes time for a plantation to mature and these are only third generation plants."

* * *

Nectario Gomez was a third generation farmer. He was fifty-four and had farmed beans, plantains, maize, and coca all his life – like his father and grandfather had done – all on the same plot of land. Originally coca was a sideline that fortified chocolate or found its way to a light, refreshing drink. Over the years, Gomez dropped the nutritious product lines, which were difficult to market, and grew only coca, which brought in money. He'd no choice than to sell to Grannobles' monopoly for a dozen years now, but, for the past few, he'd been paid to grow only leaves from specialized seedlings that Everett supplied. That was fine with Gomez – as long as he got paid.

Everett's new plants were taller and produced a much thicker leaf than before. These plants took more time to tend, but Gomez had plenty of time and tending coca was the sole support for his family. It paid for seven children to eat, have shoes, go to school and, most importantly, being needed to help process coca kept the children from being forced into service with the FARC, the Feurzas Armidas Revolucionarias de Colombia.

Gomez's expectations weren't high, and he didn't expect to solve America's drug problem. But America's problem became his problem back in 2000 when President Clinton authorized Plan Colombia, a national security initiative that furthered the war against drugs. It financed a $1.3 billion U.S. initiative against the guerrilla-dominated Colombian cocaine industry, which supplied ninety percent of the drug entering America and its coke-starving allies in Europe and Canada. Clinton's plan stepped up chemical fumigation, voluntary eradication, military intervention, and economic development programs designed to wean peasant farmers off their dependency of growing and selling only coca products.

At first Gomez obliged. He uprooted his plants, expecting compensation, but that was cut off by the FARC who saw absolutely no value in cooperating with Plan Colombia. The FARC were the left-wing military guerrillas of the Colombian Communist Party established in the 1960's, spreading Fidel Castro's self-serving ideology. They became a prominent political force in Colombia, funding themselves primarily through the sale of cocaine – not so much from actively trafficking the drug – rather by supporting the plantations, facilitating exportation, and extorting the industry for its protection, which they politely termed *vaccinating.*

* * *

In the past, like every *cocalero*, Gomez not only grew natural plants, he'd also run a *kitchen* which processed coca leaves to a semi-refined *basuco* paste or what you call *pasta*. This was made by soaking chopped-up leaves in a pit lined with a polyethylene sheet and filled with gasoline, which Gomez had his boys stomp to a mash with their bare feet, then squish by hand, before draining off to a liquid containing the narcotic base. Then, Gomez added ammonia to separate the components. He diluted this milky-white mixture with a slight bit of water, a splash of sulphuric acid, and a fistful of bicarbonate of soda. This became a brownish slop to be scooped up, drained again, and given by pail to the girls, who'd spread it out to dry in the sun. They sat in a circle, singing cheery songs, hand-molding the paste into *bricks*.

Grannobles, and only Grannobles, would buy every brick the Gomez family could press out. He demanded their weight be exactly one kilogram with precise moisture content, and he accepted not a slight slip in purity. Gomez got a flat price of $650 USD each. Non-negotiable. Though his plot was larger than most, it produced only forty kilos per year. Offsetting marked-up material costs that Grannobles supplied on interest-charged credit, a brick left Gomez $250 net. That was meager income, after Granobbles vaccinated another half for the FARC.

Gomez had no control over the next steps in the traditional cocaine manufacturing process, let alone distribution of end product. Nor did he care. Grannobles would go on to collect many bricks of pasta from other cocaleros in the region, transporting them to a central refinery. Here, more chemicals were added. The pasta was washed in vats of kerosene, then chilled and the kerosene was removed from the tanks, leaving gas crystals of crude cocaine at the bottom. These were dissolved in methyl alcohol, re-crystallized, and dissolved again – only this time in sulphuric acid. Then a wash, oxidation, addition, and separation process took place using potassium permanganate, benzole, and sodium carbonate, which left a pure white, pure benzoylmethylegonine, base of HCI – hydrochloride salt. This was now a stable, water-soluble powder.

* * *

When absorbed in your blood stream – blood being fifty percent water – cocaine smacks your central nervous system giving immediate and incredible pleasure, as it does to the aspiring actor from Tribeca, who'd snort it and become an instant idiot in the evening lights at a Manhattan socialite party; the neglected house-wife, who'd smoke it, then regret getting planked by a trucker near Albuquerque; or the decrepit soul, who'd no choice but to keep on injecting, hopeless in despair, but high in a few moments of bliss, squatting in a piss-puddled alley at daybreak on the downtown-eastside of Vancouver.

* * *

Gomez exposed his bales that were bound by the fabric mesh, allowing air to circulate. Trapped air, especially hot jungle air, would rot the plants and these plants were far too valuable to risk rot. He pulled two dried leaves for a sniff.

"These are better than the last ones. They will get better yet with every crop," Gomez said.

Grannobles wiped his furrowed brow with a soiled red bandana. He stuck it back in his rolled-up fatigue sleeve and grinned, gripping a huge Habano cigar that he'd just torched-up. He watched Everett take the leaves from Gomez, crumpling them in his hand, and tasting a pinch.

"Good. Thank you," the scientist said in broken Spanish. "Very bitter. Proper."

Dale Everett wasn't a scientist. He wasn't anything except a drug trafficker, but he was a master at that. His grasp of the Spanish language was functional, however his grasp on Colombian political and military structure was significant. Everett had good tutoring, though. He left Canada years before on Art's orders, building his association with Tracy's relatives, the Orejuela family of Cali.

The brothers Gilberto and Miguel Orejuela ran the Gentleman's Cartel; not that they were particularly nice guys, but because they resorted to bribes and payoffs, not with terror and torture which was how their competitor, Pablo Escobar of Medellin, operated. The Cali cartel worked under a strict residual-income based cell system, as Art organized them, with a series of independent downline distributors known as *cartiletos*; not a greedy, paranoid, and autocratic structure like the thugs of Medellin ran. Their low-key style let them operate openly while the authorities around them were consumed with battling Escobar, a psychotic narco-terrorist who grabbed headlines. The Colombian army finally shot Escobar dead in '93. Then, the authorities turned on the men of Cali.

It took thirteen years to break the Orejuela brothers. Their network had tendons in every arm of Colombian society – political, financial, legal, military, police, arts, and entertainment. Everett sat back with his splinter group, privately calling it the Canadian cartel. Patiently, they replaced the Cali. Slowly, discreetly, and methodically, they helped the Colombian government destroy the Orejuela family. It was deemed good for the Colombians. Good for the Americans. Good for the Canadians. And it was done within an agency's covert plan; a much bigger picture to the world of drugs.

If Everett learned one thing over the years, it was to ally with those who taught best. He was a keen student, whether of chemistry or security. On the chemistry side, he'd hired the brightest Pakistan had to offer, paying him fabulously to genetically modify the coca plant. On security, he had the FARC. Grannobles held high rank in the FARC, which Grannobles intended to keep, and he intended on keeping Everett as security.

For years, the FARC pushed limits of international acceptance with vehicle bombings, extortions, and non-conventional military tactics aimed against both Colombian government and civilian targets; even going so far as to employ the IRA, Irish Republican Army, to instruct them in terrorist tactics. Bogata was finally forced to recognize the FARC, giving them status in an attempt to slow the recruitment of child combatants and reduce the statistics of kids being slaughtered in their service. Venezuelan President Hugo Chavez weaseled a deal with the squirrely government of Colombian President Alvaro Uribe, where the FARC was recognized as a State of Belligerence under the Geneva Conventions. Grannobles was instrumental to the negotiations.

It established free zones, or *despejes*, for the FARC, in which they were allowed to operate unimpeded. One was in the temperate zone of the Puntamayo Department, or State, and the other was in Caqueta, where Gomez farmed. These were rural areas, sacrificial to the central government, but it was here where local will still held strong. Gomez, along with hundreds of cocaleros, marched on Puerto Asis to protest

Plan Colombia's failure to compensate, till he realized taking a blast of #6 birdshot in the leg did nothing to feed his family. He bandaged up, hobbled home, and went back to what he did best – grow coca.

* * *

Grannobles flipped his switch from auto to safe, slung the AK47 off his chest, and hung it over his Quad's greasy handlebars.

He and the one-eyed gofer hand-bombed the tightly-bound bales onto the springy, galvanized trailers, cinched them with orange nylon straps, fired-up the ATV's, then dragged the load downhill and aboard a rusty scow where it was weighed on a cast-iron shipping scale. Gomez was paid out. Grannobles pocketed his fee. Everett gave parting compliments and the visitors shoved off down-river, stopping at other plantations and collecting more bales, before docking at Solano to meet a canvas-covered, backfiring old military truck that would take the tons of potent leaves to an airstrip where Everett's DC3 sat waiting for a flight back over the Andes; two hundred miles northwest to the settlement of Santa Barbara on the Rio Isculande at the Pacific side.

Here the cartel's factory would refine the leaves to a paste, then a powder, then condense it eight-fold, shipping to their warehouse far north at Bamfield on the Canadian west coast. Slowly, as required, they'd adulterate the purity and release it upon the streets of North America, scoring a profit sixteen thousand times more than what Nectario Gomez received.

It wasn't fair, but it let the children eat, and lessened the kids' chances of being shot in the service of the FARC.

Chapter 22

Wednesday, May 23rd, 2012
09:05 am
RCMP Headquarters
Vancouver, British Columbia

Sergeant Bate sat at the conference table. Her leg vibrated, fingers tapped, and her eyes darted about.

She glanced at the Commanding Officer, Deputy Commissioner Mary Gillespie, who appeared disinterested, but was acutely aware of what this meeting was about – the most intricate and expensive narcotics investigation under her leadership. Inside the hushed, bug-swept room were twenty black, leather chairs seating the key law-enforcement players of Project E-Pandemic, targeting the Hells Angels.

Bate glanced at other halogen-shadowed faces, many she didn't recognize. There were no uniforms here. Most of these caffeine-lit police officers had rarely worn a uniform in their service, and they'd feel as uncomfortable wearing yellow stripes as she felt sitting-in with them.

The faces glanced at Bate. Some were middle-aged men checking her out, but all wondered who she was and why she was here. Bate saw one, at the opposite end of the stretched, birdseye table, kept staring at her. He was dark; a Caucasian, but could have passed for Lebanese. He looked like a seal to Bate – long face, long nose, with a huge black mustache. She'd get to know Sergeant Jake Bush. He was from Special I, the section installing electronic intercept and tracking devices.

She glimpsed to her left side, at another cop who'd been ignoring her, pecking away on his BlackBerry – bleached hair, wispy goatee, wrap-around instant-asshole shades, and splattered in jail-house tattoos. She'd get to know Corporal Raymond G. Peach, too – the undercover operator riding with the Angels. Sergeant Brent Stoner, a knuckly grey lunker, sat beside the CO. He was on Special E, the biker squad. Sergeant Terri Vale, a feisty thing next to him, was with Special O, the surveillance team. Inspector Jim Claymore stood, muscled arms folded.

I know who he is, Bate recognized. *He was on the ground at Teslin with Monagham.*

Claymore was now in charge of Emergency Response Operations.

I'd die for a chance to speak with him privately.

Superintendent Nolan Church was the OIC for Vancouver Island. It was in his jurisdiction where the takedown was planned. Staff Sergeants Linda Stanton and Deano Surtees were supervisors. In various ranks, like a mix of Tommy Girl and Old Spice, were the drug investigators; Christina (the 10) Athena, Norman Jones, Derek 'Boots' Tobacco, Joe Protosavage, Etienne Brule, Donnie 'Tripod' Cordell, and low and wide Gerri Bodnarski. Angela Fernandez and Manh Nguyen were both investigators and translators. Garfield Woods was the only black in the room; the liaison from the DEA and the American handler for Archibald Wiggers – the agent in Colombia. Not present was the Canadian agent embedded in with the Angels, known only to Peach, Moloci, and shortly to Bate.

Wolfgang Kresslauer sat off to one side, peering over his glasses. The old German was a trusted ex-cop who privately contracted his services. Kresslauer was a vital part of this operation.

"Good morning," Moloci said, standing up – his back to a large projection screen. "We're getting closer to D-Day now, and I'm going to update you on the operational plan. Also, since our last briefing, we've got two new members in the room. I say members because Mister Kresslauer, here, was in the Force long before I applied. For those of you who don't know, Wolf is our eyes and ears in the international political and intelligence worlds. He's been back of the curtain since the start of our project, but this morning he's going to make a presentation so all of you get a look at a much bigger picture to the world of drugs."

Moloci stopped to survey the room. "Wolfgang makes sure we're not infiltrated."

Kresslauer peered over his glasses.

Moloci looked everyone in the eye, including the CO. "We do the infiltration. We do not get infiltrated."

Some sensed their spine shiver. Some squirmed in their seat. Some just sat still, shut up, and stayed silent.

"At the far end of the table is Sergeant Sharlene Bate."

Heads turned. Bate blushed and gave the room a slight wave. Heads nodded acknowledgement.

"She's come over from I-HIT to be my personal assistant in co-ordinating Ray Peach with our Canadian agent as we move to the final phase. It'll be Sergeant Bate's responsibility to ensure evidence obtained by the agent... and by Corporal Peach... is admissible in court."

Heads looked at each other. Back at Bate. All grinned.

"Hope you drink rye," Surtees said.

The room broke out laughing. Peach didn't react, but Bate turned beet red.

"Okay." Moloci wasn't able to hold off a smirk. "Back to business. Here's what's happening. We now expect a seizure of eleven tons. Possibly more."

A bunch of gasps and some "Holy Fucks!"

"I don't have to tell you the street value." He smiled to more than a few whistles.

Bate's jaw leaded.

"It's going to land in Barkley Sound, somewhere near Bamfield. That'll be our call when the time gets near." Moloci clicked his PowerPoint, bringing a nautical chart up on the screen. It showed the central west coast of Vancouver Island.

Bate's eyes locked to it.

"The Broken Group is composed of a hundred wooded islands and a thousand rocky islets. There's an unlimited amount of off-loading spots. We know the load is going to be the whole thing. No drop-offs in Mexico or the States this time because the change of dynamics has forced things our way. That's part of the new business model, which Wolfgang will brief you on. The Mexicans will now shoot large importers on sight, and the Americans are preparing to kill them..."

He slacked off on the mouse.

"Slowly and legally. Thanks to the Kingpin Act, and its amendment which proposes capital punishment."

Moloci thumbed-up Woods. The others did too. Kresslauer just peered over his glasses.

"So we're a pretty attractive place to do business." Moloci eyed each member. "But we're putting a stop to that. We have the perfect opportunity to cut off a major supply route through Canada, and this is how we're going to do it."

He had the table's interest. Especially Sharlene Bate's.

"First of all, we have excellent Intel in Colombia, thanks to Special Agent Woods and the DEA. We would never have known about this if it weren't for our American counterparts."

He eyebrowed Woods and continued.

"You're probably wondering why the Americans don't take the shipment out as it passes their coast, or take it in international waters like they've been doing. Well, they're having some growing pains with the DTVIA and their Constitution. Till that gets sorted out, if there's no proof of intention to land on U.S. turf, they're not going to touch it."

Moloci switched images, showing the gold, wing-spread eagle of a DEA badge.

"The DEA has a Colombian plant in position to control the delivery to Canada. We also have great Intel here at home… an agent controlling the receipt… along with Corporal Peach, who'll make sure it's in HA possession when we take it down. So, you see, we're in control of both the shipping and the receiving departments. We'll take care of the accounting department later on."

Moloci paused, took a sip of Dasani, and went on.

"There are a couple of challenges. One is to be sure full-patch Angels show and it ends up in our targets' hands. That's Corporal Peach and our Canadian agent's role. Sergeant Bate will be responsible to make sure all evidence they produce is legally admissible in court. She's got a big job ahead of her. Our agent will eventually be testifying, not like the Colombian who'll get cut free. That's part of the deal."

Bate looked at Peach. He still ignored her. She looked at Moloci. He winked, then scanned the room.

Bate sat right up. *What was that?*

Moloci continued. "There's a new cartel formed in Colombia. We call it the Canadian cartel and our west coast HA's have a direct alliance with it. It's sophisticated, highly organized, very experienced, and they retain top lawyers to direct them on international law. They're depending on us to be the dunces."

Bate's eyes shot about, seeing the players captivated by Moloci. He switched to an image of an SPSS.

"They're using a transport like this. It's a robot. A water drone called a Self Propelled Semi Submersible." Moloci changed screens. "The one you see here is an older model. It's manned and holds six to seven tons, takes a crew of three to four to operate, and has limited range. The one coming at us is a next-generation craft. Larger, with greater capacity, and it's unmanned during travel. It's remote controlled, but still has something in common with earlier models. It can self-destruct and sink quickly. No evidence. No witnesses. Nothing left. That's why it's vital to let it come in unimpeded and take it down near shore. That's the other challenge."

Moloci motioned to Jim Claymore. The huge, Fu-Manchu'd man with the shaved head was still standing with his arms folded, dressed in black combat pants, boots, and a tight black T-shirt – a loaded 9-mm Sig Sauer strapped low on his left thigh. Bate saw a tattoo on his right bicep. It looked like a scrolled sword with a pair of wings.

"Inspector Claymore and his ERT boys will be responsible for the physical takedown once we set it up for them. They've been practicing water assaults, as speed and stealth is going to be crucial to prevent a scuttle, or sending the Angels flying in all directions. We've got a little technical insurance policy, though. We'll know where it is at all times."

Moloci switched to a screen similar to Google Earth, showing a map of the Colombian west coast. He zoomed the cursor in on a wide river delta, flew it upstream, clicking the image closer, stopping on what was clearly a blackish-grey submarine docked along the caramel-colored river with a large tug-boat moored behind it. The resolution was impressive. IMINT, Imagery Intelligence, showed people packing parcels across the wharf.

"This, folks, is live feed. Incredible technology, thanks to our military," Moloci said. "Those people are Colombians and those bundles contain ten, one-kilo bricks of pure cocaine. They started loading the sub yesterday and should be finished today. We're counting pieces so we'll have an accurate idea just how much will be on board. The Colombian agent tells us eleven tons, but one of the Angels told the Canadian agent that there's more. I know what you're calculating… When's it arriving? We don't know that yet. It'll probably leave Saturday the 26th, taking two days down river before heading out to sea near the Equator."

Bate watched Moloci click to a color-splotched map showing the west coasts of South and North America.

"It has to travel forty-nine degrees in latitude north and forty-eight in longitude west. That equates to nearly a hundred degrees total distance but, diagonally, it's around forty-four hundred nautical miles. The sub runs at eleven to twelve knots. Given it can only travel totally undetected at night, or in low light, it has at best twelve hours a day running time. So… doing the math… probably thirty, thirty-five days.

That puts it here around the beginning of July. There are a number of variables, though. Currents. Storms. Salinity. Mechanical issues."

Moloci enlarged Central America.

"But, there's a very real risk it may be accidentally spotted and intercepted. Remember, the route passes the coastlines of nine sovereign nations, all of which would love this seizure. Although the DEA is right on top, but keeping their distance, these countries all have routine patrols by their Coast Guards, Navies, Air Forces, Fisheries, etcetera, all who are out there watching. That includes other American agencies, especially their Navy, who are particularly adept at surveillance. For security reasons, we can't fill them all in, so we have to take some chances. During the day, the sub will stay submerged beside the mother ship, its escort and filling station, and that's under the control of the Colombian agent. But we'll know where they are until takedown."

Moloci sipped again. "Any questions?"

* * *

"I'm going to say something."

Inspector Jim Claymore's voice blasted the room like a landmine had detonated. The mean Mister Clean unfolded his arms and stepped forward. Bate recoiled, hearing the British accent. He stopped. Pivoted. Facing Bate square-on as if she were a target down-range. Her skin flashed like she'd been spattered by gunshot residue, as his eyes tapped her twice in chest.

But from deep inside Jim Claymore, something else put a third visual round to the center of Sharlene Bate's forehead. Something evil. Deceitful and deadly. Something that could trick her. Kill her. Steal her soul. Or invade her alive, riding silently inside – maybe for decades – till the energy of her possessed soul ran low. Something that sensed she'd been schooled in the ways of the ancients. Something comprehending that her sacred knowledge presented a perilous threat to its existence.

It was something Grandfather Heiclaamaax warned her of.

Long, long ago.

* * *

Claymore about-faced, addressing the room.

"I control the takedown. How it happens will be on my terms. The Sergeant coordinating the Canadian agent and the undercover operator will respond to my directions during that phase. I recognize the importance of admissible evidence. I'll do my best to respect that but, when it comes to arrests, I'll not put up with any nonsense."

There were a few snickers. One was from Stoner, who'd recently sicced Claymore and his boys on an Angel-run strip club.

"I'm not much concerned with resistance from the Angels themselves, nor any of their strikers, but Intel says the Colombian off-loaders will be armed. These sods have no concept that we're forced to play fair up here. Where these lads come from they're shot, not arrested. My concern is miscommunication, but I have a plan. Part of it means no unauthorized members inside the perimeter until containment. That includes all of you in this room. Except Peacher."

He drummed his fingers on his Sig, glaring about.

"You'll not be there if a fire-fight starts."

Claymore shot a scowl at Bate, blasting more off at the others.

"I'll hand over the prisoners, but they won't be chartered. That's up to you. You get the evidence once it's safe to handle. You deal with it then. Not before. Once we're deployed there is to be no interference. By anyone."

He eye-cleared the room, cross-hairing Bate.

"Understood?"

No one spoke. To Bate, it was as if Claymore was about to rip off her head and shit in the hole.

What did I possibly do to piss him off? She was tense as a trigger finger in a standoff.

"Good." Claymore broke the stare and stepped back, folding his shape-shifted arms.

* * *

"Thanks, Jim," Moloci said. "You folks also need to know the international scene. The big picture, as the cliché goes." He reset the Powerpoint. "This will put into perspective how important this operation is, not just for national security, but for where you, and your Force, fit into the world of drugs. We've been taking a hell of a beating in public image lately. Rest assured your management is aware of this. We can't offer you a raise, but we can give more meaning to your careers. Wolfgang?"

Kresslauer stopped peering over his glasses. He got up and took over.

Moloci sat back, assessing his members. Specifically Sharlene Bate.

Claymore stood.

Watching her, too.

Chapter 23

Thursday, May 24th, 2012
1:35 am
Vancouver International Airport
Richmond, British Columbia

YVR was hectic for this time of the morning. More hectic than usual.

Cathay Pacific Flight CX889 from JFK was one of five international arrivals within the same hour. There was no watch yet issued for its deplaning New York passenger, soon to be designated a Foreign Narcotics Kingpin, thanks to information supplied by her cousin, Ezekiel Cardenas. She cleared customs without incident.

Tracy Williams travelled light, carry-on only. She bypassed the chaos of the baggage carousel, hiking straight out towards the pick-up shelter. She looked to her left through the downpour, past the mess of taxis and shuttles, seeing headlights flash on an approaching dark truck which pulled alongside. She opened the rear passenger door, tossed her bag on the seat, hurried up front, leaned over, and gave the driver a kiss on the lips. Her assistant pulled out, merging in traffic, heading towards their home moored on False Creek at Yaletown in downtown Vancouver.

"Good flight?" Robert Haslett asked.

"I slept most of the way," Tracy replied. "That is the real perk about first class. You can stretch out and not have someone with booze-breath next to you snore and slobber. I feel guilty about the price, but it is worth it. Especially at night."

"You feel guilty about everything."

"Oh... I know, Bobby." She smiled, leaning towards him. He put his hand on her damp linen shoulder. A couple of moments passed before she spoke again, over the warming rush of the defogger. "I am not going to feel guilty about Ghomes."

"So what's up?"

"I met with Raymond yesterday. God, I feel good around him. He is so calm and reassuring."

"Like to meet him one day."

"Maybe. He is very careful about that."

Tracy sat upright. Haslett glimpsed, seeing her turn the visor down and the night-lite on, checking her eye in the mirror.

"His plan is sensible," she continued. "You and John are going to be the main part of it, so we need to get together with him in the next day or two."

"Next week. Going back to Bamfield Saturday. You should come with me."

"It is tempting. Especially at this time of year."

Tracy paused again, taking a small saline container from her purse, giving both eyes a drop. "But there are some urgent things I must attend to. Even being away three days takes its toll."

She flipped up the visor, settled back in the seat, arched her head way back, and let out a long, silent sigh. Haslett gave her some time.

"I am going to be so, so glad to get out of this," she said, suppressing a yawn.

"Won't be long," he said. "Moloci figures first week in July for the takedown. Then a month to clean up. By August we'll all be gone."

"I would go right now." Tracy took a deep breath. "Anyway... patience... patience... I know. By the way, how is Bamfield going, Hon?"

"You know? Pretty good." Haslett glanced at his mirrors, changed lanes, took a toothpick from his shirt pocket, and stuck it in the corner of his mouth. "Old cannery's done. Dive shop's smooth. First shipment's nearly run out. Shits about the second one gettin' picked off, but Wiggers is loadin' the next up right now. Also, I need some coin. There's two more short rubber boats to be paid for. Also a bunch of utility bills and some wages to square up."

"Of course. I will look after it in the morning." She turned her head to him. "What are you doing there this weekend?"

"Narrowin' down the off-load spot. Gotta calculate tides and currents before fixin' a date. Then I gotta give Moloci a heads-up. Also Ghomes. They need time to put their crews together."

"Flying or driving?"

"Boat. Got the big Zodiac over here. Had the engines serviced and the whole thing gone over." Haslett shoulder-checked and looked in his mirrors. "Make sure it's ready for the big day. I'm towin' it back to the Island, then dumpin' in at China Creek and runnin' down the inlet." He watched their way through the wipers. "Ghomes wants to come along."

"That is another reason not to go with you."

"Maybe I'll do some crab fishin' with him."

She laughed. "Now that is a better exit plan than Raymond's."

Haslett looked at the road and the rain. Tracy relaxed, closed her eyes, and clasped her fingers, laying her hands in her lap. She began to hum a familiar tune. Haslett listened as he drove on, staying silent till they arrived home, pulling into the parking lot at Quayside Marina at the foot of Davie Street where he shut off the lights and the engine.

"So how'd you make out with our other problem?" he asked before getting out.

"I spent today at the archives and spoke to someone knowledgeable... well, I think knowledgeable. She thought I was crazy, but told me who we need to contact. I checked his credentials on the Net and made some phone calls. He seems legitimate and supposedly the right one, but then I am no expert in this field."

"Makes two of us."

"I sent emails to three different addresses. I even offered a donation to assist in his research if he would agree to help us. I received an automatic reply from one, stating he was unavailable at the moment, and I have not heard back from the others as yet."

"Who's this guy?"

"A professor named Sorenson. Holger Sorenson. At the Australian National University in Canberra. He is said to be the world's leading authority."

"Australia," Haslett said, looking out the rain-splattered, fogging-up windshield. "You know? Might be a good place to hide out." He turned to Tracy and took out the toothpick. "We're gonna need one."

Chapter 24

Friday, May 25th, 2012
8:10 am
Settlement of Santa Barbara, by the Rio Iscuande
Narino Department (State), Western Colombia

"She's full, b'y."

Archibald Wiggers nodded at *The Big Easy*, chucking the butt of a still lit, hand-rolled smoke off the wharf as Dale Everett approached along the creaky, grey boardwalk leading up to the processing factory. Everett stopped. He shook his head, seeing Wiggers' cigarette floating away in a purple puddle of diesel fuel that overflowed to the bath-warm, peanut-butter brown river from the tug's auxiliary tank.

Everett came from observing the Pakistani chemist run a gas chromatography – mass spectrometry examination on the Gomez leaves which showed they produced better than he expected. Better than anyone expected. That meant more money – a good thing to them – and the only reason why Everett and Wiggers worked the drug trade, unlike some other members of the Art Williams Organization who believed in a much bigger picture.

Everett had invested a lot of time, and a lot of the Organization's money, in developing the genetically-modified coca plants. He'd also spent a pile in perfecting the technique allowing HCI salts to be concentrated. But he'd spent far more, much earlier, experimenting with the losing propositions of chemically synthesizing the drug and hydroponically growing coca; neither proving anywhere close to cost-effective.

The erythroxylum bush is a finicky thing, from a horticultural perspective. A coca plant needs natural conditions, specifically the heat and intensity of UV rays, plentifully available near the equator where it evolved. From a business perspective, it needs labor, which the Gomez family provided cheaply. It also needs security. Grannobles supplied that brutally.

Everett was pleased with the payback now, but not pleased the Organization was disbanding, though he'd known the day would come when Art would pass-on and they'd fend for themselves. He'd made plans for that, but right now his prime concern was dealing with Wiggers. Then with Ghomes. Everett made plans for them, too, but he gambled that Ridge, Moloci, and Kresslauer would stay in the game a bit longer. He also knew Tracy would fold now that her dad was gone, and that's why he'd never invested with her.

Not like Ghomes did.

* * *

"I want to synchronize the radio codes one last time, Arch," Everett said, opening a briefcase-sized, black polycarbonate case he'd brought down from the factory.

"We's done dat tree times already. I'll be giving ye me GPS coordinates twice a day by Internet till I hears from that Haslett guy off the Canadian coast."

"Yeah, I know. Just do it again."

"All right, b'y. But makes it quick. I's got a catch ta deliver."

"Yeah, yeah." Everett thumbed towards the tug.

Wiggers sneered, taking Everett onboard to retrieve an orange, plastic Pelican case from a footlocker in his cabin and hand over an encrypted Irridium 9555 Sat C. It was small, about the size of an iPhone, and disproportionately powerful.

Everett booted his laptop, plugging in Wiggers' device. He checked the drive and ran a sync. Satisfied of no glitches, he handed the radio back. Wiggers slid it shut, stuffing it back into the foam-padded, watertight container.

"Remember," Everett said. "Don't call on that unless there's a problem. From now on, look for all your directions straight up from Moloci."

Wiggers frowned. "I's always looking straight up at Moloci. The b'ys tall enough ta jerk off a giraffe."

Everett laughed. "And only from Moloci. Only on Facebook."

"Yes, b'y," Wiggers growled, scratching his testicles through a torn jeans pocket.

The pair stepped off the corrugated, metal gangplank hooked to the tug and onto the slippery, wood dock. Everett stood, sweltering in the sun, which had just popped out after a quick, tropical shower. He looked at the fathom line on the robin's egg-blue hull of *The Big Easy*, then studied the SPSS, floating ahead. *I'm surprised it floats at all, given the size of the load*, he thought, seeing it showed little freeboard.

Wiggers' crew mustered above, waiting to cast off. The sub held fast to tight lines, its engine idling – the only output a gurgling of oily, exhaust bubbles gassing out to the slow, muddy flow. Captain Nemo had shrunk this sub's profile from the previous plagues of heat, carbon dioxide, radar, and sonar signatures, but visual detection was still touchy, even with its image-flat cloak of paint. To be safe, they'd run it at night, once in the ocean, and this sub ran nearly twice as fast as the old ones, maxing at sixteen knots.

"You know, Archie," Everett said. "Think of the changes in technology. When I first started in this business, I used to drive my old Cutlass between payphones with a bag full of quarters and burn U-turns to slip off surveillance. We've come a long way."

"Arr," said Wiggers, with a wrinkled wink. "When I started, we was usin' sails and fought 'em off with a cutlass."

He let go a smoker's cackling laugh, climbing aboard. Everett watched the old knave throttle up – the yellow stack on *The Big Easy* belching thick and black as if it poured out of Wiggers' lungs.

The crew cut both ships loose. The joystick waggled. The sub lurched forward. The tugboat heaved to. Wiggers leaned out the starboard window of the tall, white wheelhouse, a new rollie hanging off his lip, giving Everett a two-fingered salute.

"Safe passage, my friend!" Everett yelled, the boats shoving off.

* * *

Archibald Wiggers made safe passage down-river, till he hit saltwater and pushed eighty miles northwest.

At dawn on the third day, an EA-6B Prowler from CVN-76, the carrier USS Ronald Reagan, flew south at 37,400 feet on a routine, national security, drug-interdiction patrol. The Prowlers had evolved with the SPSS boats, now scanning the Super High Frequency radio waves, looking for remote control signals.

"This is interesting," the intercept officer said, intercoming through his oxygen mask. "Intermittent transmissions on 26.4 GigaHertz." He switched to RF location scan, isolating the source to their east side, now behind them.

"Let's all have a look," the Missouri pilot said, steering the plane sharply port, bearing north and back for a high altitude flyover. They turned on the cameras.

"This is interesting," the intercept officer repeated, zooming the hi-res image of their blue, white, and yellow floating target, reading its name and registration. "It's *The Big Easy*."

"We all put 'er away once already."

"No kidding. What the hell's she doing loose?"

The Prowler banked, port again, 180 for another pass south.

"Now this is reee...ally interesting. By the way, she's got a sub with her."

"That surprises ya'll?"

"Naw. Not the sub, skipper. Two, thirty-second pulses at 56.9 KiloHertz. Somebody's got bugs on 'em."

"Now that is mighty interestin'," the pilot drawled. "I think we're gonna do somethin' 'bout this."

Chapter 25

Friday, June 1st, 2012
4:35 pm
Electronic Surveillance Monitor Room
RCMP Headquarters
Vancouver, British Columbia

"What's their position?" Moloci asked.

"Two hundred fifty-six nautical miles due west of the El Salvador–Guatemala border," Bate replied, stopping her notes and showing the chiclets. "They're stationary, but moving again in under an hour when it's dark their time."

Moloci had logged himself into the bunker-built monitor room, checking on targets and on her, ensuring everything was in control, as he'd been away for two days.

"Making real good time," he said, observing her LED pins on the electronic map. "What do you think, Sharlene? First of July for the fireworks?"

Bate looked up from her dimly-lit work station, surrounded by digital recorders and high-resolution desk monitors, to an image on a monster, wall-mounted, flat-screen fed by IMINT, an Imagery Intelligence reconnaissance satellite. They could see *The Big Easy* and the sub, lying lazy on the water like a welfare-mom sitting with her fat kid.

For the past week, Bate had shadowed four Special I monitoring officers in this static-charged mole-hole, minding the wiretaps, internet intercepts, audio listening devices, GPS tracking units, and surreptitious video cameras that electronically surveilled the targets of Project E-

Pandemic. Nineteen others focused in sound-suppressed cubicles, divided depending upon files. They paid no attention to E-Pandemic. Each had their own priorities; tracking other drug investigations and informers, political extortions, anticipated gang hits, and an armored-car robbery about to go down.

This was a room of the highest security. Monitors came and went, recording fingerprint scans for computerized identity, rather than signing in with a pen and a badge; the ancient practice back when Moloci started in the world of drugs.

"Maybe before that, the way they're going," Bate said. "Weather reports for the next week are great."

"Colombian agent behaving himself?" Moloci asked with a smile.

"Reports on the clock. Twice a day. An hour and twenty-five minutes, he'll check in again." She started to chuckle. "If only the administrators at Facebook knew what this discussion group was about."

"Works like a damned and doesn't cost the government a cent." Moloci chuckled, too.

Bate twirled her pen. "I'm really curious about who this guy is but... I know... need-to-know only. This stuff is like living in some kind of thriller novel."

Moloci cut to a half-smile. *I've long thought about writing a book. Maybe someday in retirement. All the crooks and chases of my career into one page-turning, bestseller. Few of the characters I'd have to make up, though. Truth is... real characters are far more dastardly than fiction. Especially characters like that old snake, Archibald Wiggers.*

"Believe me." He rolled his eyes, shaking his head. "You do not want to know this guy... and you definitely don't want him knowing you. But next week I'll hook you up with my Canadian agent. This guy's solid. You can depend on him a hundred percent. He's gone on a bit of a mission, but he'll be back Monday, and we need to debrief him. I wanted you to get some time in the monitor room first, so you get a look at the targets. Some feel for the big picture. There's a much bigger picture to what we're doing here."

Moloci winked, turning away, adjusting the resolution on a small, video screen showing the open, bay door of the Vancouver East End clubhouse where some hairy-ass slob with a winged, deathhead backpatch was straddling a full-dresser Harley.

She stared at him – a shot of adrenaline subsiding, realizing that was the second time he'd done that.

Moloci continued as if he hadn't dropped the message. "Remember, it's vitally important that you make written notes only of your conversations and directions to this agent. No electronic voice recording whatsoever. We don't want any lawyers twisting the script."

"That's so different from homicide investigations," she said, still watching him. "If statements aren't recorded, the courts don't even want to hear about them."

"Well, Sharlene," Moloci said, leaning and scanning her notebook. "You were trained to investigate crimes that have happened. You're now investigating a crime about to happen."

"Hmm." She looked down. Back up again. "Right."

"You're used to finding witnesses. I'm used to making witnesses. There's a big difference. Keeping order and keeping legal can be a fine line in the drug business. Sometimes, despite all the planning, unexpected shit happens, and this business gets nasty."

He looked from her notes and right at her.

"Then it's best if there are no witnesses."

Chapter 26

Monday, June 4th, 2012
9:10 am
Air Force One
32,400 feet above Beckley, West Virginia

Unexpected shit happened.

Outwardly, the President of the United States appeared calm. Internally, his guts whirled, and he'd had the runs for a second day straight. He'd revamped his schedule, now twenty minutes out of Andrews Air Force Base, near Washington, en-route to El Paso, Texas, across from Ciudad Juarez. It was a show of leadership; an attempt to restore order to chaos at the border following Saturday's assassination of the Mexican President.

The Commander-in-Chief listened intently to his national security advisers, deeply perturbed as Mexico collapsed into anarchy, a narco-state to his south. The scenario had been considered unlikely by his transition team. Their only contingency was to mobilize the National Guard, seal the border, and attempt to block a Hispanic exodus to the States.

Despite the main crossings being blocked, the White House was thrashed by hundreds of reports – car-jackings, robberies, hostage takings, and murders – everywhere from the east at Matamoros to the west at Tijuana. Panicked people fled through gaps in *The Barrier*, that seventeen foot high, steel security fence which sliced hundreds of miles of international boundary, protecting lower America like a giant, gated community. But now his advisers calculated that cutting off Mexico would only alter the flow of cocaine, which caused the chaos, and send it through the backdoor at Canada.

I'll never like those slack-ass lefties to the north, the President thought, nearly snapping his pen while scribbling his signature on yet another paper in his pressurized office. *I still got the goddamn A-Rabs in Iraq. The shit-on-terror in Afghanistan. Iran biting my balls. And now the fuckin' Spics. The last thing I need is a drug war on both borders.*

The President worked the air-phone, gaining support from international allies. Now late in his first term, he'd established a decent rapport with most of the free world's leaders, but he knew this martial law recourse would suffer a severe backlash over human rights. He'd wear it hard at the UN.

"The Prime Minister of Canada, Sir." An aide handed the President a secure handset.

"Good morning, Prime Minister."

"Mr. President. Let me say you have available the full resources of my government and the complete support of our citizens as well."

"We appreciate it, by God. We're going to need all the help we can get. You've seen we've taken a hard line till we get some grip on this thing. This was not a political coup, you know. It was a cold-blooded murder by drug traffickers. Organized criminals. No ideology here. Just a bunch of thugs lining their pockets."

"Agreed."

"I knew the Mexican President personally, and I admired the man. He had an almost impossible job of bringing Mexico's authoritarian past to its democratic present. He governed that dusty junction of the developed and developing worlds the best he could. May God rest his soul."

"You'll have our full support at the UN as well." The Prime Minister understood how quickly this international quandary would escalate.

"Much needed."

"What can we do for you immediately?" The PM already knew the answer.

The President got straight to the point. "Border security. Tough law enforcement. All our intelligence indicates there'll be a massive swing in the flow of drugs, and it'll come from your way. Show a hard line, Prime Minister. A very hard line."

"You have our full cooperation, Mr. President."

"Let me be perfectly clear. I do not want to be forced to fence off my northern boundary, as well."

The President made no veiled threats. Border security had been high on the agenda at their first summit, and they'd discussed it by phone six times since. The President clearly said that Americans, the people who it was his sworn constitutional duty to protect – the people who elected him and would decide if he were to be re-elected in November – were fed-up with Canada's lenient law enforcement.

It wasn't that the Prime Minister, himself, was soft on crime. Far from it. Politically shrewd and fiercely intelligent, he was stick-handling a semi-socialist country infected with a deep seated, anti-American mentality, entrenched over years by liberal elitists in the French-dominated east. The PM was an Anglophone, a Conservative from the west, who'd robbed the Liberals of power, holding only a thin, minority government. He'd been elected on a platform of justice reform and economic prosperity. A closed American border would devastate the Canadian economy and a soft stance on crime, especially drugs, would end his weak grip on power.

The Prime Minister finished their exchange and began calling markers. One was an old German, tight with an agency operating entirely in the interests of national security.

Chapter 27

Monday, June 4th, 2012
1:35 pm
Stanley Park
Vancouver, British Columbia

"Sergeant Sharlene Bate... Bob Haslett."

Moloci introduced the two.

"Pleased to meet you, Sergeant."

Haslett extended his hand. Bate shook it, feeling like she was gripped by a lobster. Haslett felt clamminess off hers, as if he grabbed hold of one, too.

"Likewise." She broke eye contact, flashing a sunglassed glance at Moloci.

He'd said little about this agent, except that identity was sensitive. Very sensitive. She'd been told that he'd been placed deep undercover; years ago embedded with the HAs as an associate, not a patched brother. It was obvious Moloci trusted Haslett and that was good enough for Bate.

"Reserved us a spot." Haslett gestured to some pink-flowered trees on the grounds outside the Vancouver Aquarium, out of earshot, but in the smell of freshly-mowed grass and the conspiring caws of organized crows. Two little kids were perched on a green, concrete picnic table. Haslett gave each a dollar and they gleefully scampered off. Bate slightly smiled.

"Popcorn, Sergeant?" Haslett offered. He'd picked the rendezvous site, moving in forty minutes before, buying a buttery bag full, wandering a bit before settling back, blending in, and absorbing who was about.

Bate looked at Moloci, who returned a slight nod.

"Why not." She smiled a bit more.

Haslett handed-off the paper bag. She promptly dropped it, dumping half on the pavers, scrambling a squadron of pigeons.

"Oh God! I'm so sorry. I can be such a klutz."

Haslett and Moloci saw Bate's fingers tremble – exactly where they wanted her.

"There's no salt. Salt does that to me. Makes the heart race." Haslett pointed at Bate's hands, tipping her further off balance. "Gotta keep your wits about you in this job, you know."

They sat down. Haslett on one side, his back to the sun. Moloci with Bate on the other.

Haslett checked around, then said "I see some major shit in the news comin' outa Mexico."

"That was bound to happen," Moloci told him.

Bate glanced between them.

"Think it's gonna hit here even worse?" Haslett asked.

"Has to. That's why getting this done is so urgent," Moloci replied.

What does he mean by that? Bate had no idea it was planted for her.

Moloci kept on. "I've handpicked Sergeant Bate for the final phase of our project, Bob. She'll be your direct handler, now. I'll be stepping back, but the rules will be the same."

Moloci wasn't telling Haslett anything he didn't already know, though they had to go through with the act.

"It's all right." Haslett surveyed Bate once up and once down. "Goods'll be the same no matter who buys 'em."

He'd been briefed on Bate. On her career. On her daughter. On her boyfriend and on her brother. Haslett knew of her aspirations. Her strengths and her weaknesses. And especially her heritage. Moloci made sure of that. He and Haslett, as well as the entire Williams Organization, had far too much at stake than to let Sergeant Bate run loose without a handler.

"I was over at Bamfield on the weekend," Haslett reported. "Ghomes came along for the ride."

"That's Robin Ghomes, Nanaimo Chapter?" Bate cut in, eyes checking with Moloci.

He'd given her an overview of the players in E-Pandemic; profiles, records, photographs. Ghomes was top of the list, appearing as a kingpin to Bate.

* * *

But there's something you need to know, that she'd never know.

Over many years, Moloci had built an intricate police file on Ghomes, documenting him as a coded informant; labelled E-1694 – starting the day after their meet in the musty, black Suburban. Now, Moloci was strangling the script, ensuring Ghomes would not be arrested; never charged in E-Pandemic. It was part of Plan B and the takedown. Part of Ridge's exit plan. Part of closure to the Williams Organization and a squaring-up from a long time ago.

It was part of a much bigger picture to the world of drugs.

* * *

"Right." Moloci turned from Bate to Haslett. "What'd he have to say for himself?"

"He's been kinda spooked lately. Some shit went down close to him, I heard." Haslett had one foot casually up on the seat, head bobbing about. "Peach has his work cut out if he's gonna get Ghomes red-handed at the off-load site. Don't think he'll bite."

Bate sat, silently contemplating something. Haslett saw that. He shifted towards her, raising his finger.

"I think you're gonna hafta go on Peach n' my evidence alone for conspiracy on Ghomes. Not direct possession on him."

"I know Ghomes," Bate said, matter-of-factly.

Moloci's adrenaline spurted. He shot a look at Bate, then at Haslett. Haslett didn't move. Moloci, too cool a performer, recovered immediately. Bate didn't catch the reaction.

"Oh, yeah. How?" Moloci asked.

"A few years ago. I was in Surrey. We had an execution-style murder of an HA striker-turned-fink found sitting in an SUV with a bullet in the head, wrists duct-taped to the wheel, in front of his burned down house. Out in a rural area. No doubt Ghomes ordered it. My partner and I went to interview him. I came on kinda hard and he just... Frickin... Flipped! I never, ever, heard as foul a mouth as on that guy. He turned words into phrases I never even imagined. Then things started happening."

Bate stopped. She looked to Moloci and nodded faintly towards Haslett.

"Maybe I shouldn't..."

"It's okay. Bob's solid. And he's tight with Ghomes. He needs to know this stuff."

Bate focused on Moloci, not on Haslett. "Anyway. Anonymous

calls on my home phone. Harley drive-bys of my place. Bottom-rockers at my car when I came out of Safeway. Then I got a blank e-mail with a photo attached of my daughter in her schoolyard. That did it. Old Stoner from Special E paid Ghomes a visit. I got transferred, and it stopped."

"Ever hear from him since?" Moloci knew of that informant's execution; not about Bate meeting Ghomes.

"Not personally. But I had this investigation where he owned a property…"

Bate stopped like her brakes had been dynamited. Moloci stayed expressionless. Haslett appeared disinterested.

"Nope. Not till now." She looked down, diverting by taking her police notebook out.

"Put that away," Haslett said, crowing again. "I'll have everything you need in my report."

Moloci put his hand over her book, quietly telling her "Bob documents all his evidence, then e-mails it in. We back it up, and he also keeps it secured. You should never bring that out in meets."

"Oh God, I'm so sorry." Bate knew how it looked. She slid the notebook back in her bag. Moloci and Haslett sat silent as she struggled for something to say.

"Ah… I'm impressed. You, ah, operate alone, Bob?"

"It's safer."

"I would have thought riskier?"

"You know, Sergeant? In this job, sometimes you gotta take some risk. Who dares wins, you know."

He took a toothpick from his shirt pocket, putting it in his mouth. Moloci and Haslett began discussing Bamfield. Bate sat back. Thinking. Observing Haslett.

He doesn't seem like a biker, and he sure isn't a cop. There's something about him. Something I can't put my finger on. Something low-key. Non-descript. Something hard-core, yet very… Professional.

Bate couldn't see his eyes. He had mirrored Ray-Bans on and a black ball cap pulled low. She saw excellent teeth. No facial hair. No jewelery. Just faded Levis and a plain-black, short-sleeved, collared shirt. Not even a logo on the hat; nothing at all in his dress to draw your attention. But what would draw your attention were two jagged scars down the right side of his face, stretching from the top of his ear to the base of his jaw.

"Got a good off-load site, now, with a back-up," Haslett said. "What do you figure the date might be?"

Moloci signaled Bate to proceed.

"This morning they were off Manzanillo," she said. "Making good time. We're thinking takedown at the end of June. Definitely by the first week of July."

Haslett pulled out his iPhone, poking away. Bate caught a glimpse of something on his right bicep, peeking out below the sleeve – a yellow and black tattoo looking like the blade of a sword with some words scrolled across.

"Monday the 27th is best," Haslett said. "Low slack tide at 00:41 of 4.0 feet. High of 9.2 at 06:28. Sunset is 21:22. Sunrise 05:09. Moon's in the first quarter. Weather should be flat calm under those conditions. Site I picked is sheltered from swells. Got a long, rocky beach. Also secluded and dark. Should be no one travellin' around in the middle of the night."

"That'll be part of the operational plan, clearing the area of civilians," Moloci told Bate. "We want to go in the dark. The off-loaders will only do it then anyway. We know the load won't beach. It's to be transferred directly from the sub to some mule boats the Angels are supplying. Based on how fast it loaded in Colombia, it should unload within the darkness available. We'll hit them part way through. That'll establish intent of a large importation, not just a drop off. We've done that dance with the courts before."

"It's best to go at low slack," Haslett said to Bate. "If they scuttle the sub, it'll be easier to hook on and salvage. The cove bottom is shallow and flat, I made sure. Also... I don't trust those Colombians, or whoever they bring for off-loading. Where these guys come from they're shot, not arrested, so they'll either start shootin' first or split. Hopefully not both. That rocky beach at low tide'll slow 'em down if they make a run for it."

Bate listened intently. *Whoever he is, he knows his way around.* She was starting to get a feeling about Haslett. Something was starting to connect. Bate remembered seeing a similar tattoo, making a mental note to Google the image.

"So our next step," Moloci said, "is to tighten up the off-loaders. What's happening there?"

"You know," Haslett said. "Peach is more up on that than me. Couldn't meet him today. He went on a club ride on the weekend and stayed with another chapter. Last week he was setting up the mule boats with Ghomes. Also, he was workin' out who was gonna be on the crews, but they keep scrappin'. He and Ghomes don't get along, you know.

They're like two badgers in a bag."

"He's a piece of work, this Ghomes," Bate said. "Be careful around him."

Moloci sent her a slight frown.

Bate flushed. "Sorry, Bob. I guess you know that."

Haslett looked at her. Out came the toothpick. "Oh, he's a dangerous fucker, that Ghomes." He paused a moment. "Come to think. Best not have Ghomes at the takedown at all. I know he packs a nine-mil Beretta. If he was cornered, he'd go down shootin' for sure. We don't need that fuckin' show."

"Good point," Moloci said. "Let's make that part of the plan. We'll isolate him. Keep him out of there. Then take him under a controlled, separate plan. No sense putting anyone at unnecessary risk."

* * *

Moloci and Haslett had good reason to make sure Ghomes was isolated. Tracy did, too. It was Ridge's plan, and that plan didn't call for Ghomes being taken into Canadian custody.

Chapter 28

"We have a crisis."

The Prime Minister eyed each face in the packed, stuffy office of his official residence. His wife was touchy on his bringing work home, trying to raise their youngsters in some sense of normality. Tonight, she understood, was an exception.

"As you know," he continued. "The President of Mexico was assassinated Saturday when his aircraft was struck by surface-to-air missiles at takeoff. The Sinaloa drug cartel has announced responsibility. They have declared civil war against Mexican government forces. There have been mass desertions from the Federal Police and the Army. The chaos of refugees flooding into America is overwhelming. The United States has deployed their National Guard, sealing their southern border... and we all know that amounts to..."

The PM dragged his words.

"Martial law."

There was whispering among the attendants. The PM's Chief of Staff. The Solicitor General. The Minister of Public Safety. The Defence Minister and his Chief of Defence Staff, who was the head of the armed forces. The Commissioner of the RCMP was present. So were his counterparts – the Director of CSIS and the President the Canadian Border Service Agency. The room included the Foreign Affairs Minister, several aides-de-camp, an independent intelligence contractor, and a recording stenographer. All knew how important this meeting was for national security. And for the security of the PM's minority government.

He pointed at the attendants. "The events of the last three days have been tragic not only for the citizens of Mexico, our free-trading partner with whom we share this continent, but also for the entire civilized world. To have a democratically elected leader removed by an act of violence is absolutely unacceptable."

There were coughs of agreement.

"This was not a political coup. It was a cold-blooded murder by drug traffickers. Organized criminals. There was no ideology here. Just a bunch of thugs lining their pockets."

The attendants murmured and nodded.

"We would not tolerate this in our country, and we're not going to accept it among our allies."

The room buzzed. They'd been briefed. They knew what was coming.

"I called the American President this morning and gave him my assurance that he has Canada's fullest cooperation in security. Mexico is in chaos. America has declared martial law at that border. It is not going to happen on ours. I am directing each of you to make this issue the highest priority in your portfolios."

The buzz stopped. They knew where this was going.

"I am asking each of you for your views on domestic security and suggestions on how to effect them."

They'd no doubt what he wanted. Some sensed their spine shiver. Some squirmed in their seat. Some just sat still, shut up, and stayed silent.

The Foreign Affairs Minister pointed his pen and went first. "I've imposed a travel ban on my citizens going into Mexico, and I'm working with my military, getting out those wishing to leave. This is an enormous task, I've got. I figure I have a hundred thousand of my people in Mexico at any given time. The resort areas are stable. For now. But I've evacuated my embassy in Mexico City. My house there is ready to blow any second."

The PM rolled his eyes. "Situation at our border?"

The President of the CBSA answered. "Routine. Ripple effect hasn't hit. But it will."

"Contingency plan?"

The Solicitor General spoke up. "Emergencies Act proclamation prepared for morning. Parliament recalled within the day. All MP's on standby. Any abroad ordered to return."

"All leave for military and federal enforcement agencies is cancelled," the Minister of Public Safety reported. "All unnecessary projects are on hold."

"What do our intelligence sources tell us?"

The CSIS Director responded. "We have limited concern for a wave of Mexicans crossing our border. They'd have to get up here first. The concern is our refugee policy. There are thousands. No. Millions of innocent civilians are at risk in the crossfire down there. We're going to have to take in our share as legitimate refugees. Our position on human rights demands it. Otherwise, we're going to be the biggest bunch of international hypocrites."

The PM shuddered. *Billeting a hundred thousand wetbacks across the nation. Gawd!*

His Chief-of-Staff grimaced, reading his thoughts.

"The drug scene. That's what's behind this." The PM looked at the RCMP Commissioner. "You've managed to hold a lid on that mess out in Vancouver. What's happening there?"

"Ahem. Beh. Beh." The Commissioner cleared his throat. "We report no significant changes in operation."

The PM kept looking. "With supply being cut off at the Mexican-American border, it seems to me that we'll be pounded with imports headed for the States being diverted our way. Especially through B.C."

The Commissioner eyed down, tapping his pipe. "Beh. Beh. Yes, we've been investigating that possibility."

"I don't want to know what you're investigating. I want to know what you're doing about it."

Everyone could see the PM was pissed with the dinosaur he'd inherited from his predecessor, but neglected to replace.

"Ahem. Beh. Beh. Yes. We, ah, have a few things on the go."

Wolfgang Kresslauer saw the Commissioner struggle. Kresslauer had watched him struggle since the two were constables, watching as the Peter Principle struggled him to the top of the Ottawa ranks. And now, he watched as young Mounties struggled with their image, tarnished by years of door-knob direction.

Kresslauer spoke out. "I'm sure the Prime Minister would appreciate being briefed on Project E-Pandemic."

The Commissioner was relieved to have someone take over. Kresslauer seized the moment and stood up.

"Go ahead, Wolf," directed the PM, who respected the man. He also owed part-success in the last election to information being supplied through Kresslauer's sources.

"E-Pandemic is the investigation targeting the west coast Hells Angels and their cocaine importing route, now direct from Colombia into Canada. It's a spin off from the international intelligence community's effort to restore some balance of power to the drug world following the collapse of the Colombian cartels."

Kresslauer had their attention.

"A bit of history. The failed American policy of destroying the Cali and Medellin cartels resulted in the shift of power to Mexico and the disaster now there. Mexico is caught between the supply in Colombia and the demand of the American, Canadian, and European markets. It's never been much of a producer nor a consumer of drugs, but it became the facilitator. We warned the previous administrations in Washington that their war on drugs would bite them in the ass and... here we are. We're working on a new... a more, let's say... civilized cartel. A Canadian cartel based in Colombia. It'll remove some pressure off Mexico."

Kresslauer took off his glasses, wiping them with a handkerchief from his suit jacket.

"Continue," said the PM.

"From a policy perspective, we accept that we're never going to stop the demand for drugs. Altering the state of consciousness is as basic a human desire as food, sleep, and sex. All we can ever do is regulate the supply, putting some order to chaos. Prohibition has never worked. Not since little green apples in the Garden of Eden. Didn't work for alcohol. Doesn't work for prostitution. It's not going to work for drugs. Whether drugs are good or evil is best left to public debate but, right now, our situation is life and death. We need to control the supply immediately. Before Canada... specifically British Columbia... becomes another Mexico."

"Where are you at, Wolf? Operationally," asked the PM.

"We have one large shipment of cocaine coming into the west coast of Vancouver Island under our watch right now. It's destined for the Angels and set for takedown around the end of the month. It's huge. Pushing fourteen tons."

There were a bunch of whistles and some "Holy Fucks".

"Who's doing the takedown?" The PM looked at the Chief of Defence Staff. The General looked baffled, and he genuinely was.

"I don't know anything about it, Sir."

The PM glared at the Commissioner. "You've got the largest drug seizure in our history coming your way, and you don't have the military involved?"

"Ahem. Beh. Beh. I'll see that they're briefed."

"No. Not fucking briefed! The military's taking over." The PM's fist smashed his desk. "I want this thing hammered. This is all about border security. Tough law enforcement. Showing a hard line. Am I understood?"

Perfect, thought Kresslauer.

The meeting adjourned. The attendants mingled and murmured, then shook hands and departed, leaving the PM and his Chief of Staff alone.

"Contact our friends," the Prime Minister instructed. "I need as much exposure on this as possible."

Chapter 29

Wednesday, June 6th, 2012
9:50 am
RCMP Headquarters
Vancouver, British Columbia

"What... The... Fuck... Do you mean... I'm not doing the takedown!" Claymore's veins bulged like a roid monkey's; his face flashed red as a tracer round.

Bate cringed in her boss's office and kept on writing.

Moloci expected it. He'd known Jim Claymore since their days in the north when Claymore converted from the British army to join the police force after serving as an instructor with Malcolm Atkinson on the 1982 ERT course.

The RCMP had recruited two SAS soldiers back then, to give up life in the Regiment for law enforcement operations in Canada. Both were from G Squadron of the 22nd – Claymore from Mountain Troop – the other soldier from Boat Troop, who the Mounties placed deep undercover. Claymore was sent to the Northern B.C. team where he hooked up again with Buday and Monagham. Despite extensive combat experience, Claymore was new by seniority and subordinate in command that day on that frozen lake.

"This came from way over my head," Moloci said.

"From who?" Claymore demanded.

"Right from the Prime Minister's Office."

"So now it's an army job?"

"That's what the CO was just told."

"How'd this change? Weren't the Forces monitoring this and

waived their interest?"

"It's the Mexican disaster. The PM wants exposure. Border security, I'm told. Tough law enforcement. A hard line, he said."

"A fucking kick in the nards is what it is."

"There's nothing we can do about this. It's political and out of our hands. The deal's going to go down, and it's our job to make sure it does. Regardless of who gets the credit." Instantly, Moloci realized he'd said the wrong thing.

* * *

James Claymore was an intense man. On the surface – absolutely honorable. His true character was far above ego. Far above self-gratification. Far above seeking glory. His outer agenda was entirely good. Get the job done. Keep his men safe. And, above all, alive.

But, unknown to his conscious self, Claymore's soul had long been held hostage. It anguished horribly and strived to be set free. His invader, his possessor and captor, was something from far, far, below. Since Teslin, it remained dormant, riding silently inside, but now Claymore's spiritual energy was running low.

* * *

"That's a fucking crock, John, and you know it. My lads are more than capable of taking this down."

"You'll still be there, Jim. Just in a supporting role. JTF 2 will do the assault and hand the prisoners over to you for processing."

For Moloci, the Mexican mess was a manna. Turning the takedown over to the military would lessen the odds of Claymore meeting Haslett, and that worried Moloci right from the start.

"I'll follow orders. You can depend on that." Claymore left-wheeled and marched out.

Bate knew more about Claymore, now. A lot more, having Googled the Isis-winged Sword of Excalibur tattoo, identifying it and its motto on the web.

She watched him leave. Gave him two minutes. Then stood and peeked down from the window.

Claymore was there. One story below. Square-on, glaring right back up through the glass. Bate recoiled as if a death adder had fanged at her face. Claymore scowled, tapped his fingers on his snap-holstered 9-mil, then mouthed something simple, crude, and effective. He turned and carried on towards the lot.

A minute passed, as she recovered.

Then, a powerful surge of suspicion swept over Sergeant Sharlene

Bate. Skulking downstairs, she trailed outside to confirm. Blending in with the overhang's shadows, Bate spied on his approach to his vehicle. Claymore stopped.

* * *

His invader had sensed her. Ethereally, it knew she was there. Claymore's big frame turned. The shapeshifter altered state. Rose to the surface. Manifesting as large, local consciousness, it scanned and sought the one it knew had been schooled by the ancients.

Anxiety bolted through Bate like she'd been shot from a crossbow. *Something's seriously wrong with this man*, she realized.

She choked back a swirl of acid reflux, instinctively breaking eye contact, and missing the fiery flash hidden behind mirrored sunglasses as The Kushtaka imprinted her image with one long, hard stare.

Slowly. Silently. It sank back to the depths in-between, recording Sharlene Bate as its next source of energy.

* * *

Claymore stayed stiff at attention, watching Bate beat-it back into safety. He stood at ease, then opened his shiny new Suburban's front door and got in.

There's some other reason Moloci wants me to stand easy and keeps that bitch hanging around, Claymore thought, as he started his black truck. *Something strange is going on here.*

Chapter 30

Thursday, June 7th, 2012
10:40 pm
Aboard the 100 foot Sunseeker luxury yacht *Bandazul*
Quayside Marina at False Creek
Vancouver, British Columbia

"I told you never to wear that here!" Tracy fired eye-daggers and jammed her forefinger at Ghomes, who wore his winged-skull Hells Angels colors as he ambled aboard her yacht.

"Hey! I rode the bike over. It's my fuckin' uniform." Ghomes shot back. "Sorta like his red coat." He lip-pointed through the folding glass door at Moloci who was seated at the candle-lit, dining table with a nautical chart spread in front of him. "Besides it's fuckin' dark out. No one's gonna see."

Ghomes started from the warm, salty air and the buzz of the city's background, into the class of the yacht's main deck salon. Tracy raised her palm.

"Put these on, please."

She handed him a pair of disposable foot covers. Ghomes took the blue booties, chucking them aside and stomping onto her India hand-dyed rug with his grease-splattered Daytons.

"Right. Like I'm gonna wear some fuckin' slippers."

"Have some respect for my property, Robin."

"Chill out, Trace."

Ghomes pushed by. Tracy smelled both liquor and BO – quite the inverse to Michael Buble, who softly crooned in stereo from a background of E.J. Hughes original watercolors.

"Don't be an asshole," Haslett said, descending the half-flight of curved jatoba-wood stairs from the bridge.

"Up yours, Bob." Ghomes flipped him off, grinning through gappy, gold teeth.

"All right. Settle down everyone," Moloci said. "We're here on business. Let's get on with it."

"In a minute," Ghomes told him. He lumbered on through to the galley, yarding open her stainless fridge door. Tracy forbade alcohol onboard the *Bandazul*, so Ghomes helped himself to a Pepsi, shook it, and popped the top. It fizzed, dripping onto her travertine floor. He slurped its rim, wiped the can with his black, leather sleeve, then hulked back to the salon and plunked it down on her inlayed walnut table, parking himself across from Moloci.

Tracy lifted the drink, placing a glass coaster with the ship's monogram underneath, then slid back a chintz-covered dining chair and sat to Moloci's left; her arms and legs crossed, giving Ghomes a look like he'd pissed in her sink.

He took another slug, let out a hot-pepperoni and pickled-egg belch, putting the sticky can back on her bare wood.

"So what's this fuckin' shit about the army gettin' involved?" Ghomes asked.

* * *

Tracy rarely let Ghomes in her home, though she'd managed his finances for two decades.

She found the Sunseeker five years earlier after spending a weekend on it with some friends who'd moored the vessel on Rhode Island. It was love at first sight for Tracy. The *Bandazul*'s lines were gorgeous, her gleaming white-lacquered superstructure contrasting perfectly against a navy-blue hull, set off by smoky-black, polarized glass and bright, polished chromium fittings. Being Sunseeker's top-end, the yacht reeked of European artisanship – from oiled teak planks on the lower aft deck to a seductive steam spa on the upper, near the bow.

Moreover, it was a reflection of Tracy herself. Imaginative and innovative in design. Elegantly appointed in fit and finish. A stunning work of art. It was also the perfect medium through which to integrate a whack of cash she'd been hoarding.

Tracy had no nautical experience, but she planned to contract that out. Regardless, the *Bandazul* was too large and complex a vessel not to be managed full-time. She'd discussed the yacht with Moloci, as she considered its acquisition. He suggested an acquaintance who could survey it, pilot it back to Vancouver, and continue maintaining it for her. The man sounded qualified. He'd been through hard times, Moloci said, and was just getting back on his feet. Tracy suspected an informant of Moloci's – some parolee just released from the joint. As Moloci put it, he'd been institutionalized, but would be discreet and keep a low profile. The man had limited possessions, no family, and needed little pay. Caretaking the yacht would keep the man occupied, giving him a purpose and a place to reside, Moloci told her. He guaranteed the man was dependable and promised to supervise him. Tracy thoroughly trusted Moloci, and she agreed to have lunch with them at the Provence Marinaside.

The first thing Tracy noticed about Robert Haslett was the two scars down the right side of his face. She watched him fidget, nervously sipping his bouillabaisse, and he had a habit of keeping a toothpick in his lips. He was clean, notably well-groomed, but she could tell he was an addict in recovery.

Most of Moloci's finks are druggies, Tracy thought. *But then that's the business we're in.*

They talked for two hours, and she came away with a nice feeling about the man. A week later, Tracy flew with him to Newport to inspect the yacht, being impressed by his knowledge. She sensed him quiet, but intense, and found herself quite liking the man, though not in any way physically attracted to him. After completing the purchase, Tracy flew home, leaving Haslett to hire a hand and skipper the *Bandazul* back via the Panama Canal.

Over time, Tracy got to know Haslett through and through. She increasingly took him into her confidence, relying on him to maintain her yacht and her vehicles, running errands – even bouncing investment ideas off him. It didn't happen in one night. Or in one month. Or even in one particular year. But, once Tracy came to understand Bob Haslett, she fell hopelessly in love with him. Eighteen months earlier, Tracy sold her Yaletown condo and moved in with him onboard the *Bandazul*.

* * *

"I did not see that coming, Robin," Moloci said, being honest. "It came from way above my head. All we can do now is damage control."

Ghomes guzzled the last of his pop, crushed the can in his hand, tossed it aside, and leaned back. "So how do these fuckin' guys operate?"

"I really don't know," Moloci replied. "Bob's more up on that stuff than me."

211

"How the fuck would he know?" Ghomes thumbed at Haslett, who was standing off to Moloci's left side.

"Read a lot," Haslett said.

"Yeah, well, I jack off a lot, but it don't make me no fuckin' smarter."

* * *

Tracy glared at Ghomes. It went way beyond his current behavior. An incident with Ghomes many years ago shaped her life, her relations with men, and tore at her very soul. Tracy long tried to repress what memories she had, but, one night – seventeen, innocent, and at a party – Ghomes slipped something in her drink. Tracy woke, knowing she'd been violated. She never told her father out of shame, but the guilt was overwhelming and still with her today.

* * *

Haslett ignored Ghomes.

"Danger with the military is their technology," Haslett said, moving to sit down at Moloci's right, then staring up and away. "They got stuff we got no idea about. We gotta give 'em the stage. Let 'em do the takedown and give us the hand-off." He turned his head to the three. "When they're gone… we go to work."

Moloci pointed at Ghomes. "You make sure your people are not armed. No weapons. We don't want anything stupid happening there."

"They'll do what they're told." To Ghomes, that applied to his full-patch Angels and the strikers he'd scammed into being patsies. Not to the Vietnamese mules, who he'd love to see shot full of holes.

"Another thing," Moloci said. "The military have no idea who any of us are. They don't care. I have no control over them… who they grab and who they leave. Bob, you have to be in there, but you know how to handle them."

Ghomes frowned. *How the fuck would that scrawny prick know military shit?*

Moloci pointed at Ghomes again. "But I don't want you anywhere near the takedown. We do not want you grabbed by the armed forces."

"I got no intention of bein' there. That's why I got strikers."

The four continued their post-takedown plan. The warehouse, the concentrated product, and the synthetic buffering agents. The dive shop, the tanks, and the inflatables. The new routes. The disbursement of profits. And a lot more that was involved in Plan C.

There was nothing specifically said. Or even not said. But, as the meeting went on late in the night, you could feel it. So could Ghomes.

He sat back, becoming quiet, studying the others, and calculating.

Hmmm, Ghomes thought, twisting his gold, deathhead ring. *Gotta make fuckin' sure Wiggers plays on my side. Sumpin strange is goin' on here.*

Chapter 31

Wednesday, June 20th, 2012
2:40 pm
26 nautical miles due west of Cape Flattery
Pacific Ocean off the State of Washington

Archibald Wiggers squirmed in the wheelhouse chair.

His real leg vibrated as he pecked out a Facebook reply. He punched send. Rolled a smoke. Lit it and got up. He half-stepped outside and stood there, gripping the gunwale and squinting out over the wide-open, flat-ass calm of the Pacific as there were four days left till the takedown, and he'd got a message to call Ghomes.

"Jesus, Mary n' Joseph. This thing's giving me the scudders," he muttered, relieving himself with a long, thin stream overboard. "A b'y don't know whether to shit 'er go blind these days."

* * *

The Big Easy had made excellent time. She was holding now, just outside the Contiguous Zone of American jurisdiction at the entrance to the Straight of Juan de Fuca, twenty-nine nautical miles southwest of the off-load site in Barkley Sound.

Wiggers already received the drop time and location coordinates from Moloci, but held off telling the Colombians, who'd ride the SPSS in. He'd wait in international waters until Saturday. Right after dark, he'd run the sub north, safe into Canadian sovereignty. He'd hold again till Sunday evening, then hand off the laptop and joystick to Haslett, who'd rendezvous with him at the pre-assigned position and take control. Then, and only then, he'd give the site information to his off-load crew. As a back-up, the Colombians could manually steer the sub, but

Wiggers didn't trust them knowing details till they absolutely had to. It wasn't that Wiggers mistrusted Colombians with sensitive information. Wiggers mistrusted everyone. He knew plans had changed and the military were doing the takedown, but he didn't care about that. That was someone else's problem. Not his. He and *The Big Easy* weren't going anywhere near the takedown. He had a document – signed in America and also in Canada – that guaranteed his freedom, and he'd had another destination in mind long before it was signed.

What did concern Wiggers were conflicting messages within the group. He'd read the posts. He'd sensed the dissension, and it wasn't good. Especially this late in the game. For some reason, Ghomes had his face in it, and Ghomes wasn't a Facebook-type guy. Wiggers, on the other hand, chatted with all his Friends in the group. He stayed friendly on-line, keeping his options open. He'd play out his cards in the deal he'd cut with Moloci, and the side one he'd scammed over on Woods. He knew he could negotiate with Everett, and he was cautious enough with Ridge, but you have to know that Archibald Wiggers was shit-scared of Wolfgang Kresslauer.

Like he always operated, Wiggers' only allegiance would lie with the highest bidder. In this case, whoever he thought gave him the best odds of staying alive. Right now – that appeared to be Ghomes.

* * *

Precisely at 15:00, Wiggers cracked open the orange, plastic Pelican case. He pulled out his device, clicking it on, poking the code, and keying the mike.

"Ghomes from the Easy. Ghomes from the Easy. Comes in, b'y."

"Hey, you old fuckin' codfish. How's yer trip?" Ghomes radioed back, his voice a raspy mix of Budweiser, BC Bud, and garbled static.

"Sneaky b'y, but I's here with the prize."

"Good thing, or you'd be having a fuckin' drink with Davy Jones. Over."

Both crooks laughed, but neither gave a shit for the other. There's a thing called a symbiotic relationship and, in this one, host and parasite tag-teamed. For years this pair survived off their wits, by keeping their heads and covering behinds. There was no reason to change MO's now.

Wiggers knew there was a problem, and that Ghomes had an angle.

"So what's spooking ye, Ghomes? Over."

"The coppers, Arch. That boy's club's upta something. Can't put my finger on it, but I'm gonna be prepared."

"So how's it affecting me, b'y?"

"If I go down. You go down."

"That's if I can fuckin' be found."

"Anyone can fuckin' be found, Archie. Anywhere. Anytime. Got it? I got my boy's club, too. Over."

Wiggers knew Ghomes had a point.

"So how's I to make ye feel comfortable, b'y?"

"You keep yer eye to the sky for some air mail. Sunday afternoon."

"What's ye got coming?"

"Call it the insurance policy. Anything happens to me. You make sure it ends up with you know who."

"If I don't?"

"You'll be haunted by Angels. Over and out."

"Lard Tunderin Jeezus!" Wiggers cursed.

He was in a bind. A snarl, the old Newfie would say. But, then, he'd been in snarls before. He stood, gripping the gunwale, looking out over the jail-cell-grey water and calculating how to save his ass this time. He knew exactly who Ghomes meant and that scared him shitless.

* * *

Archibald Wiggers had no intention of ending up like the two other old informants he'd sold out, ten years before.

Chapter 32

Wednesday, June 20th, 2012
3:35 pm
China Creek Marina
Near Port Alberni, British Columbia

Sergeant Bate pulled into the gravel parking lot and was smacked by a déjà-vu.

Haslett was standing outside his truck, dressed in faded Levis, a plain black collared shirt and black ball cap, with polarized Oakleys shading his eyes. She'd had a lot of contact with him over the past few weeks, but something was more than familiar here, she knew, though couldn't quite place it given the commotion that'd been going on in her life.

She'd nearly missed the ferry to Vancouver Island, running late after her alarm failed, then fretted about, second-guessing if she'd packed enough for what she thought would be only a week on the road. She'd arranged to meet Haslett at the China Creek marina, on the salt-water west of Port Alberni, where they'd leave their vehicles, then go west some more, an hour down the inlet by Zodiac and join up with the command post – a warship of the Canadian Navy. Bate's job now moved from HQ out to the field where there was a pile of coordination coming at her once she boarded the frigate.

She parked her car and jumped out – bungeed right back by her handbag strap, claimed as its own by the seat belt. Haslett stood, witnessing her struggle for freedom. He shook his head, then strolled over and helped with luggage from her trunk.

"How was the drive, Sergeant?"

"That is one windy frickin' road," Bate said, showing him the chiclets. "Hope the boat trip is straighter."

"Weather's breaking. Got a full week of sun and calm ahead. Couldn't be better."

Haslett took her bags to his 4X4, putting them in the passenger-rear next to his. He motioned Bate to the front.

She looked at him. "I thought we were going by water?"

"We are." He opened her door. "First, I'm gonna ask you to wait a bit. A thing come up, and I gotta go get some line, weights, and a couple buoys from across the way."

Bate's brow tightened. Haslett pointed east, up the inlet towards the town site, out of sight and around the bend.

"Like you to stay put and guard the gear till I get back, if you don't mind. Be gone half, three quarters of an hour, maybe."

"Fine with me, Bob." Bate pushed back in her seat, flexing her shoulders, and fixing a stare on her BlackBerry.

She welcomed the break. It'd been a hectic start to her day. Up early in time, but late on the clock. The rush to the ferry. E-mails. Notes to catch up. Weak cell signal on the ship. Family problem calls. Then a fast, rainy drive across Vancouver Island.

Haslett left her settling into his Ford. Disinterested, she saw him cross the lot, go down to the float, and step into his big Zodiac – a large, grey and white, rigid-hull inflatable with two powerful outboard engines. He cast off, idled past the breakwater, powered up, and streamed towards the town site.

Bate tried to relax. The sun just came out, quickly heating the inside of Haslett's dark truck. She bumped her tinted window down half, taking in the smells of moist air mixed with salt-beach at low tide, and hearing the endless squawks of circuiting gulls above the distant rumble of a log-boom tug. She touched the seat lever, reclined way back, closed her eyes, placed both hands overtop, and let out a long, loud "Hhhhhuuuhh."

She'd been giving the come-on to a melt-down for years. She thought of the happy things in her life and how she'd neglected them. She thought of Emma, who she'd left at her brother Terry's last night. She thought of Graham and their talk in bed. She thought of Carolyn, whose sister just passed on. She thought of her father, her aunt, and her grandfather and of what their culture had taught. She thought of her career and the responsibility laying ahead in handling evidence in E-Pandemic. She thought of Mahle and Moloci and of finally getting her white-shirt.

Sharlene Bate thought of a lot of things, but no matter what she thought, her thoughts returned to what was now an obsession – Alfred Monagham and the mystery of why the informants had to be murdered.

* * *

It started with her gut feeling again.

Nothing strange. Nothing unnatural. Just that sense that a savvy and seasoned cop gets. It was beginning to add up to her now. She straightened, turned, and looked back at Haslett's gear; a large olive duffle bag, a hard black case about two feet long, and a soft-sided nylon one, holding his computer.

Feeling like a voyeur, she checked up the inlet. Haslett was turning the bend and heading for town. She got out. Snuck behind the truck. Stopped. Looked down at the heavy boat trailer hitched to the framework. Stepped over it. Then opened the driver's rear door.

She stared at the logo on Haslett's green army bag, recognizing the motto scrolled across the blade of the winged sword, then unzipped it and dug around inside. It contained mostly clothes, but there were a couple of books whose titles made her jolt. She zipped it back up, lifting the hard and black case. It was secured by two clasp locks and a peculiar flex-strip of a type she'd never seen. There was no rattle and the weight said it contained about eight pounds. She set it down. Took out his laptop. Her hunch turned to an overwhelming urge.

Passwords can be infinite, but it took Sergeant Bate only four tries. It was something he'd said and the words she'd just read. Bate jolted again. A verse popped up on the screensaver, appearing as an engraving on a grey stone backdrop.

We are the Pilgrims, master; we shall go

Always a little further; it may be

Beyond that last blue mountain barred with snow

Across that angry or that glimmering sea

Poetry? Who… is… this… guy?

She began by scanning his emails. They were minor, like grocery orders and honey-do lists; also stuff about a renovation project, mostly with someone named Tracy. Bate checked the drives. There was a lot of activity to a data-stick but, without it, drew a blank. She suspected these were investigation notes. She opened Internet Explorer, checking bookmarks. *Whoa… This is interesting.*

History showed considerable Facebook activity. The same password refused entry to his profile, but Haslett being on FB didn't surprise Bate. She knew the conspirators communicated that way, but it was the bookmarked sites that really grabbed her attention.

Her hands trembled as she tried the C-Drive. There were PDFs, JPEGs, and digital photos on it.

She opened the first.

Then the second.

And a story unfolded.

"OH… MY… GOD!"

Her palm shot over her mouth.

"Oh My God!

No one will believe this without seeing for themselves! I have to seize this computer!

She gripped it with both hands.

Wait… I can't… I don't have a warrant. No… I have to preserve this as evidence. This is way too serious.

She stared at the screen.

Hhoa… What am I doing? Salt Spring's not my investigation no more. I don't have any right to… Oh My God! I have absolutely no right to be looking in here. Not without a search warrant. But… this is evidence. Hang on! I don't even have grounds for a warrant. Not without knowing this first… Aw Fuck! Double fuck!

Her thumbs turned white.

There's no way of getting a warrant without disclosing how I know this! I can't tell the truth how I found this… but I sure as fuck can't lie. Oh, man! What a horrible, awful, dilemma! Think this out… Think this out… I have to tell someone. It's my duty. Some investigator… whoever's case this is now… has to know this. That's the right thing to do. Tip them off. This is major evidence of a major crime.

Knuckles locked.

But… Hang on… Oh Christ! I broke the law myself. I invaded privacy. I'll end up the criminal for disclosing. Oh God! Have I screwed up royally again! Let me think… let me think… If I tell, it's going to break Salt Spring wide open. But that'll take the main agent out of this drug operation and… that's going to be the end of E-Pandemic. Like right now. Oh God! That cannot happen!

Throat constricted.

This huge operation… years of work… millions of dollars… taking down the Angels... all that work down the tube? I don't think so! Oh Gawd... and my career! My promotion rides on this operation!

A glance out. Up the inlet. Back at the screen.

Aw, Fuck! If I tell, I'd be forced in court to reveal how I got the information. Right! That'll go over just great! Ah... Your Honor... just on a whim I broke into a man's private computer without reasonable cause or any judicial authorization and, gee, look what I found! Wrong, Sergeant Bate! You're charged with a serious criminal offense, punishable by five years imprisonment... And you blew any chance of ever being commissioned.

Head shook.

Finally I have my white shirt right in hand and... Oh No! No way! I cannot lose that! I have to ignore this. Just turn a blind eye.

Face squashed in hands.

That's the right thing. I have to keep my mouth shut and play along.

Hands clasped hair.

But it's wrong. It's so wrong! God... let me think... think this out. For now it's only information I have... It's not evidence... it's not evidence until it's seized... and it can't be seized because there's no legal right.

Eyes closed.

If I don't tell... no one's going to know any different. Right? It's only just information in my head... that's all it is... it's not evidence unless it's recorded... so I'm not suppressing evidence and I'm not committing any offense. Right! No one will ever know except me.

Fists clenched.

But I'm duty bound to report this to my superior. Wrong! Go to Moloci with this? Moloci? Of all people, for Christ's sake!

Stomach in knots.

But I have to live knowing about this. God! What do I do? Oh God... tell me... what is the right thing to do?

The dichotomy of right and wrong sliced through Sergeant Bate's brain like a double-bladed axe of morality – duty dripping off one edge, self-interest off the other, and it chopped her conscience in half.

* * *

Bate had the computer stashed away and was back in the front when Haslett streamed in at the breakwater. He cut his throttles and glided to a tight mooring spot at the float, stepping off in one fluid motion as the big RHIB snuggled in, then secured the lines with the quick ease of tying his shoe. She watched him ascend the gangplank, saunter across the lot, and slide in the driver's seat beside her.

"We'll leave soon as I get this." He patted his iPhone. "Waitin' a call back from Moloci."

Bate didn't respond. She sat as if cast of bronze.

Haslett picked up on it. He looked at her. She at him. Bate's expression gave her away. Haslett glanced back at his gear. The army bag seemed okay. So did the hard, black case. The security strip was intact and impossible to defeat without the right cutters. But the computer was backwards from how he'd placed it; a zipper screaming partially open.

He turned and stared out the windshield.

"See anything interesting while I was gone?" he finally asked.

She swallowed. "How you operate interests me."

"Huh?"

"How you operate is impressive. Like the boat. Where'd you learn how to operate a boat like that?"

He knew she was up to something.

"Been doing it pretty much my whole life. 'Cept for some time here 'n there."

"Where was the here and there, Bob?"

Haslett's toes curled. Bate never got personal before.

"Don't think you need to know that, Sergeant."

He took a toothpick from his shirt pocket, put it in his mouth, and gazed out the side window.

She turned and touched his knee. "Why are you doing this?"

Haslett chewed on his crutch. Both knew his contract had no monetary reward. Simply go deep undercover. Infiltrate. Then testify.

He thought of an answer. "Call it a sense of duty."

"I'm you're handler. I need to know."

He shuffled in his seat.

"I don't want any surprises come trial." Her voice was slightly above whisper.

Silence.

"I know something else is going on."

Still silence.

Bate couldn't help herself. She tried something risky. You'd think it irrational – downright foolish – but she felt no fear, even though she now knew just what this man was capable of. She reached. Lifted his right sleeve. And exposed the tattoo. "I know what that is."

He stayed silent. No hint of anxiety.

"And I know what you've done."

Haslett squirmed like she'd grabbed hold of his balls. Bate leaned back to her side. They sat – for what seemed like eternity – both minds grasping that, here, right now, what was wrong was the right thing to do.

Bate spoke first. "I'm not going to compromise this operation by saying something. Probably no one would believe me anyway. But, in trade, I want you to promise me… one day you'll tell me why."

Haslett showed no reaction. Bate knew she'd pushed as far as she could. She switched tactics.

"I'm concerned about your safety, too. You should have backup."

He stared through the side window.

She kept at him. "If nothing else, it will corroborate your evidence."

A long pause.

As if time stood still.

Then Haslett leaned forward.

"You know, Sergeant?" he said, now staring out the windshield. "I like travellin' alone."

He took out the toothpick, turned, and looked Bate right in the eyes. "There's no witnesses to nothin'."

Chapter 33

Wednesday, June 20th, 2012
6:35 pm
Marble Cove Anchorage
Tzartus Island in Barkley Sound
West Coast of Vancouver Island, British Columbia

Unum Cum Virtute Multorum
* * *

"One With The Strength Of Many" is the motto of FFH338, the HMCS Winnipeg, a Canadian Navy Halifax Class Patrol Frigate. At 440 feet in length, 50 feet in beam, displacing 4,770 tons, carrying a complement of 225 sailors, and holding an arsenal of sophisticated weaponry, the haze-grey Winnipeg was an intimidating sight to Sergeant Bate as she approached at over 50 knots in Bob Haslett's big Zodiac.

"Steady yourself," Haslett cautioned, at the port side of the center control console.

Bate braced as he cut power to the screaming, twin 250 horse Suzukis on his 26-foot RHIB. Bate was sucked forward as the inflatable settled out of its plane and laid down in the water, spraying salt mist over her lips and under her Serengetis. She could begin to hear again as the decibels of wind and engines subsided. For a moment, Bate had a twinge of guilt that she was being paid to take a trip that others would dearly pay for.

Her guilt switched to anxiety, seeing a uniformed figure training a belt-fed .50 calibre Browning on her from behind a flak-shield at the Winnipeg's stern. The sailor relaxed when Haslett hand-signaled as friendly.

Bate sneezed from a waft of exhaust fumes as Haslett dropped the big RHIB back into gear, idling past a No-Go marker towards the warship. She could see little of his face now – blaze-orange floater-coat pulled up, dark goggles on, black ballcap backwards, with an olive-drab bandana wrapping his neck and hiding his chin, covering some of the scars. Haslett pointed. Bate turned. Moloci was standing above, giving a welcome wave.

Haslett pulled starboard to a retractable gangplank, letting Bate stagger onto the corrugated metal platform. Two sailors took her bags, allowing her a two-handed grip at the square-tubing rails as she wobbled on high-angled stairs. Moloci reached, helping her up. Bate turned back, watching Haslett pass the marker and punch the throttles; the long RHIB leaping out of the water and speeding off, foaming a silver-white wake from its transom.

"Welcome aboard," Commander Mike Ferguson said, shaking Bate's hand as Moloci introduced them. He ordered an Able Seaman to take the cases containing her laptop and cipher-communication equipment, and to follow him, along with Moloci, towards the superstructure. Another sailor carried on with her personal bags, heading towards a different portal. Bate looked both ways as she removed her life-vest.

"He's taking them to your wardroom," Chief Petty Officer Dave Bass, the ship's Coxswain, told her – smiling after checking for rings. "We've put you up in our quarters."

Moloci steered Bate away from Bass, who now leered at her chest.

"Galley's only open for a bit more, Sharlene, so let's grab something now." Moloci made a move towards a companionway. "We've got a briefing tonight, and it's going to be lengthy." Bate stayed put. "Sounds good. Just need to get my balance first. I wasn't born on the water like him."

Moloci looked back as she thumbed at Haslett, now just a dot in the distance.

"Interesting guy. Interesting history, I'm sure." She gave a wink. "Like to hear his story sometime."

Moloci didn't bite. Bate turned and gazed about the bay. It looked like an armada to her.

Beside the command ship, Winnipeg, were the support and auxiliary vessels, also at anchor. FFH334 Regina was another helicopter-carrying, fast frigate of the same class, but with a different role – coordinating a craft Bate couldn't see, but one that'd seen Bate from high in the air the day she stood in the Esquimalt pub parking lot.

A huge Iroquois Class destroyer, DDH283 Algonquin, was astern with her Sea-King ready. Three Kingston Class coastal defense vessels offered armed intercept capabilities; Whitehorse, Saskatoon, and Brandon. Five Ocra Class training patrol craft held the takedown teams – Grizzly, Raven, and Renaud housing JTF 2 – Cougar and Orca quartering Claymore and his ERT prisoner restraint teams. Two 58-foot RCMP catamarans, Lindsay and Higgit, sat silent as watchmen. So did a dozen assorted tugs, service, and supply vessels.

Bate was amazed at the magnitude of the military response. You'd think total overkill – exactly what the PM wanted – but the timing coincided with a routine naval exercise held most summers off Vancouver Island. For the military, having a live target to pounce on was a windfall.

Bate turned to Moloci, who was holding the companion-hatch door open.

"Sorry." She released the railing. "I'm a bit overwhelmed by the firepower."

Moloci just smiled and ducked inside, halting at the base of a steep set of steel stairs to let a very fit figure descend. Bate stopped, bending down to retrieve her shoe caught on the coaming. She stood up, just as the soldier hit the landing. They met face to face.

"WHAT THE FUCK!" Ryan Wedge yelled, dumping his coffee. "Not you again!"

"Yeeeeow!"

"What the fuck are you doing here?"

"Ow..w..w! Oww! Oww!" Bate tore her steaming-wet sleeve off her scalded arm.

"Aw Fuck!" Wedge scrambled. "Fuck. I'm sorry. Ah, shit. Here..."

"Yikes!"

He stripped off his T-shirt to mop at her forearm. "I'm so sorry. You okay?"

Bate stopped tugging. "Ohhh God that's hot," she said, looking up at Wedge standing there half-naked.

And they had to laugh, including Moloci.

"I've changed jobs, Ryan," she said, gritting the chiclets. "I'm here on the takedown."

"Hope I'm not the takedown again."

"No, but we've got a dangerous way of doing coffee." Her grimace switched back to a grin.

Moloci was curious. "I take it you two have met before?"

Neither Ryan Wedge nor Sharlene Bate were opening up that crypt.

* * *

With dinner over and more intros done, Bate retreated with Moloci to the dimmed CIC, the Combat Information Center, along with senior military officers. She felt like she was entering some billionaire's home theatre. An image of Barkley Sound was prominent on a screen bigger and clearer than anything she'd seen. The Winnipeg's XO, the Executive Officer, called the operations room to order and the CO of Joint Task Force 2 took over.

"We're confident in takedown at 00:40 on Monday, the 25th," said Colonel Dave May. "The moon is in first phase, tide is at low slack, and weather appears to be at the peak of a high pressure ridge." Colonel May clicked the PowerPoint, showing a glass-water image of the open ocean horizon. "It's made to order for us."

Bate sat, gyrating her foot and gripping an Aloe Vera wrapped wrist. She had no idea who May was. Next to him, though, was a familiar figure. She'd never seen the face, but she recognized the hands. P90 man. Captain Lange ignored her. He and May had been briefed on Bate and her role, privately agreeing the past remain past.

May finished with logistics and motioned to Moloci, who stood up.

"Our agents are now on site and ready to go," Moloci said. "The tug and sub are stationary at the holding point off Cape Flattery."

Moloci changed the PowerPoint to live feed from low orbit, showing the entire west coast of North America from Mexico to Alaska. Like Alice going through the rabbit-hole, the image zoomed onto a dot in the open Pacific displaying *The Big Easy* and the SPSS, each flashing orange from a light. Bate watched the image become so clear that she could see a deckhand cut open a cardboard box and take out three purplish cans of garbanzo beans.

"This, folks, is the mother ship with our target."

Murmurs went through the ops room.

"It's carrying a crew of seven, including the skipper and two mates. The other four are South American flunkies who'll ride the sub in and unload the cargo to the mule boats."

More murmurs and some coughs.

"The mules are already crewed, but will hold, waiting instruction. They will not know the exact time, nor position, of the off-load site until absolutely necessary. As a precaution, we're doing a series of diversions, or false meets, with them over the next three days. We're wary of piracy by these people. We need to be satisfied that we're in complete control before directing them to the takedown site. Then, from our point, the evidence collection point, we're good to go. Here's who to expect."

The image switched to a feed showing the *Helms Deep*, a fiberglass crab boat, tied to a dock back at China Creek. A click of the mouse brought up the *Bottomline*, an aluminum prawn fisher, anchored south at Pachena Bay. Another click showed the *Jolly Roger* and the *Do Boy III*, rafted together in Ucluelet harbour, on the north side of Barkley Sound. The image split into four quarters of the screen, each showing the positions of the mule boats within a backdrop of a digital nautical chart. What all had in common was the orange flashing light.

Bate looked at Moloci, then at Sergeant Jake Bush, who was beaming. She'd not been briefed about bugs on the boats.

Moloci clicked to a feed which Bate recognized – a live, full screen image of Haslett's RHIB, now moored at a wharf in Bamfield. Orange flashed on the Zodiac she'd ridden in.

So what else don't I know? She kept watching.

"Our Canadian agent will be operating this inflatable," Moloci continued. "He'll be alone and will rendezvous with the Colombian agent at the off-shore position, here at a point in the open water known as Miller Reef."

He displayed an image of a nautical chart showing the outside of Barkley Sound.

"This is set for 18:15 on the 24th when he'll take over the remote controls to the sub and guide it straight in from there. The Colombian agent will be granted free passage to leave with his ship, as guaranteed by the collective agreements with the DEA and the RCMP. He will not be interceded with, or impeded upon, in any way. The same goes for the Canadian."

Bate saw Moloci nod to Garfield Woods, who glanced at Bate and nodded back to Moloci. Wolfgang Kresslauer, directly in front, peered at her over the top of his glasses. She turned, shuddering to see Claymore had circled a body-length behind her, standing arms folded, seeming to melt a hole straight through her. She looked left to the Colonel. Right to P90. Then she glanced once again at Wolf Kresslauer. She sensed the old German knew far more than he'd told them back in Vancouver, and she suspected there was far more going on beyond E-Pandemic than she was allowed to know.

"Our agent will then steer the sub to the offload zone, which is here."

Moloci showed an image of a beach at Kirby Point on the northeast side of Diana Island, one of the first sheltered spots in from the vast Pacific.

"The sub will contain the four foreign nationals, who will unload to four boat crews, which have five individuals per boat. That makes a total of twenty-four for arrests. There will also be several high-value targets present, as well as our undercover operator. We expect two full-patch Angels, but the conspiracy evidence we'll obtain goes far beyond those arrested on site. This operation will take down the top of the food-chain."

Moloci took a sip of water. He looked at May, then at Claymore, who loomed back of Bate.

"We've some assurance that the off-load crews will not be armed, but I can't give that guarantee. Expect this to be dangerous."

Armand Lange already assumed the worst. The JTF 2 bricks repeatedly practiced the takedown. They had a plan, but the men were restless, waiting a green light.

Moloci kept the Ops room captive. "When the sub is delivered, 22:45 being the time, all four off-load boats will be on site. Cargo transfer will commence immediately and should be one-third complete, dividing product evenly among the boats according to a strict, rotating inventory controlled by our operator. The strike will be executed by Colonel May and his Special Forces starting at 00:40, which is right at low slack tide. We, the evidentiary agency, will standby to receive the prisoners and the contraband, once the site is safely contained."

Moloci motioned.

May spoke up. "We, call us the tactical agency, require a wide perimeter to safely diffuse this situation. No one, especially civilians, are allowed inside the zone until the operation is concluded. We'll be taking measures to sweep and secure the area prior to execution. Upon neutralization, Inspector Claymore and his ERT members will enter the takedown zone aboard the Kingston Class vessels and receive the prisoners. The processing of the contraband can then take its time."

Moloci grinned and spoke to his police members. "There's good reason for us not to be in there."

May picked up. "Yes, you bet. The tactics we use are classified. In fact, quite volatile. It's best you sit back and watch it play out on the video. I guarantee you'll enjoy the show."

May, Lange, and Moloci laughed.

Kresslauer took off his glasses and wiped them clean.

* * *

Claymore shifted, big arms folded – creeping right up against Bate from behind.

Chapter 34

Sunday, June 24th, 2012
3:50 pm
Bordelais Islet in Barkley Sound
West Coast of Vancouver Island, British Columbia

"Ze-ro. Gold Key," radioed JTF 2 Signal Operator Corporal Mason Kong. "We got another civilian aircraft out here."

Kong was a sentry, hovelled on a tiny, windswept rocky nub at the edge of the wide-open, crashing Pacific leading to the off-load site.

The bright, sunny airspace became restricted to military exercises at 2:30 pm and a Sea King from the Regina had just removed an amphibious Beaver fixed-wing, escorting it at door-gun point to a paved strip at Tofino, north of Barkley Sound. Ground interception found a CTV crew claiming they were producing a documentary on whales, despite the spring migration long gone. Two journalists, a cameraman, plus the pissed-off pilot, were held for interrogation. The Winnipeg's CO was sure some informant had tipped-off the media. He fumed about, suspecting a highly-placed rat, and was bent on ferreting it out.

"Gold Key. Ze-ro. Copy that," replied the Sig Op onboard the controlling Winnipeg. "Got it on Doppler now. Slow response to RF direction. Second Sea King preparing for intercept. Can you read call sign? Over."

"Negative," Kong responded. "Too far out. Over."

"Ah, stand down, Gold Key. We're turning the drone on it now. Over."

"Copy, Ze-ro."

"Appears compliant. Now exiting restricted space."

"Visual has it bearing 040. Gold Key out."

* * *

Kong and a partner had been embedded in their OP, Observation Post, six days before by a JTF 2 RHIB; grateful now for a break in weather. They'd been flogged non-stop by Mother Nature, who beat their bones as if sending a cavalry of soaking-wet, salty rag-mops, charging in on a pressure change from the great big sea.

The OP's protection was the leeward side of a stony outcrop, walled-off by a wispy grove of twisted, old, dwarf Sitka spruce. In it they'd built a hooch – an improvised shelter – after their tent got deep-sixed in the landing. Insertion also beat up their stomachs, starting with heaves due to monster swells, then the corpse-stinking reek of a rotting Humpback, wedged in a crevasse directly below on the basalt beach.

A lack of bottled water and decent food didn't help. Their grub box had been Titanic'd, along with the sleeping bags, after a rogue roller did them like a release of the Kraken. That left them hooched and trapping rainwater for washing down cold IMP's, Individual Meal Packs, which survived as would cockroaches after a nuclear strike. But they'd hung onto what was really important – their optical, transmitting, and receiving equipment.

Despite advances in technology, military operations will always rely on human watch and endurance. Kong and his partner had a 360-degree view on the entrance to Barkley Sound, which they watched with enduring equipment: Rockwell Viper Laser range finders, KillFlash binocs, and AN/PVS-7D night vision goggles. These were great from the ground, but good as their amplified sight was, they were nearly blind as three mice compared to their help in the air.

* * *

The occupants of the offending Cessna Skywagon had no sense of being watched, never mind by what, or how sophisticated the eyeball was. It was at 33,100 feet in altitude, but its discreet imaging SAR, Synthetic Aperture Radar, could read the 185's call letters as if on a replay at Cowboys Stadium.

The small airplane was climbing out of a starboard bank and bearing northeast, 460 feet over Imperial Eagle Channel, when the AVO, Air Vehicle Operator, at her GCS, Ground Control Station, onboard the Regina locked on. Through her ROVER, the Remotely Operated Video Enhanced Receiver, Captain France DeClerc fed a live video stream to Kong's PTAC Secure Rugged Data Terminal on the ground, to TACCO, the Tactical Coordinator on the Sea King and to 'Zero' or Command, the Combat Information Center onboard the Winnipeg. Here, Bate and a roomful of others watched the MTI, Moving Target Indicator, give a real time, multi-dimensioned, situational picture.

The CU-170 Heron UAV, the Unmanned Aerial Vehicle that DeClerc controlled, was a drone-on-loan from Israel to the Canadian Air Force with an agreement that Canada would purchase four of these tactical surveillance aircraft once tested. CFB Comox, on Vancouver Island, had been operating this Heron for two months now, including at JTF 2's scenario request to spy on Sergeant Bate outside the pub in Esquimalt.

DeClerc turned on the UAV's hi-resolution Electro-Optical camera, gyroscopically balancing the image of the little plane as if it were being filmed from a studio tripod. She jerked her joystick and fingered her keyboard, arousing the SAR hung under the drone's belly pod and erecting split-screen images of the 185's occupants. Bate nearly crapped her pants when she saw the passenger.

* * *

"I picked up some side-band," the Sig Op told Bate. "Not on the aircraft frequency. It was garbled, like from an encrypted Sat C. I think the plane was communicating with a surface vessel. Probably our Colombian target, 'cause there's no one else out there. I couldn't make actual conversation, but something was going on. For sure."

Bate phoned Moloci on his cell. He'd gone to the galley for a break, knowing the hand-off to Haslett would happen in two hours, and he wanted to be in control from then on. "Sir, come back to Zero, please. There's something you need to see."

Captain DeClerc, call-signed Hotel-One, was waking her Heron from sleep and orbit mode. The drone alerted DeClerc to something in its memory bank. She was checking as Moloci rushed back in Command.

"What have you got?" Moloci asked, entering the dimmed, blue-hued room full of optics and operators.

"Take a look," Bate replied. "A private Cessna circling the tug and sub, well past curfew. It may have contacted the Colombian. Now it's on its way out."

Moloci bent over her monitor, seeing the image of the aircraft's registration. "What's this about?"

Bate clicked to the split screen, showing occupants. "In the passenger seat, Sir. It's Ghomes."

Moloci looked like he'd seen a ghost. "What the fuck is he doing out here!"

Bate shot back in her chair. *That's the first time he's ever dropped the F-bomb.*

The Heron was now wide awake, acquiring new targets. DeClerc called the alarm.

"Ze-ro. Hoh-tel Wun. I have a foreign contact on the water. 48.9803 North. 125.7601 West."

The two Mounties stared at the wall screen. An image developed; clearly a periscope with a long, blackish-grey cigar lurking below. The XO ambled over with his coffee.

"You got a submarine here, too?" Moloci asked. He was rattled, and Bate knew it.

"Not ours," the XO chuckled. "It'll be the Americans. Doesn't surprise me, though. They've probably been watching this all along."

DeClerc called again. "Contact in the air. There's another drone with us."

It took eight seconds to download the image to Zero's screen – an RQ-4B Global Hawk from the USAF 9th Reconnaissance Wing at Beale AFB in California, loitering 61,300 feet over the international boundary.

"So they have been following us." The XO grinned like a stoned hyena.

Bate looked at Moloci. He was tense. Really tense. She glanced to Kresslauer, detecting a gleam from behind his glasses. She looked at May, who was typing in numbers. Then at Lange. Then back to Moloci. He stared vacantly. She looked to the chipper XO. He took a sip and stood back, knowing the takedown would be filmed from space.

He also knew the Prime Minister would delight in the lead story on the CNN morning news.

Chapter 35

Monday, June 25th, 2012
12:40 am
A bay at Kirby Point
Diana Island in Barkley Sound
West Coast of Vancouver Island, British Columbia

Diversions can be wonderful things, as Malcolm Atkinson once said.

* * *

Ngoc Van Nguyen was the first to see it come down. He was a lookout on the *Bottomline*, one of four lookouts on the mule boats at the off-load site.

A bright, white light switched-on low in the southwest sky. He squeezed his eyes and looked again. It was closing fast. Nguyen called in Vietnamese to the man on the *Do Boy* who also looked. They saw a second white light flash-on beside it, streaking straight at them.

"Gai Lum Bob! Gai Lum Bob!" the pair yelled. They had exactly 7.7 seconds to sound the alarm, causing everyone to look up as the lights screamed silently by, 580 feet overhead. The off-loaders had another 2.3 seconds to watch trails of fire arch upward before –

BAAAAA – BAAAAAAAANNGGGG

Two massive sonic booms blew out eardrums and shot blood from the noses of the exposed workers in the bay. Shattered glass, fiberglass shards, ripped fabric, and debris of all sorts blasted everywhere within the shock-stricken target. Half the off-loaders were unable to stand, let alone hear the mind-fucking roar of afterburners. The CF-18 Hornets pulled six G's going vertical from their Mach 1.2 run, climbing thirty seconds, wing-tip at wing-tip to 26,000 feet, banking sharply north, returning to CFB Comox.

Mason Kong uncovered his head, shutting off his laser beacon, which guided the jets in. He swung, yelling "Fuckin' Irene", both thumbs up at the disappearing fighters.

The site was chaos. Lighting dropped back to night's dim for those who could see; panicked cries for those who could hear. Crematorium smells and toxic tastes overwhelmed; mostly burnt JP-8 fuel, but also puke, piss, and shit. Two full-patches emerged from down in a cabin, trying to police order, but Ray Peach stayed below. He knew what was next.

WHHOOOOOOOMP

A magnificent fireball of diesel set by C4 lit up the eastern bay. The Angels instinctively turned to it, taking heat and concussion right in the face.

SKREEEE-EEEEE-AAKAKE

Electronic infrasound was the next diversion, highly amplified at 158 decibels, timed to be the third wave in demoralizing the site. Its long, low release – same frequency as dragging an immense set of sharp fingernails down a gigantic blackboard – registered on the skull, regardless if eardrums were intact. The HAs dropped to their knees, gripping their heads, as four Colombians popped-up from the sub like death-wishing whack-a-moles, bailing into scrap-strewn water.

BWUUUHHHAAA HAAA HAAA EEEEHEEHEE

Vincent Price laughed from the loudspeakers.

Five bricks of JTF 2 assaulters were held back at Fleming Island, two nautical miles northeast. On queue, their RHIBs hit full-throttle when the second F-18 light turned them on. Corralling the site, they cut back, awaiting one final diversion. Through night vision goggles they caught a pathetic green scene of tough-guys-now-tit-suckers; clinging to buoyants, whimpering for help, and reduced to quivering, diarrheic messes. Brandon and Whitehorse moved in, securing the cove's exits.

A brick had been inserted on Diana Island to control the diversions and stop anyone fleeing to land.

"Standby... Standby... GO!" the brick leader on shore called to three assaulters who fired on command.

FEEEEEEEEEUUUUUWWWW

Rocket-propelled, luminous parachute-flares were the last diversionary tactics, exploding over the site and raising the light to near bright-as-day. The assaulters replaced their NVGs with tinted visors and moved in, but there was no fight to be found in the bay. The scene was simple to secure now. JTF 2 members restrained and tagged captives, surrendering them to Jim Claymore's forces. A triage was done. Surprisingly, the most serious injuries were to the Colombians, mauled by two dogs set on shore with the speakers. Prisoners suffering more than shock and shot eardrums were transferred to the Saskatoon, a medical post; others to the Brandon, a floating jail. In total, thirty-one arrests were counted. Four Columbians as expected. Two full-patch HAs, seven strikers, and eighteen Viets – all sucked-in by Ghomes like krill through a whale's baleen.

Captain Lange's Delta-5 brick were the same guys who'd made off with Sharlene Bate; Sergeant Fury, Master Corporal Wedge, Corporal Durrani, Corporal McKee, and Corporal Dubas. They'd been detailed to search the submersible. McKee, the coxswain, snapped on the searchlight and idled his RHIB parallel, letting Wedge hop onto the hull; his C8 threatening the hatch. Durrani, gripping an MP5, stepped next, followed by Dubas, then by Fury, and then by Captain Lange.

"Stand-by... Stand-by... NOW!" Fury yelled. Dubas fired a Flash-Bang down the hole.

BAAAAAM

Four glow-sticks followed. Wedge passed his rifle to Lange, drew his Sig, dipping head-first into the white-lighted guts. Fury and Dubas held his ankles, sweeping him 360.

"Clear!" Wedge called, dropping in.

"Whadda ya see?" Lange yelled.

"The fuckin' motherlode. She's still packed!"

"Ze-ro. Dell-Tah Fife," Lange radioed.

"Dell-Tah- Fife. Go," the Sig on the Winnipeg replied.

"Confirming target secured. Contraband onboard. Over."

"What's it look like, Fife?" Colonel May called back, sitting in with Signals.

"Tons! Fucking tons!"

* * *

Archibald Wiggers witnessed the diversion, but it was of no concern to him. He had another purpose right from the start. Wiggers was home free, running lights out, well into the last leg of *The Big Easy*'s voyage to Canada.

Sharlene Bate watched it go down on the Winnipeg's big screen, live via feed from the Heron. She'd never seen anything like it. *What a great book or movie plot this would make!* she thought. But Sergeant

Bate had no thought yet, same as you, what the real plot was – why the informants had to be murdered, what secret the ghost would entrust her to keep, and just how deadly The Kushtaka will be.

John Moloci watched from a different perspective. His was of relief. This phase of the operation was over and, by all accounts, a huge success – despite Ghomes nearly blowing it wide open. Moloci was confident the final phase would be smooth, though. He was back in control with a month to implement Plan C before his retirement, then a few days afterwards to do-in Robin Ghomes.

Tracy knew the takedown went well. Moloci texted her right after the arrests, but she didn't care for sensational stuff. She could see that on the news. Right now, the financial markets were opening in Europe, and Tracy had her hands full starting the sting.

Raymond Ridge and Wolfgang Kresslauer watched. Kresslauer on site. Ridge far away in a room without windows.

The PM was informed. He couldn't believe the good fortune.

The CO of the Winnipeg was still on the hunt for the informant while his XO was online with the Minister of Defense, who'd tell the Americans what they already knew.

Ghomes waited in the safety of his clubhouse.

* * *

It was 3:40 am now, Pacific time. Mason Kong and his partner were packing for extraction come daylight. Kong stopped. He stared through the darkness, northwest to the open ocean, past Folger Island.

"Something's out there."

"What?" the partner asked.

"Sounds like a boat."

"No one's supposed to be there."

"I know," Kong said. He dug in his kit bag, pulling out NVG's, scanning the dark as the pixeled, green image of a large, twin-engine Zodiac emerged. A lone rider was ripping right at them.

"Who the fuck is this?"

"Call it in."

"Ze-Ro. Gold Key. We got an unidentified RHIB in the approach zone." Kong gave co-ordinates.

"Gold Key. Ze-Ro. Not ours. Turning the drone on it."

Bate watched the Sig respond with a call to DeClerc whose Heron clicked and whirred, devouring the digits she fed it.

The vessels pinned with tracking devices were accounted for, Bate could see; all flashing orange on the screen. Haslett's beacon was still east of Dixon Island where he'd been instructed to hide after guiding the sub in. *The Big Easy* showed stationary at Miller Reef, the rendezvous spot off shore. The sub and the mules were corralled in the bay. It was Colonel May who saw they'd been scammed.

"Dell-Tah Fife. Ze-Ro," May radioed, over-riding the Sig. "Break off to intercept unidentified vessel. GPS location being downloaded."

McKee looked at his nav-screen. "It's bearing 124, right at Gold Key. What the fuck?"

"Dell-Tah Fife. Lone helmsman," Kong called. "Straight by me. Like fast. Hard turn. Now east-northeast, bearing 091."

"Intercepting," McKee called, powering up, telling his brick, "It's coming at us from 271. Brace!"

Delta Five hit max speed – 50 knots – southwest passing the Whitehorse, entering Trevor Channel, bearing 198 in the black.

"Fuck!" Haslett cursed, rounding Edward King Island in his RHIB, now heading 080, seeing the oncoming brick through his NVG's. *Shoulda known they'd placed a sentry.*

Getting caught out of place was not in the plan. He'd fixed his SatTrac device to a buoy attached by a line to a weight anchored back at his holding point, then he'd gone out to do the same for Wiggers, letting him and *The Big Easy* run free.

Haslett swung hard port. He cut, stopping at the entrance to Dodger Channel, a narrow passage west of Diana Island. Timing Delta-Five's approach, he hit the throttles. One forward wide-open – the other half in reverse – burning three water donuts, boiling a huge, whirling pool – hammering both full-forward; the big RHIB leaping up, nearly standing on end, launching north towards the shallows.

McKee saw the hole – too late to avoid.

"Hang On!"

JTF 2's inflatable hit hard, swinging violently starboard, ripping back 180, turning on its side, nearly capsizing. Anything not secured hurled overboard, including Dubas, losing grip on the support stick. Delta-Five died in the water, its kill-switch ending both engines.

McKee restarted. Lange activated the searchlight. Dubas bobbed in his floater vest, waving hard.

Haslett looked back, seeing Delta-Five fishing Dubas from the chuck. *No choice* – he faced forward – *Gotta gamble* – getting away through the shallow channel, full speed at 63 knots.

A sickening rock-smash stripped Haslett's stainless-steel props clean off of their shafts; engines free-wheeling in werewolf shriek-howls, exploding as hot piston-shrapnel.

"Yesss!" McKee fist pumped, powering up, his man back on board. Lange shot the spotlight forward. Haslett was silhouetted – his back to them – standing still in the stalled big RHIB. Wedge aimed as McKee idled in.

Slowly. Carefully. Haslett stretched his hands high, high, up. Locked his fingers. Downed them behind his head; elbows straight out.

He turned to face the brick.

"Surprise, Cock-Fag!" Wedge said with a huge grin, C8 centered on Haslett's mass. Safety off. Finger on.

Haslett stood firm in his rocking boat and stared in the young soldier's eyes.

"Stand easy, lad," he said. "I'm one of yours."

Chapter 36

Friday, July 27th, 2012
9:50 am
RCMP Headquarters
Vancouver, British Columbia

"My very, very best to you, Sir." Bate showed the chiclets with a part smile, giving Moloci a light squeeze. "It's been a real privilege to serve with you, even though it was far, far too short. Enjoy your retirement."

He took her right hand. "Drop the Sir thing. It's John, now."

"Thank you for having faith in me, John."

Bate saw a bit of moisture in his eyes, too – a human side to the all-controlling Superintendent she'd come to know, respect, and genuinely like. They stood in the boisterous reception area of Federal Drug Enforcement Branch, as he worked a well-wishing lineup. The usual cheap, paper cups holding machine-dispensed mud were replaced by glass flutes of Dom Perignon and fresh OJ.

First thing this morning, Moloci turned in his government-issued 9-mil, his cell and his pager, his handcuffs, and the keys to his car. His computer passwords were erased and his security clearance now eliminated. His thumb print and retina profile were no longer recognized. His badge would be sent for acrylic encasement and, shortly, his first pension cheque would appear in the bank, guaranteed monthly till the day he'd be dragged from the pasture.

"You're going to make a hell of a good officer, Sharlene. Treat your people right. Fair but firm."

Bate flushed as Moloci wrapped his right arm around her shoulder.

"Remember, it's what you know that'll make your career," he whispered, pressuring her wrist. "There's a group you may be interested in getting involved with. They'll be in touch."

Moloci stepped back, giving a quick index finger to his lips.

A rush went through Bate like taking a hit on a crack pipe. *What in the Christ is he up to?*

He continued his byes to the parade of co-workers. Most shook his hand, but some gave him hugs mixed with teardrops. Then, after thirty-six years of loyal service to the Royal Canadian Mounted Police, Giovanni Moloci walked out the door of headquarters for the last time.

Bate stood at the window and watched him cross the parking lot. Without the slightest look back, Moloci hit the remote, opened the door to his Escalade, and got in. He sat for two minutes – not reflecting – rather planning – then put the black truck in gear and drove off.

She smiled and couldn't help shaking her head.

* * *

Bate wandered back to her office, shut the door, and sat behind the grey, metal desk. She put her hands behind her head, locked her fingers, leaned back, exhaled, and drifted deep into thought. *So what... Is... Really going on here?*

Her BlackBerry toned, jolting her back into consciousness.

"Sergeant Bate."

"Yeah, Bate? Staff Sergeant Surtees here. I'm at the lab. Something bad's goin' on with the shit from Bamfield. You better get over here."

* * *

Bate locked up and hurried across the street, this time signing in with her destination as Chemistry Section. Hiron Chan, the senior chemist, buzzed her into the Pine-Sol smelling room. Bate looked at Deano Surtees, then at Chan, and then at Constable Gerri Bonarski, who'd been assigned as exhibit-man and had requested random purity testing on the thousands of bricks seized from the sub. They looked part-pissed and part-stunned.

"W-What's wrong?" Bate asked.

"This bizarre, to say the least," Chan said. "I analyze twenty-seven sample so far, each from separate package. These were from different part of submersible and from different stacking level, so it give me proper grid for random selection. Normally, any large cocaine seizure, I see average purity percentage around ninety-five with only small deviance. Here, we have maximum purity at twenty-six, all the way down to lowest at two. That not even enough to numb your tongue. I get average so far at twelve."

"This is fuckin' shit stuff," Surtees said. "They'd never cut it like this on import. Something phony's goin' on."

"What do you know about the source of this shipment?" Bonarski asked with suspicious eyes.

"No more than you." Bate's darted between theirs. "You-you saw the video of it being loaded in Colombia just like I did. Where it came from before that... I have no clue."

Chan cut in. "Something else you need to know. I did molecular profile on better sample. This not same as other cocaine I see. This product has entirely different signature. It much more concentrated. It appears to me this originate from some sort of experiment with hybrid. Some sort of genetically altered plant. We heard rumor this being developed, but I know of no other seizure yet. Also, low purity is not explained by buffering. It just weak. It... it like it come from sick plant or something."

"You think we got a war goin' on now," Surtees said. "If this crap hit the street, rippin' dealers and addicts, it'd be ten times as bad. This fuckin' reeks. Somebody fed us a shipment of dog shit to take down."

"Where does our case stand?" Bonarski asked.

"Purity level is irrelevant," Chan said. "It all cocaine, and I testify to that. It still illegal."

"Yeah," Surtees agreed. "Purity's got fuck-all to do with legality. The case still holds, but it's gonna look real dirty in court. Like we got sent on a fuckin' goose chase." He pointed at Bate. "It's just a huge red herring that defense is gonna make you swallow raw."

"M-Me?" Bate pointed at her chest.

"Yeah. You." Surtees pointed, too. "Your fuckin' agents had to know this. And you, the coordinator, are gonna look like a fuckin' idiot tryin' to explain on the stand how you got scammed this bad."

Her limbs hinged.

"Or worse... The Angels are gonna think you tried to fuckin' rip 'em."

Her backbone buckled.

"You been set-up, lady."

She knew Surtees was right – she'd been strung like a marionette – now she knew there was way, way more going on in E-Pandemic than she'd been told.

"I'm going to make some calls." Bate said, mouth dry, voice a hoarse whinny. "Just keep this quiet till we figure out what's going on."

"Well, I'm sure as fuck not gonna say anything." Surtees pointed at Bonarski and Chan. "And neither are you."

* * *

Bate signed out with a scrawl and tore back to her office, grabbing the secure phone, punching in Moloci's own cell.

"The number you have reached is no longer in service."

She called his home. Same thing. She tried Haslett. His cell was active, but cut to voice mail, as her anxiety pot boiled over.

"Bob… John… Somebody call me ASAP. There's a major problem with the stuff off the sub. I need your help… Please!"

Haslett got Bate's message. Moloci listened, too. They knew of the purity problem, and they'd get back to her. But, at the moment, they were dealing with another problem.

One far more dangerous to the Art Williams Organization.

Part Five

The Payback

Chapter 37

Diversions can be wonderful things, like Akker said.

The jets, the lights, and the blasts. The smells, the tastes, and the sounds. The weights, lines, and buoys that cheated the tracking bugs. *The Big Easy.* The SPSS. Sacrificial Angels. Strikers. Viets. Tons of garbage cocaine. Even Kresslauer's PowerPoint. All were diversionary devices.

In fact, the whole takedown was just one big diversion.

But only a few knew about it.

* * *

Ghomes lumbered out of the old cannery and clomped down the boardwalk, packing a large, steel Scuba tank; five kilos heavier now than when he'd dragged it inside. He tramped onto the dive shop's concrete wharf, lowering the tank down to Haslett who stood on a Douglas-fir float. Haslett dunked it in salt water, swishing off residue and giving it back. Ghomes slid it beside seven, yellow and black others in the shade by the fuel shack, then undid his fly and pissed in the water.

"Fuck, man. Have some class," Haslett said. "There's a woman standin' right there."

"She'd rather see it than be blind." Ghomes grinned through gold teeth. He shook it and zipped up. "So, you takin' these fuckin' tanks and that little inflatable over to Vancouver tomorrow or Sunday?"

"Today." Haslett was back up on the dock.

"When'd that change?"

"This mornin'."

"Why the fuck's that?"

"Tracy called. Says she needs to talk."

"She got you so pussy-whipped. What the fuck's she want this time?"

"She's got some issue with finances. Sounds upset."

"What's this about?" Ghomes was curious.

"Don't know exactly. It's gotta do with Ridge. Tracy thinks he's been skimmin' off the top or sumpin like that. She's been suspicious for some time, I guess."

"What! Why the fuck's nobody told me?"

"Said she just got proof today, but didn't wanna getcha all worked up. There's probably nothin' to it. Don't know the guy myself, but I can't see that happenin'."

"The fuckin' cocksucker! If he is, I'll cut his fuckin' bag off myself."

"Yeah, well, I'll find out tonight and letcha know."

"Fuck that. I wanna hear this for myself. I'm coming with ya."

And, with that, Robin Ghomes took the bait right down his gullet.

* * *

The old cannery, now a warehouse masquerading as a dive-charter shop, was under renovation before Ridge drew the exit plan for Ghomes.

The fake dive shop was Haslett's idea. He included Ghomes in building it, keeping him close as in Moloci's Sun Tsu philosophy. But Moloci's scheme to put Haslett close to Ghomes started much earlier, and it was for an entirely different purpose.

Preparations for the warehouse, however, began three years before when the Williams Organization realized they were losing control of Colombian cocaine routing through Mexico. The American government was waging their war on drugs. Violence in Mexico was rocketing. Distributors were dropping. Seizures of product and cash were stifling. And sentences handed out in the U.S. for large importers were paralyzing. The Kingpin Act was proving brutally effective.

Art wanted to abandon coke trafficking well before his real death. He never did like the stuff but, by now, the others were addicted to its sale for supporting their downlines. Art genuinely cared about his organization. They were family to him. Out of loyalty to his group, he agreed to Plan A. Canada was the logical site for the new route, he well understood, and every look at the business case supported it. Reluctantly,

Art committed the Williams Organization to move forward; confident, as it was approved by another organization even more secretive than his.

Plan A was to ship huge volumes of condensed cocaine by sea, warehouse it at Bamfield, then dilute and release the drug under a controlled rate to the North American market. It was overseen by Ridge and monitored by Kresslauer, both answering to a ghostly council concerned with a much bigger picture. The plan also defined roles for team members.

Everett was tasked with developing the submersibles and perfecting the Santa Barbara factory. Both took longer than expected.

Moloci was tasked with diverting authorities from the business plan; keeping them occupied with projects that would justify budgets, organizational positions, and look good on the news.

Tracy was tasked with her forte; financing the venture, then accounting for income, expenditures, and hiding all profits.

Wiggers was tasked with testing the vessels, charting the route, and feeding false information. This went smooth, until he ran afoul of the DEA. Wiggers and *The Big Easy* were vital to the business plan and that forced Moloci to develop Plan B, which appeased the Americans. It was a small price, though, as it sprung Wiggers free with his ship. Moloci, Ridge, and Kresslauer were used to bailing Wiggers out – they'd been running him for years. He was a handful, but he always produced.

Haslett and Ghomes were tasked with distribution through Canada and back to the States. Haslett reasoned the lowest risk was by water, his comfort zone. Large shipments by land or by air were logistically unsound, and the new route would have to be something that was dependable. And repeatable.

He came up with the idea one day when he and Tracy cruised the *Banduzul* in U.S. waters near Orcas Island in Puget Sound. They slowed, approaching a sports diving site. Haslett stopped and chatted the dive master, who freely passed the international boundary every day, picking up clients and gear. The master said he'd been doing this twenty years and checked only once for safety issues. Never for contraband.

"My air tanks and the compartments on my inflatable could be filled with drugs, bombs, and guns," he said with a chuckle. "They'd never know."

Haslett filed it away. He'd scuba-dived in the past and decided to take it up again – only this time as a business.

Ghomes had a machinist who built custom bikes for the Angels. Between them, they fabricated air tanks with removable lower sections that unscrewed by fine threads. This accessed an inner compartment which held up to five kilos, hermetically sealed in clear, poly bags. The machining was precise, nearly impossible to discover with a naked eye. Any contamination from loading was eradicated by immersion in salt water; the only detection being scanning through X-Ray. But these tanks would never be scanned.

Next, they modified the inflatables. Tracy purchased five, 14-foot Bombards, in which they built false floors. The boats held fifty kilos and could be driven or towed to their destination. One shipment alone, an inflatable with eight scuba tanks, could move ninety kilos – worth 2.5 million bucks. That was before being stepped on. Ounced. Cut multi-times. Then grammed-up, or rocked-out at the street.

While Ghomes made the tanks, Haslett found the warehouse. The old fish cannery at Bamfield showed up on a court ordered sale. Tracy bid it for a song, flipping it for a ridiculously inflated price to her new company, High Seas Charters. She took the profits, along with those from another laundering venture – the patent on the improved diving tanks – socking them in an offshore account labeled 'Retirement Fund'.

High Seas fronted as a legitimate operation. They'd renovated the cannery to appear as a lodge complete with chef's kitchen, dining hall, and common area, as well as hotel-type rooms for the guests. What wasn't legitimate was the warehouse, accessible only through a passageway, disguised much as Art had once done with his lab.

They replaced the dilapidated floats and the collapsing fuel shack, then bought all new equipment. An F-350 dualie pick-up and a white, logo'd cube van for moving gear. A passenger van for their guests. Trailers for inflatables. Scores of steel tanks; some with compartments, some without. Racks of dry suits, masks, regulators, buoyancy compensators, weights, and the like. Their signage and web presence projected a professional image. They were properly licensed. Even current with compo and good with the tax man. Soon, High Seas was swamped with reservation requests; all turned down – always booked up – full of Angels and trusted associates.

Groups of two, three, or four would come in, stay several days, head out on the water and out of sight, then return in the evening. Sometimes they'd actually go diving. They'd be driven in by the van, or flown to Bamfield's gravel strip. They'd bring in empty tanks; sometimes an inflatable. Then, they'd leave loaded; heading back to one central location. The Lake of the Woods, near Kenora in northwestern Ontario on the Minnesota border.

Through Ghomes, the HAs out of Winnipeg, Manitoba, built an identical charter business run by a particularly treacherous biker named Jinx. The lake crossed miles of international boundary, holding hundreds of islands with thousands of bays, in both the Province of Ontario and the State of Minnesota.

An impossible border to secure.

* * *

The Bamfield warehouse ran smooth from the get-go; processing one small, four-ton load before *The Big Easy* was snagged in the fall, enroute with a second, seven-ton shipment. That forced Plan B. The diversion. It was pure serendipity – the perfect solution to securing the big picture, feed the political needs of a large seizure, and get Archie Wiggers off the hook.

There was enough product warehoused to withstand a delay. That gave Moloci time to work his illusion. It was so simple. They had the reject stockpile at Santa Barbara to dispose of. The sub would be scuttled anyway. And Ghomes had some housekeeping to do. *The Big Easy* would accompany the sub; otherwise it would run empty. Both the ship and the sub were under the control of the RCMP and the DEA. Wiggers had conned a contract to go Scott-free with his ship, once the sub was handed-off.

But no one said where he could go after.

And no one said what else he could bring in.

The Big Easy was long gone now, nearly back in Colombia for a refill. It had run straight to Bamfield, lights out, while the takedown was underway.

Eighteen tons of cocaine concentrate, stashed in her hold, had been quietly removed and stored in the warehouse; already letting out in a controlled manner to the streets of North America.

That was secure.

* * *

But what wasn't secure was the future of Tracillina Williams, Robert Haslett, and, of course, Sergeant Sharlene Bate. They had one common threat to be dealt with.

One even more murderous than Ghomes.

Chapter 38

Friday, July 27th, 2012
6:25 pm
Access Self Storage
Richmond, British Columbia

Ghomes and Haslett made a fast drive to the Vancouver ferry, catching the 3:15, heading straight to Richmond and a mini-storage compound near YVR where they secured product in transit.

They locked-up the loaded Bombard with its coke-laden tanks, then waited inside Haslett's truck. Haslett thumb-drumming the wheel. Ghomes slouching in the passenger side. It was hot and humid this early evening, and they kept the engine running with the air conditioner growling away. Ghomes insisted the windows stay closed, avoiding any chance of eavesdropping. In fifteen minutes, Tracy pulled up, parked her Audi, and got in behind Ghomes with a burgundy, leather folio bag in hand.

"So that sunavawhore's been stealing my fuckin' money!" Ghomes smashed his meat-hook hard on top of the dash.

Tracy recoiled. "Ridge has been stealing *our* money, Robin. There is a business relationship here. Remember? It belongs to all of us."

"Yeah, well I know what part of him's gonna be your share. You'll be able to hold the fuckin' thing in one hand and lick..."

Haslett cut in. "Yeah, well, we're still gonna have to get a hold of the bastard first."

"There is no way he is coming into Canada. I am sure of that," Tracy said. "But I know how to get him close. And I doubt that he knows we suspect him. He has hidden this carefully."

Ghomes glared at her. "So where's the proof?"

"It is all in here." Tracy produced a manila folder with yellow hard-copies. "It establishes a pattern of significant funds being owed to the Organization by his downline. Exactly one point eight-four million dollars is unaccounted for. My calculations clearly put the shortage under his control, and I have no doubt he has made false returns. I will show you."

Ghomes snatched Tracy's balance sheet. He grabbed a calculator and pen from his black Harley vest. Checked figures. Inked a few notes on the back of his wrist. Grunted. Then checked and re-checked again. He sat twenty seconds, brown face gone red, before roaring a "Fuuuck!", crushing the calculator with his bare hands, and firing plastic bits on the floor.

"So how long's this fuckin' shit been going on?" Ghomes turned at Tracy, crumpling the papers into a ball, chucking, and just missing her face.

Haslett tensed, about to drop Ghomes, but Tracy's quick signal held him off. Ghomes stared at her, arm over the seat. She stared right back. Ghomes broke eye contact, shoving himself back towards the dash. Haslett leaned against the driver's door, taking out a toothpick, clamping down hard with his jaw. Tracy stayed just as she was.

"Ever since the new route started," she told him.

"How long you known 'bout it?"

"Well, I have been suspicious for a month. I spoke to Ridge twice, but he gave me reasonable answers. It was not until early this morning when I ran an audit that I became sure. He has gone to a lot of work to cover it up, but he does not understand my system. There is no other explanation. The money is missing and he damned well knows about it."

"Why didn't you say sumpin before now, Tracy?"

"I was unsure, Robin. I was not going to make this type of accusation without proof. That would be stupid of me."

Ghomes thought a bit. "Yeah, okay. So, what're we gonna do before I cut his fuckin' throat?"

"I have a plan," Tracy said, never taking her eyes off him. "I would not be here without a plan."

Ghomes frowned.

Tracy smiled. "We will steal it back."

Ghomes took a long, hard look at Tracy, then at Haslett, who sat with the toothpick in his teeth and a nearly invisible receiver in his left ear.

"Now yer talkin' my language," Ghomes said, glinting gold out his mouth.

"Here is what I suggest." Tracy kept smiling.

* * *

Moloci smiled, too – so did Ridge – listening-in through a bug in the truck.

Chapter 39

Monday, July 30th, 2012
4:35 pm
Clearwater Diving Charters
Kenora, Ontario

"Bob. Meet my bro, Jinx." Ghomes introduced Haslett to the tattooed, hairy, sawed-off little biker.

Jinx eyed around, giving Haslett the thumb-locked shake. They stood in the sliding-glass doorway to Clearwater Charters on the picturesque waterfront in downtown Kenora, by the north shore of the Lake of the Woods, 120 miles east of Winnipeg, Manitoba.

"Welcome to suckin' 'n fuckin' Ontario," Jinx said, voice idling like an old, two-cylinder Knucklehead. He was a full-patch with the Winnipeg HAs, but lived in Kenora most of his life, except for eight years in Stony Mountain on a beef, plea-bargained down to manslaughter.

Ghomes and Haslett had left Vancouver early Saturday morning, this time in Ghomes's black truck, crossing western Canada in three days. Ghomes insisted on taking his Suburban, towing the loaded inflatable containing the eight full, sealed tanks, now simmering in the sun on Clearwater's west side.

Tracy insisted Haslett go along – not as a second driver – but to keep Ghomes in line.

"No violence until we get money," she'd told him.

Surprisingly, Ghomes agreed. But, then, Ghomes had a different definition for the term violence and a different mission in mind for Haslett.

Jinx scoured out back, then strode them away from the shop, up to the parking lot where heat waves miraged off gooey-grey asphalt, feeling safe from electronic eavesdropping here. They stood in a circle. Jinx rubber-necked, then huddled in tight for a talk.

"Ya know? This really fuckin' surprises me." Jinx rumbled, knurling his deathhead ring in a palm. "I known that cocksucker a long time. I never got no fuckin' suspicion he'd ever rip us. This don't make no sense to me."

"I seen the proof," Ghomes confirmed.

"This all comes from that Tracy broad? The money bitch?" Jinx grilled him.

"She always been a hundred percent," Ghomes assured.

Jinx jabbed at Haslett. "She's your ol' lady, right?"

"Right."

Jinx revved right up. "She fuckin' well better be right if we're gonna pull off sumpin like this…"

Ghomes interrupted. "I known her way longer than even Bob here." He one-arm hugged Haslett. "And you know who her fuckin' dad was. She'd never fuck us over. She even looks after my own money, for fuck's sake."

Jinx gawked about, nose twitching. He'd been born in the business, instinctively not trusting anyone outside the brothers. Especially not citizens like Tracy or Haslett.

But he trusted Ghomes. He'd been Ghomes' brother a long, long time, and there was a saying within the brotherhood: *Angels Forever – Forever Angels.*

"Yer fuckin' convinced her shit's solid?" Jinx had throttled back.

"She's no sweetbutt," Ghomes defended.

Jinx paused. He scanned the sky at some contrails, then brought himself back down to earth. "Okay. Good 'nough for me. So this is what's happenin'." He squinted far left, then hard right, and his tone muffled out. "Ridge is expectin' the ninety keys you guys brought in with the tanks and that little fuckin' blow-up so we cut a deal at twenty-seven nine per key but it's rounded out to a flat two point five even."

Ghomes was pleased.

Jinx's looked over his shoulder, then chuckled with a black, bushy grin. "I give him a little discount for cash up front."

Ghomes nudged Haslett. "Gotta like it."

"Gotta fuckin' love it!" Jinx cracked wide-open, punching Haslett's arm.

Haslett said nothing. He'd been watching Jinx wander – one eye looking at you, the other one looking for you – sizing Jinx up as a psychopathic, leather-clad munchkin.

Jinx backed-off on his larynx. "All in U.S. hundreds. That explains why he's cool showin' up hisself. That's some major fuckin' coin, and he ain't gonna risk it to no one else."

Ghomes scowled. "A lotta fuckin' coin that's owed to me."

"But it's fuckin' risky, ya know." Jinx sniffed and stared south. "It's in the fuckin' States."

"Fuck the States," Ghomes said with a grunt.

Jinx head-snapped, frowning up at the brother. "Careful on sayin' that. Them fuckin' Americans play hardball."

"So does we." Ghomes made it known.

Jinx checked his back. "Okay, so we're takin' your rubber fuckin' boat and tanks and stayin' at the shack tonight."

"Where the fuck's that?" Ghomes demanded.

"An island. Just on our side. Then, tomorrow, we run the border 'n meet up with the Minneapolis bro's. Ridge, he'll be at the Warroad airport just before noon. He's flyin' in to pick up the load which is goin' to his Newark downline."

Ghomes nodded approval.

Jinx stopped. He surveyed the lake, then ripped out a straight-piping laugh.

"How things fuckin' change, eh? I been usin' this route with Ridge for years now, but always gone Minnesota to here. Summer by boat. Winter by snow machine. Now it's goin' the other way." He cracked his knuckles. "Hehh! Fuck! But it's been a long fuckin' time since I put my hands on the shit myself." Jinx fisted a palm. "That's what I got fuckin' strikers for."

"Thank fuck for strikers." Ghomes grinned, glinting gold, and grinding an elbow into Haslett's left side.

Jinx glanced around. "So I got two fuckin' strikers comin' with us to drive the inflatable and follow with a guard boat. You guys come with me in the speedboat. Two more'll meet us at the dock in Warroad. They got two vans over there to drive us to the strip."

Jinx crowed some more, sniffed, and squeezed his nose. Haslett felt like he was watching TV with someone that had both ADD and the remote.

"Bob, you n' me drive one van with Robin stashed in the back. The strikers, they drive the goods in the other. We do the motions. Ridge, he checks quality 'n quantity. Then I sucker him to Robin. Bob, you stand six with your piece. Robin 'n me'll get the cash off the plane. Then we all fuck off with him in the van n' the coin 'n the load."

Ghomes fist pumped. Jinx rubbed his hands, eyes like paranoid pinballs.

Ghomes turned. "Then, Bob, you whack him 'n dump the fucker. Simple."

Jinx nearly came in his pants.

Ghomes gleamed at Haslett. "Fuckin' classic rip."

"Like the old days." Jinx hit it wide-open.

"The good old days." Ghomes slapped their backs.

"Let's ride," said Jinx.

* * *

Haslett went to the rear of Ghomes's Suburban, taking out his green logo'd army bag, the hard black case about two feet long containing a weight of eight pounds, and the soft-sided one, holding his computer. He packed his gear down to the dock, set it in the bow of Jinx's speedboat, and got in.

Ghomes backed his blacked-out 4X4 down a ramp, letting the Bombard float free from its trailer. A short, fat striker climbed onboard, firing-up the little RHIB's outboard, casting away. A tall, skinny one followed behind in an open, sixteen-foot aluminum.

Ghomes parked his Suburban, humped it down, and put himself into the speedboat. Jinx flicked the key. The engine caught. He dropped it in forward. They sputtered out of the marina to an open stretch where he hit it, speeding south towards the maze of treed islands. The strikers chased along with the product.

Jinx opened a red plastic cooler, cracking a Molson's. He gave it to Ghomes, popping another, handing towards Haslett, who declined.

Ghomes took a big slurp and let out a belch. "Fuckin' pussy don't drink."

"His fuckin' loss." Jinx snatched it back, guzzling down.

"I'm looking forward to this," Ghomes said, wiping foam from his mouth. "I think I'm gonna really fuckin' enjoy it!"

"I sure as fuck am." Jinx lit a doobie, toked, and passed it on over to Ghomes.

"Hope you both do," said Haslett, holding a toothpick.

Chapter 40

The Beechcraft King Air that flew Raymond Ridge into Warroad was an asset of the American government, though its registration said corporate. It scorched on the grey, concrete tarmac with its fuselage door open, stairs resting down.

Ridge stood at the base, sweating – a bit from humidity – but mostly from the effect of a Kevlar vest. He watched as two white, unmarked, Chevy panel vans crawled up to a chain-link fence topped with loops of razor wire.

The Beech pilot punched a code into an electronic control box, letting the security gate rattle aside. He waved the vans towards the airplane, where an ExxonMobil fuel truck sat idling on its far side. Three workers wearing red, long-sleeved coveralls milled about. One moved the fuel hose. One checked tire pressure. One inspected the port engine through an open hatch.

Ridge gave the first van a hi-sign, seeing Jinx grinning behind the wheel with Haslett expressionless on the other side. Both vans backed-in against a large, green, metal-clad hanger. Jinx got out, gawked around, then strolled towards the Beech.

Haslett exited, made distant eye contact with Ridge, turned, and slipped away, carrying the hard black case. Ridge saw him disappear in the shade behind a small, yellow, wooden hanger, but couldn't see Haslett unlock the clasps and snip the flex-strip with a tiny, diamond-edged cutter.

Ridge knew what was up. He'd arranged to have Haslett designated as another type of federal asset, permitted to carry firearms. He'd also arranged a designation for Ghomes.

* * *

"Hey Ray. Long time." Jinx gave Ridge the thumb-locked biker-shake.

"Good to see you." The big American smiled, handing a vigorous one back.

"You, too, man." Jinx chuckled and eyed about.

"So how's your old brother, Ghomes?"

"Gettin' old. Fucker sends his regards."

"Likewise. Haven't seen the peckerhead in long while. I'm looking forward to it again someday."

If you only knew, asshole, you'd be fuckin' runnin', Jinx thought.

If you only knew, you little fuck, you'd be long gone, thought Ridge.

"Product's in the other van." Jinx nodded to it.

"Cash is on the plane. Let's do it."

They walked behind the second van where the tall, thin striker cracked the doors. The fat one and two sweaty others were inside with the tanks unscrewed and the kilos neatly laid on a Teflon mat. Fifty wrapped bricks from the Bombard floor were systematically stacked to one side.

Jinx climbed in. Ridge followed, carrying a blue, nylon sports-bag. Fat boy had an electronic scale set up which Ridge calibrated with brass weights from his bag.

It was warm as a senior citizens home in the van. Jinx got out and hung behind, crowing his pin-pricky eyes. Haslett stood in the shadows by the yellow hanger.

Two vehicles pulled up. One, a mechanic's truck with two occupants. The other, a FedEx cube-box with a lone driver.

The process started. Ridge took a field test-kit, slitting brick after brick, randomly sampling for purity. For twenty minutes, he probed and weighed, wrote figures, did longhand, then stuck out his head and thumbed Jinx.

"Weight is exact. Purity average of ninety-seven percent. Fucking excellent!"

"Nothin' but the best for you, m'man." Jinx said, laugh as fake as an old porn-star's climax.

Ridge got out, slapping Jinx on the shoulder. "It's all good. Time for your cash."

Ridge stepped ahead. He walked by the first van and on towards the King Air. Jinx trailed a bike-length behind, head swiveling.

"Hang on, Ray," Jinx called. "Got sumpin in here for ya." He'd stopped and opened the first van's rear door. Ridge came back and looked in.

"Hello, you thieving cunt," growled the voice from the darkness.

Ridge saw a glow of gold teeth and the glint of a silver blade as Jinx pulled a .380 ACP, sticking it to Ridge's ribs.

The mechanics saw it. They gathered their tools. FedEx readied to roll-up his door. Fuel-man replaced his hose, picking up something else. Hatch-inspector moved to greet the mechanics. They seemed to pay no attention as Ghomes, Jinx, and Ridge approached the airplane steps.

"Play it easy, guys." Ridge kept his hands in the open. "Money's in bags at the front. And put that thing away, Jinx, you fucking idiot. You're a fucking heat-score. There's no need for that."

"There is for this." Ghomes held his knife by the grip, blade up his sleeve.

Jinx gloated. Ghomes grinned and head-snapped at Haslett, who'd caught up. Jinx glanced to his right, seeing Haslett move ahead with a blackish-grey metal box in one hand. A worker seemed distracted. Jinx looked about, thought twice, and shoved the little heater back in his pants.

"You guys fuckin' stay here and watch him." Ghomes pointed at Ridge, then at the steps. "I'm goin' in."

Ghomes tromped up the stairs and entered the plane. His cardiac nearly arrested.

Two men were in uniforms. A tall third, at least 6-5, in plainclothes with slicked-back silver hair, turned and smiled.

"WHAT THE FUCK!"

Ghomes's voice was the last thing Jinx ever heard. He was raising the .380 at Ridge's head when two 9-mm bullets drilled Jinx an inch apart in the middle of the chest, dropping him like a lead balloon. Instinctively, a third signed Jinx's forehead. Right in the center.

One plane-width back, FedEx rolled-up the door. Grenades flash-banged in both the white vans as black-kit figures swarmed into magnesium smoke, taking out the tall, the fat, and the other stunned bikers. Fuel-man raced the stairs. A third uniform stepped from the plane's cargo curtain, placing a hair-triggered Glock at the base of Ghomes' brain.

Ghomes didn't need to be told. His eyes cored a hole through Moloci. His grip released. His knife clattered. Fuel-man snapped on cuffs. One uniform began to speak.

"Robin Ghomes. United States Marshals. We have a warrant for your arrest under the Foreign Narcotics Kingpin Designation Act. You are a prisoner of the American government. You have the right to remain silent. Anything you say, can and will..."

* * *

You could hear the roar out of Ghomes back in Bamfield.

Chapter 41

Thursday, August 2nd, 2012
11:40 am
United States Federal Correctional Complex
Terre Haute, Indiana

"Where's my fuckin' money, Tracy!" Ghomes screamed into the phone. "I need my fuckin' money to pay my fuckin' lawyer! That slippery cocksucker Sleeman won't do fuck all without money up front!" He smashed his palm against the thick, riveted-steel door locking him inside a tiny, vomit-green, concrete communications booth, then kicked it hard with a shackled-up, woolen-socked foot.

Three trollish guards eyed Ghomes through a foot-square, Lexan window at the center of the maximum security United States Penitentiary where Kingpins were held. It also held federal inmates facing execution. They were kept in a nasty quadrant called the Special Confinement Unit, the place where Ghomes might face the end of his days.

"You no longer have money, Robin," Tracy said, on a disposable cell phone from the aft deck of the *Bandazul*.

She'd made sure of that. She'd also made sure she was long gone from Vancouver by the time they had this conversation.

"Whut the fuck you mean?"

"Robin. I want you to listen carefully. I am only going to say this once."

"Whut?"

"I have destroyed you financially."

"Huh?"

"I have drained your bank accounts. Your investments no longer exist. I have sold off your stocks, your bonds, and your GIC's. I have liquidated your bullion. I have also shut down your credit cards and closed your lines of credit. All that cash in the safety deposit vault? It is gone. The same with your valuables in my safe."

Ghomes gaped at the cinder-block wall.

"Listen further. John has had proceeds of crime forfeitures placed on your properties, vehicles, and material assets. I have given information to the tax people which put you massively in arrears. I have also developed a profile on your credit rating which appears horrible."

"Whut the fuck you talkin' about, Tracy!" Ghomes managed a croak.

"You are broke, Robin. Flat busted."

"Whuuut?"

"You heard me."

"Fuck you, Tracy! You filthy slut! You get my fuckin' money right fuckin' now or my guys'll come and carve your fuckin' cunt out!"

"That will not happen, Robin."

"You know it will. Yer all fucked if I go down."

"That will not happen either."

"Yer fuckin' rights it will!"

"You know that package which you gave to Wiggers?"

Ghomes hesitated. "How you know 'bout that?"

"You should have been much more careful about who you trusted with such sensitive information. Some of your funds went to purchase that back from him."

"Yer dead, Tracy."

"You are at much more risk of that than me. John has released his coded informant file on you to the Nomad chapter."

Ghomes was the color of a ghost.

"And I would like you to hear something else."

Ghomes could not speak.

"I would like you to think back many years to the time when you poured salt on a poor little slug on my parent's walk. You delighted in its suffering. You forced me to watch, and I shuddered in horror. And that night? You know of it. You fucked me when I was defenseless. Now I have done it to you. It is your time to suffer. I have transferred all your wealth through untraceable accounts, and I created a philanthropist who has donated it all to charity. The children's hospital."

"You Fuckin' Slut!"

"Rot in hell! YOU FUCKING BASTARD!"

Tracy slammed the cell into the deck. It bounced across the planks, through the rails, spiraling down into the cold, green-black of the Pacific.

She stood, said a silent prayer, and made the sign of the cross.

Chapter 42

"That does it for your depositions, Mr. Haslett," the prosecutor said.

He'd flown straight back to Vancouver on the Beechcraft with Ridge and Moloci, right after Ghomes's arrest; now in a carpet-stained, harshly-lit interview room, clearing up legal obligations.

"There's no preliminary hearing for E-Pandemic," the prosecutor told him. "We have direct indictment on these gonads, so we're going straight to trial. Stay in touch with Sergeant Bate, here. And don't worry. Testifying will be safe. We'll do it by video link. The security risk of having you in the courtroom would be unacceptable."

The prosecutor got up, shook their hands, and took his papers, leaving the two sitting across the scarred-up, golden-oak desk. She looked at him. He at her.

Bate broke the silence. "I'm depending on you to explain in court why the purity was so poor. That really worries me. It's going be a disaster if you don't clear it up."

He shrugged.

"Seriously. If anything happens to you... I'm screwed."

He shook his head. "Simple. Like I told you on the phone. I'll just tell 'em the truth. It was a scam by the Colombian agent. He was in a bind with the DEA to save his ass, so he sent them a shipment of shit from some hybrid experiment they had go wrong in Colombia. Don't matter. It's still coke. Sure the clowns here were expectin' pure stuff, but they're still guilty of intent to traffic, even though they got suckered in. And that's straight goods."

She saw the usual toothpick in his lips. They were alone. The operation was over. The evidence was disclosed. Bate took her best shot.

"I asked you before. You didn't give me straight goods, and I need to know this. Why did you do this? I mean. You didn't get paid. It's not your job. You took huge risks. You know the Angels are going to be after you forever. You don't even want the witness protection program."

He stared up at the single, bare bulb.

"Between you and I," she said. "And I guarantee it stays right in this room. What is really going on?"

He thought. She waited. His gaze dropped to hers.

"You know, Sergeant? Sometimes you just gotta do the right thing."

Bate saw intensity in his eyes. "What is the right thing?"

"To finish off sumpin that got started a long time ago."

"Try me."

"Couple a things goin' on here, Sergeant." He shifted positions. "One is people I owe sumpin to."

Bate listened.

"Moloci. He treated me real good. Changed things around to give me a new start when I was down 'n out. And there's a lady who took a chance on me. We all had problems to be dealt with. That's over and done now, but I still got an old friend out there... somewhere... who needs a hand yet."

She kept listening. He kept talking.

"The Angels? Fuck 'em. I tangled with a demon far more dangerous than those assholes ever will be. I'll keep my wits."

Bate reached out and touched his knee. "For myself. I need to know."

He glimpsed down. "You got it figured out, mostly. I know you snooped in my computer. You just don't know why."

She kept at him. "I know who you really are."

No response.

"And I know about that thing."

He took a fresh toothpick from his pocket. "Well, I'll tell you this... The drug thing? It's way bigger than you might think. The takedown? Just a big fuckin' smokescreen. A diversion."

Bate's pulse quickened.

"Sure, it caught some crooks, seized some shitty coke, and looked good for the troops. But that's nothin' compared to what they really got goin' on."

"What are you saying?"

He looked up and away. "They're tryin' to maintain social order. Tryin' to prevent these wars from breakin' out when things get outta balance."

"I don't understand."

"They know no one's ever gonna stop the demand for drugs, so the best they do is try n' control the supply. Keep it flowin' smooth, you know? I just helped 'em out a bit, till I finished a thing of my own."

"Who are 'they'?"

"Some kinda outfit no one's supposed to know nothin' about."

"I...?"

He looked back at Bate. "You know that old guy that keeps showin' up? The one that peers over his glasses?"

"You mean Kresslauer?"

"Yeah. Well... I don't know if that's his real name, but it don't matter. That guy is a spook of the highest order. He's behind it. He and a big, black American. Moloci's part of it, too. They're all tight."

Bate gasped.

"Oh, no. Don't get it wrong. Moloci's not crooked. Oh fuck! Far from it. Done sumpin stupid early in his career, but made it work best for him. He never done nothin' that wasn't best for what they call the big picture, and he never pocketed a dime for himself. The man lives in a real world. Not in some politician or some lawyer's dream. He knows it gets ugly and keepin' moral ain't always keepin' legal."

Bate swallowed.

"No one agonized more n' him when these drug wars broke out. He warned people for years this shit was gonna happen. These guys know the war on drugs is stupid and can never be won. See... They believe there's much more to human existence, and they think drugs are just a necessary escape. Like some kinda portal to another world of consciousness. That's why people want 'em. It's natural. They know the demand has always been around and always will be. No one can stop it. So they try n' keep some kinda orderly supply goin', so the balance of power don't get upset and a war starts. They say it's all for national security. The big picture, they call it."

Bate swallowed again.

"And believe me, they're fuckin' serious about it. So, over the years, Moloci did his best to help 'em control things. I hear 'em talkin' a lot, but that shit's way beyond me. I got my own issue to work out."

He paused and wiggled the toothpick.

"By the way... Don't be surprised if they approach you to get on board. They like you and they need a police contact here now that Moloci's gone."

"God! I can't believe what I'm hearing."

"Straight goods, Sergeant." He pointed at the recorder they'd used for his depositions. "Noticed that thing wasn't turned on."

Bate reached for it.

"If this goes outside the room, I'll just deny it."

She smiled faintly. "It never will."

"You know? Probably no one would believe you anyway."

He winked, got up, and moved towards the door. She put her arm straight out.

"The other thing?"

He stopped.

"Why those two guys?" she asked.

He looked Bate right in the eye. "That was justified."

"Justified?"

"What goes around, comes around."

"Try me again."

He shifted his focus vacantly beyond her.

"You know, Sergeant? I will some day. I trust you. You coulda ratted me out and you didn't. You were good to me and that's worth sumpin. But first, I need to do a little... call it... soul searchin'."

* * *

She stood at the window and watched as he walked out of Headquarters, crossed the lot, and got into his Excursion.

He sat there and thought; thinking of a lot of things. Order and chaos. Life and death. Good and evil. Those sorts of things.

He thought of Tracy. And of Moloci. Of his mom, his dad, and his granddad. Of Bude. Kaash Klao. The Kushtaka. And the informants.

But mostly he thought of Maria and Gabriella. They never left his mind no matter how much time passed. He opened a watertight container, took out their photos, and wondered just how different his life would be if they were still here.

Sharlene watched as the ghost put his black truck in gear and drove off.

Part Six

The Soul Search

Chapter 43

Thursday, August 30th, 2012
9:55 am
School of Archeology and Anthropology
A. D. Hope Building at the Australian National University
Canberra, Australian Capital Territory

"Now mind me platypus duck, Bill. It's me cobbers from cooee! Foinly 'ear in down under! A rip snorter!" Professor Holger Sorenson beamed out of a scruffy, grey, hedgehog face squashed on top of a Tilley-clad, Humpty-Dumpty torso. "And tar for d'quid to gets me snoosin' around. A fair sucka the sav, oid say."

Tracy and Haslett just looked at each other.

"That's banana-bender! Sneeeee! It's Queenslander! Means pleasure to meet you and thanks for the donation to my research. Very generous! Hee-heh-hee-heh-hee-heh-hee!" Sorenson giggled away like a creaky old porch swing, then jabbed his right index finger straight up. "As in proper shirty! Big bonza bik-kies makes me cracka fatty. A ridgy-didge it is! Hoo-Hoo! Better 'n a brass razoo. Keep me flat out like a lizard drinkin'."

"Pardon me?" Tracy asked.

Sorenson squealed and full-on belly laughed. Then stopped.

His cheeks sucked in and his eyes bulged out as if suddenly grabbed and probed up the anus. He let off a "Hhoorrrh" then a "Nnheee", going headlong into a hacking fit, bending over and beating his breast like a low-land gorilla giving itself CPR. Out popped a hard wad of something similar to tangled coconut fiber coated with a purply-black glisten. It hit the stone floor between Tracy's feet, hip-hopped through, and was long-gone under the banister behind her.

Haslett turned to split. Tracy grabbed his wrist and held fast.

The Professor recovered from his conniption, seizing their hands and pumping like priming a well, then spun Tracy, pressing his palm to the small of her back. He gripped Haslett by the shirt, herding them across the marble mezzanine, through huge, double Blackwood doors and into his private space overlooking the university's Chanceley Annex and the Fellows Oval green-space.

Haslett stopped in his tracks.

A menacing collection – dozens of abominable, indigenous masks – gawked right back at him; suspended by thin, stainless cables, eye-hooked to Tassie-oak, amber wall panels and spot-lit by bluish-cool beams of halogen. The room was more museum than office – a magnificent man-cave, or a tomb yet to be raided. A frankincense mist of balsamic-sweet fragrance swirled in lemony hues from a liquid diffuser and waltzed up their noses at the composure of Wagner who maestroed Die Walkure; slowly turned on a vinyl disc, needle-scratched within a Malaysian teak console.

Tracy stayed rigid, soaking it in.

The right wall rose eighteen feet – floor-to-ceiling with claret-stained, rasped Kepelan-plank shelves straddling a massive, draped Palladian window; stacked with books, scrolls, and bundles upon bundles of dusty documents. Some had been leather-bound and buckled tight, hundreds of years before. Some were of parchment and some were of papyrus.

The opposite wall, one tightly cross-hatched with inch-round poles cut from bamboo and Malacca cane, was slathered with cob-webbed paraphernalia straight out of Indiana Jones – shields and symbols, wrought iron hatchets, feather-trimmed blow-guns with obsidian-tipped darts, long flaring didgeridoo horns, a moldy green canvas haversack stuffed full with teeth and hair and who-knows-what-else, blanched bones, bullroarers, boomerangs, and beaded but-but bags.

Haslett squeezed Tracy's arm, jerking his head to left-rear.

Three shaggy clumps with tiny raisin eyes dangled from komodo-skin thongs knotted to a woomera-clad war-spear, horizontally impaled deep in a blonde, tallowwood post. He was sure they were shrunken heads.

Then – Haslett jumped nearly clear out of his skin. Behind the wee noggins, wedged in the corner, was a bi-pedal figure, cloaked in ragged brown hides with a hideous face and fiery eyes.

Sorenson caught the reaction. He grinned like a rooted-out wombat and wound up with a turbo-prop whine. "Nnnnnnyyyeeeeeee! That's Bakwas! The Wild Man of the Woods! He does that to people! eeeeeEEE."

Haslett looked at Sorenson. Then back at the monstrosity. He shuffled away, eying over his shoulder, keeping the devil in sight.

"He's a gift from the Kwakwaka'wakw people up the northwest coast of Canada, near where you're from." The portly man bent forward, putting his arms high with hands dangling down, tip-toeing towards Haslett. "He shifts his shape to steal your soul and spin it off to the dark world of ghosts."

Sorenson let go a Gatling-gun laugh, trailed by four wheezy pig-snorts, and just about got punched out.

"Don't fuckin' do that, man! It freaks me out." Haslett's fist clenched; bicep tensed. Tracy reined him in.

"There is something you must know, Professor," she said, clasping Haslett's hand, cinching him tight to her side. "There is more to our being here than I told you in emails. What you just said... and the sight of that creature... is exceptionally traumatic for him."

"Oh! So sorry, mate." Sorenson whacked Haslett hard between the shoulder blades. He plunked himself down on his desk and pointed to two tortoise-shell, high-back chairs built into a carved wooden pulpit. "Come. You two sit for a yabber. Tell me the yarn. Give 'er a good cracka the whip."

* * *

The Williams Organization was disbanded now. Tracy had fled Canada three days before the phone call from Ghomes – to sanctuary onboard the *Bandazul*, already moored across the line in Washington State. It was planned that way. Part of Ridge's plan.

Haslett caught up after finishing his depositions with Sergeant Bate, driving the black Excursion to the Olympic Peninsula and leaving it for Moloci to pick up at Port Townsend, where he'd hidden the yacht two weeks before; taking with him the reason of why the informants had to be murdered.

Moloci had manufactured new identities for the pair – just as he'd once done for Haslett – back in the Monagham days. The *Bandazul*'s name and registration were also changed, now the *Walkabout*, flying the Southern Cross out of Cairns. It'd been stocked with provisions during planning. Tracy made sure their affairs were in order and it would appear relocation. She notified the banks, the utility companies, and the government. She'd paid all their bills – credit cards, insurance, fuel and moorage, cells, satellite TV, and post-office box. Even their taxes. Then she closed the accounts with a forwarding address to Saint Kitts and Nevis in the Caribbean.

Tracy Williams planned to go out clean.

She also planned on going to the other side of the world.

Their escape, down-under to the land of Oz, took twenty-five days; stopping first in Hawaii, then taking on more fuel and fresh water at stops in Tarawa and Vanuatu before arrival in Brisbane. There, they got land-legs, then flew on south in their quest to Canberra.

Tracy had been referred to Professor Sorenson during her trip to the archives at the National Museum of the American Indian in New York. They'd corresponded by email, discussing her and Haslett's interest in mythical beings and soul retrieval. She'd arranged for a private meeting, sending him a generous donation as a gesture of good faith.

Holger Sorenson was a Dane, a Nobel-prize-runner-up Dane, long ago drifting off to the southeastern Ring of Fire and becoming an anthropological expert in indigenous mythical studies.

He was also a passionate believer in Shamanism.

* * *

"Now that is a whopper!" Sorenson said. "I'd think you'd come me the raw prawn if I didn't know it was bloody oath. And so sorry, mate. This is nothing to jib of. Nothing at all. I'd no idea. No worries, though! I'll kark Bakwas if he makes you wobbly."

"It's alright," Haslett said. "You get used to him after awhile."

He'd eased a bit. For years he'd told no one the Teslin story of Kaash Klao and the Kushtaka – except for Tracy, Moloci, and some small, bearded shrink who'd laughed before getting stuffed in a garbage can.

Tracy spoke. "Now you understand what he has been through, Professor. Are you at all able to help?"

Sorenson pointed at himself. "Fair dinkum if I can't." He waved the back of his hand over his shoulder towards the north. "But I know of a Sheila who can... Doctor Nez. Remember, I am a scientist. Not a spiritualist. In no way do I claim to be a Shaman. Now she, mates, is one."

"She?" Haslett asked. "Like a Shawoman?"

"Haaaa! A Sha-Shelia! Ne-heeeee. Nnnin-ahww." Sorenson jumped up, stomped a sock-footed jig in his Birkenstocks, then stopped and blinked his blue eyes. He smacked both his ears, bobbled his head, and focused his sight on the pulpit. "Tan me hide when I've died, Clyde. These are misunderstood people! Though they've been around least forty-thousand years. Long before any of the pommy religions we have today."

Tracy glanced at Haslett from the corner of her eye; he doing the same thing to her. She unclasped her hands and leaned forward.

"Professor," she said. "When Bob first told me about Kaash Klao, the Tlingit Shaman, I had a vision of some witch doctor casting spells by dancing about a fire with a bone and a chicken. But when I started reading... in the library, at the museum, and on the Internet... I had no idea just how complex and legitimate Shamanism is."

"Oh! These are men of the highest degree." Sorenson stopped. He snapped his head, hummed, and grinned at Tracy. "And women, too. In fact, historically there were just as many females, I'll call 'em nicely, in Shamanic practice. They earned the highest respect in their societies. Shamanism was of immense social significance for the health of the group, who largely depended on faith in the powers of the Shaman for their survival. Not just for physical and spiritual health, but to locate food sources. Predict the weather. Dispense justice in the community. These powers... you can call them psychic powers if you'd like... must not be readily dismissed."

Haslett went to speak. Sorenson stood, raised a finger, and kept on.

"No! These people had taken a degree in a secret life. A step which implied discipline. Intelligence. Mental and physical training. Courage and perseverance. But our... Eh Eh Ehem... modern and enlightened world... has blown them off. Tarnished them as rogues, charlatans, and ignoramuses. Ockers. Blokes several palings short of a fence."

Tracy smiled – till Sorenson brought out a blotchy-green bandana, blew his nose, and sat back down.

"But far from it. Their powers are not primitive. Not make-believe at all. These are people who have specialized in the workings of the human mind... in the influence of the mind on the body, and... on other minds."

Sorenson scratched his bushy old beard like a dingo ditching fleas, wiping a runny brow with the handkerchief. Tracy slid her hand to her mouth.

"So what exactly is Shamanism?" Haslett asked.

"Well, my boy. Core Shamanism takes some serious squizzing, so let's start with peeling furfie and strike some good oil. This'll be no jiffy, so take a more comfy seat."

He patted his chin with the snot-soiled scarf, stuffed it in his shirt, got up, lifted three wooden Zanzibar spice crates from a tattered chaise lounge, and gave them a quick motion over.

Tracy coughed as she rose, but was instantly clothes-lined by the Professor who'd spied a penny-sized, black spider sporting a red dorsal stripe, defensively backed in a fold of the long chair. He raised his palm like a traffic cop, grabbing something shoe-hornish from a shelf, scooping up the venomous vermin, laying open the window, and flicking it out on the ledge. He shut the sash, gave the pair a barred-tooth sneer with a forefingered-slice across the carotid, seated his guests, dragged over a hefty-legged stool, perched in front as if nothing at all had happened, and started in – now sounding like the worldly professional he really was.

"Quite simply, a Shaman is a man... or a woman... who enters an altered state of consciousness... at will... to contact and utilize an ordinarily hidden source of reality in order to acquire knowledge, power, and methods to help themselves and other persons."

He hauled out the hanky, horked, and hid it back in his pocket. Tracy turned away with a gag.

"Shamanism represents the most widespread and ancient methodology of contacting pure consciousness known to humanity. The knowledge survives today, primarily among indigenous people, some of whom still have primitive cultures. No modern malarkey to mock their intelligence, mates. It was acquired over hundreds of generations, learned, and passed on with virtually no written records. It's from these descendents that we learn Shamanic principles. Remarkably, the methods are near universal, despite these people being totally isolated. Over thousands of years. Continents apart. Through trial and error, people in diverse cultures and ecologies came to the same basic principles of Shamanic power."

He paused, ran both thumb nails across his lips, sunk his head into his shoulders, and peered as if reading their minds.

"Why you ask? Because it works."

Sorenson stood up, waddled to the wall shelves, and pulled out a thin, dog-eared book.

"I must defer to my friend and colleague, Michael Harner, who authored *The Way of the Shaman*. It's the Shamanic Bible. Now, he, has the academic expertise to profess on the subject, though he'd be first to disqualify himself as a true Shaman. Michael spent decades with the tribal peoples. Studying their ancient cultures. Publishing books and papers. He's been a driving force behind the Shamanic renaissance."

He handed the soft-cover to Tracy.

"Before then, Shamanism was rapidly disappearing from the planet. Missionaries. Colonists. Governments and commercial interests. Bless their greedy, coin-sucking hearts. They overwhelmed the native peoples and the ways of their ancients. During the last twenty years, however, Shamanism has returned with startling strength, even to urban bastions such as London and Los Angeles. But this has been subtle. Most of the world's masses are unaware of Shamanism, let alone its return."

Tracy glanced between the book and the Professor.

"There is a rapidly growing movement that's taken up Shamanic practices and made it part of their life. Many educated and thinking people have left the Age of Faith. They no longer trust ecclesiastic, fulla-kangaroo-shit dogma to provide them with evidence of the spirit... that being passed down in anecdotes of competing, culture-bound religious texts from other times and other places. These are simply not convincing any longer."

Tracy leaned back as Sorenson pulled out his mucous-messed mopper.

"No! Not nearly enough to provide paradigms for their personal existence. So, they turned to the New Age. A take from the Age of Science. Now, children of science, myself included, prefer to arrive first hand, experimentally, at our own conclusions as to the nature and limits of what we perceive as reality. Shamanism gives us a way to conduct these personal experiments, for it's entirely to be discovered within one's self. For one's self."

Tracy watched Sorenson scrunch his eyes.

"It's a methodology. Not a religion."

Haslett sat, gazing to the side. Thinking.

"The Age of Science also gave us drugs to alter our state of consciousness. Fast acting, synthetic drugs like LSD, DMT, MDA, and that horribly addictive white lady, cocaine. Not the slower, safer, natural entheogens like marijuana, ayahuasca, psilocybin, mescaline, or even ethanol, which indigenous practitioners incorporated over millennia. Many who've found their way to Shamanism have experimented with psychedelic trips for enlightenment. And for entertainment."

Haslett started to speak. The Professor cut him off.

"True Shamans would be aghast of this! But, most of these day-trippers came of age in the sixties and seventies. They'd no framework. No discipline. No maps for their experiences. This was a hit and miss approach."

Sorenson lowered his voice.

"It's primal human nature... an instinct... to seek out an altered state of consciousness. Many crave the use of drugs to achieve it, rather than allowing the mind to find it naturally, but the easy way out has always been the case. So, as long as there's humanity, there's going to be a demand for drugs. Therefore, there'll always be a supply... as long as someone can line their pockets by distributing them."

Sorenson paused, sizing Tracy and Haslett up and down.

"Unfortunately, ingestion of drugs results in serious ramifications. Not only to the individual, but to society as a whole. I think you get my drift."

Haslett glanced at Tracy. She stared at the floor.

Sorenson set down the sniff-scarf, unbuckled his fifty-four inch belt, zipped open his trousers, and tucked his crinkled, cotton shirt overtop of his boxers.

Tracy stared up at the Professor. Her eyebrows said it all.

Sorenson casually did himself up, and plopped back on his stool to continue.

"The Age of Science also produced the near-death experience on a large scale, thanks to medical breakthroughs which brought many people back from the brink after cardiac arrest. Ironically, many were from drug overdoses. These experiences proved profound. They changed the survivor's convictions of reality and beliefs in the existence of spirit. These people, too, searched for maps and many turned to the ancient Shamanic methods in their quest for enlightenment."

Sorenson grabbed Haslett's arm.

"This includes the out-of-body sensation, the fear-death experience, you report from your encounter with The Kushtaka. We'll yack about that big, bad bastard in a bit."

Tracy squeezed her eyes as the Professor produced his babushka, cleared his throat, spit in, and spoke out.

"What are Shamanic methods, you might ask? Well, they start with ways to induce an altered state of consciousness. This is the state you must achieve for the benefits of enlightenment by contacting non-ordinary sources of information. They require a relaxed discipline with concentration and purpose."

Tracy opened her eyes. The cloth was closing. It looked like it'd captured an oyster.

"Contemporary Shamanism, just as in tribal cultures, primarily uses monotonous percussion sound, the binaural beat stimulation of rhythmic drumming, to induce a hypnotic or trance-like state. This classic, drug-free method is entirely safe. If practitioners fail to maintain focus, they simply return to a normal, waking state. There is no preordained period of entrapment, such as when under the influence of psychedelic drugs."

Sorenson winked and waved his snuff-flag.

"Drugs certainly give no guarantee of a pleasing performance."

He frowned, stuck out his tongue, and kept going.

"Many New Age practices are holistic in approach. They recognize the body must be treated as a whole and is much more than the sum of its parts. Thought field therapy is interesting. So are energy therapies, like Reiki and Shiatsu."

Tracy was on red alert for that thing.

"And then there's the mind-body interventions. Aromatherapy. Biofeedback. Hypnosis. Meditation. And, of course, good ol' yoga. All these use the mind to help healing of the body and maintain wellness, both physically and mentally. This health field represents the rediscovery of many individual methods once widely known in tribal and folk practice. Some of these are quite effective."

Sorenson raised his reading glasses from a lanyard, held them up to the light, and gave them a good rub with his rag. Tracy looked like she'd chewed-up a lemon.

"But Shamanic methods are the full quid. They work surprisingly quick and are bloody efficient. Most people can personally experience in a few hours of Shamanic training what may take years to achieve with meditation, prayer, or chanting. So this makes Shamanism ideally suited to the busy lives of contemporary people, just as it suited the lives of indigenous people who were also consumed with the struggles for survival... running from head-hunters during the day... then jungle, and now corporate... but both having evenings to relax in their cave."

He put on the glasses, squinting through.

"Consider Shamanism as a system of embodying this ancient knowledge that can be devoured timelessly. Shamans seek and get solutions for problems, whether physical or mental. Shamanistic techniques are about changing the state of consciousness to allow for assistance from the non-ordinary source. The spirit world. The world of infinite imagination. Infinite information. Infinite intelligence. Pure thought!"

Sorenson gripped his glasses, licking the lenses and cleaning them hard. Tracy thought she was going to throw-up.

"Another appeal of Shamanism today is that it's spiritual ecology. We have a worldwide environmental crisis looming and Shamanism provides something totally lacking in the world's anthropocentric, mainstream religions. That is reverence for, and spiritual communication with, the other beings on the planet. And with the planet itself. This is not nature-worship. It's actually communicating with the awesome spiritual power of the Earth and all its inhabitants. The birds and the bees. The rocks and the trees. The air and the water. All our relations, as the Lakota Sioux would say."

Sorenson had hidden his hanky. He closed his left eye, leaning back, and retracting his head tight to his shoulders like a ticked-off turtle.

"Do you know what animism is?" he asked.

Tracy and Haslett shook their heads.

"It's the belief that everything has a soul. A life force. The essence to existence. The conduit of consciousness. The intangible field of intelligence that connects with all else including humans, animals, plants, celestial bodies, and the forces of nature."

Sorenson shut his other eye and tugged on his nose, then popped both eyes wide, wide, open. Tracy jumped. He rocked to and fro, humming away, then continued right on with his sermon.

"The ancient Shamans were able to speak with nature. They recognized the power of life and death which the environment held over them. They knew communicating with their relations was essential for survival. That included all their relations. Physical and spiritual. Not only could they heal the sick and prevent illness. They could predict the weather. Track food sources. Instill good. Exorcise evil. Expound wisdom. Entertain in storytelling. Even telepathically spy on their enemies."

The Professor's left hand went horizontal to his curly, grey uni-brow; right index finger up to puckered pink lips, eyes squinting, and head roaming side to side.

"The ancients. Oh, the ancients! They observed the positive and negative system of dichotomies. Good and evil. Life and death. Order and chaos. Those sorts of things. They knew that reality is composed of the world of the living and the world of the dead. They practiced animism, knowing both worlds are controlled by spirits. Everything, they knew, possesses a soul. A life force."

He slid from his stool and crouched like a linebacker.

"They also knew the other world holds mystifying beings. Shapeshifters that take human or animal form. They are evil. Deceitful and deadly. They trick you. Kill you. Steal your soul. Or invade you alive, riding parasitically inside... sometimes for decades... till the energy of your essence expires."

Sorenson lifted his bulk, jabbing his thumb.

"Like The Kushtaka, who is Bakwas over there. The Wild Man of the Woods, who eats only raw meat."

He sat, pulled up his specs, put them on cock-eyed, and peeked overtop at Haslett; already having him diagnosed.

"A Shaman is the protector of souls... an intermediary in the world of the living, and the world of the dead, and also the ghostly world in-between where souls get trapped. In-betweens are dysfunctional souls... not enjoying life among the living, nor finding rest with the dead. They are minds without bodies, who anguish horribly and strive to be set free. Freeing trapped souls is a skilled task... an ancient task... which only a Shaman can perform."

They stared at him.

"In such cases the Shaman undertakes a metaphysical journey, transcending the human condition and passing to a different cosmological plane, somewhere in-between the darkness and the light, to recover that lost... or stolen... spiritual energy, and return it to the patient."

Sorenson stared at them.

"This has proved perilous on occasion. For both Shaman and patient."

Haslett swallowed.

Sorenson mumbled something about '*shooting through*'.

Tracy missed what he'd muttered and spoke up. "We have done a lot of our own research, Professor, but really, we do not understand. We just know that we both need help. All we know... there is something seriously wrong... spiritually... with both of us, and we believe that it lies somewhere in our souls. Whatever that is. If even we have any left... after everything that we have done."

Sorenson saw a tear trickle. Haslett put his arm around her shoulder.

"Oh, your souls are out there, my dear," Sorenson said. "That's not something that can be created or destroyed. They just get sidetracked from time to time. It's going to take some work to reconnect, but that's not something I do."

The Professor touched her knee.

"What I can do is help you understand, by preparing your mind as to what we know about the soul and how it functions. It will make the retrieval process easier. What I do is inform you of the science. It's critical to understand that whatever the mind can conceive and believe, it can achieve. You must believe in the process, as it's the mind that achieves the reconnection to the soul. You must arrive in the proper mindset. You must believe."

Tracy dabbed her eyes. "I am sorry. Please excuse me. I have been holding this in far too long. I just feel terrible, so guilty, about what I have done with my life."

Haslett squeezed.

"Or have not done," she said, almost inaudible.

Sorenson touched her again. "Guilt is in your mind, my dear, not in your soul."

Tracy pondered what the Professor just said.

Haslett held a toothpick to his lips. "So how does all this retrieval stuff work?"

Sorenson grinned. "Well. I'm not going to try and explain the inner workings of Shamanism. That will be much better done by Doctor Leslie Nez. Now, she, mates, is a Shaman. She is the expert. And she's aware of your interest. From our emails, I suspected you'd need her expertise, so I've arranged sessions with her after this. She wanted me to ground you in the science of souls before she takes over."

"So how'd you get into this?" Haslett asked.

"Ah! My original expertise is in physics. That was before I got bored and took up anthropology. I find talking to cannibals in Papua New Guinea much more engaging than sitting with eggheads at Cambridge contemplating quarks, leptons, and gluon fields, as well as chasing after that elusive little bugger, the Higgs Boson, who some call the God particle of quantum entanglement."

Tracy sat upright. Sorenson cupped his hand over his mouth and spoke through it.

"Who I suspect may just be the soul!" he whispered, then let go a hyena-pitched cackle.

"The what?" Tracy's brow rose.

"I'll get around to Mister Higgs. Just bear with me. After I finish, ah, let's say... indoctrinating you... that's a better term than brainwashing. Nyeeee! You'll be having sessions with Doctor Nez near Brisbane, where she's doing her sabbatical at the healing center."

"Seems like she wants to weed us out first," Haslett said. "In case we're some kinda nutbars."

"That may very well be true," Sorenson replied. "But it's time to have a serious discussion about the physical world. The local world. Doctor Nez will explain the spiritual, or non-local world."

Sorenson picked up a long, hollow, tapered object looking very much like a Huli penis-sheath. He tapped it in his palm. Tracy shot a glance at Haslett, grasped his wrist, and looked right back at what the Professor was gripping.

"No one understands why the soul exists," Sorenson said, shaking the sheath. "No one understands why anything exists. The only thing we, as humans, know for sure is that we do exist. As the philosopher Descartes put it, 'I think therefore I am'. Perhaps it's our purpose, our meaning as humans, to discover existence. To witness it for ourselves. Without existence, there'd be nothing to witness, so there'd be no witnesses to nothing. Nnnnyyeeeeee! I love that line! Nnnnyyyaaaw!"

Haslett wrinkled his nose, cocking his head with a squint.

"Now, there are two parts to our human existence. The mind and the body. The mind-body duality. The mind operates in the non-local, spiritual world of consciousness. The body operates in the local, tangible world of physics. The soul operates as a connector, a conduit between the two, allowing a flow of information. It's like a computer system where the body is the hardware, the brain is the software, the mind is the processor, the soul is the server, and consciousness is the information available on the world-wide-web."

Sorenson sucked in some breath.

"The body is finite. The mind is not. The body follows a molecular process. It is conceived. It forms and grows. Repairs and reproduces itself. Then dies and decomposes back to the molecular level. The body is physically created and destroyed, but the matter it's composed from cannot be. It can only be changed. The mind exists outside of the body, outside of physical locality, so the same rules don't apply. Basic stuff, right?"

The Professor pointed the sheath at them. They had to nod in agreement.

"Leaving the mind aside, I know I have many times," Sorenson said with a grunt. "Let's take a look at the physical field in which the body operates. Thinking of a field is the best way to understand the known, local universe. It's like a ball game. Right now, we think of four physical realities in locality. Space. Time. Energy. Matter. But… there's a fifth reality. One that is not physical. One that cannot be measured. One that exists outside of locality… Intelligence. We term this combination STEMI, and we know far more about the first four than the fifth."

They nodded some more.

"Think about space being the ball field itself. It's where we play. We need to play somewhere, right? Time? That's just the measurement of how long we're going to play. The duration. Can't keep it up forever, right, Bob? I know I sure can't no more. Nnnnyyyhaaaaaaaaaa!"

Sorenson erected the pointer and broke into a fit of nearly hysterical laughter, ending in a chorus of camel-like sneezes. Haslett squeezed Tracy's hand. She just rolled her eyes.

"Moving on," Sorenson said, catching his breath. "Energy is the dynamics, like getting off the bench and getting going. Keeping it moving. Hitting it out of the park and getting the crowd roaring. Matter is the ball, the bat, the uniforms, the players, the fans. You know, little stuff like that. It'd be a boring game if no one showed up. Intelligence is the rules... the ideas for the game. It'd be a pretty wacky game if there were no rules."

Tracy smiled. Haslett rubbed his chin.

"Let's look at each of these concepts. Space is that dimension in which objects and events occur, and have relevant position and direction to each other. We know on earth to observe the three dimensions of height, width, and length. It keeps us from walking in front of a trolley. Then there's the fourth. Space-Time. It's also obvious, although most don't recognize it. These four dimensions are fundamental to understanding the physical universe. Oh, there are many theories floating about of additional dimensions. Branes, warps, strings, and M-Theory are fun to ponder, but the four dimensional model works very well."

Sorenson paused. He raised his brow, pulled out his time-piece, swacked it with the stick, and continued.

"Time can be a problem, though. We move freely about in space, but not in time. Time is linear. It's a temporal measurement. Pretty much a one-way street. Time travel makes a great plot for *Back To The Future* and *The Twilight Zone*, but in reality, as the Yanks would say... it ain't never gonna happen. Time is nature's way of preventing everything from happening all at once. Or from doing it over again."

Sorenson paused again. He set down the watch and the wand, taking a swig from a canvas-covered, metal canteen hanging from a strap on the back of a chair. The hanky came out, and he wiped at the spout, generously offering his guests a pull of their own.

Tracy waved a fast refusal, reaching to her bag, and removing a vacuum bottle of chilled, lemon water. She sipped, quickly handing off to Haslett.

Sorenson fell into a long, vacant stare. Tracy waited, looked around, at Haslett, back at the Prof, then interrupted with a hand-circling signal. He startled, snapped his head to one side, and let out a sharp, squeaky "Hmmmmmm".

"Energy. Ha! Some days I have none," he started up. "But energy is a scalar, physical quantity describing the amount of work performed by a force. There are many types of energy, my friends. Nuclear, chemical, kinetic, potential, thermal, sound, gravitational, and that biggie of all, electromagnetism, which is transmitted in waves."

They nodded a bit.

"Now a basic law of physics, the law of conservation of energy, tells us that any form of energy can be transferred to another, but the total remains the same. The total inflow of energy into a system must equal the total outflow. So, all the energy available since the Big Bang is still available to us, and always will be. It changes form all the time, but the fundamentals do not."

Haslett saw Sorenson eye him up, then reach for his rod.

"As an example, Bob... you're a slim fellow, but the potential energy within your roughly hundred and seventy pound mass would be about seven times ten to the eighteenth Joules. Enough to explode with the force of thirty, very large hydrogen bombs... assuming you knew how to liberate it... and really wanted to make a point. You see, everything has this trapped energy, but it's very difficult to get out. Even a uranium bomb, the most energetic thing human beings have ever produced, releases less than one percent of its capability."

Tracy and Haslett were listening. Sorenson touched his tool, winked, and kept on.

"Matter is composed of particles. Anything that has mass, and occupies a volume or space, is matter. But matter needs energy to exist. Like your adversary. The Kushtaka."

Haslett tensed.

"Matter stays matter, until it is accelerated to the speed of light, then, in theory, it converts back to pure energy and ceases to exist. $E=mc2$ and all that crap. But relativity doesn't allow that to easily happen in practice. Remember being taught in school that matter was made up of molecules which are made up of atoms?"

Tracy slid back as he shook his staff.

"Well it still is, but back in your high school days, you were taught that atoms were as small as it got, stopping at protons and neutrons being circled by electrons. We're learning more about quantum physics all the time… aka quantum mechanics. It's the small, small world where the interacting building blocks of the physical universe… fermions of leptons and quarks… are held in check by force fields of gluons and bosons."

"Bosons? What is this Higgs Boson that you mentioned?" Tracy asked. "You referred to it as the 'God particle'?"

"He who has never been seen!" Sorenson shrieked, sticking the sheath straight at her. His voice lowered. "But exists as the connecting force between local and non-local reality. It's the messenger that channels information from the spiritual to allow the physical to exist. The conduit of consciousness. The voice of God."

Tracy and Haslett sat motionless as the Professor swiped it back and forth like a wooden windshield wiper.

"The Higgs Boson gives mass to particles. He's not seen as a wave, nor a particle, unlike his colleague, Mister Light, which can be both. Light, which arrives in the form of a photon particle riding an electromagnetic wave, exists in locality and has a finite speed, whereas Mister Higgs has no physical bounds. He's just a quiet, wee wanker who goes about his day acting as the bridge between localities. The fundamental stop in smallness. The life force that can only be thought of as the common denominator… the essence to existence… the neutrality between positive and negative. As a neutral whole, our tiny Higgs-meister maintains an intelligent, harmonic balance of opposing spin. Half rotating in positive. Half in negative."

He spun the spike faster, then reversed it much slower; rocking a hand to and fro.

"When one rotation increases or decreases momentum, the other compensates, so existence remains in a timely, balanced space of energy and matter. But, when Higgy's balance is excessively disturbed…"

He let his thing droop.

"Then some serious supernatural shit happens. Order is upset by chaos, life is overcome by death, and good is dominated by evil. This little fornicator services the really big dichotomies."

The Professor paused and put his pole on the pulpit.

"Great cocktail discussion. Eh, as you Canucks would say."

Tracy half-smirked. Haslett sat with the toothpick in his lips.

"Back to basics," Sorenson said. "Today we follow the standard model of particle physics. We recognize the four fundamentals of gravity, electromagnetism, the weak nuclear force, and the strong nuclear force."

The snot-rag was back out, sending Tracy on guard.

"But... there's a problem with it. Gravity, which holds the inner and outer universe intact, cannot be accounted for at the quantum level, right down where Monsieur Higgs is hiding. Gravity has dick-all to do with nuclear resonance... maintaining the quantum spin correlation."

He mopped his forehead and put the rag away.

"That's Higgs' job. And his direction must come right from the Big Girl herself. Infinite Intelligence."

Sorenson locked his fingers, stretched, then motioned his head towards the window. Haslett glanced out, but Tracy kept watch on the Professor who'd snuck for the sheath.

"Now, electromagnetism is a strange duck. We best know it as light, which is what we see with our eyes, but then our eyes evolved to see what was available to them. You see, light got here long before we did... light on the visible spectrum which is emitted by the sun and the stars. From our earliest recorded observations, humans have interpreted light as a phenomena of STEMI, but light, on its own, is not the super-size, full-meal-deal that so many New Agers love to chew up."

He stroked his shaft.

"Take Genesis from the Hebrew Bible. They got the process a hundred percent right in the first sentence. *In the beginning* (Time) *God* (Intelligence) *created* (Energy) *heaven* (Space) *and earth* (Matter). It was not till the third line that God said *Let there be light*. She'd already whipped up the universe before turning on the lights."

Tracy's eyes lit up, but stayed on Sorenson's hand.

"Light is a by-product of energy and matter, albeit an important one, I'll agree. You see, those sages telling the creation story were able to access this knowledge through the same consciousness that we have available today. Certainly some individuals over history were a little brighter than others... possessing an enhanced intuitive awareness. Jesus, Buddha, and Mohammed come to mind, as do DaVinci, Einstein, and today Hawking, but they all got their information from the same bin."

Sorenson paused, now twirling his baton like a fat old cheerleader.

"I'm afraid I'm rambling."

"No, no. This is fascinating," Tracy said, motioning him to continue.

"The nuclear forces are unremarkable, except for silently keeping us alive, but I have to mention a group... the four states or phases of matter. Solid, liquid, gas, and plasma. Funny how so many things are packaged in groups of fours. That's an interesting number... four. Half of four is its square root, two... the prime number and the base for dichotomy. Half of two is one... the positive number of the zero-one binary code. Half of one is one-half... as in half positive and half negative, which is exactly the spin balance that Higgy-boy juggles. Just numerological co-incidences, I'm suggesting."

The Professor stuck the stake between his legs and wobbled the backs of both hands.

"All four states of matter are interchangeable, depending upon their give and take of energy. Recently, we're learning about other peculiar states of matter like the Bose-Einstein condensate, neutron stars, quark-gluon plasma, and transparent aluminum. We're aware they exist, but they're poorly understood. And that's all we know about matter. The good matter, that is."

Tracy glanced at Haslett, who was finger counting.

"What we don't know anything about, whatsoever, is anti-matter. The evil spirit of the physical world. All we know is that it exists. This is degenerate matter, like in a black hole, where negative attraction of gravity exceeds positive repulsion of matter. It's where the ugly galactic guy hits on the cute solar chick, sucks her in, drives her home, and strangles her dead in the garage."

Tracy chuckled. Haslett deadpanned. Sorenson got up, used his stick as a back-scratcher, and sat down.

"Then there's dark matter... for lack of any other name. It's out there in reality, but does not emit nor reflect electromagnetic radiation waves. We observe it from gravitational effects on visible matter. Dark energy is another reality. It exhibits the anti-gravitational influence that accelerates the expansion of the universe, but we cannot measure it either. On a pie chart of our perception of the universe, just four percent of the cosmological constant... that great reservoir of critical density... is ordinary luminous and non-luminous matter. Twenty-three percent is dark matter. And seventy-three percent is dark energy."

The Professor put both palms over his eyes.

"So, ninety-six percent of the entire universe? We know absolutely fuck-all about. Current theories suggest that's where the rules are booked. Dark matter just may be information. And dark energy just may be thought."

He put his fingers to his temples.

"The blending of these two just may be the unified theory that Einstein spent the second half of his life searching for, tying local reality to non-local consciousness, and that search just may lead to the source of intelligence. The gal who went to the trouble of thinking all this into existence."

He looked at the two, lifting the limb to his mouth, and giggling. "I told you being a dinner guest of cannibals is more fun than pondering the unified theory!"

"I have always believed in God as the creator," Tracy said, to no one in particular.

"A grand design of a grand designer." Sorenson's voice raised. He smiled and winked. "Just sayin'."

Haslett took the toothpick from his lips. "So this Higgs Boson guy might be good science but, emotionally, I'd like to know... what is the soul? That's what I'm missing out on."

Sorenson jabbed at him. "Ah! Ya been listenin', m'man! The age old question. Humans have been pondering this since we evolved into a state of self-awareness. This is where science and religion meet. Science doesn't know, and religion asks you to accept it on faith."

"Emotions seem to be what I'm missing."

"Emotions belong in the non-local half of existence. Science can't explain what love and hate, or happy and sad are, except that we intrinsically know emotions are intangible, yet very, very real dichotomies of existence. No doubt the soul channels our emotions, so it goes along that someone whose soul is dysfunctional would have difficulty in experiencing these feelings. Even though they were still of mind, brain, and body."

"I still seem to have some of that."

"Personally, I feel humans are on the verge of another huge leap in our evolutionary path, the expansion of our personal consciousness towards knowing the soul."

"I heard some guys talkin' about that."

Sorenson squinted at him, then continued. "You can thank the Internet for part of it. So much information, from so many sources, coming together in the same medium. It profoundly amplifies our local awareness. The Shamans have been way ahead of the game for a long time, though. They had their mind-form of internet, connecting to non-local awareness, but the ignorance... no, the sheer arrogance... of western society and organized religion has been profound. To assume that someone who moved to the beat of drums and smoky-hot chants around a fire with a bone in his hair can't be clued-in is preposterous."

"Do you see God and the soul as part and parcel, Professor?" Tracy asked.

"Excellent question again. But let's look at what we know about the source of information first. All societies, without exception, recognize the presence of a creator. That's as obvious as a pair of dog's balls. We exist, so therefore we were created. By what, is the prize-winning question. This is where science leaves us and philosophy and religion step in."

Tracy nodded. Sorenson dropped the dowel on the desk, crooking both index fingers and waggling them.

"A few quotes about God and the soul I like. One is by the old cock, Walter Russell, who said the soul is the marriage between science and religion, where the body is merely a machine made to express thoughts, and those thoughts are the ghost in the machine."

Haslett was thinking of something from his past.

"Einstein?" Sorenson went on. "About quantum entanglement, which describes the Higgs Boson's ability to allow particles to communicate instantly in non-locality, he called it 'Spukhafte Fernwirkungen' or spooky action at a distance. When asked about the Big Bang, Einstein said 'I have no problem with the fact that everything in the universe was created from one infinitely small and dense point. Where that came from, only God knows.' He also famously put it 'I want to know God's thoughts. The rest are details.' No, the reality of consciousness is something we know very little about, but it goes like this."

Sorenson took another gulp of whatever was in the canteen.

"For any conceivable question there is an answer, although sometimes it's just plain *No*. Questions and answers are infinite, and they don't exist in the physical world. They are thoughts. Information is the fuel of thought and is everywhere in both localities. It's in the instructions bar-coded in your DNA, to the owner's manual of your car, to the secrets of the universe. Our mechanism to access this vast library comes through the conduit of the Higgs Boson, which is in-between both worlds. The phenomenon of intelligence is accessed by our ability to think with our mind... by using our brain."

Both nodded.

"Access to thought? We are information-seeking, thought-driven beings. It seems to be our purpose to seek our true selves, aside from daily routines of eating, sleeping and, of course..."

The professor glanced about, putting his hand to the side of his mouth.

"Doing the naughty to procreate. Hee! Hee!"

Haslett gave Tracy a nudge. She lightly frowned back.

"We understand our physical bodies to some degree, including a bit about the operation of the brain, which is just a physical organ through which the mind operates. The mind is not tangible. It is best understood as a metaphysical transmitting and receiving set for waves, and it's my belief that information travels to and from the mind on thought waves, instructed by... ta da... Mister Higgs."

Tracy and Haslett nodded again.

"You didn't know you were doing that."

"Doing what?" she asked.

"Bobbing your heads. You also weren't thinking about your heart beating, your lungs breathing, your stomach soon telling you it's time to eat, or your bladder saying I gotta go pee. That's all going on subconsciously. Good thing, or we'd be exhausted by day's end, then die in our sleep if we had to think about routine shit all the time."

Tracy caught herself in another nod.

"So let's look at the mind and what we know about how it operates. You know about being conscious. You found your way here, so you know that it works. You sought out information, processed it, and made the conscious decision to come here. And you're listening to me in an awake state, and you're consciously processing the information I'm offering. Whether you believe it or not, that's up to you. That's where local intelligence kicks in. It has to make sense to you."

They kept nodding and listening.

"But back to the mind, thought, and the levels of consciousness. We have our own individual thresholds to entering the levels, but there are four main groups. They are awake, asleep, sub-conscious, and super-conscious. There you go again, the number four."

He held up four fingers.

"So, what are thoughts, you ask. Well, you get an idea which just pops in your head. Where did that come from? Most likely you were thinking about it beforehand, like... I need a new way to hide money from the government."

Sorenson saw Tracy cross her legs and fold her arms. He filed that away.

"So you try to consciously think about what's the safest place with the best return. Maybe you jot some things down with pen and paper, but the answer doesn't come to you. So you put it away and forget about it for now. But, the next day, you're happening about your business and the solution just pops into your head. Now how did that happen? And where did it come from? Certainly not from the revenuers."

Sorenson picked up his pecker-pole and pointed at Tracy. She looked down.

"Well, it arrived by a thought, traveling on a wave. When your conscious mind gave up, your subconscious took over and broadcast the question out in the ether. To the realm of intelligence. Seeking the answer."

She looked up. The Professor swiped as if playing a Wii.

"And it was there. Like all answers are. And it was broadcast back to your mind, which received the information subconsciously. This, in turn, was processed by your brain, so your body could go ahead and manipulate your money.'

Sorenson winked at her.

"This can happen instantaneously, or… it can take years. It depends a lot on the demand or urgency your subconscious places on it. Take a reaction in the heat of battle, for instance, compared to dreaming up the words for a new song."

Haslett removed his toothpick. "You know. I think I'm gettin' this. You, Trace?"

"Yes, mostly," she said. "But how do the mind and brain interface? I understand that Shamanism is dependent upon the mind altering its state of consciousness to access information available in the spiritual world. But, it must use the brain to do so?"

Sorenson made an OK circle with a thumb and forefinger. "How is it possible for conscious experience to arise out of a clump of grey matter endowed with nothing but electrochemical properties?"

"Yes."

"Outside of being a phenomenally complex organ that runs our central nervous system, the brain is the housing for the mind, which is the transmitting and receiving set for processing information. Physical information from our local environment, such as light and sound, travels to our brains on local waves picked up by our senses. Spiritual information arrives in the brain by thought waves originating in the infinite, non-local, world. Therefore, not subject to the strict, finite laws of physics."

"Fascinating," Tracy said.

"Yes. Now, a local wave is a disturbance of energy that propagates through space and time. They are measured in frequencies and occur everywhere, all the time. We, as humans, are restricted by our five senses to receive certain local frequencies, but, fortunately, we have been endowed with a sixth sense to process non-local frequencies. It's a common sense. Unfortunately, a lot don't apply it."

"With you on that one," Haslett said.

"EMR, electromagnetic radiation, which governs our daily lives, crosses a broad wave spectrum. These we can measure... unlike thought waves, which we can only speculate upon. EMR is rated in the term Hertz. It starts at brain waves, then increases in rate of vibration to audible sound, then to radio waves, microwaves, infrareds, into the narrow band of visible light, then to ultraviolet which causes sunburn, upward to X-ray, then to Gamma rays which is the highest energy vibrations we have been able to record. So far."

Sorenson stopped, making sure not to lose them.

"That shit'll scramble your DNA."

They were with him.

"Current theory is that thoughts are actually waves of a much higher vibration. Far, far, exceeding the light-speed barrier which, till recently, was considered the limit... but, then, we also once assumed nothing could break the sound barrier... so, if the theory holds true, then thoughts travel at a limitless speed."

They ducked as he swept his sword over their heads.

"Theoretically, if two minds were thinking about each other from each end of the universe, using non-locality, the distance would be irrelevant, and they would be able to communicate instantaneously. Experiments at the quantum level have recently proven that physical particles are, in fact, able to get away with this. The culprit that lets them gabber so fast is..."

He held it like a unicorn's horn.

"The Higgs Boson! And we've just recently caught the bastard at it. To me, it makes sense, and there is huge progress in the capacity of our brains being able to capture it. This is the evolutionary breakthrough I'm speaking of."

Tracy flashed a glance at Haslett, then back at Sorenson who'd shut his eyes and massaged the missile as he spoke.

"Brain waves have been subject to extensive study. EEG, or electroencephalography, is the recording of the brain's electrical activity produced by the firing of neurons, the brain's nerve cells. They are clearly recorded in escalating wave lengths. Delta waves occur in deep sleep, between one and four Hertz. Theta is the meditative state at five to seven. Alpha, at eight to twelve, is a relaxed but awake state. Bata, thirteen to forty hertz, is our normal thinking state, approaching arousal. Gamma is the high capacity, super-conscious, fight or flight and hyper-aware, clairvoyant state. This runs from forty all the way up to one hundred. The Gamma cycle, not to be confused with Gamma rays, is intrinsically localized in the thalamus, the reptilian zone of the brain."

The Professor popped his peepers and prodded the pointer at Haslett.

"This is the brain activity in which you experienced the out-of-body state, Bobby-boy!" he yelled. "It was achieved spontaneously. An automatic response to the extreme danger of your encounter with The Kushtaka. Your fear-death experience!"

Haslett leaned into the lounge. Sorenson pulled back the projectile and lowered his voice.

"Or… it can be carefully obtained by people of intense discipline, like Buddhist monks and, of course, our Shamans. In that altered state of consciousness, your brain continues to keep contact with your mind… even though your mind is in an entirely different metaphysical plane. Your perception is that time stands still, and you are hyper-aware of your entire surroundings, allowing you to react with the proper response of self-preservation."

Haslett relaxed. "So I wasn't imagining it just 'cause I was scared shitless?"

"Heavens no! Having the shit scared out of you just triggered the state. It let you react as you did. You were fortunate to come out of it alive. Unfortunately, though, with an apparent spiritual deficiency."

"What in the fuck was that thing?"

"This is better for Dr. Nez to answer, clinically. My studies have found that every indigenous culture has their version of The Kushtaka. Like Bakwas over there."

Haslett looked back at the hideous face with fiery eyes set on ragged shoulders and he shuddered. The Professor looked at it, too.

"The Kushtaka is the embodiment of badness!" he shouted again, thrusting high. "It's a monstrosity of the world in between local and non-local realities. A black hole in the world of ghosts. It feeds off quantum energy… by stealing the negative spin of Higgy's rotation. Soul food, you may say! It functions in the physical world, but belongs in the spiritual, and it's capable of shifting its shape to many forms."

"Incredible," Tracy whispered.

Sorenson toned down. "This seems to be done by willfully altering its DNA through a biological process. Probably SNP, single nucleotide polymorphism, which realigns its genetic coding."

"How?" asked Haslett.

"No one knows," he said with a shrug, laying the lance down. "But it has to be accomplished by thought waves, meaning the entity thinks itself into different physical and metaphysical forms. Just as a chameleon or a cuttlefish thinks itself into camouflage. This happens in a flash. It's of no coincidence that DNA also appears to receive instructions through messages transmitted by the Higgs Boson, so that suggests a likely spot to pilfer."

"Wow!" Tracy whispered again.

"That *thing*, as you put it, was very much real and, if mythology holds true, still very much is... even though you... or something acting through you... were able to kill the human body it possessed."

"So it's like a ghost?" Haslett asked.

"Not exactly. Although it haunts the world of ghosts," Sorenson calmly replied. "Ghosts are quite straightforward and easy to understand. They're residual energy of human souls trapped half-way between localities. In their anguish to be freed, the unbalanced quantum spin interacts with electromagnetism. Sometimes it manifests as a state of matter, reflecting the visible light spectrum. That allows ghosts to occasionally be seen by the naked eye. It can be quite the color show, I hear."

"So what is it?"

"The Kushtaka was never a human soul. It functions as quite the opposite and sustains itself through high-grade energy obtained from conquering human prey. It needs the soul's energy for its survival and is known to stockpile souls, like food in a cache. It can lie dormant for ages, as it exists outside of space and time, and it's not known what sets The Kushtaka off on a rampage again. Probably because it gets hungry."

Sorenson stopped and thought for a second.

"Or something pisses it off."

"So it's still out there?" Haslett asked.

"Unfortunately, yes. It has only one purpose, and that is to manifest evil."

"Yikes!" said Tracy, utterly absorbed.

"So what the hell happened to me and Bude?"

"It seems that in the gun-fight with The Kushtaka, you were all spiritual casualties, but something intervened, so none of you got quite finished off."

"So it's still out there?"

"Yes. Possibly wounded. And it would view you and your partner's souls as its property."

Tracy's mouth gaped.

"Don't think I care much for that idea," Haslett said.

"I'm not qualified to lecture on the spiritual world. I just know it exists. If there are good spirits... then it follows that there are bad ones as well. It seems you encountered a particularly nasty deity, my friend. Let's leave that for Doctor Nez to resolve."

Tracy swallowed hard.

"So what really is the soul, you must be wondering," Sorenson said. "Plato, a pretty bright guy, was the first to tell us that thoughts are ideas. *Forms*, he called them. That's where the word *in-form-ation* originated. He argued the mind-body dichotomy... that the body is from the material world, and the mind is from the world of ideas or spirits. He professed that the soul is our connection between the physical and the spiritual worlds."

Tracy's hand covered her mouth.

"Since the soul does not exist in the realities of space, time, energy, or mass, as the body does, it is able to access universal truths directly from intelligence. The soul, Plato said, was only temporarily connected with the body and could come and go at will... sometimes taken away by tragedy or tremendous grief... sometimes stolen by interference... sometimes partly missing... sometimes wholly gone... but, nevertheless, at the physical death of the body, the soul would return to world of Forms."

Haslett was unable to smile, and the Professor understood why.

"Plato believed that our true purpose is to achieve the ability to grasp the world of Forms with one's own mind. To achieve true happiness and freedom. *Nirvana*, it's known in eastern cultures. In physics, the Higgs Boson... the God particle... seems to offer the best scientific solution to the soul. In spirit, it's simply our connection to God."

Tracy gripped Haslett's hand. Sorenson finger-combed something out of his beard while eyeing his scepter.

"Twenty-three hundred years ago, Aristotle defined the soul as the core existence of a being. This, I believe, is still the best explanation."

He reached and picked it up.

"One thing's for sure. The soul is the only thing you come into life with and the only thing you take going out, so you better be comfortable with it. It's our source. Our spiritual energy. Our immortal connection with the truth. And sometimes we lose it. But, fortunately, some people understand enough to help get it back."

The Professor knighted both on the shoulder with his penis-sheath. "This is Doctor Nez's expertise."

Chapter 44

Tuesday, September 4th, 2012
10:55 am
Narajmata Healing Center
Near Alstonville
New South Wales, Australia

It was abnormally warm outside for a late-winter morning, but comfortably cool inside Doctor Leslie Nez's office where she sat, rich coppery face resting in one hand, absorbing Haslett's story of Kaash Klao and The Kushtaka, which he repeated – precisely as told to Holger Sorenson the week before.

God, I hope she believes this, Tracy thought. *If I were her, I would chuck us both out on our tushes.*

Tracy stayed silent, seated beside Haslett on a soft-cushioned couch – partly listening, and partly soaking in the surroundings which brought a taste of the American southwest to the northeast of Australia, where they'd checked into the Narajmata holistic healing center.

A waft of sage mixed with sweetgrass, smoldering in a baked-clay bowl, meshed with hollow, haunting tones of the flute played by Native American musician, Ronald Roybal, drifting from speakers secluded somewhere within the room's desert palettes – fiery reds, yellows, and burnt oranges of the sunrise, trapped in Navajo tapestries and draping both sides of a north-facing window – airy pinkish-purples of a sunset sky, woven into a topper above the bronzed glass – mulchy browns, cactus greens, and driftwood greys of the earth, patched into fabric furnishings – and watery blues with foamy whites, splashing off a rough stucco wall.

Leslie Nez, too, was a study of color.

A stylish, petite woman of fiftyish, she'd penetrated Haslett with coal eyes accented by bluish liner and sharply-cut bangs becoming two braids of raven hair. Her few motions revealed a flash of feathered earrings, much like the flick from a red-winged blackbird taking flight; both contrast and complement to silver and turquoise jewelry, hung and pinned on the backdrop of a midnight dress.

"Amazing!" Nez said.

Tracy sank back as Haslett locked his fingers and stretched his arms. Nez reached for a pottery pitcher of iced tea set on a sandstone coffee table and topped off their glasses.

"Extraordinary! I've heard of this entity. I know another person who's encountered it."

"You know, Doctor," Haslett said, not comprehending what she'd just said. "What I told you is straight goods. It's exactly what happened. So, you think you might be able to help us out?"

Nez set down the pitcher, grasping Haslett's hands and gazing off, seemingly deep in thought. Two minutes passed. Haslett glanced at Tracy till Nez released, swallowed, and made a pinching rub between her left thumb and fingers. Through coral lips and a smoky voice she murmured a barely audible, "All my relations."

Haslett nudged Tracy, who smiled and lightly gripped his thigh.

Nez frowned and leaned forward. "It is my duty to help. The spirits have spoken through my soul."

Tracy and Haslett sat upright.

"Relax!" Nez broke into a day-lighting smile, showing a twinkling set of Hollywood teeth. She chuckled and waved her right hand toward the sky. "I'm not a kook! The spirits are simply thoughts. Thoughts that are out there, in that infinite mass of information, running free in the non-local world, but available to all of us trapped here in the local world. And the soul is the translator of those thoughts. I just took a quick journey, thought for a bit, did some translation, and got some direction."

Both sat silent.

Nez thumbed-up. "I'm good to go."

No reaction.

"Professor Sorenson... explained this to you... didn't he?"

"For sure." Haslett cleared his throat. "He covered the science stuff, but said you were the expert on the spiritual and soul retrieval thing. Seems that's where our problems lie."

"*Our* problems?" Nez looked at Tracy. "As in both of you had a go-around with The Kushtaka?"

"No, Doctor Nez." Tracy said. "But we both have personal issues to resolve. From our time with Professor Sorenson, it has become clear that my problem... the void in my soul... is entirely self-inflicted and relatively minor, whereas Bobby's is a matter of, let me say... supernatural robbery."

"Interesting perspective, Doctor Williams. I understand that's your proper title, but I'd prefer we be more casual. Please, it's Leslie." She looked down, paging a file. "And you are Tracillina and you go by... Robert?"

"Bob's fine with me."

"And I am just Tracy. We have read a number of internet articles about you, Leslie, and also looked through your website. You have an interesting description of your practice. Shamanic Counseling. How is that different from what the Professor called Core Shamanism?"

"I've a few terms for what I do. Techno-Shaman. Contemporary Shaman. Eco-Shaman. Healer and Medicine Gal. Even Psychonaut." Nez laughed. "And I've a term for a bunch of con-artists who claim to practice my craft, but just rip people off. Plastic Shamans. They've developed quite the profitable business of exploiting gullible New Agers seeking enlightenment. *Caveat emptor*, though. Buyer beware, dumb-ass."

"I have read of that. But the Professor assures that you are a true Shaman. I must say, he is quite the character."

"Oh, he's a free spirit, all right, A bit strange at times. That Tourette's thing gets annoying, but the man lives in the real world, not in some academic or some preacher's dream. It makes my end so much easier when he's prepared a client on the science of the soul. Belief is the key to success in dealing with spiritual issues. You have to believe in order to achieve results. And you need the proper knowledge... factual information... in order to believe."

"Professor Sorenson was clear about that," Tracy said.

Haslett agreed.

Nez brought her hands upward and outward. "Now, a Shaman is simply one who Shamans. Just as a minister is one who ministers. By the way, most legitimate Shamans now prefer the term Shamanic practitioner, but it's really a play on words. Like bureaucrats do."

Nez gave a dismissing wave. Haslett leaned back and nodded. Tracy stayed still.

"Shamanism, at its core, is not culture bound. It's not governed by religious structure or exclusive to ethnicity. You don't need a priest or a guru to tell you what to do. It's a direct relationship between you and spirit, without a church or mediator. Core Shamanism is based on the knowing that humans are part of the totality of nature... not superior to it, not the way some mainstream religions will con you into believing."

Tracy crossed her arms.

"It recognizes that reality has two masks to the world, and the perception of each depends upon one's state of consciousness. There's the ordinary state of consciousness, the local world where we do day to day living... and there's the Shamanic state of consciousness, where the mind freely interacts with infinite forms of information. This is the spirit world, the non-local world, which the Shamanic practitioner moves their mind freely to and from, in order to obtain knowledge."

Tracy shifted in the cushions. Haslett stayed reclined, one leg over the other.

"The existence of spirits, or forms of thought, is not a hypothesis. It's an empirical fact. To someone in a Shamanic state of consciousness, these spirits are heard, seen, and felt. They're just as real as the humans they interact with in an ordinary state."

Nez read their silence.

"A Core Shaman is one who alters their state of consciousness, then journeys to the spiritual world *on behalf of others* to seek information. I do things a bit differently. I want people to find their *own* solutions. To their *own* problems."

Nez kept eye contact.

"Not have me do it for them. I don't want to hook them and keep them coming back for me to deal out their fix. I don't encourage dependency, so I teach clients to do their own journeying to the non-local world. And I avoid giving advice. They get advice directly from the source of information. The spirits."

Tracy unfolded her arms. Haslett fiddled with a toothpick.

"It's all about developing the ability to find things out for themselves. I assist my clients to do this in a modern, clinical setting. I advocate a health care approach that integrates ancient traditions with modern technology, and I call this Shamanic Counseling."

"Interesting," Tracy said to Nez, who sat across in an oversized upholstered chair, bare feet curled underneath her.

"So how'd you get to be a Shaman?" Haslett asked.

Nez sighed. "Like all Shamanic practitioners, I was initiated at a very early age. When I turned three, my grandmother beat me within an inch of my life with her Shaman stick. It makes for quick learning."

"She did *what*!" Tracy's mouth dropped.

"Gotcha again!" Nez started a light, little giggle. "Seriously, it stems from my culture. As you see, I'm Native North American."

"You remind me of someone I worked with," Haslett said.

He'd been observing Nez and saw the similarity to Sergeant Bate. Not just the features and skin color. It was their demeanor. Their intelligence. A sense of confidence and trust. And Haslett had become confident that he could trust the secret with Sharlene Bate.

The secret of why the informants had to be murdered.

If this journey succeeded.

* * *

Nez filed Haslett's comment away.

"You're very dark, too," she said to Tracy.

"Mexican, Colombian, and Limey!" Tracy replied with a laugh. "Quite the mix. And you, Bob?"

"Brit. Hundred percent. But second generation Canadian."

"I won't hold that against you." Nez chuckled, reaching out and brushing his arm. "We fought the King a long time ago, although I recall you Canucks kicked our Yankee asses around 1812."

Tracy smiled as Nez turned serious.

"But you're curious about my credentials, and so you should be. We'll be spending considerable time together and some of it's going to be intimate. Very personal. Baring your souls, so to speak. And some of it's not going to be comfortable, I caution you."

Tracy clasped Haslett's hand.

"I'm here in Australia for a year's sabbatical. Partly to teach. Partly to learn. The Aborigines have so much to offer. My tenure is clinical psychology at the University of Arizona in Tuscon, but my home is a little place called Window Rock, further north on the New Mexico border. My mother is Navajo. My father's Cherokee. I wasn't exactly underprivileged, nor raised as a reservation brat, though."

Nez took a sip and re-set the glass, drumming her fingers on it. Their eyes drew down to the tapping.

"Dad is a geological engineer, semi-retired now, and Mom is an English Lit professor with twenty-plus published works to her credit. We moved around the world a lot. Dad followed the mineral markets. Mom researched, taught, wrote, and raised kids. I spent my teens in Ecuador and Colorado. Ah… I've got two sisters. One back in the States and one in Europe. Three nieces and one nephew. No kids of my own, unfortunately. My one and only marriage was a fail. That's fail with a big f'n F."

She made a sour face. Tracy struggled to say something, but Nez stayed speaking.

"I was fortunate, though, that my parents could afford to have me educated at UC, Berkeley, then at Harvard where I received my Ph.D. in Psychology. I first worked at psychological profiling for some spooky government outfit in Langley, Virginia. I hated that, so I did private practice in Philadelphia. In my late twenties, I took a trip back to Arizona with my mom to re-connect with my grandparents. That was life changing. I found my calling."

Nez paused and took another sip. Tracy did, too. Haslett twirled his toothpick.

"It was in a Navajo sweat lodge. This was my first experience with a Shaman. He was an elderly man, actually of Hopi heritage, and it was my first out-of-body experience."

Haslett's brow went up.

"Sweats are not some sort of hocus-pocus, I caution you. They're not a sauna on steroids or some kinky, get-your-clothes-off, steam-bath orgy. Far from it. They are a profoundly powerful, spiritual ceremony. Up till then, I knew little of my grandparents' culture. Mom and Dad always chased the American dream. You know... the career success... big income... home ownership. The materialistic things."

Haslett was thinking. Tracy was listening.

"I connected with the spirits right away. I'm a natural, you know. I talk to them every day."

Haslett squirmed, but Tracy winked and smirked. Nez knew she was getting it.

"After that, I studied everything about Shamanism I could get my hands on. At first, I didn't intend on practicing. I was just fascinated. But, it became an obsession. I spent hours immersed in anthropology... at the library... in museums... with the elders. I saw the primal therapeutics were far more effective than anything I'd learned in graduate school, and I became a royal pain-in-the-ass to poor old Machakw, the Shaman. I pleaded with him to take me on as a full-time apprentice, but he flat turned me down. I was devastated. It took me years to appreciate the wisdom of his decision."

Nez rose and stirred the baked-clay bowl. Fresh, sagey-sweet smoke scented their nostrils.

"He told me I wasn't meant to be a Core-Shaman... like him. He

303

called me a bridge-person, as in a bridge between cultures. I was literate. He was not. I had difficulty undoing my literate mind and seeing reality the way he did."

Tracy squeezed Haslett's hand.

Nez continued. "But I could see that his lack of literacy would be a paradox. It would block educated people of learning from him. They'd see only his inability to read and write... not the radiance of his presence. I realized... for Shamanism to reach the urban, technological, and industrial world... it would have to come from someone like me, who had credentials in both worlds. Unfortunately, he passed before seeing my maturity."

Nez gazed upward.

Tracy released her grip. "I am sure he went peacefully among the spirits."

"Actually, no. It was quite messy. He got run over by a farm tractor."

Nez reached for a large, woven satchel – brightly dyed with indigenous patterns and adorned with beaded figures.

Inside were her tools – a taut-skin drum with its cottonwood stick, hawk feathers, a buckskin pouch with herbs, turquoise stones and white shells, yarn for tying medicine bundles, kachina dolls, rattles, dream catchers, crystals, beans, dried corn and squash seeds, tobacco, a soapstone pipe, matches, a fetish strung with abalone and black jet pebbles, an iPod with two sets of earphones, her iPad, and an iPhone.

To Kaash Klao – they'd be astonishing sights.

* * *

"So I studied Navajo healing," Nez said.

She removed a gourd shell lashed to a mesquite handle, shaking it slightly. The sound of seeds and stones soothed her visitors.

"Healing is a more appropriate term than treating. To the Navajo, healing is not taking something to get better. It's restoring and maintaining *hozho*, balance or harmony... going from the place of *koyaanisqatsi*, where life went out of balance... to *hozho nahasdlii*, or harmony restored."

Soft, warm rattling continued.

"The Navajo don't rid all problems. They find the balance between positive and negative, which western medicine ignores. The Euro-American version worships a model of illness. Not wellness. Notice how so much is *anti*. *Anti*-inflammatory. *Anti*-bacterial. *Anti*-depressant. You'd almost think profits made by pharmaceutical distributors promotes a sick system."

Nez set the rattle aside. She picked up her drum, giving two quick taps with the cottonwood stick. Sound waves resonated through Tracy and Haslett like a pebble plopped in a placid pond.

"It's difficult to describe Navajo holistic healing in a non-holistic language like English. The worldviews are so dissimilar. So few people possess the linguistic and ceremonial skills to be able to translate between the languages. You see, language is a reflection of consciousness... reflected as the perception of reality. English is reliant on the dominance of nouns. They separate and reduce the expression of thought to a static entity."

Tracy listened. Haslett watched.

"Navajo is composed of verbs, which are process and motion concepts. Among indigenous peoples, language is far more than expression. It's a manifestation of the essence of existence and of consciousness. Consciousness is knowing. It's the soul that makes it happen."

Nez tapped low, binaural beats on her drum.

"Scientists have no English words to describe what they're finding within quantum physics. As they journey into the sub-atomic world, they're seeing that reality is a flux. They're finding entities that cannot be defined as waves or particles. They're neither nouns nor verbs. The ancients had terms for these discoveries, but our people are at a loss of how to translate this into English."

Nez set down her drum and reached for a book on a side table. Tracy and Haslett felt a cool lapse from the relaxed state the beats had put them to.

"This is a quote from author Gary Witherspoon in *Language and Art in the Navajo Universe*. It illuminates the opposing foundations of reality between Navajo and Western perceptions of consciousness."

'An example of an underlying metaphysical premise would be the Western conception of the relationship between mind and body, or mind and matter. Western thought has been dominated by the complete separation of mind and matter, idea and entity, and subject and object. To western thinkers, what goes on in the mind is subjective, while that which occurs in the world of matter and energy is objective... These basic metaphysical notions, which are taken for granted by Western intellectuals, are denied in Navajo thought. Navajo philosophy assumes that mental and physical phenomena are inseparable, and that thought and speech has a powerful impact on the world of matter and energy...

Navajo interpretations of the constitution of reality and the causation of events are all based on an unbreakable connection between mind and matter.'

Nez closed the book. "And you know what they say about mind and matter?"

"What's that?" Haslett asked.

"If you don't mind. It don't matter."

She picked up her drum, giving two quick taps.

"That's a great deal of what's wrong in our western psyche. We fail to stop and use our mind. It's not that most of us don't give a shit about what matters. It's that we don't understand. We don't take the time to stop and journey inward."

Nez tapped again.

"Urban life is an ongoing emergency situation. Everything is supposed to be done yesterday and everyone is in such a big frickin' hurry. We live under incredible pressure. It's no wonder so many use cocaine."

Nez watched Tracy grip her fingers and look down.

"When Navajos speak of healing, we mean a holistic and dynamic process, interrelated with cosmic energies that is never-ending and deals with far more than idiopathic symptoms. It's a no-brainer that there has to be a diagnosis of the disease, but pronounce that dis-ease. It's in the corrective treatments where the waters part."

Two more taps.

"Western medicine likes to cut the patient open and rip out the rot, or drug them up to ease the pain. Navajo medicine treats the whole illness, which can be localized in one individual, or manifested throughout generations of families. Or the entire tribe, for that matter."

She set the drum down.

"But healing requires a physical effort from the patient to get off their ass and take part, as well as incentive from the community... a communal kick in the ass to make sure they do. And the government response of dumping more money while the problem mopes around with a 'poor-me, somebody-else's-fault' attitude just don't cut it. That cop-out plain pisses me off... but that's for another story."

Tracy looked up. Nez had her palms vertical, facing each other, rotating in opposing circles.

"Maintaining the harmonic balance of the soul is what healing achieves. It's a never ending cycle from birth to death to birth. Curing and healing are different words in English, but are the same when translated in Navajo."

Nez's palms switched direction.

"The soul, in Navajo terms, is that force that balances the interaction of relationships. *Sa'ah naaghai*, the negative, and *bik'eh hozhoon*, the positive. In both science and spirit, negative and positive forces spin oppositely, but interdependently, and all hell breaks loose when they lose control. Yet, this shit happens all the time. That's why we fight chaos over order, evil over good, and death over life. We can't get away from this natural ebb and flow, so we learn to deal with it. To balance it."

Nez lifted the drum and resumed double-tapping, noting Tracy and Haslett did the same with their fingers.

"Ceremony is vitally important to Navajo holistic healing, but not so much in Core-Shamanism. Shamans have always been pragmatic. They used what works."

She set the drum aside, reached in her bag, removing her iPod.

"If they had this back then, they'd have used it."

Tracy grinned as Nez put the digital device on the table.

"The use of music and song, however, is integral to both. Articulating the workings of the universe cannot be expressed in simple words but, by invoking the vibrations of voice and instrument, the energies of healing can be better transmitted and understood. We use a tempo beat of twos and fours. So much of Navajo ceremony involves the concept of numbers."

She held up four fingers.

"We observe the four directions, the four seasons, four sacred mountains, four sacred plants, and four sacred stones. We have the four sacred virtues; life, work, relations, and respect. And we have the four deadly sins. Money, sex, power, and chocolate."

Tracy chuckled. Nez licked her fingers and winked, keeping a straight face.

"We have the four-fold way. The warrior, the teacher, the visionary, and the healer. Our ceremonies have four acts. Singing, dancing, storytelling, and silence. We recognize four stages of life. Child, adolescent, adult, and elder. We honor the four quadrants of nature: Earth, air, fire, and water. We observe four corners to a square. When you smooth the corners, it becomes a circle... the basic concept of infinity."

She put her forefinger around to her thumb.

"And we teach the four fundamentals of mathematics to our

schoolchildren. Addition, subtraction, multiplication, and division. We even have four suits in a deck of cards. And, of course, we have four states of consciousness."

Nez picked up her drum, striking twice.

"But what is even more remarkable is the number two. We have two realities... physical and spiritual... in which everything has its opposite. Positive and negative. Yin and yang. Awake and asleep. Hot and cold. Wet and dry. Big and little."

She double-tapped with each phrase.

"Sick and well. Pleasure and pain. Love and hate. Laugh and cry. Give and take. And the basic of all human dichotomies... right and wrong."

Nez kept drumming.

"So many of the sacred Navajo ceremonial traditions have been lost with the decline in the number of *hataa'lii*, the medicine people."

Tracy and Haslett sat relaxed, yet attentive.

"Two generations of youths left the reservation, seeking work in the border towns. Only a few stayed to follow the path of the traditional healers. Those complex rites take a life-time to master but, recently, there's been a resurgence of young people returning on weekends to immerse in tribal culture, so the four main ceremonies are still faithfully practiced. That's the Mountaintop Way, the Grandfathers' Ceremony, the Lightning Way, and the Enemy Way. This has had incredible success in healing soldiers returning from Iraq and Afghanistan who were suffering PTSD, by the way."

Nez stopped drumming to take a drink. Haslett's head nodded as Tracy spoke up.

"Leslie. Earlier you made reference to yourself as a psychonaut. What did you mean by that?"

"Oh, that's just a personal thing to describe a Shamanic journeyer. An astronaut travels to outer space. I travel to inner space. I prefer being spaced-in, as opposed to being spaced-out. Besides, it's safer."

Tracy smiled. Nez picked up her player and earphones.

"In an office environment, I use this little guy to help with journeys. It does the same trick as a drum and song, but is more neighbor-friendly. It prevents noise complaints to the cops."

"I can imagine." Tracy chuckled.

"Mindset is the doorway to journey. Relaxation is the doorway to altering the state of consciousness, which is mindset," Nez said, wrestling with tangled wires. "There is a definite physiological process to altering your state, though. Physically, this occurs in brainwaves. It's neither hypnosis, nor dreaming, which are restrictive states."

"Fascinating," Tracy commented.

"It occurs on a much higher wave scale. It allows the conscious mind to change its state, to leave the trappings of the brain and travel... journey for lack of a more descriptive term... to the spiritual world where space, time, distance, and all the trappings of the physical world are gone."

"Is it all done to drumming?" Tracy asked.

"There are many ways to facilitate journeying. Some involve extreme forms of sensory depravation like fasting, sun dancing, or sweating it out in a lodge, but I prefer sonic driving which is absorbing a rhythmic beat along with a chanting background."

Nez cursed something programmed in the iPod.

"I don't advocate using entheogens to initiate journeying. By entheogens, I mean natural hypnotics with psychoactive agents like peyote and psilocybin, not the addictive euphorics like opiates and coca, and certainly not brain-frying chemicals like LSD or methamphetamines."

She looked up as Tracy looked down.

"I've never tried the hard stuff," Nez said, poking at the player. "But I have experimented with some hypnotics. These were traditional for many Shamanic practitioners, and still are in many cultures. And, of course I've smoked my fair share of weed."

Haslett shrugged. Tracy giggled.

"Duh, I was a teenager in the seventies, then went to Berkeley! It just made me goofy and a serious threat to the fridge. I also did ayahuasca, which is a South American plant made into a brew. Now, there's one trip without bonus points. I was two days puking up my socks and shitting through the eye of a needle. I'll never friggin' do that again."

Tracy let go a laugh. Nez kept prodding.

"No, personally, I just don't go for the loss of control, but I'm not naive. I know the intrinsic human nature. The need to alter the state of consciousness. It's always been there. Always will. This is as basic to our species as the need for food, sleep, and sex."

The player beeped in protest.

"It's just that drugs are so convenient, but so tragically abused as vehicles of entertainment and escape, not as elevators to higher awareness. There'll always be the demand for drugs and, as long as someone can make a buck off of it..."

Nez stood up to unstrangle the ear-phones.

"There'll always be a supply. Sorry for my soap-box. It's a rant of mine, but neither of you give me the impression of ever being around the drug scene. Now, you have to naturally block out distractions and focus on where you're going, but it also helps to have an instructor along till you get your license. Here. Let's take a little test drive."

Nez had both lie on the floor, on their backs, on a pair of roll-up backpacker mats. She fitted their earpieces and flicked the iPod, starting stereo, low-frequency pulsations, 30 Hertz apart.

"Close your eyes, relax, and focus on your happy space," Nez directed.

Tracy took Haslett's hand. She breathed long and low, picturing them aboard the *Bandazul*, cruising the Gulf Islands on a hot, cloudless day.

"You will perceive the drum beats as one," Nez began a soft monotone. "It will come from the center of your head. In your mind. Not from your ears."

Haslett's thoughts were porpoising.

"As you fall deeper and deeper into relaxation, total relaxation, you will experience a change in your consciousness. Do not fight it... You will experience weightlessness. Do not fight it... You will have freedom from the pull of the physical world. Let go of the pull... Let it go... You will experience an expanse of your lesser senses. Smells will be richer. Tastes will be sweeter. Journey beyond this. Go beyond... A silkiness of touch will be sensed, not with the fingers, but with the mind. Journey beyond this. Go beyond... Greater senses will call to you. Journey beyond this. Go beyond... Sounds will be beautiful. Go beyond... Colors will be more vibrant than you ever have seen. Ignore this. Go beyond... Look towards the light. Look towards the portal that beckons you. Go to the portal... Go to the light... Go to the portal... Go to the light... Go through the portal... Go through the light..."

Haslett went under.

Tracy did, too. She'd experienced nothing even close to this – floating in a rose-petal basket of fresh cinnamon-bread, lined with yellow chick-down and orange flamingo feathers, swirling with baby-blue butterflies, drifting in harp tones along a river of lawn towards a harvest full moon.

"Whoooah!" Haslett screeched to a metaphysical stop.

Just shy of release, he bolted upright, ripping out the earpieces.

Tracy shocked back to locality. She groped, rubbed her eyes, lifted her knees, falling back; entirely disoriented.

Nez stayed placid. "What was it that you saw, Bob?" She saw him icy-grey. "Tell me what you saw."

Ten seconds passed.

"That face! That fuckin' orange face with the flamin' eyes. It was that thing again. It was there waitin' for me."

Tracy sat up, grasping his shuddering shoulder. Nez kneeled, taking away the earphones.

"I was afraid you'd experience that," Nez said. "But you're safe. It was repressed memory you envisioned, not the entity itself. It's a psychological block. A mental wall that you have to blast through."

"You mean I'm seein' things?"

"No. It was a reflection of reality. But now I know the entity is out there and is very much real."

Nez motioned them to rise and sit on the couch. She dropped the iPod back in the satchel, sitting back in her chair. Tracy gripped Haslett's arm. He took his glass, gulping down. Nez clasped her hands and spoke.

"There is no question, from what you've told me... from what I found in my short journey... from how I see your reaction to your own journey attempt... that you truly experienced the theft of your soul. And so did your police partner."

She let this sink in.

"The only way of retrieval... is to journey to where the souls are held... and forcefully take them back. You have to seek out and face this demon directly."

They stayed silent. She pointed at Haslett.

"But it is not safe for you to do this alone. Not a chance in hell. We need a more powerful approach. A much more powerful method. I need to guide you on your journey, but we can't possibly do it in an office setting like this. This is far too serious. Far too dangerous."

"Wh-what are you suggesting?" Tracy's hands pushed against her cheeks.

"An ancient method," Nez said. "A sacred ceremony. This much I know. The entity which accosted you and your partner, Bob, is not something I've ever confronted. Thankfully."

Haslett stiffened.

"But I'm familiar with what it is. All Shamans are. And all cultures have their term for it. Polymorph. Transmuter. Doppelganger.

Lycanthrope, which is a werewolf. Rakshasa in Hindu. Kitsune in Japanese. Bunyip in Aborigine. Bakwas in Kwakuitl and The Kushtaka in Tlingit."

"Oh my God..." Tracy covered her mouth.

"Navajos know it as *Yee Naaldlooshii* which, literally, means *Skin Walker*... a shape-shifter that takes human or animal form. A Skin Walker's only purpose is to curse... as opposed to heal. It is badness in the purest form... the epitome of the evil within and without, everyone and everything... and it exists in the metaphysical realm, somewhere in-between the darkness and the light. The world where souls get trapped. The world of ghosts."

"This... thing? Is it a ghost?" Tracy asked.

"No. Ghosts are mostly harmless. They're misunderstood, but quite straightforward. They are kind of opposite a Skin Walker... The Kushtaka... who feeds off souls. Ghosts are simply restless souls without bodies or, in rare cases, bodies without souls who anguish horribly and strive to be set free."

Nez stopped. She pointed at Haslett. "Like you."

Tracy's hands dropped. Haslett put a finger to his chest.

"So I'm a ghost?

"In the sense of a body without a soul. Yes."

"That's really fuckin' nice," he mumbled, lifting up and leaning back. Tracy grabbed his arm.

"The only way you are ever going to be free in soul..." Nez swallowed. "Is to challenge the one who stole it. You must face your demon."

Tracy squeezed.

"But that will be dangerous." Nez swallowed again. "Exceptionally dangerous."

Tracy squeezed so hard that his toothpick shot out.

Nez remained calm. "If freedom of your soul... and the soul of your partner... is what you truly seek... then I am bound by the ancient duty of a Shaman to assist you. Together, we must battle The Kushtaka... and beat it at its own game."

"Don't think I care much for that idea." Haslett didn't blink.

"How is this done?" Tracy whispered.

"We're going to have it come to us."

Their eyes saucered.

"In a sweat lodge," Nez said, looking toward the window. "And I know just the guy who's crazy enough to run it."

Chapter 45

Saturday, September 22nd, 2012
1:50 pm
Alkie Springs Recovery Center
Near Cunnamulla
Queensland, Australia

"Smerchook!" Leslie Nez hollered.

"Wooo Hoooooo! Shimasani!" a long, lanky, bronze-skinned figure shouted back.

Nez shook her fist and hopped down from the motorhome, onto the hot terracotta sand, heading towards it along a dirt trail beside the silty back-eddy of a narrow, desert waterway splitting an expanse of the Outback.

The shape shifted slightly, but stayed stretched out, a hundred paces away in a hammock strung under the shade of two, chunky coolibah trees leaning over the bank of the Warrego River, watching her approach, but not in any great rush to expend energy.

Tracy stood inside their rented RV till Haslett slipped it in park, then she stepped out, following Doctor Nez. Haslett shut off the engine and undid his seatbelt, getting up for his start down the stairs. He stopped, reeling back. A rag-tag bunch of misfits were surrounding the Winnebago as if he were Custer about to last stand.

"Smerchook! You lazy bastard! Get up!" Nez yelled and shook her fist again, now two-thirds up the pathway with Tracy trucking along behind her.

Tracy glanced back, seeing Haslett trying to catch up. He looked like a sad Pied Piper. A group of seven formed a loose line of stragglers, congregating behind. Most kept an apprehensive distance, but one small fellow with a prosthetic left fore-arm had hooked his claw into Haslett's cargo-shorts as if to bumper-shine along for the ride.

Two middle-aged women trudged eight paces back, giggling, pointing at Haslett, and whispering back and forth. One was dark, very short, and terribly obese, with the inappropriate name of Dainty; the other her bi-polar opposite – a tall, pale, anorexic bone-rack suitably nick-named Gnarly. Roger came next with her head facing down, limping along and kicking up dust, but avoiding all eye contact. Gus, Speed, and Spin-Dry brought up the rear, each packing serious, but poorly-diagnosed issues of their own.

The hammock tipped. Its occupant flopped out and unfolded; towering at least a foot – more like two – over Tracy who stared eye-level at the bare, brown, ribby torso painted in dots of charcoal, stripes of white pipe-clay, and splotches of red ochre. Two squinty eyes peered at her from above wide, flaring nostrils and huge, sealed lips, topped with a frizzy, grey Afro propped up by a tie-dyed sweat band, appearing much like the cap of an old pine mushroom. Tracy gazed down to faded Wranglers, cut off above horse-like knees, and held at the loops by a braided cloth rope; one strand black, one red, and one yellow. She followed two crane-legs to the ground where they stood firmly planted inside a pair of size 20, lime-green Crocs.

Haslett hustled up and braked next to Tracy; his newly-found disciples box-caring behind. Everyone gawked up at the face.

"My name is Haru Maru Karu, Harack Marack Karack, Smerchook," the Aborigine man slowly said, frowning with eyes shut and arms tightly folded across his tattooed and metal-studded chest. He flashed open bloodshot eyes, staring first at Haslett, then at Tracy, then dipped his left hand as if an extension of the space shuttle's robotic arm. "But you may call me Smerchook for short."

Haslett awkwardly reached back. "Pleased to meet you, Mister Smerchook."

"Silence in the ranks!" Smerchook roared, directing a carrot-like forefinger at Haslett. He gently rolled his other palm upright in a polite gesture towards Tracy and quietly said, "I was addressing... the lady."

Tracy stepped back. Haslett strained his neck at Smerchook.

"Okay! Cut it out, goofball!" Nez laughed. "These are the Canadians I was telling you about."

Smerchook loosened his lips to a grin that went from earringed ear to earringed ear.

"Tracy and Bob… meet Donnie Osmand!" Nez introduced them. Tracy and Haslett just looked at each other.

"Yeah, yeah, I know. Different spelling, though," Nez said. "But he goes by his tribal name, Smerchook."

"I perfer my traditional Dharawal title, if you please. Not my university frat name which was *Gadya Gabara*." Smerchook smiled, placing one arm behind his back, wrapping the other in front, bowing deeply to Tracy.

"Your frat name means… ah?" she asked, uncomfortably trying to make conversation.

"Ya might wanna Google that." Smerchook chuckled. "So… Canadjun, eh? Never been there, but I hear it's a lot like New Zealand, only where sheep-shaggers get more respect. Mountains and Mounties I'd imagine." In a flash, he whipped off Haslett's safari hat, squashing it on top of his own head. "Always wanted one of them Mountie lids, but this'll do."

Tracy and Nez snickered, watching Haslett dance for it. Smerchook out- maneuvered him like a Harlem Clown, fake-dribbling the hat, and thrilling his dysfunctional fan-club who whistled and cat-called him on.

"All right, you wing-nut!" Nez kicked at Smerchook. "Give it back and get a grip. We're here on some serious business."

"Get a grip?" Smerchook shouted. "I'll get a grip!"

He grabbed Haslett in an armed-barred head-lock, giving a quick knuckle-noogie, setting the hat back on, and taking Haslett's hand in a thumb-locked shake followed by two quick fist-bumps. He turned to Tracy, winked, lightly placing his fingertips on the small of her back, and escorting her to a rickety, wooden picnic table at the side of a strange-looking, dome-shaped fabrication near his hammock. Haslett and Nez followed.

"Sit down, my new friends. Sit down." Smerchook snapped his fingers, code-signing little Billy to fetch a rusty, blue Coleman cooler filled with brown ice, leaves, and pop, which he hooked by one handle and dragged over. Smerchook raised the creaky lid and offered his guests a drink. Tracy selected three Raspberry Schweppes, handing one off to each Nez and Haslett.

"Stop!" Smerchook screamed. Haslett was about to open his. The three jolted as if zapped by a cattle prod. "Let me see that!"

Haslett handed over the drink which Smerchook shook and gave back.

"So you're here on serious business?" Smerchook settled into a folding camp chair, feet flat on the ground, knees forced level with his eyes. He waved the back of his hand at his group. "Well, as you can see, this is certainly no place to be serious."

Billy wagged in agreement. He'd taken a position next to Smerchook, sitting under the long, empty hammock. Roger stood behind one of the anchor trees, keeping her eyes on the ground. Dainty and Gnarly leaned against the other big coolibah, holding hands, whispering, and giggling at Haslett. Hobbit-like Gus was making Tracy jittery. He seemed to continually stare at her boobs from behind John Lennon sunglasses and stayed within groping distance. He wasn't the least bit intimidating by stature, though – unlike Speed, who tipped the scales at well over three hundred and could have stood-in for Hagrid from Harry Potter. Spin-Dry was off in a world-all-alone, silently squatting on an aluminum lawn chair directly under Speed's shadow; four hammock lengths back where Smerchook told them to stay.

"I better explain to Tracy and Bob," Nez said. "Smerchook and I go way back to our college days in California. I was majoring in psychology and Smerchook was…"

"Primarily interested in pharmaceuticals at the time," Smerchook cut in, pointing a finger straight up. "I was immersed in their research and development, which I funded through the promotion of enlightenment products, however my service ran into a bit of a misunderstanding with a federal agency. At least they were kind enough to room and board me a spell, then allowed for my airfare home." He shook his head. "To their loss, America still declines all applications for my return."

Nez laughed. "Smerchook and I've had many, many hours of philosophical discussion. He was on an exchange program between UC in Berekley and ANU in Canberra. We've kept linked-in as professional peers ever since. Smerchook holds a Masters from the ANU School of Philosophy. He's the connection as to why I'm here in Australia. He and Professor Sorenson."

"The old sword-swallower, hisself!" Smerchook grinned and motioned to his crotch. "Oops! Sorry to the newcomers. I get a little colorful out here. You see, the group I support keeps me a little bushed, and I don't get into town much these days. That and a slight jurisdictional issue I'm committed to."

Haslett looked about the grounds. It made an Occupy encampment look master-planned.

To the east of the dome, in a clearing about fifty paces out, lay a blue and orange collection of small, tarped-off sleeping tents, encircling a large, army-green, canvas cook-house; its rusty-tin chimney barely roped-up by two yellow, nylon lines. At the clearing's fringe sat a faded red and white, eighteen-foot travel-trailer with three flat tires and its tongue-missing hitch propped on an angled stump. The door was braced shut by a warped two-by-four and the word *Office* dripped in black spray-paint down the side. Old Stinky, their Land Rover, was next to the office with her engine hood up, showing evidence of a recent carburetor fire, and three Honda dirt-bikes without serial numbers leaned against her rusty rear-end; one with the front wheel missing from badly-bent forks. North of the dome was a thick stand of trees, corridoring the back-eddy's bank; a well-worn trail cut through to a murky swimming hole, complete with a frayed, hemp rope hanging from a rather thin branch.

"You're curious as to our workings, I can see," Smerchook said. "Welcome to the recovery center, mates. I run a bit of an unusual show out here but, then, my clientele tend to respond well that way."

"What sort of facility do you administer, Smerchook?" Tracy asked, most interested, but cautiously keeping Gus in her peripheral.

"In general terms, m'lady, it's a non-traditional... wellness facility. The residents you see are socially-isolated individuals who require that special attention which the mainstream cannot efficiently provide. The current enrollments are long-term cases referred to me by the Wollongong schizophrenic society, after a collapse of their disability assistance. I managed to secure new-start allowances for them through a creative approach under the auspices of the Department of Human Services. I do... ahhh... re-alignment programs, employment pathway plans, career supplements, addiction intervention, dependency counselling, spiritual guidance and, to some degree, legal rehabilitation. I pride myself on versatility by offering a wide variety of services."

"He also runs a bank," Billy said, wiggling enthusiastically. "He gets us to sign our welfare checks over to him..."

"Ah! Tut-tut!" Smerchook muzzled Billy's yap. "Our financial matters must remain strictly confidential."

Tracy glanced at them, then back to keep Gus's hands in sight. He'd been inching closer.

"I'm sure I can be of help." Smerchook gestured to the Canadians, changing the subject. "Shimisani has arranged for me to run a sweat ceremony, but was very cagey about the type." He pointed to the domed structure which was partly obscured by the rubbery, silver foliage of overhanging eucalyptus trees.

"Shimisani?" Tracy asked.

"A term of endearment," Smerchook replied, circling a finger at Nez. "From Navajo it translates to *Grandmother*. A respect for my Leslie... the Shaman." He closed his eyes, giving a slight bow to Nez, whispering, "All my relations."

"An integral part of Smerchook's recovery program is his sweat lodge," Nez said. "Smerchook is the hereditary chief of the Wodi Wodi clan of the Dharawal tribe and was raised in the sweat lodge culture. He's forgotten more about sweats than most Shamans will ever know."

"Are you a Shaman, too?" Tracy asked, getting up and moving. Gus had snuggled in tight.

"Not precisely," Smerchook said. "I'm not a Shaman such as Leslie. I don't journey as much. My method relies on making the spirits do the work. They come to me. Not me to them. I find it takes less effort."

Nez smirked, letting him continue.

"To each their own, though. We all just do what works. In my tradition we are referred to not as Shamans, but as *Clever-Men*. We're kind of the jack-of-all-trades in the tribe."

"Oh, he's clever, all right," Roger said, not looking up. "Clever enough to scam the government."

Everyone turned to her.

"Attt-tattt-tta!" Smerchook sprang up. "Don't pay any attention to Roger. She's struggling with a change in her meds. Now, let me explain a bit about sweats. Follow me."

Tracy took Haslett's hand, walking with Nez towards the dome. Gus got up, stumbling behind her. The rest of the group moved, mingling about, all seeming to know their positions. Haslett stood, examining its construction.

The lodge was a makeshift affair about fourteen feet in diameter and six high, framed in ribs of skinny poles stuck in the dirt at one side, bent over, and lashed to ones from the other. Its skin was a patchwork of once-blue, polyethylene tarps stitched together, now nearly black from the stain of soot and smoke. The small, ground-level doorway faced due east and was partially opened by a flap pulled back and fish-hooked to the upper north corner, allowing Haslett a peek inside. Brown fabric mats were scattered about the earthen floor, circling a central depression three feet across and one deep.

Haslett moved to inspect a fire-pit, sixteen feet directly east of the door. In it were forty round rocks ranging from eight to twelve inches in diameter, mixed with charred chunks. To the north was a stack of split firewood with various implements leaning against it; two shovels, a splitting-axe, a pair of log-tongs, a well-worn broom, a chain-saw, and a red, metal jerry-can full of mixed gas.

"It's not pretty, but it does the trick." Smerchook motioned towards the entry. "It's what goes on inside that counts. You see, sweats have been a ceremonial part of every indigenous culture, from every part of the world, including the Inuit who used animal fats for a fuel instead of wood. Like I said, we use what works."

Nez agreed. Smerchook continued.

"There are many different purposes to sweats... purification sweats, healing sweats, clan sweats, battle sweats, funeral sweats. The list goes on and on, but the procedure is the same. It involves mindset."

Smerchook swirled his finger around his ear.

"The ceremony has etiquette. It prepares the participants to release from everyday cares. To experience their inner self. And the outer world of the spirits. That can be done for a simple self-interest, or, as a concentrated force for the benefit of the whole. I, like all lodge leaders, have developed my own routine, but I'm flexible according to what I'm trying to achieve. Etiquette is the most important element of the ceremony."

He swirled the finger at them.

"The lodge is a community."

He swirled at himself.

"I respect the lodge, and the others inside, in order to respect myself. An offering is always given. This is symbolic of the universal truth that you must give in order to receive. What goes around, comes around."

Tracy nodded.

"My lodge will hold up to twenty, but normally we have eight to twelve participating. I do three or four a week. Some of the locals drop by, and I always accommodate. We start with a simple gathering outside, start the fire, jam a bit of music, give an offering, discuss what we'd each like to achieve, then share a few prayers, and generally get in the groove."

He pointed to his crew.

"There are certain responsibilities assigned to the more experienced... firetender... rocktender... doortender... but the general participants are expected to just relax and go with the flow. There are certain seating positions inside, depending upon the need, but we are all circular to the central rock-pit. In a circle, everyone is equal."

"Some more than others!" Roger yelled. Smerchook ignored her.

"Also, the domed shape of the lodge is equivocal to mother earth's womb which gives new life. Out of practicality, I stay near the door in the event someone is uncomfortable and needs to depart. Remember, this is not an endurance test. There is no shame in not completing. I find, to the contrary, that many don't want to leave when it's over."

"It's a way better trip than any drugs I've been on," Speed said, out loud to himself. He was standing by the woodpile with the axe in both hands and the chainsaw at his feet. Gnarly and Spin-Dry had each picked up a shovel. Dainty was already in position, holding the unhooked door-flap up with the broom, while Gus had shoved off the picnic table, shuffled over, and nudged next to Tracy. Roger stayed behind her tree.

"Hang on, gang!" Smerchook ordered. "You're getting way ahead of yourselves again."

He waved, and they set down their tools.

"Each has their job, and it upsets them to go out of routine," he told his guests. "I have Speed tend the fire. The flames are soothing to him. The two with the shovels look after hot rocks and Dainty, there, has the doorway down to a science, but she can't fit inside. Billy acts as my spirit-helper."

Smerchook gave the little guy a pat; returned with a vigorous nod.

"Roger prefers just to watch and Gus, here, we have to be a little careful with, as he's blind. He could end up hurting himself."

Tracy snapped a look at Gus. He smiled as Smerchook carried on.

"We have four rounds, or sessions, in the ceremony. Each involves a shut door creating a light-deprived environment that becomes more intense with each round. Light is the biggest detractor to our awareness, as we naturally look to light for physical guidance. In a sweat lodge, we look to the dark for spiritual guidance. We also use subtle psychological therapy… a relaxed and equal atmosphere with no hierarchy… no set script. It allows the individual to confide in their needs, their views, and their offerings. We have group discussion. We share our emotions. And we have respectful olfactory rituals, such as sweet smudging and pipe smoking."

He paused, making sure they understood.

"We gradually decrease lighting, then amplify sound with drumming, rattling, prayer, chants, and singing. During this time, rocks are heated in the fire, then carried to the central pit. We ladle water on them from a wooden spoon and bucket, increasing heat with each round. The heat becomes so intense that the individual, thus the group, must focus on their issue, not on their discomfort. This facilitates an altering of consciousness and allows access to the non-local world. The world of spirits."

His helpers were fidgeting. Smerchook glanced at the sun.

"It's mid-afternoon. The ceremony takes about three hours, so let's take a break and re-group in a bit. Dress lightly. No metals, like jewelery or watches. Also, don't eat anything, but make sure you're properly hydrated."

Tracy and Haslett turned to leave.

"Ah-Heh Heh Hem." Smerchook coughed.

They stopped, seeing the outstretched hand.

"By the way... about the offering? I take cash, Visa, and Mastercard, but no personal checks, please. I'm having a slight issue with the bank at the moment."

"Yes. Yes, of course," Tracy said, subconsciously looking for her purse. "Ah, what would be appropriate?"

Nez swatted Smerchook.

"Just kidding," he said, shielding with both forearms as she cuffed some more. "A little tobacco will do. It's symbolic. Nezzie, here, always carries some spare in her bag for a loaner."

* * *

As Haslett and Tracy headed back to the motorhome, Smerchook snagged Doctor Nez by the arm, pulling her around Gus and behind the dome for a talk.

"Okay," he said, bending over, head down near hers. "What the fuck's goin' on? These aren't your typical ass-head New Agers seeking a show by the next trendy mystic. What's their angle?"

"I couldn't tell you anything on the phone." Nez looked at her friends, two hundred feet distant, then back at Smerchook. "This is far too serious. Besides, with you, I never know who's listening in."

"Hey, I'm too old for that shit. I got a good schtick happening here. I'm not gonna screw it up and go back to the clink."

Nez scowled. "I would certainly hope not."

"So who are these guys and whadda they really want?"

"They are absolutely for real," she said. "This has nothing to do with money, or making some schmucks feel good about themselves, so don't even go there. It's real. It's one of those rare, genuine cases of soul loss. I wouldn't have brought them here if it wasn't."

Smerchook frowned, straightening up.

Nez leaned to him. "I have to do a retrieval, and the only way is through a sweat."

"Retrieval?"

"Nothing else is even remotely powerful enough."

He backed away.

She grabbed his hand. "I'll do the dirty work, but I need your help to run it."

Smerchook studied Nez. "You're serious? What you said on the phone was you had some serious clients. I thought that meant serious... as in serious coin. That's why I got all painted up."

She shook her head. He pointed back to the picnic table.

"C'mon, Les. Siddown. Give it to me straight. What's their deal?"

Nez perched on the table top. Smerchook dangled his limbs out beside her.

"They contacted me through Sorenson, asking his help on mythical creatures and soul retrieval. I was suspicious, but Sorenson screened them. They're legit. Both are Canadian. Bob used to be a cop, and Tracy's some kind of financier. I know she's loaded, but that's of no consequence."

Smerchook's brow went up. Nez's elbow went out.

"She made substantial donations to ANU and to Narajmata center, but there's no fee in this sweat for you or for me. It won't work that way. It's our duty. Our responsibility to help them. It's our loyalty to the ancients who taught us our craft."

Smerchook's brow went down.

Nez continued. "I spent the last two weeks immersed with them at Narajmata, and I think I've got her issue worked out. But not his."

"She's the one needing retrieval?" Smerchook peered at Nez.

"No. Tracy is the classic case of ghost-sickness."

Smerchook's head cocked.

Nez's didn't. "That's a Navajo term for a purely psychotic disorder where someone is convinced they've lost part of their soul and goes about life in a state of numbness. Like a ghost. It's manifested by unresolved grief, fatigue, chronic sadness, a sense of worthlessness, and a feeling of suffocation or being buried alive by stressors. Sometimes it's wrongfully diagnosed as Somatoform Disorder or Briquet's Syndrome."

"Hate it when that happens," he mumbled.

"In her case, it's pure and simple guilt that led to a complete lack of self-esteem and the inability to be at internal peace. Father-worship was her baggage. She spent her entire life in her father's service and did nothing whatsoever that she felt honorable or worthwhile about. The dad's gone now, and she wanted amends. I did a total emotional breakdown with her. Brutal journeying. Lots of sobbing and shaking, but she's vented out now, and her build-up came back real quick. She's a bright cookie, that one."

"So what's this Bob dude's thing?"

"Now he's a whole different sport. I didn't even try rehab with him. I did a test journey and ran into something real frickin' nasty."

"Huh?"

"He used to be on some police tactical squad. Years ago, some place in northern Canada, he and his partner were attacked by an entity that came at them from the other side. It killed the partner. Nearly got Bob, too. Then it made off with their souls. Or, at least part of their souls, from what I see."

"For real?"

"Yeah. It's got them trapped somewhere in-between. There's no way I can get there in a normal journey. You gotta help. You gotta trick it. Make it come to us. When it does, I attack it while Bob makes a go for the souls."

Nez looked up. Smerchook looked down.

"As I said, it's our duty. Our obligation to the ancients, to help them get free."

"Hmmm?" He squinted up. "This entity?" he asked, gripping his chin and clenching the table. "Which of them was it?"

She turned away. "He calls it The Kushtaka."

"Huh?"

Nez took a long breath and turned back to him. "You know it as Bunyip."

"Whoa-No! Oh-No! No-No-No-No-No!"

Smerchook jumped off the table, spinning around, locking his fingers in his Afro, facing Nez.

"Not having no part of that! You know that story. When I was young, old Bungaree-a-Goneda, my mentor, conjured up that shapeshifter in a sweat, and it cut his fucking throat. No way! No fucking Bunyip in my sweat lodge!"

He batted both hands, twisting away.

"You know, Smerchook. You disappoint me. I thought you had more balls."

He stopped. Twenty seconds passed till he said, "Having balls and being crazy are two different things. Going a round in the lodge with that fucking thing is suicide."

"Remember one night? In the dorm at Berekely? Remember our talk? What you told me about it and your mentor?"

No response.

"You said one day you'd face it and get even."

No response.

"You can't just keep playing silly-bugger all your life, Smerchook. Pretending things are good when they're not. You gotta deal with the bad sooner or later."

Still no response.

"And this situation is bad. Probably the toughest sweat you'll ever do. But you have to do it. It's your duty. Your loyalty to Goneda, at the very least. You owe it to him. You said so yourself."

His silence continued.

"Smerchook?"

He turned – head drooped, chin at chest – blood-shot eyes gone watery. He bent, draping those spindly arms over Leslie Nez's shoulders, pulling her in. They stood, tight in embrace. Nez felt the tall man tremble. Neither said a word for the longest time. Neither needed to – you know that their fear was understood.

Smerchook released his hug, stared up in the sky, then back down to Doctor Nez.

"Tough's not the word, Shimasani. Dangerous is more like it. Real fucking dangerous." He horse-kicked the ground. "No, I'll do the dirty work, but we need a plan."

* * *

Tracy and Haslett strolled back to the lodge-site, carrying towels after changing in the Winnebago; she now in a baggy, cream shirt over khaki shorts, he stripped to flowered Bermudas and bare-chested.

The usual suspects were milling about. Speed had his fire roaring, enjoying the flames. Dainty swept the floor mats which Gnarly tossed out and slung over a red, polypropylene rope stretched between branches. Spin-Dry squatted, hawkishly sorting the rocks by size and into groups of four, while Gus looked vacantly on from the picnic table. Roger was in transition, blowing sporadically through a long, termite-hollowed log and snickering at Billy, who struggled to unscrew the top off a large, green, Rubbermaid garbage can. Nez and Smerchook were nowhere to be seen.

"Here, let us help you with that." Tracy reached for the can. Billy unhooked from the handle and stood aside. Haslett grabbed the main barrel as Tracy gripped, twisting the lid. Haslett was face level with Billy's chest which was covered by a black T-shirt with white letters. He coughed at Tracy, nodding to Billy's design; a pattern with hundreds of tiny, randomly-placed ones and zeros, with a script reading 'There are only 10 types of people in the world: Those who understand binary and those who don't'. Tracy chuckled as the lid popped free.

Inside were Smerchook's tools – a hand-drum and its stick, a pair of Bush Stone-Curlew wings with sewn-on leather handgrips, a soapstone pipe wrapped with a beaded thong, a Ziploc baggie holding a smokeable ounce of what certainly wasn't tobacco, a blue nylon CD case containing some other dried and diced plant matter, a huge string of sea-shells, rattles, sassafras clackers, a odorous leather bag secured by a drawstring, a carved talking-stick, two bullroarers, painted rocks, bones and charms, crystals, leaves, bark, coins, stamps and a Scottish plaid sash loaded with collector's lapel pins, six Tupperware bowls full of paints and dyes, two hefty rosewood drumsticks with leather ball ends, a bundle of tattered checkbooks, pens, disposable gloves, a box with dozens of assorted credit cards, crumpled legal documents, and a phone book.

"He needs the big drumsticks first," Billy said, pulling them out and pointing to a set of four, ceremonial conga drums aligned on a large, woven, coconut-leaf mat to the south of the lodge. Tracy and Haslett moved over, examining the instruments.

"God, they are beautiful!" Tracy whispered. "Look at the engravings, Bobby. And the color and detail in the patterns on the sides. These must be hundreds of years old." She knelt and gave the smallest drum a flick on its grey, rawhide head, sending a sharp vibration to their ears. She tapped the largest with her palm, then ran her fingers over the leather webbing which tightly stretched the membrane to the rim of the shell. "These are exquisite!"

"Smerchook don't like us fooling with those," Billy cautioned her, his mouth salivating from something that he waved in his good hand. "He says they're magic drums and bring out bad spirits if you don't play just right."

"Oh, I am so sorry." Tracy retracted her hand and got up. "By the way, where is he?"

Billy hooked at the cookhouse. "He went in there with the lady doc you brought. They're talking medicine stuff for the ceremony."

Tracy looked over at the big wall-tent just as its canvas door pulled aside and Smerchook stepped out. He was barefoot, dressed in a bright-orange loin-cloth with a red, black, and yellow Aborigine flag wrapped about his forehead and draped down his chest. His face was now painted with pipe clay, ochre, and charcoal; his body patterns freshened-up, too.

Nez appeared from behind. She'd changed to a dazzling, calf-length Navajo dress in the most vivid of colors – zig-zagged patterns of ruby on taupe at the short-sleeved mid-section, horizontally banded across a royal-blue background. Her shoulder line showed an ermine-white base, set with jet-black diamonds shaped within turquoise and blood-red squares. The wide, half-moon collar was a sunrise of bright violet lines becoming fiery yellows, turning orange, then to red, pink, and purple. Below a sashed waist was a solid mix of the earth – hues of sand, clay, rock, and wood. Brilliantly dyed feathers – canary and emerald, sapphire and crimson – stood up from her headband and out from her wristbands and anklets.

Nez held a rawhide-wrapped, beaded rattle in her left hand; her satchel and a taut-skin drum in her right. Smerchook carried a folded-up, red woollen blanket intricately woven with Aborigine designs. Together, they maneuvred the tent maze, marching in parallel back to the lodge.

To you – they'd be astonishing sights.

* * *

"Shimisani has informed me of the purpose to our sweat," Smerchook said, looking sternly down at Haslett.

There was no hint of apprehension as he placed a monstrous mitt on Haslett's left shoulder.

"I expect your full participation in this journey... to retrieve your soul... and set free that of your partner. This is absolutely required. You are the one who must travel. You must travel alone, to that world in-between, seek out the place of captivity, break free your energies, send your partner's soul to eternal rest... and return with yours to locality. No one can do this for you. Not I. Not Shimisani. You must do this alone."

Haslett swallowed. "So just how bumpy's this ride gonna be?"

Smerchook kept his hand on the shoulder. Tracy glanced back and forth, gripping Haslett's arm. Nez stayed still, and Gus sat sightlessly by. Billy heeled next to his master.

"Impossible to predict," Smerchook replied. "I've met this entity once... the one you know as The Kushtaka. Hopefully this time it will be... more productive."

He let go of Haslett, shifting the shape of his blanket.

"So how does this work?" Haslett asked.

"We'll do a four-round sweat. The first two rounds are communal. Everyone who wishes to participate will be allowed in. The third is restricted. It focuses on taunting the entity. Raising its awareness. I'll provoke it. Paranormally piss it off, so to speak. Antagonize it. Then trick it with spiritual bait... the offering of a soul... a sacrifice no shapeshifter can resist."

Tracy gripped harder.

"In the fourth round, I'll call in the demon. When it appears in the lodge to face me, Shimisani will attack it and divert its attention. While it's distracted, you slip out in your journey. You circle behind its awareness... to locate and free the souls. Remember... in this state, time does not exist. Then you return to this plane of existence. It's like a supernatural jail-break."

"The spiritual bait?" Haslett asked. "This sacrificial soul? What... exactly... you got in mind here?"

Smerchook peered down. Billy's eyes turned sad as a Bassett's. Smerchook's gaze passed over to Tracy. Her mouth gaped as she touched her chest. Smerchook nodded. Haslett turned grey as a ghost.

"I see no other option," Smerchook said. "We can only have four in the lodge when the entity appears. Anymore is unmanageable. Tracy, you must be inside for Bob's spiritual support. There is a risk, but no other choice. However, I sense the bond between you two is strong enough to withstand this."

"I'll be beside you throughout, Tracy." Nez gave a reassuring grasp on her arm. "I wouldn't approve if I wasn't, ah, reasonably sure of your safety. But there's no other way. We have to use this ruse... if we're to defeat The Kushtaka and return the souls to their rightful place." Nez let her go. "Or... we could just leave things as they are."

Tracy took Haslett's hands, connecting his eyes. She needed no time for decision.

"It is the right thing, Bobby. I trust them. Totally. And my love for you is far stronger than whatever this monster can be. We have to go through with this. We have come this far already. You have to be freed..." She lifted his hands to her face. "Mike has to be freed."

* * *

Haslett stared at the ground.

In silent soliloquy, he thought of the collusion made long, long ago. He thought of the years of confinement which could finally come to an end. He thought of his loyalty, then looked to his right bicep and the motto scrolled across the blade of his winged sword. He thought of the souls, anguishing somewhere in-between the darkness and the light. He thought of Tracy. Of Maria. And of Gabriella. He thought of Bude. Moloci. Akker. Of Sergeant Bate. And of why the informants had to be murdered.

But now the more he thought, the more his thoughts turned towards confronting The Kushtaka. He brought his gaze onto Tracy. Then to Nez. Then way, way on up to Smerchook. He swallowed and squeezed back on Tracy.

"Let's do it. Who dares wins, you know."

Smerchook gave a sharp nod and a dull smile. "First we need to warm-up. It's a ritual; getting everyone on the same page. Remember. It's all mindset. I'll explain the procedure as we go along, but you just go with the flow. You do what comes natural."

Smerchook herded them all to the coconut mat where his drums sat waiting.

"Music gets the mind set," he said, placing his folded blanket down as a cushion, sitting cross-legged, and taking the drumsticks from Billy. "Roger! Bring your didgeridoo closer and join in, my dear. Gnarly! Grab a bullroarer. Spin-Dry, get on the gumleaf, and Gus, you take the clackers."

Like a rehearsed and choreographed production, Smerchook's band of social rejects took to their outback stage. Roger shuffled in to the edge of the mat, closing her eyes, and blowing low, haunting hoots on her hollowed-out log. Speed got two sassafras sticks from the Rubbermaid can, helping Gus's wee hands tap them aside Roger's didgeridoo. Squelchy-squeak-squeals came from Spin-Dry, who'd picked a dollar-bill sized, green leaf from a gum tree, lip pressed it, forcing exhales across the leathery surface. Gnarly took a bullroarer from Billy, who'd hooked it from Smerchook's tool-bin. Looking like a straightened-out boomerang with a hole in one end, it whipped at the end of a cord. Smerchook began a slow, low tone on his congas.

The beat went on and the pace picked up. A buzz off the bullroarer blended with blasts off the empty log, as more squeals and squelches spun from the gum leaf. Nez double-tapped on her drum using the rattle's blunt end. Gus clicked away to the cadence. Smerchook's fingers and palms altered thumps on the congas; tempo setting pace for the others.

The rise and fall of Gnarly's bullroarer bellowed a ghostly groan *Whoo-a-Hoo Whoo-a-Hoo Hoo-a-Woo* as the didgeridoo's flared horn emitted electrically-charged echoes *Wah Wah Wanda Wanda Wah Wah We Wah Wonna Wonna Wah.*

Clackety-Clack-Click-Click-Clackety-Clack snapped on Gus's clickers like a pair of Irish spoons. Spin-Dry's gumleaf pitched to the beautiful tone of a pinched violin, wailing *Dee Dee Wheeee... Dee Daa Heeee... Dee Daa Whaaaa... Wee-a-Whaaa... Wee-a-Whaaa.*

Nez switched to a tambourine swish of her rattle, chanting in a barefooted dance. Smerchook's arms sped faster. Then faster. Then faster, near blur. A baritone song in indigenous stanzas correlated the improvised instruments, as Smerchook mourned a metaphysical message.

Tracy and Haslett stood mesmerized. The composition was nothing they'd ever heard – a musical masterpiece by a mystical maestro, flowing in fanatical frenzy.

* * *

The two snapped from locality.

A force from beyond carried their collective consciousness as if elevated to an opera box in the trees.

Haslett relaxed.

Tracy transcended.

She floated in awe – in divine bliss – marvelling in perfect clarity as the world all around her made sense. She felt at her physical carriage – reaching over – reaching under – her hands never moving. She saw all without eyes. Heard all without ears. Smelled fragrances without nostrils. Tasted sweets without buds.

For Tracy –

Time stopped –

She became the music, the song, and the dance.

BamBamBamBamBamBamBamBam BOOM

Smerchook raised the drumsticks high in the air, sirening a screech that slashed like a sonic machete, popping them back into locality.

"Ohhh." Tracy was barely audible. She'd gone down on her knees, palming the dirt. "Whh... What happened, Bobby?"

Haslett bent, steadying her.

"That, my dear, was your altered state of consciousness," Smerchook answered for him. "Quite the experience, isn't it?"

"You okay, Trace?" Haslett helped her rise.

'Yes, yes. Fine. Wow! That was amazing!"

"As I said, it's mindset." Smerchook gave his drumsticks to Billy and a front-handed thanks to the band. "Now, to the next step in setting your minds."

* * *

They set their instruments aside, forming a rough semi-circle. Billy handed the blue CD case which Smerchook zipped open, taking a wad of the dried, diced material, and began some short sniffs.

Haslett watched, suspecting dope. "What's that stuff?"

"Rat-Root," Smerchook replied. "A tradition in my culture. Sort of like chewing tobacco or snuff. Here. Wanna try?"

Haslett's nose wrinkled, moving back.

"Don't worry. There're no hallucinogens."

Smerchook held out the case. Curiosity got the better of Haslett. He took a pinch, put it in his mouth, and bit down.

"Pttt...tttthewh. Ye-ucck!" He spat, wiping his mouth with his fingers. "Eeech! That is horrible!"

Tracy broke out laughing.

"Yeah, I know," Smerchook replied, closing the case. "It tastes like horseshit. That's why I only sniff it."

Nez moved beside Tracy as Haslett rinsed from a cup that Dainty filled from the red, metal jerry-can. Speed gave his fire a stir with the axe, as Spin-Dry shoveled five large rocks in the fire-pit. Gus looked amusedly on. Billy fished the soapstone pipe out of Smerchook's ceremonial can, as well as the Ziploc baggie. Gnarly took the floor-mats off the poly-prop line and crawled inside the lodge, Dainty holding the flap with the broom. Haslett had stopped spatting out petrol. He tried to peek in, but was barricaded by Dainty, who'd bent to boss over Gnarly.

Haslett leaped like a tasered wallaby. Roger had snuck up and goosed his backside, pointing at Dainty, mumbling, "We call her Woman-Wider-Than-She-Is-Tall."

Tracy missed it. She'd been watching Smerchook, who'd moved near the fire, whispering to Billy. He scampered away, tossing the plastic baggie back in the bin and retrieving the carved talking-stick. Nez touched Tracy's elbow, calling Haslett over. She placed a small, tied bundle into each of their hands.

"Tobacco," Nez said. "For the offering. It's customary to approach the lodge master, present him with an offering and ask for permission to take part in the sweat. Also, in the ceremony, he's to be referred to as 'Grandfather'. It shows respect for the wisdom of the ancients which he represents."

"Wisdom, my ass," muttered Roger, still by the door and blocked by Dainty. Speed heard her. He lip-cursed 'Fuck-You', fisting Roger.

She fingered him back. Billy caught it, giving an up-yours with a left hook which Spin-Dry backed-up with a razzpberry. Dainty, thinking the slam was for her, turned and broom-smacked at Spin-Dry, who ducked, and Gus got clobbered instead. He had no idea where it came from and let out a mortified cry. Speed lost it. He lunged at Dainty like an axe-wielding Saxon. Gnarly shrieked. Nez tugged Tracy to safety as Haslett stepped-in, seizing Speed's sharp, swinging splitter. Smerchook screamed a "Time-out, Kids!" and cursed them all back to the corner.

Roger refused to join in, slinking away to the tree. Smerchook let her be, putting himself between the fire and the lodge, folding his arms around the talking stick, and turning his back on the bunch.

"It's time to approach," Nez said, just a whisper.

Haslett went first. He stood behind Smerchook, looked back at Nez, then shuffled and coughed.

"Grandfather," he said. "I come to ask if I can join in your sweat lodge ceremony. Here, ah… take this tobacco and allow me to, ah, go in there with you."

Smerchook kept his back to Haslett. "What is it that you seek?"

Haslett coughed again and reached for a toothpick, right hand patting his bare chest. He looked down. All around. Then up, up, up at Smerchook. Shifting foot to foot, he clasped his hands, coughing more.

And then – a wave of calmness washed through Bob Haslett. A wave in the form of a voice. A voice from his past. A presence not felt since he'd dried himself out. Someone much more powerful than him. His body relaxed. His thoughts collected. His vision became clear as he remembered his partner and promise.

"I seek to retrieve our souls."

Smerchook turned. He peered at Haslett over his lips and his nostrils, nodding to receive the tobacco. "Your sincerity is recognized."

Tracy stepped around Gus, taking her turn. Placidly, she offered Smerchook her bundle, giving a slight curtsey. "Grandfather, I also wish to partake in your lodge ceremony. Please grant me permission."

"And you seek…"

"I seek to right a wrong," she replied without hesitation.

Smerchook smiled, accepting her offer.

Spin-Dry presented next, giving up rocks for a chance at inside. Billy followed with Gus in his paw, giving Smerchook two packs of tobacco and the pipe. Nez went last; her gift a blend of sage and sweet grass. Smerchook tossed the offerings in the fire, keeping Nez's packet for the pipe.

"All my relations," Smerchook murmured, then motioned one hand at the door. Dainty flapped it open. Speed and Gnarly tended rocks and the fire. Roger kept safe at her tree. Spin-Dry stayed out of the way, and Billy brought back four, long strips of colored cloth.

"For you." Smerchook gave Haslett a yellow streamer. "You're to sit at the north, the direction of the warrior. Tie it above your head from the frame. Tracy, yours is white, for the visionary. You're to sit at Bob's right, which is west."

He gave Nez a green flag for the healer of the south, then pointed his pipe at the lodge. "And I stay here, east, under the black banner, which is the way of the teacher. Spin-Dry, you sit still between Tracy and Shimisani, at the southwest. Gus, you're to my left, in case you need out, and Billy, you're in the usual spot to my right."

Billy dropped to all fours, clambering through the door. Smerchook grabbed him by the boxers and reefed back, yelling "Hang on! There's an order to this, or we'll be piling all over each other." He handed Tracy her white streamer. "My dear, you may go first."

Tracy slipped off her sandals and got down, carrying her towel, crawling on the brick-red dirt through the dome's slender passage. Till her eyes adjusted, she felt claustrophobic and slightly nauseous. She'd expected it to be rank, dank, and dingy but, to her surprise, the inside was pleasantly warm and smelled of fresh Radiata Pine needles, aromatic dried Chinaberry fruit, and shredded Mallee-tree bark meshed in with the framework.

Squinting about, she saw remnants of past ceremonies on the domed ceiling-cum-walls – braided grass, swatches of cloth, threaded shells with rawhide laces, tiny figurines of hair tied on bone, and little leather pouches containing secret wishes – all stained by round upon round of smoke and steam, human sweat, and many, many tears. She circled the empty rock-pit, taking her spot, sitting knees-up on a burlap mat at the west, opposite and facing the door.

"In you go, Spin-Dry." Smerchook's voice broke Tracy's silence.

Spin-Dry scuffled in, perching to Tracy's right, giving her an inquisitive look, then staring straight into the pit. Nez passed through next, carrying her drum, rattle, flag, and a crimson towel with gold accents. She reached by Spin-Dry, squeezing Tracy's arm, then set down her tools, stretching above to secure her green banner.

"Oh, right!" Tracy twisted within the tight space, tying her cloth to a lodge-pole. She turned to see Haslett duck-walk through the door. He knelt at her left, knotting his yellow band, squatting with it dangling down to his shoulder.

"Careful now," Smerchook told Billy, who nosed Gus inside. Gus groped for his mat, sitting cross-legged, haggard hands on knobby knees, and hairless head showing a toothless, crinkled smile. Billy scrambled out for the tool-can. Smerchook gave directions to the tenders as Billy trotted back, holding the leather bag, a drum, and its stick. He scampered under the flap and laid beside Haslett as if expecting a scratch on his belly.

Light faded as Smerchook folded in. He set down his pipe and carved talking-stick, taking the bag from Billy, loosening the drawstring, and carefully removing a talisman.

"This represents what I believe in," Smerchook said, showing the artifact of the ancients. "A discipline to adhere to." Detail was impossible to see in the dimly-lit dome, but it appeared an assembly of stones, bones, sticks, and shells knotted together with a crumbly, old cord. "It has been honored to me through generations of Clever-Men and manifests the commitment of service to others, despite sacrifice of the self."

Voices murmured as Smerchook placed the instrument of oracle around his neck.

"We start with the pipe ceremony," Smerchook said, picking it up, opening Nez's offering, and stuffing the bowl. "For those of you who don't smoke, I ask your courtesy to puff, but there's no need to inhale."

Gus spoke up. "This is the part I really like. It makes me happy, and I think up funny things."

Billy replied, "Smerchook only wants regular tobacco today..."

Smerchook jabbed Billy. "What'd you do with the lighter?"

"You already got it. It's in your hand. Geez."

"Oh, so it is." Smerchook flicked the Bic, lit the bowl, and took strong sucks on the mouthpiece. An orangey-red glow pierced the darkness. He passed to his right, in the direction of the sun, thanking the Creator with, "All my relations."

Billy took his turn, repeating the phrase, giving it to Haslett who took two short pulls. "All my relations," he hacked, handing to Tracy.

It was the first time in her life that she'd smoked. Carefully. Respectfully. Tracy held the pipe in both hands, drawing a breath. She expected to gag but, instead, a sweetness surprised her. She exhaled, drew again, blew it out, and passed to Spin-Dry with a soft, "All my relations."

Spin-Dry hogged the pipe, dragging away till it died, then hand-signaled Smerchook, who reached across, taking it back, filling, and re-lighting the bowl. A sense of uneasiness hung in the lodge.

"Please don't misinterpret the lack of comment," Smerchook told the newcomers. "There's plenty of respect, and the intentions are honorable. You see, Spin-Dry is a mute."

Nez took the pipe, puffing away like a pro. "All my relations," she said, passing to Gus, helping it into his hands. Gus finished, said his respect, and returned it to Smerchook who smoked away till it extinguished.

"All my relations," Smerchook said, swapping the pipe for the drum. "Time for the rocks," he called outside, pushing against Gus, as Gnarly shoveled in the first stone; a large, smoking-hot boulder, sliding it along the ground to the pit. Immediately, the temperature rose five degrees.

"We use five rocks for the prayer round," Smerchook said. "This first stone represents the creator. The next four rocks can have numerous meanings. The directions. The seasons. The tides and the times of day. Many things in our reality work off the number four."

Speed shoved in next, moving two rocks to the pit at the same time. Gnarly put the fourth through the door, and Speed followed-up with the fifth. The lodge took a sauna-like feel, but not yet unpleasant. The door remained partially open with the glow from the rocks giving just enough light to see faces. Beads formed on foreheads. Palms, underarms, and groins became damp.

Smerchook tapped his drum. "We go in a counter-clockwise direction. The direction of the sun. Each has the opportunity to offer a prayer, tell what they seek to achieve, or just vent if they wish. There's no time limit, and what's said in the lodge, stays in the lodge. This rule is never broken. There can be discussion, if problems need solving, but no two are to speak at the same time. You can choose to speak, or not to speak, but you may only speak with this in hand."

He handed Billy the talking-stick.

"Grandfather," Billy said. "I welcome our new friends and offer my prayers in support of what they seek. I also offer gratitude for your loving care to our wonderful family. If it wasn't for you, there'd be no one to look after us. I don't know how we'd survive if we lost you. All my relations." He poked Haslett. "Here, guy. Your turn."

Haslett took the stick, rotating it lightly. The lodge was still. Absolutely still. The only noise – *snap-crackle-pop* of Speed's fire, and the distant laugh of a displaced kookaburra. Haslett glanced at Tracy.

Then Nez. Then he looked to Smerchook.

"Grandfather. You know what I'm after, and I waited a long time for this chance... the chance to get back my soul... and to free an old friend. So I'm ready to do what it takes. You and Leslie know what you're doing, and I'll just follow along, but I don't wanna put no one else in danger. So we can just call this whole thing off, before it gets outta hand, if you want. I know that thing we're going after is really frikkin' terrible, and I'm not afraid for myself, but I don't want no one else gettin' hurt. 'Specially not you, Trace. I guess that's all I gotta say." He handed Tracy the talking-stick, followed by, "And, ah, yeah. All my relations."

Tracy held it in a prayer position. "I support this ceremony, no matter what the risk to my safety. I have faith in God. I believe that good always defeats evil, and I know that this devil will be defeated. All my relations."

She gave the stick to Spin-Dry, who hand-signed Smerchook.

"That won't be necessary, Spin-Dry," Smerchook said. "Just give the stick a little rub and pass it on."

Leslie Nez took the talking-stick and motioned it over her face. "Grandfather. This ceremony is about restoring harmony. Harmony in life, and harmony in death, is what we, as souls, all strive to achieve. It is my Shamanic duty to help Bob and Mike restore harmony in their souls, which were so wrongfully taken from their rightful place. I would like to say a Navajo prayer.

Hozhoogo naashaa doo In harmony I walk.

Shitsiji hozhoogo naashaa doo With harmony before me I walk.

Shikeedee hozhoogo doo With harmony behind me I walk.

Shideigi hozhoogo doo With harmony above me I walk.

Taa altso shinaagoo hozhoogo naashaa doo With harmony all around me I walk.

Hozho nahasdlii It has become harmony again.

Hozho nahasdlii, hozho nahasdlii, hozho nahasdlii

All my relations."

Nez motioned the talking-stick across her breast, then placed it in Gus's small hands. He fondled the stick and began to speak.

"Grandfather. My eyes no longer work, but I still see in many ways. I see you and Doctor Nez about to challenge an entity that exists in a polar dimension. This being can also see, but it does not see as you do. It sees as the opposite. I hear Tracy speak of good and evil. This entity's concepts are reversed. In theology, I was taught that goodness is a complex, broad spectrum of behavior which produces the best consequences upon the well being. Evil is simply the opposite. Goodness is based upon truth. Evil is based upon falsehood. In law, I was taught to analyze the adversarial view and compel the opponent into accepting that my premise was in their best interest, regardless of what is ethically right or morally wrong. Confronting The Kushtaka is no different than dealing with a lawyer. You have to confuse its thinking, or it will just do what comes natural to it. It will act instinctively to conquest, never with compassion or with compromise. You cannot blame it for that. That is the nature of the beast, but you cannot let it prevail. I also hear Tracy speak of God and of righting a wrong. I, too, have faith in God, but I am not below questioning how God stands on right and wrong. May I say something from a Bodhisattva?

If there is a Creator of the world entire
They call God, of every being be the Lord
Why does he order such misfortune
And not create concord.
If there is a Creator of the world entire
They call God, of every being be the Lord
Why prevail deceit, lies, and ignorance
And such inequity and injustice create
If there is a Creator of the world entire
They call God, of every being be the Lord
Then an evil master he is
Knowing what's right did let wrong prevail.

So, what is wrong for us, is right for The Kushtaka. And vice-versa." Gus paused and felt-up the talking-stick. "The way I look at it, right and wrong is pretty much a matter of opinion."

"Thank you, Gus," Smerchook said. "You always have something enlightening to offer."

"You're welcome. Sometimes it's easier to see when you can't." Gus smiled and passed-on the stick. "All my relations."

Smerchook set it aside, picking up his drum, giving it two quick taps. "Time to move on to the rounds. Hand in the pail!"

A big, hairy arm shot through the door as Speed shoved in a wooden bucket of water. Smerchook took the ladle. The doorway flapped closed. The chattering stopped. In total blackness, a bullying blast of steam bitch-slapped the faces.

Tracy gasped, immediately covering her mouth and nose with the towel. Haslett groaned, sticking his head in his lap. Billy curled-up on the ground, panting, while Spin-Dry sat soaking it in.

"Heyhey a yaya, La sha na sha hwey ya, La sha na sha hwey ya." Leslie Nez began a Navajo chant, rattling away with Gus gumming along.

Boom-Boom Boom-Boom Boom-Boom Boom-Boom

Smerchook did a steady beat on the drum. "Grandfathers!" he yelled. "Grandmothers!" he cried, wailing out indigenous lyrics. *"Crah-yah Hee-lah, Cunni-lah-lah he-lah, Crah-yah Hee-lah, Cunni-lah-lah he-lah."*

His song stopped. The bucket swished. A second smack of steam scorched the heads. Haslett hit the ground as if his backbone exploded. Tracy held fast, knees to her face, forcing her focus on Haslett. Billy panted harder. Gus stayed perfectly calm. Nez rattled to Smerchook's drum, banging binaural beats that altered awareness.

One minute. Two minutes. Three minutes. Four.

Light flashed – Dainty ripped open the door. Tracy felt like her ears had been blow-torched. Haslett stayed flat on the floor; mouth in his arm-pit. Nez reached to Tracy. She reached for Haslett.

"Are you okay, Bobby?" Tracy coughed, grappling the nape of his neck.

"Yup. I'm alright. Jeezuz! Was that hot!"

"It'll be more intense as the rounds progress," Nez said. "This is what forces you to alter consciousness. It'll come natural, I promise. Right now, let's get some air."

Smerchook was already out. So were Billy and Spin-Dry, but Gus stayed happily inside. Dainty hauled Haslett and Tracy to their feet, and Gnarly handed them a bottle of water. Haslett swigged as Tracy wiped her face with her towel, smearing a charcoal-dirt mix around her eyes like a drunken racoon's mascara.

Smerchook had his Curlew wings by the straps, swinging them to and fro. "They act like big fans to break up the steam, so no one gets scalded by water drops." He grinned, pointing at the fire. "We'll add eight more rocks, cranking the heat, and I'll jack up the water as well. This time, completely concentrate on your purpose."

Nez spoke. "Make sure to cover over with towels. It's critical to tune into your quest, not to your discomfort. You have to move past the heat. Move out of the dark and into the light. You'll see the light when you let yourself go."

"Back inside!" Smerchook ordered.

The group clustered in; same sequence as before. Tracy bunched against Haslett, clutching the sooty, damp towel. Haslett gripped his feet. Gnarly and Speed shoveled in rocks. The flap shut. Black hit and heat struck. Tracy stuffed her face into cloth, squeezing on Haslett like a leghold trap.

"Grandfathers! Grandmothers!" Smerchook wailed. "Give us your truths! Give us your wisdom. Give us your guidance!"

A ladle of liquid crashed on the rocks, sending a blast-furnace sear to the back of their heads. Ferocious flapping followed, as if an immense eagle took flight, attacking from inside the lodge.

Haslett towelled Tracy's head and hung on.

The flapping stopped as Nez sang.

"Hi, Hi Hi Ha, Hi Hi Ha, Hi Hi Ha... Hiiiii, Hi Ha, Hi Hi Ha, Hi Ha... Yaaa."

Another splash. Vicious steam. Flapping furious and faster.

Oh God! Tracy prayed. *Give me strength. Give me courage. Give me focus. Give me focus.*

* * *

Haslett snapped. He did something he'd not done in a quarter century. He started to cry. It began with a choke. Then a whimper. Then he burst into sobs. Big, heaving sobs. Gut wrenching sobs. Bawling from heartache and anguish.

Tracy tossed the towels on his head, throwing herself on his back like a human shield as he collapsed in a fetal ball, withering sideways on the mucking-up ground. His eyes compressed. His fingers clawed for a desperate hold, clinging to the edge on a crumbling cliff, head smashing-in under a stampeding crush.

Through a dusty haze, he saw the finks' faces.

Two filthy, white-bearded faces like those of bull bison, one grey and one green – impaling black horns and huge, flame-snorting nostrils – charging at him on legless torsos, becoming two shirtless old ghost-riders, one fat and one thin, showing holes of the bullets in the middle of their chests and the center of their foreheads.

"I am the Alpha!" cried the thin. "Omega!" moaned the fat. "We are the first and the last. The beginning and the end. And we live on in the eternal hell where you sent us."

In a whirl, they imploded into transparent streams of golden-black silica, funneling down a foaming-lead hourglass and captured within a hot, icy cube, exploding to a globe of cold fire. Out of it appeared two more faces. One dark and strikingly pretty. The other innocent in fresh, girlish youth. Maria blew a kiss as Gabby fluttered her small goodbye.

Assembling as one, they drifted off; dissipating as a mirage on the horizon of an endless sky.

Frigid in heat, Haslett screamed at them to come back.

Tracy held tight, her back and bare legs defending a third scalding slosh, hissing from Hades-hot rocks.

Flaps. Chants. Drums. Cries. Sobs. Rattles. Singing and praying. Panting and hacking.

The sound in the sweat overpowered sight, smell, and taste; only trumped by intense sense of feel.

WHOOMP

The doorway whipped open.

Dainty dodged a bellows of supercharged air. Smerchook crawled out, wobbling to his feet, handing Gnarly his wings. Gus keeled over and felt for the door. Billy scuffed through, kneeing Gus in the ribs, spread-eagling out in the sand with Spin-Dry coiling beside. Nez shuffled to Tracy. She was lying on Haslett, sucking sharp, shallow breaths and stroking his hair. He was decked out. Totally drained. Tears indistinguishable from what was sweat, what was steam, and what was suffer.

* * *

As Haslett lay still, he took his first steps towards re-birth.

Not in the spiritual sense – that would come – but in the psychological. He'd lost care about heat and discomfort; replaced by a perception as never before. He wriggled his toes, then his feet, then onto his legs. His hands came alive, as did elbows and arms. He raised his head, rolling over, collapsing with Tracy above.

Nez crawled to the couple.

"I sensed something happen," Tracy said, holding onto him tight.

"He let something go," Nez whispered back.

"Someone," said Tracy.

Nez understood, though she'd never been told. She got to her knees, her dress and adornments a soiled mess which she wore like a badge of distinction. "Now. Time to recharge. Two more rounds yet… it's going to suck us right dry."

Tracy rolled aside, helping Haslett crawl out; staggering like a drunk shit-kicked in a biker-bar brawl.

"Feeling lighter, my friend?" Smerchook slapped his big, grimy hand on Haslett's gritty shoulder.

Haslett started a sputter.

Smerchook stopped him short. "No need to explain. I saw what went on." He shook the talisman and winked.

Nez cut in. "Bob, you had to endure that. You couldn't possibly journey without purging first."

She gave him a water bottle. He slurped, puckered, and shoved it right back.

"I know. It's piss-warm," she said. "But, whatever you do, don't drink cold stuff right now. You'll cramp like your hoop was jalapenoed." She gave him a nudge, passing to Tracy, who downed nearly half.

Smerchook had been into his Rubbermaid bin. He set a tiny, wooden charm in Tracy's hand. "Keep this in your fist as we go through the third round. There's only four of us now and your concentration will be much more demanding. Focus on it. Hold it tight and squeeze hard. We're going to antagonize the entity."

Speed readied his rocks. Dainty held back on her flap. Nez crawled through to the left. Tracy to the right. Haslett ducked under, finding the temperature now almost toasty. Smerchook had a wooden flute mounted in a fabric neck cradle. He blew two chirpy squeaks, then grabbed his drum, bent, and contorted inside.

"Rocks!" he instructed.

Gnarly shoveled in the first of eight more. Temperature soared with each stone.

Tracy leaned forward, shielding her legs with her soggy, stained towel. Haslett sat straight up – focus clear – purpose definite.

Smerchook began a short double-tap, signaling Nez to join in. Their binaural beats began a slow, sensual bliss, forcing Tracy's eyes to blur and go heavy. On cue, the door flapped shut.

Boom-boom Boom-boom

Low drumming reverberated off the walls.

"*Hi Hi Hi Ha, Hi Hi Ha, Hi Hi Ha, Hiiiii, Hi Hi Ha, Hi Hi Ha, Ha Ha Hi.*"

Nez's voice soothed a balance to the echoes. She picked up her rattle. Smerchook blew his flute like a harnessed harmonica, marking time with his drum.

The music mesmerized Tracy. She fell to a trance. Light at first. Then heavy... heavier... heaviest. Haslett focused on his task, drifting to a state of suspension.

Fluting faded as Smerchook said a low, rumbling ramble, "Grandfathers. Grandmothers. I call on your powers. Your energies. I call on your righteousness. Your goodness. I call on your eternal wisdom and your truths. I call on your guidance. On your directions."

Boom-boom Boom-boom

His drum beat stronger.

"And I call on your assistance. I call on you to intervene with a spirit that exists in the darkness. A spirit that is evil. Deceitful and deadly. A spirit that is cowardly and tricks to sustain its existence. A spirit without the courage to appear before me and negotiate for control of a soul. A soul I have as an offer. A cowardly spirit."

Booom-booom Booom-booom Booom-booom Booom-booom

Tracy lost all sense of locality. Haslett transcended. He hovered about as her guard. Neither here. Neither there. Nowhere. Yet everywhere. Defending her soul like a bubble.

"Spirit! I call on you. Appear before me! Spirit! I call on you as the Bunyip. Appear before me! Spirit! I call on you as The Kushtaka. Appear before me! Spirit! I call on you, The Kushtaka. Appear before me once more. Do you dare? Kushtaka? Kushtaka the coward. Ha Ha Ha! Kushtaka the coward... the coward... the coward..."

Boom-bam Boom-bam Boom-bam Boom

The lodge shook.

Boom-bam Boom-bam

"The Kushtaka! I offer a trade."

Boom-bam Boom-boom

"Soul for souls!"

Boom-boom Boom-bam

"New for old!"

Boom-bam Boom-boom

The ether shuddered.

Boom-boom Boom-boom

"The fresh soul of a woman!"

Boom-Boom Boom-Boom

"For the spent souls of two men!"

Boom-Boom-Boom-Boom

"A fresh soul of this woman. For old stolen souls of two men."

BOOM BOOM BOOM BOOM

"The Kushtaka! Show yourself! You chicken-shit bastard! Show yourself! Yellow-bellied scumsucker! Bottom-feeder of the spirit world. Show yourself!"

Steam like Old Faithful geysered as Smerchook sloshed the full bucket on the rocks.

BAM BAM BAM BAM

Nez pounded for all she was worth.

BA-BOOOM

Smerchook smashed his stick on his drum. Picking up speed. Screaming obscenities at the demon.

Nez's hands were a whir. Beating like never before.

Haslett held fast around Tracy. She sat still as stone. Sensing not heat nor grave peril.

"KUSHTAKA! KUSHTAKA! KUSHTAKA! KUSHTAKA!" The two mystics taunted; voices in shrilling sharp shrieks.

* * *

An inversion formed in the rock-pit.

Invisible at first, it began to haze and swirl in a direction away from the sun.

A chill blew through the sweat; no effect on drumming and chants.

Haslett watched from a dome-pole as the entity amassed.

Colorless at first, it shifted shape from pure gas to part plasma.

Spinning. Gyrating. Faintly translucent, it molded to a PlayDoh-like texture, looming larger.

And larger.

Yet still larger.

Till its mass became two twisting columns.

Serpent in shape. Double-helix in form. Connecting the pit on the floor to the roll of the roof.

The spectacle ignited as a spectrum of light.

Phosphorous pink to burnt umber. Reddish-blue to key-lime.

A vomitous stink saturated the dome as a scorching stream of spectral spew shot Smerchook straight in his eyes, melting them clean from their sockets, boiling right through to his brain, and sucking his life-force off to the other plane of existence.

It circled behind Tracy.

Haslett saw the face. That hideous face with fiery eyes set on ragged shoulders.

Shoulders that became arms.

Arms that had hands.

One with a cache – a tiny, stick cache. Suspended on a rope of raw sinew.

In the other – a blade.

A bloody, bone blade.

Cutting through Tracy's bare throat.

* * *

For Haslett –

Time stopped.

In the center of the cache – in the core of a nightmare abyss – were their souls.

Miniature souls.

Not the souls you'd expect.

No!

Pathetic souls.

Emaciated souls.

Ghostly, wee souls without spin – waif-like and castaway – spiritually starved, spent, and shackled together, impaled on infernal spear-points in a devilish dungeon – telepathically screaming out

TRAP!

Haslett's body stayed frozen.

His mind drop-kicked the cache, busting the in-between inmates wide, wide open.

Leslie Nez shot through with a watchful, old *icht'a* as they attacked the aberration – slashing and stabbing, wailing and hissing, biting, clawing, strangling – groaning – gasping – collapsing – convulsing – ceasing – flat-lining to ethereally exist; now one form en masse.

Haslett snapped back to locality, frantically compressing the towel to Tracy's trachea.

* * *

Doctor Nez died that day, too – in physical form, that is – on the ground in that sweat lodge, a vibrant woman sacrificing herself in a metaphysical match that sent the shapeshifter spiraling back to a corner of the paranormal.

At exactly the same time, Inspector James Claymore dropped in his Vancouver driveway; the anatomical cause of his death undetermined.

Part Seven

The Confession

Chapter 46

Friday, September 28th, 2012
3:15 pm
Cambie Street Whitespot Restaurant
Vancouver, British Columbia

Diversions can be horrible things.

* * *

Sharlene Bate sat in the restaurant booth, showing the chiclets. She was having coffee with Jill Prunty and Barb McCormick, who'd just come from another autopsy at Vancouver General, only this time the murder didn't happen on Salt Spring. It was a Red Scorpion found dumped out in Surrey.

Prunty now had her dream job as an investigator with I-HIT, and she was exhibit-man in this homicide. McCormick had been to sixty-four more death scenes since she'd examined 1745 back in May, and she'd taken a move as the Regional Coroner for the Greater Vancouver area.

There'd been changes in Bate's life, too. She'd taken a month off to work things out with Emma, and her new position let her be home every night and weekend now. Like Moloci promised, the Commanding Officer had promoted her.

Something else was going well for Inspector Sharlene Bate.

"That wasn't there before." Prunty grinned, pointing at Bate's left ring finger.

"Ooh! Other congratulations are in order, I take it," McCormick said.

Bate blushed like a schoolgirl, showing her platinum set, triple diamonds. "Last weekend. I'm so happy!"

"Who's the guy gettin' lucky?" Prunty asked.

"Graham Sheehan."

Prunty drew a blank, but McCormick didn't.

"The prosecutor?"

"You know him, Barb?"

"Yes. Yes, I do. Rather well, in fact. He's acted as counsel on several of my inquests. I see his name and face in the news regularly. I expect he's heading for the bench soon?"

"He's been approached. But, right now Graham has other things in mind."

"Ahh... politics."

Bate smiled, but hid the chiclets.

"Oh, don't take that wrong," McCormick said. "I was a journalist long before I decided that dead people are much more interesting than live ones. I've covered my share of politics. I'm sure you'll find it quite, how shall I say... "

McCormick's pager went off.

"Ah! Saved by the beep. Must get this, if you'll excuse."

Prunty slid out, letting McCormick by, then sat back across from Bate.

"I gotta ask. I know you're not with the file no more, but I'm real curious if anyone good ever come up on our Salt Spring guy?"

Bate looked away. She thought a bit and swallowed. "A name surfaced, but it turned out the suspect was already deceased."

"Yeah. Guess it's kinda hard for a ghost to do it." Prunty chuckled.

Bate smiled faintly. She was about to reply when her BlackBerry toned. She glanced down, then jolted like she'd bitten a ball of tinfoil.

It made Prunty startle, too. "You okay?"

Bate stared at the email subject on her screen.

>>WHY THOSE 2 GUYS<<

"Sharlene?"

"Oh... ahh..."

"You okay?"

"Sorry... ah... something, something came up that I wasn't expecting."

McCormick returned. "Must go. Business calls. Nice to see you again, Inspector, and give my regards to Graham."

Bate nodded. McCormick put cash in the folder, setting it on the table. Prunty got up, following McCormick to the door. She stopped and turned her head, seeing Bate still in the booth.

She couldn't see Bate's hands tremble, opening the message.

>>Congratulations on the promotion, Inspector. I heard about it from Moloci.

You'll be a good officer. You're smart. You understand people. You'll treat them right. Fair & firm. You were good to me and that's worth something. You figured me out and didn't squeal, so I think I owe you the explanation on why those two guys like you asked.

You know? Feels good to finally get this off my conscience. Been doing that a lot lately - baring my soul. Wish I could describe what years in-between is like, but till you been there yourself, you could never understand.

I know you read my file and looked in my computer, so you know all about me and my past. But, then, I know lots about you, so we got common ground.

I hit bad times, like you know, and worked at getting my shit together. Took me a long time to understand what went down at Teslin and what happened to Bude and me. Basically we met up with a monster that made off with our souls. You can choose to believe that. Or not. But that's straight goods. It's exactly what happened.

Funny how you think and act when you got no soul. You don't have to play by the same rules no more, but you're just empty. You can't rest like you're dead and you can't enjoy nothing like being alive. You just feel horrible and all you want is to be set free. You go around half alive and half dead. Like a ghost. But that's under control now. I finally got happiness.

So you asked me why those two guys. Simple. Cause they fucken deserved it and if they came back to life, I'd kill them again in an instant. They say when you got no soul, you got no remorse, and that may be true. But even with my soul back now, I got no remorse over those two assholes. Never will. But you know? I brung this whole thing on myself.

It was back in the summer of 83. I took a little holiday, traveling alone up to the Yukon, and thought I'd try out some gold prospecting. I run into these two dirtbags at a camp and got drinking with them in a cabin on a claim outside Atlin. They found out I was a cop in my day job and try selling me information on a guy called Archie Wiggers, who owned the place. They tell me Wiggers is some kinda big fish, in with the Angels and all, and how he runs drugs by sea. I realized this was outta my league, so I introduced them to my buddy Moloci who just got in charge of the drug squad up north at the time. He starts running these slimeballs, and I guess with good results, but I never seen them again till they looked down the spout of my Ingram.

Things were pretty good back then. Moloci got his sister, Maria, a job as a police dispatcher before I got up there and she and I become an item. How she put up with Bude and me, I don't know, and she took it real hard when Bude got killed. I was just empty after it happened and I went downhill from then on. Even when our daughter, Gabby, was born I couldn't feel nothing except when I was hammered. I could only feel when I got in a stupor. The professionals, they now call it an altered state of consciousness. I like that term.

Anyway, I could communicate with Bude when I was wasted and I knew he was trapped in some kinda world in-between and he was begging me to help get our souls loose like I promised. But I didn't know how. I tried to function in the normal world, but I got worse all the time. After Maria and Gabby died, I spent all my time with alcohol and with Bude. I was about to give up. But then I found out something about 1745 and 1804 from Moloci, and it gave me and Bude a purpose.

Moloci had bought a tip off Wiggers about what those two shitstains had done. Wiggers said they were hiding out in his cabin near Atlin, so I took a trip up there and scouted the place out. Sure enough, 1804 was there, but I missed 1745 by a whisker. I watched from a hill most of the day. He'd come in and out, taking a piss and stuff. Towards dark I snuck down, dressed in winter camo, white balaclava and all. I threw a block of firewood on his steps and he opens the door to check out the noise. You shoulda seen his eyes. The last thing that scrawny prick saw was a ghost standing there holding a submachine gun.

But I was sloppy in what I done and they got on to me. There was a smooth old detective named Mahle who fucken near got me to confess, and I knew I couldn't hang on much longer so Moloci put together a plan for me to disappear. We made it look accidental as a suicide woulda fucked up my insurance and I had a couple people from my past I wanted to look after. So we set up the fake boat thing.

I was pissed and fucken near bled to death after the boat hit the rocks cause I ripped my head open on the sounder bracket. Then I damned near froze, even though I had a wetsuit on under my rain gear. Moloci was by shore with a skiff and had a warm van running with a change of clothes and he bandaged up my face the best he could. That's where them big scars come from.

Moloci made me promise to quit drinking and he hid me out at a rehab place in the States. It was tough, but it worked. I spent a year down there drying out, then he snuck me back to Canada with a new identity to finish off our business with 1745. He'd worked out a plan to find the fucker. The fat slob figured there was a hit out on him, so he went deep underground.

Moloci got me a job looking after a boat for a lady who moved money for an organization run by her father out of Mexico. Some of the HA's worked under him. It took a long time to get her trust but, eventually, like Moloci planned, going through her got me next to that Angel named Ghomes who knew where 1745 was hiding.

I feel guilty now for using the lady, but she turned out to be the best thing that coulda happened to me. So I owe my life to Moloci, and I owe getting my soul back to the lady, and I'd gladly die for either one of them. Anyway, back to why those two guys.

Ghomes had no idea who I was. I bided my time till he slipped up one day, making a comment about having to 'go see Pops'. You see, 1745 spawned Ghomes. He was Ghomes' old man.

I put a GPS tracker on Ghomes' vehicle and followed him over to Salt Spring, up to a grow-op he's got going not far from where we faked my death. So I parked by some mailboxes and sneaked through the trees and watched, confirming it was him. Fucken lizard-jizz had been right under my nose and I didn't even know it. I went and moved my truck, dressed in black combats with a black balaclava, grabbed my Ingram, and went back. It was fucken hot out that day and I waited three hours till Ghomes left, then another hour to make sure 1745 was alone so there'd be no witnesses to nothing.

Once the sack of maggot-schmeg went into his trailer, I crept up and threw a rock on his steps and he opens the door to check out the noise. You shoulda seen his eyes. The last thing that festered pissflap saw was a ghost standing there holding a submachine gun.

So there you have it. I admit I shot both of them and now I'll say why.

By 2000, Moloci turned 1745 and 1804 over to some high-flying young Inspector named Haugland to run. They had a cocaine undercover operation in Richmond go sideways and the two fuckheads kidnapped Haugland's wife, holding her hostage over some payment beef. Moloci brokered a back-door deal which senior management secretly approved. All they wanted was to save Haugland's wife and they were shit-scared this mess would get found out.

1745? He was a violent, volatile cokehead. No doubt he woulda killed her if he didn't get his deal.

1804? He was a follower, but far as I'm concerned he was there and also deserved to die.

It was near Christmas. Dark. Pissing down rain that night. I was drinking with the boys as usual, waiting for my wife to pick me up for a ride home. I'm not trying to make no excuses, but if that fucken thing never ripped off my soul, I never woulda been sitting drunk in a bar. I woulda been home like a decent father, and a decent husband, and none of this shit woulda ever happened.

Moloci and Haugland were out tailing the assmonkeys. The two fudgepackers were driving a stolen car and blew a red light, piling into an innocent SUV, flipping it upside down. Those cornholers made their choice right then and there. They coulda helped out. But instead, like Wiggers caught them bragging on tape, 1745 took out his lighter and torched the leaking gas tank to create a diversion. Then they fucked off on foot.

My wife and my little girl. Moloci's twin sister and his niece. They were in that SUV. 1745 and 1804 left Gabby and Maria to burn to death.

What goes around comes around, both in life and in death. Took me years, but I got both the cocksuckers and if you think I took drastic action – that's fuck-all compared to what Bude had waiting when they hit the other side.

I was glad to see that fucken Ghomes go down. He's an evil bastard, but not nearly on par with The Kushtaka. I know I'll be looking over my shoulder for the rest of my days, but I'll keep my wits. And don't bother looking for the weapon. I still got my Ingram.

You know? From what I been through? It's like I heard this little guy say. Right and wrong is pretty much a matter of opinion, so you do what you think is right with this information, Inspector.

Regards, Al Monagham<<

* * *

Sharlene Bate hit delete.

A little boy with his Pirate-Pack in the booth across the isle wondered why the pretty lady in the white police shirt was crying.

Chapter 47

Saturday, September 29th, 2012
11:15 am
Combo Waterhole on the Diamantina River
Near Kynuna Station
Queensland, Australia

He shut down his laptop after sending Bate the email. Tracy came from the kitchen of their motorhome, putting her arms over his shoulders, squeezing the scars on his cheek against the stitches on her neck.

"That took you awhile, Honey," she whispered. "You are tense. Is everything all right?"

"Yup. Just some unfinished business with the cops."

"What is happening?"

"First trial is in a couple weeks, so we gotta be somewhere to get a secure video link so I can testify."

She paused, pulling back to look at him. "We are already heading to Darwin for that. Any reason to change?"

He sat vacant.

"Sweetie?"

"Sorry, Trace. Just caught in a moment from the past."

"You promised to accept closure, love. You know you cannot bring them back."

"Sorry. Right." He shoved the computer away, giving her a slight smile. "You know? I got every freedom in the world right now. Never been so free. Gotta learn to enjoy it."

"That makes two of us," she said, her voice now a permanent

struggle. She swung and sat on his lap, resting her chin on his shoulder and gripping his back. "I am so, so happy. For the first time in my life, I am truly happy. I am free. Finally free. And I am with you."

Her hands rose to his face.

"When I was a girl, I would spin my father's globe, pick a place, then run there in my mind. Oh, the places I would go and the freedom I would have. I was in love with Peter Pan. I would be Tinkerbell, and we would travel to magical lands and fight pirates."

She stopped, her bottom lip quivering.

"Peter Pan grew up and went away. He left me all alone. I was so sad. I lived my life in sadness. And one day you showed up. Peter came back, and I was Tinkerbell again."

She dabbed at her eyes.

"Look at me. I am so happy, yet I am crying."

"It's all right, Tink. Just hope Capn' Hook don't return."

"Oh God, Peter! Do not even say that."

"He'll never take us alive, Tinkerbell!"

They giggled as teenagers. She coughed to catch her breath.

"Do you know why I insisted we go out of our way to stop here? At this spot?" she asked.

"Nope. I'm curious. Seemed important to you."

"It is symbolic, but very meaningful. I promised myself... if I ever found freedom, I would visit here. Ever since a girl, I would sing a song... a song of freedom. I believe the greatest song about freedom ever written."

His forehead wrinkled. "What's that?"

"Waltzing Matilda!"

"Right. You hum it a lot. That's the anthem down here. No?"

"Actually, it is not. Most think it is. And many around the world know the tune. Even the words."

"So what's with this spot?"

"This used to be Dagworth Station. A sheep ranch where Banjo Patterson wrote the song in 1895."

"Really? Nothing here except this little pond."

"It is called a billabong, silly."

"I know." He grinned. "I even know that down under a sheep's called a jumbuck, a food pack's a tuckerbag, a tea pot's a billy, the rancher's a squatter, cops are troopers, and a crook is a swagman. And Matilda is the swaggie's bedroll, so when he's travellin' alone with his gear, he's waltzin' Matilda. On the run. Sorta like us."

"How do you know all of this?"

He kept grinning. "Internet. You hummed it so much, I got curious and looked it up. I just didn't know where it was wrote."

"So you know what the song is about?"

"Pretty much about a loner who pulls off a heist, then turns hisself into a ghost rather'n getting caught and losin' his freedom."

"That is exactly it!"

"But I got no idea what a ghost is." He laughed – something not able to do for a quarter century.

"I think you have some first hand experience with that, my love." She pushed his chest and got up, taking the laptop. "Come. Let me get a signal outside."

They stepped from air conditioning, to the brilliance of the Australian springtime sun. She set the computer on a rickety, wooden picnic table under the shade of a large, leafy tree and Googled *Slim Dusty Youtube*, finding an image of an older man in a leather vest and an outback hat, sitting in front of a camp-fire holding an acoustic guitar with a wide, monogrammed shoulder-strap.

"This is the best version of the song ever recorded. It brings tears when I hear him sing it."

"Who's this guy?"

"Slim Dusty!"

"Don't know of him."

"The king of Australian country music! He is like Hank Williams down here. I saw him live once. He sang it at the closing of the Summer Olympics in Sidney. I was there, in the arena. One guitar. A hundred and ten thousand backup singers. It was magic that night. Pure magic."

Tracy kicked off her sandals, standing in bare feet on sizzling sand. She cranked the volume, clicked the play arrow and, with the ghost of Alfred Monagham in her arms, led them on a waltz of freedom.

Pure freedom.

Once a jolly swagman camped by a bill-a-bong
Under the shade of a cool-a-bah tree
He sang as he watched and waited 'til his billy boiled
You'll come a-Waltzing Matilda with me

Waltzing Matilda Waltzing Matilda You'll come a-Waltzing Matilda
with me
He sang as he watched and waited 'til his billy boiled

You'll come a-Waltzing Matilda with me

Down came a jumbuck to drink at the bill-a-bong
Up jumped the swagman and grabbed him with glee
He sang as he shoved that jumbuck in his tuckerbag
You'll come a-Waltzing Matilda with me

Waltzing Matilda Waltzing Matilda You'll come a-Waltzing Matilda
with me
He sang as he shoved that jumbuck in his tuckerbag
You'll come a-Waltzing Matilda with me

Up rode the squatter mounted on his thoroughbred
Up rode the troopers; one, two, three
With the jolly jumbuck that you've got in your tuckerbag
You'll come a-Waltzing Matilda with me

Waltzing Matilda Waltzing Matilda You'll come a-Waltzing Matilda
with me
With the jolly jumbuck that you've got in your tuckerbag
You'll come a-Waltzing, you scoundrel, with me

Up jumped the swagman, sprang into the bill-a-bong
You'll... never... take... me... alive... said he
And his ghost... may be heard... as you pa- aass by that bill... a... bong
You'll come a-Waltzing Matilda with me

Waltzing Matilda Waltzing Matilda You'll come a-Waltzing Matilda
with me

His ghost...
May be heard...
As you pass...
By that bill-a-bong...

You'll... come... a-Waltzing... Matilda... with me

Chapter 48

From Somewhere In-Between The Darkness and The Light

Bude watched the two dance in freedom and laugh in happiness; something neither was able to do for half their lives.

His soul is free now, too – thanks to his partner, Alfred Monagham.

He could easily drift off to eternal rest, but he's going to stick around and keep watch with Doctor Nez, Smerchook, and Kaash Klao.

You see, it's not Tracy that's in immortal danger. Alfred can handle things if Ghomes ever gets loose, or the Angels catch up.

No, it's Sharlene Bate to fear for.

The Kushtaka has her number, and it's going to call for a new ride.

Like Alfred said –

What goes around comes around, both in life and in death.

Sharlene was good to him. She kept the secret of why the informants had to be murdered, and that's worth something.

Loyalty has no earthly bounds, and they're not about to leave Inspector Bate unprotected with The Kushtaka now hunting for her soul.

* * *

To be continued in the sequel '*No Life Until Death*'.

Acknowledgements

Foremost, my thanks go to Guy Lepage, Senior, for his support and encouragement during the two and a half years that it took me to research and write *No Witnesses To Nothing*. Guy, you'll never know just how much I appreciate your help.

Secondly, I extend gratitude to the Buday family of Alberta, Canada. Mike was a brother to me as well, and this book is my way of keeping his spirit alive.

Sincere appreciation goes to Delorise Munro for her help in story, structure, and content editing, as well as to Heather Adkins of CyberWitch Press for her wicked eye in line editing, proofreading, and formatting.

Other invaluable editing information came from books by Renni Browne and Dave King of The Editorial Department (*Self-Editing for Fiction-Writers*) and from Jessica Page Morrell (*Thanks, But This Isn't For Us*). Vital information on the craft of writing came from William Strunk, Jr., and E.B.White (*The Elements of Style*), Stephen King (*On Writing*), and Lisa Cron (*Wired For Story*). Every writer will benefit from the phenomenal knowledge which these works provide.

Many thanks go to my internet friend, Joanna Penn of *TheCreativePenn.com*, who is a gem. I continue to learn so much from Joanna. Ali Luke (*Publishing E-Books for Dummies*) was a big help in the publishing process. Derek Murphy (*Creative Indie Covers*) designed the cover and Bruce Byfield provided the image of the Bukwas mask from his collection of First Nations art.

Insight into Shamanism came through the works of Dr. Leslie Gray, Michael Harner, Gary Witherspoon, James Endredy, and Roger Walsh, M.D. Research into consciousness was provided by Pim Van Lommel, M.D., and Bruce H. Lipton, Ph.D. Information on quantum physics came from Bill Bryson, Brian Clegg, Peter Russell, and Stephen Hawking.

A long salute to all the women and men who've had the courage to wear a uniform in the service of their country. As Winston Churchill put it 'We sleep safely at night because rough (men) stand ready to visit violence on those who would harm us.'

And, above all, I thank my family and The Creator. "All my relations"

Garry Rodgers, February 2013

About The Author

Garry Rodgers has lived the life that he writes about.

Now a retired Royal Canadian Mounted Police homicide detective and forensic coroner, Garry also served on RCMP Emergency Response Teams, trained with the British Special Air Service, and was recognized by the Canadian Courts as an expert in the operation and identification of firearms.

Garry is currently writing a series centering on Sharlene Bate, as well as a non-fiction work, *Lone Nuts – A No BS Guide to the JFK Assassination*, set for release in November 2013; the 50th anniversary of United States President John F. Kennedy's murder.

Garry is active on social media and welcomes your questions, comments, and reviews. Feel free to contact Garry in Vancouver, Canada at:

Web / Blog: www.dyingwords.net
Email: garry@dyingwords.net
Twitter: @GarryRodgers1
Goodreads
Facebook
LinkedIn

26550886R10205

Made in the USA
San Bernardino, CA
01 December 2015